Martin Middleton was born in London in 1954 and his family emigrated to Inala, Brisbane, in 1960. After attending Corinda High School he joined the army and spent most of his time at Lavarack Barracks in Townsville. Middleton now lives in Beaudesert, Queensland, with his wife and children.

He has always been an avid reader of science fiction and fantasy novels, and for him it was a logical step to move from being a reader to a writer during a period when he was a house husband.

CIRCLE OF LIGHT

Book One of the
Chronicles of the Custodians

MARTIN MIDDLETON

PAN BOOKS

First published 1990 by Pan Books (Australia) Pty

First published in Great Britain 1995 by Pan Books
an imprint of Macmillan General Books
25 Eccleston Place, London SW1W 9NF

Associated companies throughout the world

ISBN 0 330 33105 1

1 3 5 7 9 8 6 4 2

A CIP catalogue record for this book is available from
the British Library

Typeset by Excel Imaging, St Leonards, Australia
Printed and bound in Great Britain

To my wife Kate who can spell

CONTENTS

1	THE COMPANIONS	13
2	DEATH OF A FRIEND	22
3	THE WASTELANDS	31
4	JOURNEY TO BEESTRONE	44
5	JON	58
6	THE WYERNT RIVER	66
7	THE MERCHANT ARDEMUS	76
8	ELRED	85
9	THE BLACK SHIP	99
10	THE SEARCH ENDS	113
11	THE TRUTH	126
12	A FRIENDSHIP RENEWED	132
13	RAFE	139
14	THE OSSEAUX SWAMP	149
15	AMBUSH	156
16	THE ANCIENT CITY	165
17	USARE	176
18	THE TRUE PRINCE	183
19	A TASK OF GREAT IMPORTANCE	190
20	TALISMAN	198
21	REYA	213
22	THE PURSUIT	227
23	THE TRAP	239
24	CHAGRIN	251
25	RHYHL	261
26	THE CIRCLET AND THE DAGGER	272
27	RETRIBUTION	282

28 THE VRIJBANE   294
29 PLASTRONS   308
30 WELCOME TO THE FREE STATES   318
31 DEATH LORD   329
32 CHIMERA   337
33 THE MESSAGE   348
34 THE REGENT   357
35 THE STRANGER IN GREY ROBES   366
ARMOURY   377

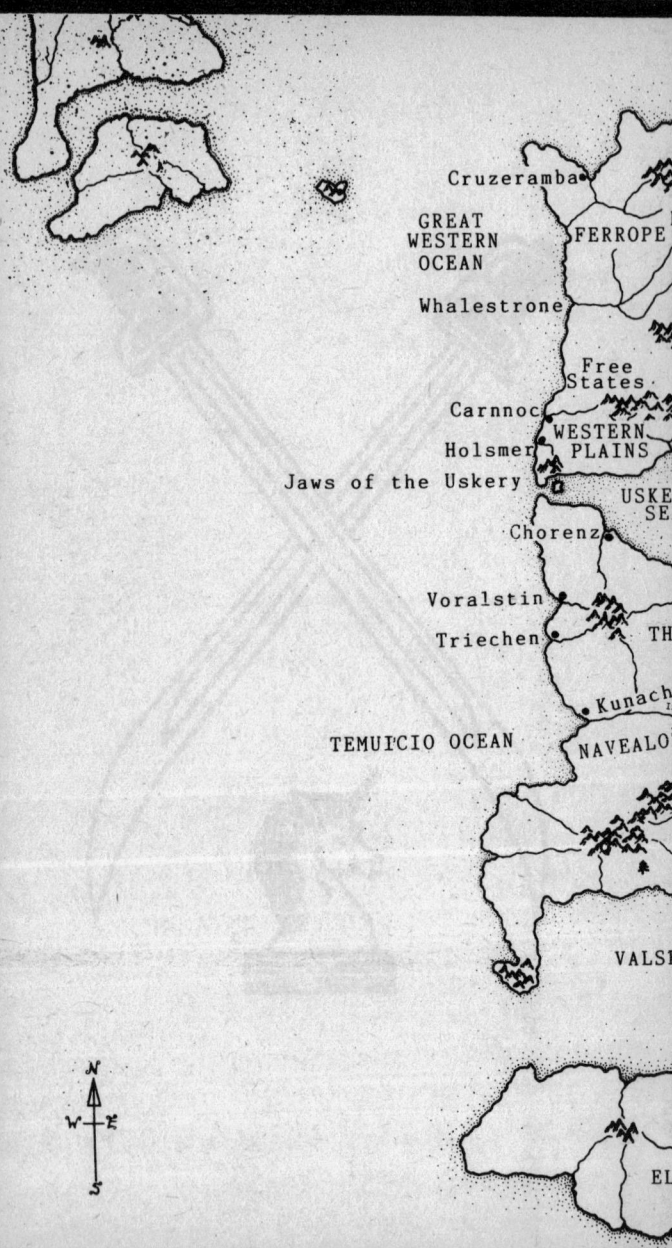

Cruzeramba

GREAT
WESTERN
OCEAN

FERROPE

Whalestrone

Free
States

Carnnoc

WESTERN
PLAINS

Holsmer

Jaws of the Uskery

USKE
SE

Chorenz

Voralstin

Triechen

TH

Kunach

TEMUICIO OCEAN

NAVEALO

VALSE

EL

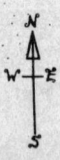

N
W E
S

CHO
Yalthen

RUSMAYO
gium
Erg
s

STERN
AINS
erweld
C

Firnall
Kelturk

Wirrilac

Todismal
forest
Osseaux Swamp
Velliach
Murztal

Focharber
Mtns

Falham River

Falham

Kelturk River

Osseaux River

River

Erg

WESTERN PLAINS

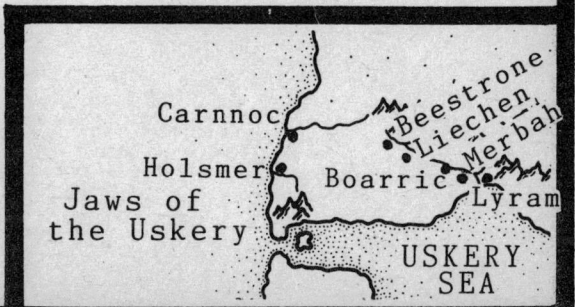

Carnnoc

Holsmer

Jaws of
the Uskery

Beestrone
Liechen
Merbah
Boarric
Lyram

USKERY
SEA

1

THE COMPANIONS

THERE were four of them. Their hair was long and matted, and they were unshaven. Their clothing was stained, and showed signs of wear from a long hard journey. They hung over their saddles as if they were asleep, but their eyes showed that they were far from it. Tired, yes, but they were alert to their surroundings. Their heads bobbed and rolled as they rode past, but this too, I realised, was simply the easiest way for them to watch the surroundings without being too obvious.

I had seen their type before — Runners, from over the mountains. What they were running from no one had ever told me, but this time each year brought a few of them through our streets.

The mountain ponies they rode were in worse condition than the riders. Their heads were bowed almost to the ground and their tongues were hanging from their mouths. Their coats were cut and scraped in places as if they had been pushed through thick scrub. While the men's eyes were alert and continually moving, the eyes of the animals were dull and unseeing. There seemed to be no life behind those blank orbs.

The four moved to the far end of the street, and stopped in front of the livery. The smallest of the riders swung down from the saddle and walked into the darkness of the livery. While he was out of sight, the others remained mounted and continued to watch the houses and street. Eventually he stepped back out into the street, and began to talk to the other three.

After a short conversation between all four, with the smallest man doing a great deal of the talking, they dismounted and led their weary animals from sight into the livery.

I had been in the tree since the first thing that morning, and as the day was quiet, I decided to stay hidden in the tree rather than return to the tavern and continue my work.

That morning, after I had finished my early chores, I had slipped out by the rear door of the tavern and climbed to the upper branches. I spent most of my free time in that tree. The branch I sat on was about ten feet above the ground, and from there I could see either end of the main street without being seen myself. I could also see both doors of the tavern, and therefore would know when Harnet came searching for me.

In the time I had been bonded to Harnet, I had learnt how to avoid the beatings I often deserved. At first they had been frequent, but since learning the secret of how to handle Harnet, beatings had been rare. Whenever I saw Harnet leave the tavern looking for me, I would climb down from my vantage point and enter the tavern through the other door, so that when Harnet eventually found me I was hard at work. In answer to his questions about where I'd been, I would simply stare up at him with an expression of utter confusion. I would never actually lie to him — it was hardly my fault if he chose to believe that all the while he had been searching for me I had been working hard somewhere else.

Harnet was not the quickest man in the village, but he was hard-working and respected by all the community. His tavern was the only one in the village — the last resting place that travellers encountered before entering the Wastelands. Large and small caravans stopped at the tavern for a night's lodgings and to rest their mounts. While in the village they replenished stocks and picked up guides.

The Wastelands was a very different place to travel through. Water could only be found with the help of a diviner or guide, both of which the local villages could supply. The Wastelands was an area choked with bramble-covered ridges and large thorn trees. Burr bushes also grew in abundance. It was usually travelled only as a last resort, though these days it had become common practice to cross the Wastelands to the river town of Beestrone. The lower Plains were alive with bands of Brigands and the Uskery Sea was swarming with Corsairs. The Wastelands had become the safest way to travel in these troubled times.

The strangers stepped out into the light and began to march across the street towards the tavern which was also the direction of the tree in which I was hiding. I followed their progress as they came towards me. Gone was the look of fatigue. They moved with a sureness of step which showed they were not the usual type of Runner.

Most Runners came to our village to find food, and to trade their tired mounts for fresh ones before continuing their journeys. While in our village, they spent the entire time looking behind them as if they believed the slightest pause would allow whoever was chasing them to catch up.

But these four were different — they were watching the village itself, not their backtrail. Now they seemed to be moving with a purpose — their heads were held high and their step had quickened.

As they passed beneath me, one of them suddenly looked up and fixed his gaze upon me. His eyes looked deep into mine, as if trying to look into my very soul. I could not break the stare which held me, but, as I began to panic, his eyes softened and a faint smile turned up the corners of his mouth. As soon as his eyes left mine I was free. He reached into a pouch and took out a coin which he flicked up to me. He then turned and followed the others into the tavern.

I looked at the coin. It was a double copper piece. I glanced back at the strangers as they entered the tavern. The one who had thrown the coin stopped and turned.

'Tend the horses,' he said to me, and then disappeared into the tavern.

Dropping from the tree, I crept over to the window of the tavern and peeked in. I could just make out the shapes of the strangers as they moved through the smoke-filled tap room of the tavern. The smallest one again took charge and began to talk with Harnet. As they obviously discussed prices, the one who had spoken to me suddenly turned, and our eyes locked again. Without even knowing I was there and through the smoke, his eyes had fixed straight to mine.

I turned and fled across the street to the safety of the livery. Once my eyes became adjusted to the dim light, I saw the animals belonging to the strangers at the rear of the building. They had been placed in individual stalls and feed had been given to them. I began to work on them with a handful of straw, then a brush and comb, stopping occasionally to give them more feed or water.

At last I was finished. I leaned back against the railings;

my arms were on fire and I ached all over. I was about to leave, when I caught sight of the strangers' belongings in one corner. The saddles were old and worn, and each had a small knife fixed below the saddle horn. Each had a blanket roll, and one had a long bundle with a smaller one tied to it. I decided it would be best to leave the gear where it was. They had obviously placed it there for a reason.

I hurried back across the street towards my tree, but while I was still in the centre of the street, Harnet came out of the rear door of the tavern. He beckoned to me.

'No time for your dreaming today, Teal. Galt is sick and I've a tavern full of guests. You'll have to help me in the tap room tonight. Understand?' As he spoke, he gave me the usual tap on the top of the head as if trying to push the idea into my head.

I nodded and followed him into the tavern. I was never allowed in the tap room once it was opened in the evenings. Galt was Harnet's helper and he did not like the way Harnet treated me. On several occasions I had heard him telling Harnet I was a lazy boy and he would be better off without me. Each time Harnet answered that he would think about it.

The first time I heard this, I was so terrified that I worked until I dropped, trying to show I was worth keeping. I was carried to my bed and told to rest for the next few days. When I came to, Harnet was bending over me telling me it was all right. Galt was standing behind him with a smile on his face nodding and saying, 'I told you he was useless'.

That night I was helper to Harnet. I raced back and forth with both empty and full mugs. It was also my job to wipe down the tables and to clear away the empty platters, which I returned to the kitchen, where if I was quick, I could palm myself a piece of pie or pastry. Harnet's wife and his daughter, Jayne, worked in the kitchen, while he

17

tended the roast turning slowly over the fire in the centre of the room. The smell of the slowly roasting meat drifted to all corners of the tap room, and many stopped their conversation and turned to watch as old Harnet basted the roast. All eyes followed the spoon, as it moved from the pan of juices to the top of the roast, where it slowly tipped, and the juices poured down the sides of the roast. Hands passed over mouths and tongues moistened lips in anticipation.

Harnet always started his roast early, so they only needed a few more hours once he was open for business. With the roast went warm fresh bread and vegetables which Jayne had picked during the afternoon from the small plot behind the tavern.

After the meal had been served and the platters cleared away, the customers settled down to the serious work at hand, and soon the tap room was full of singing, though somewhat off key. This was followed by stories, and tales of the past. That night we were lucky enough to have a Chronicler as a customer. Most landlords allowed travelling Chroniclers to stay free-of-charge, since a good tale about the olden days, or of magic and monsters, could increase the tavern's business.

The pattern for the usual night was set. Eventually the room would clear until only a few unconscious patrons were left under tables or in corners. These were placed in a back room with an open door to the yard at the rear of the tavern. The door to the tap room would be locked and then Harnet would take himself off to bed. Next morning he would rise early and scrub down the tables and prepare the roast for the evening meal. He would also check the stock room to see what stock remained. All these things I had seen many times before. But this night was to be different.

On other nights, Harnet and Galt had raced around the

tables in such a manner that it made them seem tireless. But that night, I was exhausted by the time the roast was ready for serving. The rubbing down of the animals this afternoon, and the rushing back and forth from the tap room, was beginning to take its toll.

The strangers came down late and took a table, one of the last, at the rear of the room away from the fire. From a distance it was nearly impossible to see them at all, as their dark travelling cloaks blended with the shadowy background. I moved towards their table. As I neared them I saw that they had shaved, and combed the tangles from their hair. The grime of the trail had been washed from their faces and as they had now opened their cloaks, I could see they had put on clean, fresh clothing.

The smallest one sat to the right, while the one who had spoken to me was on the left. The two in the centre had to be brothers; even in this poor light the family resemblance was remarkable. Both were young and had brown hair. One had a scar on his face — it ran from the corner of his right eye to the lobe of the right ear. The scar was long and thin and seemed to shine in the light from the lamps.

The smallest one spoke as I reached the table. 'Three meads and an ale.' He turned to the others and then back to me. 'We'll have four meals to go with that as well, if you'd be so kind.'

As I turned to leave, the fair-haired one on the left smiled and said, 'You did a fine job on our mounts. Thank you.' I nodded and left to fill their order.

I returned shortly with their drinks and then later with their meals. They sat and ate in silence, and when they had finished they talked together quietly. They kept apart from the other guests, and did not join in the singing or other forms of entertainment.

As the night wore on, the strangers left the tap room and retired upstairs to the rooms they had rented for the night. By the time the last customer had left or been dragged to the small room in the back, I was hardly able to stand. The fumes from the beverages had finally begun to overwhelm me. My eyesight blurred and my thoughts became slow and confused. I bade Harnet goodnight and made my way slowly to my room in the attic.

Once in my room, I closed the door and stumbled over to the window. I needed fresh air. After a great deal of effort, I managed to get the window open. As I leaned out and breathed in the cool, fresh air, I was startled to see a figure in the compound below. Thinking it was one of the drunks, I was about to call out to him, when something struck me as strange.

There was something wrong. I realised that the man was going to great lengths to stay in the shadow. I spotted him when the moon came out from behind one of the many clouds. He froze in the dim light, and I was able to see him quite clearly for some time. Then the moon disappeared behind a cloud, and he began to move once more.

In my muddled state, it took me a while to realise exactly what I was seeing. Then it became clear — a thief.

I stood and wondered what to do. A thief, here! It was unheard of. I left my room and crept along the corridor towards the stairs to tell Harnet about the intruder. As I crossed the tap room towards Harnet's quarters, I heard a faint scraping noise coming from the back door. The thief was trying to gain entry into the tavern. Obviously not satisfied with what he had found in the stables and stores shed out back, he was now actually trying to enter the main building.

The effects of the alcohol fumes were gone. Caught in the middle of the room, I froze as the rear door opened and closed. A sound of scuffling feet could be heard as the intruder moved towards the stairs I had just descended. Should he turn, he would be sure to see me.

But he did not turn. He moved quickly to the stairs and climbed to the next level — the level on which the strangers slept.

Should I warn Harnet or follow the thief? I decided to follow the thief. At the top of the stairs the entire corridor was enveloped in shadows, cast by the solitary lamp hanging outside the furthest room. The thief was merely a darker shadow against the dim light. He stopped at the second door and listened, then slowly began to turn the knob, which gave a faint squeak in protest, before finally turning.

On the floor near my right foot was one of the stone wedges used to hold open the doors of the empty rooms. I bent down and picked it up. My plan was simple. I would sneak up behind him and strike him on the head with the stone. Then, I would wake up Harnet and be a hero — and prove my worth.

2

DEATH OF A FRIEND

EVERYTHING went well with the plan . . . until I took my second step. The thief stopped, and turned. Something had alerted him to my presence. I could have sworn I hadn't made a sound. He placed a finger to his lips and waved for me to come closer with his other hand. The waving hand held a slender-bladed dagger which caught and reflected the light from the lamp.

His penetrating eyes held me transfixed as the eyes of the smiling stranger had done — only this time there was no smile, only a slow chill spreading throughout my body. I dropped the stone and began to walk towards him, powerless to resist.

Suddenly his eyes left mine and opened wide in surprise. There was a noise of a small object whipping past my ear, and the hilt of a knife appeared in the centre of his chest. He turned and began to run for the window, as though the knife had never been thrown. But even as he did so, a second knife buried itself deep between his shoulder blades. The force of the blow sent him staggering against the wall of the corridor. He regained his balance and continued towards the window at the end of the corridor. A third knife struck him in the back: his knees buckled and he fell forward on his face.

A person pushed past me, and then another. Sounds could now be heard coming from several of the rooms around us. I shook my head. I was still standing in the middle of the corridor. Two of the strangers were bending over the body of the thief. They were talking in a strange tongue which, somehow, seemed familiar yet foreign at the same time. They were asking the thief something. They kept repeating the same thing over and over again. But he never answered. Slowly he slipped from their grasp and folded to the floor, to lie in a pool of his blood. As I watched, the pool grew noticeably larger.

At last Harnet arrived to investigate the disturbance. His face hardened at the sight of the body. I was taken back to my room where Harnet's wife gave me a drink which made me drowsy. For some time I lay and looked up at the ceiling. I wasn't sure when I fell asleep, but I awoke looking at the ceiling as though I'd done so all night.

Then the ceiling disappeared as Harnet's smiling face peered down at me. He spoke; but it sounded as if he was talking from a great distance. His voice sounded faint and muffled. I smiled back and tried to speak, but found I couldn't. Harnet nodded and stroked my forehead. This time I tried slowly and managed to ask him what had happened. He told me to be patient and to rest.

I dropped back to sleep and found myself back in the corridor. This time when I looked, it was me who was lying in the pool of blood, and Harnet was bending over me smiling and telling me to wait and see. Behind him was Galt. 'See?' he was saying, 'As I told you, absolutely useless.'

When I woke again, I felt much better. I left my room and made my way downstairs. In the tap room, the four strangers and Harnet were talking. With them was the Keeper of the village. They were sitting at one of the tables and there was a large platter of food in front of them. The sight of the food reminded me of how hungry I was. 'Come join us,' Harnet called, and pointed to the seat beside him. While I ate, the rest of them talked over what had happened the previous night. I was asked several questions, which I answered as well as I could. I told them about seeing the thief, and how I went downstairs. I told them how I decided to follow him upstairs and capture him myself, with the aid of the stone wedge. On hearing this, there were a few laughs around the table and a great many smiles.

The Keeper rose and bade all farewell. He had other duties to perform. As soon as he had gone, the strangers and Harnet began to converse in the strange language I had heard two of them use last night with the thief. Harnet seemed to understand the language because after listening for some time, he began to answer them. As I listened, I was surprised to find I was able to pick up small pieces of the conversation, yet apart from the few words hastily spoken in the corridor last night, I did not think I had heard the language before. From the little I could gather, they had come to Dienall explicitly for the purpose of speaking to Harnet. I had no idea why.

They talked for some time. I drifted in and out of the conversation, missing small sections of it. They were talking about finding something-or-other before some person had the chance to catch up with them. What they were after, or who was after them, was lost to me.

The four strangers stayed on at the tavern for several more days. In this time their mounts filled out, and once again

24

resembled sturdy mountain ponies. Though small in size, they were sure-footed and could cross terrain which would make a mountain goat think twice. They were hard to come by, and were extremely hard to train. So, a well-trained mount could bring a considerable amount of money. To see them in the condition they were in when they arrived, was indeed strange.

When the strangers spoke together, they acted as if I was a piece of the furniture; at first this disturbed me, then I realised they didn't realise I could understand a little of what they were saying, and the more they used their northern language, the more I understood it.

On the fourth day of their stay, we received word which terrified the village. A caravan had been attacked as it passed through the Wastelands. This in itself was nothing major. These attacks happened all the time. The thing that had the people worried was the caravan had been attacked by two clans raiding together. This was a bad thing for the people of the area. The clans usually spent so much time attacking each other they had no time to worry about the villages located on the edge of the Wastelands. But every so often, two clans would find they had no blood feuds existing between them, so they formed a shaky alliance for the purpose of attacking caravans or the outlying small villages.

· After hearing the news, the four met again with Harnet. I entered the tap room on an errand, and found them deep in discussion. I had by now become quite good at listening in on their conversations, while seemingly ignoring them.

'What do we do now?' asked the smallest of the four. He looked at his companions as he spoke, but I had the distinct feeling the words were meant for Harnet.

'As I see it, Roebert, you have little choice. The way via the Capital is sure to be watched. Your only hope is to cross the Wastelands and reach the river where you can get transport to the coast.'

'You believe we could still cross the Wastelands?' asked the brother with the scarred face.

'Yes, Danel,' Harnet said. 'At first the clans will raid for weapons. That's why the caravan was attacked. Then using the newly-acquired weapons, they will attack the surrounding clans to weaken them and ensure they are no threat to them while they are away raiding. Only then will they turn their attention to the surrounding villages, like this one.'

'Will you and your family be safe here?' the other brother asked.

'Yes. We have held the clans at bay for years. We will take a few casualties, but the village will be quite safe,' Harnet answered.

'All right! We'll still cross the Wastelands. When would you suggest?' Roebert asked.

'As soon as possible — tomorrow morning, first light,' Harnet answered.

'We should have left earlier,' the other brother said.

'It would have done you no good to leave any earlier. Your mounts were all in. If you had pushed them much more you would have lost them. Even now, they have not had sufficient time to rest and regain their full strength. But you can't wait any longer,' Harnet told them.

Danel stood. 'Tomas and I will see about getting another pack animal,' he said.

Harnet watched the brothers walk towards the door, then he rose and said, 'I'll be off to find you some supplies. I won't be long.' In our language, he added, 'You'd best come with me, Teal.'

We left the tap room and went out back to the storage sheds. Once inside, Harnet pointed to a side of bacon, a sack of flour, and assorted dried vegetables.

'I'll finish off here,' he said. 'You go to the kitchen and put a dozen of the cooked birds into a sack. Then get several loaves of bread and bring them to the livery.'

I did as I was told, and in no time I was standing in the livery watching Harnet and Danel tie the supply packs to the two animals.

'Tie your sack to Mikal's saddle,' Harnet told me, 'and then get yourself back to the tavern and give Galt a hand to set up for this evening's custom.'

The evening was going well. With Galt and myself to work the tables, things were much easier. We were delivering platters of roast chickens to the tables, when suddenly the front door erupted.

Before the broken segments of the door touched the floor, the open doorway was full of armed men. Screams could be heard coming from neighbouring buildings. Tables were thrown onto their sides as customers rushed to escape from the room. Roebert and his companions raced towards the small room where the drunks were placed for the night. They were only halfway across the floor of the tap room, when the door to the small room burst open and more armed figures could be seen.

The intruders were wearing mail armour, covered by a loose coat of red. In the centre of their chest was a white circle, surrounding a small green tree. The heads of the intruders were covered by full helmets which showed only their eyes. They were wielding a variety of weapons, though the most common seemed to be a sword with a short wide blade.

'Upstairs!' Mikal shouted, and pushed Harnet's wife and daughter ahead of him as he crossed the room. Harnet and Galt appeared at the door of the kitchen; both were carrying meat cleavers. Galt's was covered with blood.

'Not this way!' shouted Harnet. While he was shouting, Galt was closing the door to the kitchen. I could see more

27

armed men through the door before it closed.

Harnet saw his wife and daughter disappear upstairs. Calling for Galt to follow him, he began to make his way to the base of the stairs. Several times he was blocked by the armed intruders, but each time he avoided their attacks with a speed and skill I had thought beyond him. He saw me hiding behind one of the upturned tables and veered towards me. 'This way, boy. Stay close to me.'

Without waiting to see if I followed, he turned and began to batter his way across the final distance to the stairs. One attacker blocked his path, only to have his sword turned away with the cleaver while a massive backhand threw him to the floor.

Harnet had never insisted that his patrons leave their weapons at the door, as was the practice of taverns of the other villages, so fierce fighting had broken out in all corners of the room. But more and more of the attackers poured through the broken doors and threw themselves on the beleaguered defenders.

We reached the stairs, and climbed to the second level, where we saw Danel standing at the end of the corridor. He waved for us to follow him, and disappeared into a room. We raced down the corridor, and reached the room in time to see Harnet's wife being lowered out of the window by Mikal. There was a look of horror on her face — I remembered that she was terrified of heights.

Shouts could now be heard coming from the direction of the stairs. Harnet and I went out the window, followed by Mikal. This left only Danel in the room. I reached the ground and jumped out of the way as Harnet slipped from the rope and fell to the ground beside me. Danel was now out of the window and climbing down the rope when the head of an intruder was thrust from the window above him. Seeing us in the open below, the intruder turned to shout to the other intruders but he made no sound as an arrow from Tomas' bow passed cleanly through his neck and disappeared into the room behind.

'Quick! Into the stable,' Danel said, as he reached the ground. In the stable, the tavern's supply wagon had been readied and Roebert was leading the team towards the rear entrance of the building.

'We must get to the livery across the street,' Roebert said.

'Your best bet, Harnet, would be to head east and then south towards the Capital. Once we get our mounts from the livery, we will catch up to you and see you safely on your way.'

Harnet nodded and climbed aboard. He flicked the team with the reins, sending them racing out into the street. Galt was in the front of the wagon beside Harnet. He was cracking the whip over the team. I was in the rear of the wagon with Harnet's wife and daughter, holding tight as it careened out into the street. The four travellers raced across the street behind us and entered the livery. Weapons clashed from within, and then all was quiet. I watched from the rear of the wagon and was about to jump to see if I could be of any help, when the four galloped out of the livery and spurred their horses after us.

As we left the edge of town I turned and saw many horsemen in pursuit. Harnet was standing in the wagon, steering the team between the trees. Suddenly an arrow flashed from the trees on the right, missing me by inches. I turned to tell Harnet, and as I did, I heard a gurgling sound. The arrow had taken Harnet's wife in the throat. She was dead by the time she hit the floor of the wagon. Jayne leapt to her mother's side. Horsemen broke from the trees all around. One moment Jayne was bending over her mother; the next she sat back on her heels and keeled over backwards. Her head struck the side of the wagon with a thump. She had been felled by a blow from one of the horsemen.

Two horsemen tried to grab the reins from Harnet but Galt was keeping them at bay with the whip. One of the riders leapt to the rear of the wagon, and was about to strike me when he straightened and fell forward, the shaft of an arrow protruding from his back. I looked up and saw Tomas as he let fly with another arrow. This one too struck another rider. Using his spear like a lance, Mikal rode past and knocked a third rider from his horse. Danel, sword in hand, was fighting to cover his brother's back as he continued to send arrows into the attackers. Roebert had ridden from the trail and had charged his mount directly at the largest group of attackers. With the buckler on his left arm he warded off blows from his opponents as he stood in his stirrups, swinging his flail left and right. With each blow he sent a rider crashing from his horse to be trampled by the mounts of the other attackers.

As we cleared the trees, three armed men dropped from the branches above into the wagon. Snatching the dagger from the attacker killed by Tomas' arrow, I threw myself at the first. My attack caught him by surprise, and he tumbled backwards with me on top of him. He slipped and we both fell from the rear of the wagon.

3

THE WASTELANDS

.   I WOKE to find myself lying on
the forest floor with Danel sitting beside me. We were in a
small grassy glade surrounded by enormous trees. He
looked down at me with a relieved look, and said, 'Just lie
there. You have a nasty bump on your head. You've been
unconscious for hours.' As he was talking, he was continually working a whetstone along the three and a half foot
blade of the sword which rested across his knees. I tried to
get up, but my head began to pound. I slowly leaned back
against the rough bark of a tree. 'What happened?' I asked
groggily.

'After you fell from the wagon, Mikal stopped to see if
you were still alive. When he found you were, he threw you
over his saddle, and joined us as we chased off the last of
the attackers.'

'You beat them all off?' I asked. 'There must have been
dozens.' I found it incredible that just four could have
beaten off all those attackers.

'It wasn't hard — they weren't really well trained, and
as soon as they started to take casualties most of them

tried to run. A few of them were Wolves — though they fought more like jackals — and it was these who put up the most resistance. Once they were dispatched, it was all over. Whoever planned this action had obviously positioned all his best men in the village.'

'What happened to Harnet and Galt?' The wagon was nowhere in sight, but its two horses were a short distance away with the ponies.

'They're both dead, I'm afraid,' he answered quietly. 'After you had fallen from the wagon, Galt forced another of the attackers over the side with the whip before being killed by the third. Harnet left the team to fight this attacker and the horses panicked. The wagon flipped, killing Harnet and his attacker.'

I could see he was affected by the loss of Harnet as much as I was. I remembered hearing them speak of old times and wondered just how well they had known each other.

'Where are the others?' I asked, turning from the painful subject.

'They are laying a false trail to lead the enemy into thinking we have turned south towards Tharrac,' Danel answered. 'Once they have finished, they are going to see to the bodies of Galt, Harnet and his family.' Again I could hear the loss in his voice. He continued to work on the blade of his sword.

'What type of sword is that?' I enquired.

'It's a Vahian glaive,' he answered. 'It is made of the finest quality steel and is a rare weapon even in Nuevah. It was my teacher's, as was the longbow my brother now uses. He gave us the weapons when we completed our training.'

'I have never seen a sword with a blade that long.'

'It's three and a half feet in length and gives me a nice

edge over those who prefer the two-foot short sword,' he answered.

I rested my aching head back against the tree and fell asleep.

I was awoken by the sounds of movement coming from the bushes nearby. I turned to Danel to see what we should do, but he was not there. There was no sign of him anywhere. I got unsteadily to my feet, in time to see Tomas stride from the forest. I turned around and Danel was again standing beside me. The look in my eyes must have given away my confusion because he smiled and pointed up. I looked above me and saw the low branch he must have swung up to when he heard the noise.

'No sign of pursuit,' Tomas said. 'I see the newest member of our party is awake at last.'

Roebert and Mikal entered the small glade. Mikal had several small rabbits draped over one shoulder. 'Awake at last?' he said with a smile. 'It's about time too — you've been resting long enough. How about earning your keep?' With that he handed me the rabbits and a knife. 'See what you can do with these.'

'Anything will be better than the burnt offerings we have been forced to eat on the trail lately,' Danel said.

'Is that so? I haven't noticed you losing any weight,' Mikal answered.

I moved to the edge of the glade and dug a small hole. I prepared the rabbits the way Harnet had taught me. The offal went into the hole which I then filled in and covered with a few large rocks to keep the scavengers out. Then I pegged out the skins. Once this was done, I took the prepared rabbits over to the fire and, placing them on one of the packs, I cut them into pieces. Pulling the large skillet from one of the packs, I greased it and set it over the fire. I rolled the pieces of rabbit in flour, seasoned with salt and nutmeg, and basted them in the pan. I kept rolling the pieces until they were sealed on all sides, then I turned my attention to the rest of the meal. I poured some dried peas into a pot of water and set it on the fire. The potatoes were old, so I placed them into the coals on the edge of the fire. I then busied myself setting out the travel plates and jacks. I had placed a large jug of cider in the supplies and from the look of the seal it was untouched.

I had been so busy with the preparation of the meal, I hadn't noticed what was going on around me. When I finally looked up from the work, I found my new companions were sitting a short way off watching me with a great deal of interest. Checking the pieces of rabbit once more, I turned and called to them.

They moved over quickly and picked up the plates I had laid out for them. There were only four plates, so I waited till one of them had finished. While I waited, I took the jug around and filled up their jacks. They were made of waxed leather, so as not to leak, and were hardier and lasted longer than other types of mugs.

Watching them eat, I got the first chance to study them up close. The brothers, I could now see, were more than that; they were twins. There was no mistaking it. Both were tall with mouse-brown hair and deep blue eyes. If not for Danel's scar, it would have been hard to pick them apart at first glance. As well as the longbow, Tomas carried a short sword or gladius on his saddle, though I had not seen him touch it yet. Danel, on the other hand, always seemed to have his right hand resting on the rounded pommel of his sword. He did not use a shield like Roebert or Mikal. Instead his lower left arm, from elbow to fingertips, was encased in a steel sleeve and glove. The fingers of the glove were scaled to allow them to flex, and there were small spikes along the outer edge of the sleeve. Protruding from the elbow was a short spike. He used this on anyone

34

foolhardy enough to close with him from behind.

Though slightly shorter than his companions, Roebert's great dexterity made up for his lack of height. His eyes were blue, which seemed to be a Vahian trait, and his hair was slightly darker than that of the twins. Roebert used the flail with deadly effect. The flail was a steel ball covered with spikes. This was attached to a chain, which was, in turn, attached to a wooden handle a foot and a half long. The force that could be applied to a blow was enormous. I even saw it dent the shields of several of the attackers.

As well as the spear and shield, Mikal carried four throwing knives in a belt across his chest, and one on either hip. He had given me one of these to use on the rabbits. Mikal's smile was always open and pleasant, yet it was hard to tell the true colour of his eyes, without being drawn into their depths.

'That's the best I've eaten on the trail for a long while,' Mikal said.

I washed his plate and filled it for myself. As I was eating, I thought of poor Harnet. I would miss him; he was the only person I'd ever thought of as family.

After my meal, I cleared away the utensils and supplies. My four companions sat around the fire, with a second jack of cider.

'We have travelled east since leaving Dienall,' Roebert said. 'Tomorrow, we turn north.'

'North!' interrupted Tomas.

'Yes, north. Raimend's Wolves will expect us to turn south toward the Capital, Tharrac. Then to follow the coast road to Lyram, or Esherweld.'

'They will believe it because that is the only way we can go,' Danel nodded.

Roebert looked at them and smiled. It was the first time I had seen him smile. 'We will turn north towards home.

They will not expect that. Then we will turn west and cross the Wastelands.'

The other three looked at each other in amazement.

'You're joking! We're almost two days from the Wastelands. If we have to swing well north of Dienall, will our supplies stretch that far?' Tomas asked.

'We have enough for six more days,' Mikal answered.

Danel looked at me. 'How long to cross the Wastelands?'

'Usually six days once we reach the rim, though at this time of the year, it could take eight.' I was happy to be included in the conversation at last.

'Why, what do you mean by "this time of year"?' Tomas asked.

'The northern tributary of the Wyernt River can sometimes dry up this time of year. We may have to travel to the West Wyernt before we find water,' I told him. 'I have crossed the Wastelands with Harnet on several occasions, none of which I liked.'

The brothers looked at one another and then turned to Mikal. 'It makes sense,' Mikal told them. 'Turning north will confuse them — then turning west should throw them off completely. If we find a guide to lead us to water, we can cross — a few days without food won't hurt us. The only problem is Teal: what do we do with him?'

I stood up and tried to make myself as tall as possible. 'I'll be coming with you,' I told them. 'As I said, I've crossed the Wastelands before, and I know where the waterholes are. I can help you.'

'How old are you, Teal?' Danel asked.

'Harnet thought I was four or five when I was bonded to him. That was eleven years ago this winter.'

'Who bonded you to Harnet?' Mikal asked.

'I don't know. I can remember very little about myself before I came to Dienall. Harnet simply told me I had been

36

acquired at a public sale in Tharrac, and I had been abandoned by my parents, and indentured to pay their debts.'

'They must have been large debts to have you in bond
for so long,' Tomas said.

Mikal was watching me, and could see these memories
were causing me pain. 'So, sixteen,' he said to change the
subject and turned to the others, 'Danel, two years ago
when you and Tomas were sixteen you had just completed
your training at the Collegium. If he wants to come with
us, why not? We need a guide. Why not him?'

'Okay,' Roebert said, 'You come with us. Now, let's get
some sleep. We will need to get an early start.'

Danel, Tomas and Roebert rolled themselves up in their
blankets. Mikal sat with me by the fire. 'Aren't you going
to sleep?' he asked.

'I'm not really sleepy. Can we talk for a while?'

'Of course we can,' he answered. 'What about?'

'When we were still in Dienall, I heard you speak of
finding something. You also said you would be followed.'
All my questions seemed to come out at once. 'Where are
we going?'

'When did you hear this?' he asked.

'The morning after the assassin was killed,' I answered.

'When we were speaking with Harnet?'

'Yes.'

'But we were speaking Vahian. How is it that you know
our language?'

'I don't know,' I answered. 'I just seemed to understand
a word here and there.'

This caused Mikal to pause, while he thought over what
I had just said. Then, apparently having made up his
mind, he continued.

'We're travelling to Lyram. About five months ago, the
King of Nuevah died. If you have not already guessed, we
are Vahian. The death looked to be natural, but several

days later, before the coronation, the heir apparent was found dead — stabbed in the back. The King's daughter, Princess Loriet, is next in line to the throne, but she is only thirteen. There's a law in our country which says a person must be eighteen before they can inherit estates. The King's second brother, Raimend is acting as Regent until she comes of age. This is quite normal, and happens all the time. If a person is not of age, then an older relation will act in their stead.'

'Did they find who killed the Prince?' I asked.

'Roebert was set the task. He is an Aron of the Royal Guard and is well-known. He followed what leads there were, and at last found the murder had been committed under the order of Raimend — the current Regent. Roebert told me of his find, but Raimend controlled everything by then, so it was useless to report it. We informed Princess Loriet of what he had found, but we were overheard by one of her handmaidens. Roebert and I were forced to flee. The Princess is safe. Should anything happen to her, the throne would go to the King's older brother, Grehem. Grehem and Raimend have been enemies for a long time.

'Roebert and I were riding south when we met Tomas and Danel. They were riding to Cruzeramba, the Capital, to tell of a discovery they had made on the southern border.' He stopped to pour himself some of the cider, and emptied his jack in one draught.

'They had been riding the southern border, when they discovered a party of Lyramians, who had been slain by Tribesmen of the Erg. In the process of burying the bodies Tomas and Danel had found a message pouch addressed to Raimend. Realising that none of the Erg Tribesmen would be able to read, the brothers then began a search for the message the pouch had contained. They did not take long to find what they were after. Once the Tribesmen

38

discovered the pouch contained nothing of value, they discarded the worthless piece of paper.'

'What was the message?' I asked, as he paused to refill his jack.

'It was from a merchant of Lyram, called Geerge. He claimed to have something of value for which the Regent would be willing to pay five thousand pieces of gold. Tomas and his brother believed it must be very important to be worth that amount of money, so they were hurrying to get the message to the Regent. When we came across them one evening and shared their fire they told us their story. Roebert then told them of his discoveries.'

'Does the merchant have the killer of the Prince?' I asked.

'No, the Prince's murderer was found by Roebert, but he was slain before he could name his Master to anyone else.'

'Then what has he got?' I asked.

'Roebert believes it is a who rather than a what,' Mikal said.

'Who?' I asked.

'About three years back, the King's second son disappeared in a skirmish with Tribesmen of the Erg on the southwestern border. This happened just north of Carnnoc in the Free States. Although the bodies of his Liegemen were discovered, his body was never found. It is possible the Prince was taken alive and has somehow, whether as a slave or a prisoner, found his way down to the coast town of Lyram. This is what Roebert believes the message was about.'

'Does that mean he is the rightful heir?' I asked.

'Yes. If we were to return the heir, Prince Nels, to Neuvah, it would be Nels, not his sister, who would take the throne. That would spoil Raimend's plans. He intends to marry the Princess before she is of age to rule, thus placing himself on the throne. Once he has achieved this, he will be untouchable.'

'If the Regent gets his hands on the Prince, he will have him quietly killed. We have to get to Lyram before his Wolves and free the Prince. Right?' I asked.

'That's right,' Mikal said. 'Now you had better get some sleep.'

We were on the move as the sun cleared the horizon. We headed north and around midday turned west. The pace was fast: we had to get to Lyram before another messenger could be sent to Raimend. Roebert believed the attack was directed against him because of what he had found out, and Harnet and his family and Galt had been killed, not because they had aided us, but because the Regent's Wolves, as Mikal had described, were jackals who went for the easiest victims. They were often contemptuously referred to as Jackals rather than Wolves.

By dusk on the second day we were slightly north of Dienall. Roebert sent Mikal ahead to spy out the village to see if anything could be learnt of our pursuers. He returned in the morning with grave news. The village had been burnt to the ground and all the people had been slain. At first glance it looked to be the work of the Natives of the Wastelands, but Mikal found evidence that it had been soldiers — Wolves — who had done the damage.

The clans of the Wastelands continually warred with each other, but for them to leave the protection of the Wastelands and attack a village of the Plains was a rare occurrence. The land of the Plains bordered the Wastelands on three sides, west, east and south; the north being walled by the Cordilleras.

'They are obviously trying to cover the fact that they attacked a village of the Plains. Many of the dead have had arrows placed in the original sword wounds. After a few days, it will be impossible for anyone to tell the difference,' Mikal said.

'What if somebody else should come across the village as you have just done? Won't they be able to see it was not the Natives who did the damage?' Tomas asked.

'The Jackals left three of their number behind to ensure that did not happen,' Mikal answered, and placed his right hand on the throwing knife at his hip. 'They were somewhat lax in their duty, so now they too, are part of the massacre.'

Roebert stood and moved towards the horses. 'We'd best be moving on. We'll travel through the night. It will get us out into the Wastelands, well beyond sight of any Jackals Mikal may have missed.'

We stopped briefly for a bit of food at midday, after which we continued westward. Mikal scouted ahead of us, looking for any sign of Natives. I was leading the two pack animals and the second horse from the wagon team; I was riding the other. Tomas was well back. He covered any tracks we left, and was watching our backtrail to make sure we were not being followed.

The Wastelands was not a desert. There was ample water if you knew where to look and the soil was as good as the surrounding areas. A variety of bramble had taken hold. The bramble was a large bush with very sharp spikes. It had a large root growth which made it extremely hard to clear from the land. In amongst the bramble were assorted burr and brier patches. And towering over them all were mighty thorn trees which grew to a height of fifty feet. If settlers were allowed enough time they would eventually be able to clear all these obstacles away, but the Natives had made it quite clear they did not want outsiders on their land. Just before last light, I led the group to a small waterhole where we drank our fill and replenished the supply we carried.

'That looks like a good place to spend the night,' Mikal said, pointing to a small flat section in one of the arroyos close by.

'Nuh — no good!' All eyes turned towards me as I spoke. 'The snakes will seek places like that as well. During the day they keep in the sun usually on the ridges like that one . . . ' I pointed up to a large flat area of rock before us. 'Once the sun sets, the rock loses its heat quickly, and the snakes seek warmth elsewhere. We need a place which has a stone floor where it will be too cold for them. Unfortunately this means it will have to be out in the open.'

'Where do you suggest?' Danel asked.

'Up there,' I answered, pointing to the raised area of rock I mentioned before.

'No fire?' Tomas asked.

'Not up there. However, we will have one down here. Once the meal is prepared, we will put the fire out and then move to the higher ground,' I answered.

'Anything else we should know about?' Roebert asked.

'Only that you should not venture into the arroyos once the sun sets.'

'All right! Danel, you stay here with Teal and the pack animals. The rest of us will go on ahead and see what the night's accommodation looks like,' Roebert said, and spurred his pony up the slope towards the area I had indicated.

I got a small fire going and started unpacking the stores. Danel stood a short distance off, watching me. I sliced bacon and placed it in the skillet. I heard a scuffle behind me and turned in time to see Danel stoop and snatch a snake from a nearby rock. He studied it and then walked over to me.

'What do you call this type of snake?' he asked. He held it out for me to see. He had it by the neck in his armoured left hand.

'It's a Dethshed. When it is about to strike, it raises its head and a hood opens. On the front of the hood is a mark like a human skull. That's how it gets its name.' As I spoke, I leaned back. The bite from a Dethshed was deadly. Danel threw the snake away from him and I went back to my work. At last the meal was ready, the fire was out, and all the gear was reloaded on the pack animals. With Danel leading, we started up the slope towards the rest of the group. As we climbed, I watched Danel. It was easy to see he was a Vahian. He was typical of his race, taller than the people of the Plains by at least a head, and of a much more solid build.

Nuevah was far to the north. I had heard many people say if not for this the Vahians would have invaded us long ago. There were two types of Vahians, the Lords or True Bloods and the Vahian vassals. The latter were not of the same stature and strength as the Lords, but they were still of Neuvah. They made up the farmers, merchants and common soldiery. They were the remnants of the original people who possessed the land before the Vahians arrived, but were now totally loyal to their Lords.

Nuevah was an area the size of the Plains and was located north of the Cordillera — a large series of mountain ranges. Beyond the ranges was the Erg — a great expanse of desert which made the Wastelands look like a farmer's vegetable patch. It took weeks to cross and was frequently subjected to terrible storms. There was very little water to be found and only small snakes and scorpions could be found in the heart of the Erg. Around its borders were found savage tribes.

We kept to the arroyos as we travelled. This slowed us down, but it kept us out of sight. Once in the distance, we caught sight of a party of Natives, but they were moving away from us.

43

4

JOURNEY TO BEESTRONE

SEVEN days after entering the Wastelands, we sighted the Wyernt River. The ponies sensed the water and had to be restrained while Mikal scouted out the water's edge to make sure there were none of the Jackals about. Mikal gave the all clear, and we raced to the river. The water was cool and fresh. I laid on the bank and scooped handfuls of it over my shoulders and head. Soaking wet, but refreshed, I got the water bags from the pack ponies and filled them up as well.

'Will we be staying here for any length of time?' I asked. 'I've noticed several ripples in the water — a feed of fish would go down well at the moment.'

'No,' Roebert answered. 'We'll continue downriver till last light. We can't be far from the ferry, and should cross the Wyernt and West Wyernt Rivers as soon as possible.'

We rode for several hours before it began to grow dark. We made camp in the trees away from the water's edge. The river was full of rather hungry fish, so it was not long before we had a nice meal cooking over the coals of our small fire. The aroma of the cooking fish had my companions and I waiting at the edge of the fire.

'The river seems far from dry,' Mikal commented.

'There must have been a great storm in the mountains at the river's source,' I answered.

'Is any of this familiar?' Roebert interrupted.

'Yes,' I answered. 'I believe we are only a few miles north of the ferry. Once over the Wyernt, we will be only three or so miles from the West Wyernt, and Beestrone, though the ferry is as far as I've ever travelled.'

He nodded and returned to his conversation with Tomas. Sitting waiting for the fish to cook and listening to the sounds of the river and night life around me, I began to fall asleep.

I was awoken by Danel. 'I think they're done,' he said, as he gently shook my shoulder.

I rubbed the sleep from my eyes. 'I think I'll go down to the water and wash my face,' I said, talking to no one in particular. As I walked down I heard the same sounds which had caused me to fall asleep. Now, instead of being restful, they were frightening. I hurriedly splashed water onto my face and turned to make my way back to the camp site. I took only a few steps when I realised something was wrong. I stopped and listened; but I heard nothing. I kept walking, slower now. Again I stopped and listened, but still I heard nothing. Then I realised that I *did* hear nothing . . . nothing at all. No animals of any kind. I dropped to a crouch as I had seen the others do, my hand searching for a sword that wasn't there.

Danel had been instructing me on the basics of swordsmanship — the stance and grip. But I had not had many lessons, and even if I had, there had been no spare sword for me to carry. I looked around the ground at my feet and saw several rocks. I picked up two, both slightly larger

45

than my fists. With one in each hand, I retraced my steps to the camp.

I could see the fire of the camp through the trees ahead. As I watched, a shadow passed between me and the fire. I stopped and looked around, but I could see nothing else. I looked back towards the camp site and saw another shadow flit across the light of the fire.

I crept up to the edge of the camp site. The fire was still burning, though somewhat lower. My companions were wrapped in their blankets and looked to be asleep. I found it strange that all four would sleep with no thought of sentries. That they would do so before my return, also puzzled me.

A shadow straightened before me and I heard the sound of a sword being drawn. The shadow cried out and began to move towards the camp. At the cry, other shadows leapt from the darkness, drawing weapons as they did so. I also cried out — a warning to my companions — and launched myself at the closest shadow. I struck at the head with all the force I could muster. The shadow went down, but almost immediately began to get to its feet. I dropped one stone, and, grasping the remaining one in both hands, I brought it down on the head of the rising shadow. This time it went down and stayed down.

I searched the ground trying to find the fallen sword. I looked into the camp and saw one of the attackers tumble and fall. My hand found the hilt of the sword. As I pulled it towards me, I saw another of the attackers trip and fall. Neither he nor his companion rose. As I was watching I saw a third shadow stumble; this one was closer to the fire, and in the failing light of the dying campfire I saw an arrow protruding from between his shoulder blades. A fourth and fifth fell before a cry issued from the attackers. They turned and began to search the shadows. Danel stepped from the furthest edge of the camp and drew his glaive. The intruders saw him and attacked; five of their number were down and at last they saw something physical to attack. They rushed forward for the kill, only to be met by a flashing shield of glove and glaive. Regardless of which direction they attacked the lone figure, their blows were blocked by the glove, while the long blade of the glaive reached out effortlessly and took the life from all opponents.

Roebert moved from the shadows and engaged the attackers from the rear. Four were smashed to the ground before warning was given of the attack from behind. Six turned to engage the new source of danger. Two attacked and were swept away with blows from the flail. The others were more cautious, and spread out into a half-circle in an attempt to rush him from all sides. One of them fell, an arrow in his throat. A second took an arrow in the back and fell beside his companion. The other two turned and ran. Danel stopped a blow with his glaive and almost tore the face from his attacker with a smashing left. The remaining intruders were set upon by Roebert from the rear. After a few half-hearted blows, they turned and fled.

Tomas dropped from a tree beside me and walked out into the camp; he had an arrow nocked but not yet drawn. Danel and Roebert moved over to the fire as well.

'Teal! Build up the fire. We will be back shortly,' Roebert said, and with Danel and Tomas close behind, disappeared into the shadows in the direction that the remaining intruders had gone.

Once the fire was ablaze again, I looked at the ruined meal strewn about. I sat down and began to pack away the remaining supplies and gear. I dropped the sword I had taken for the skirmish next to the body of its owner. I did not want a weapon which had been used to spill the blood of innocent people. That very sword might have been used in the massacre of the people of Dienall.

Danel and Tomas returned and helped me to repack the animals. The last strap was being tightened when the others returned.

'They're still running,' Mikal said. 'There were a few Wolves amongst them who would not dishonour their Lord, but they did not have much experience and short work was made of them.'

'Mount up. We'll put some distance between us and this place before the sun is up.'

We rode west in silence. When we came to the river, Roebert led us into the current. The packs on the animals were nearly empty so they did not have too great a problem with the swim. My mount, on the other hand, being somewhat older and not as versatile as the others, began to tire before the other bank was reached. Just as I thought I would have to swim the remaining distance, Mikal moved up alongside and pulled me over to his mount.

'Hold tight to my waist, Teal,' he told me. 'We're almost there.'

At last our mounts found footing and began to climb from the water. I dropped to the ground; my legs were shaking from the cold.

Roebert turned south. I mounted up and followed them. Danel had gathered up the leads for the pack animals and as I neared him, he passed them to me and smiled. I drifted in and out of sleep as we rode. How I managed to stay in the saddle was a mystery to me. I was still mounted when Roebert finally called a halt. The others dismounted, while I simply fell unceremoniously from the saddle. Danel took the ponies and horses away while Roebert brought out flint and steel, and lit a fire. Tomas and Mikal had disappeared, but I forgot about them as I saw the small flames take hold of the wood. I walked shakily over to the fire and sat beside it.

Mikal returned and told us we were not being followed.

The first I knew of Tomas' return was when three brush turkeys were dropped beside me. With one of Mikal's knives I set to work on the birds. Soon they were cooking and filling the camp with a pleasant aroma. All the while, Tomas had been sitting by his gear and drying off his longbow. When at last he felt it was dry enough, he picked up a small roll of material and walked over to me.

'Here!' he said, and threw the roll to me. I picked it up and held it in front of me. 'Well, open it — it's no good as it is.'

I unwrapped the material. The last wrapping fell away to reveal a knife. Not the short-bladed, balanced weapon that Mikal had, but a knife with an eight inch blade, double edged. Beside the knife was a sheath of leather decorated with strange symbols. I held the knife up and the light of the fire reflected from the blade of the weapon. On the blade above the hilt were the same symbols that were on the sheath.

'I wouldn't make a habit out of attacking an armed man with a rock — it may stunt your growth,' he said. This drew a laugh from the others.

'That's true, Teal,' Mikal added. 'The next time you try it, he may turn around and take the rock from you and make you eat it.'

This brought even more laughter from the others. But I didn't mind. I hardly even heard them. My full attention was on the knife in my hands. I slipped the knife into the sheath and this in turn I slipped onto my belt. I stood and walked around; the weight of the knife felt good. I looked up at the others and saw they were no longer laughing. Each had a strange look in his eyes as if thinking back to the time he had received his first weapon.

I sat down by the fire and drew the knife once more. 'What do these words mean?' I asked. They looked like small twists and squiggles. I had no idea what made me think they were words.

He took the knife from me and held it up to the light of the fire and said. 'This symbol means Victory, and this one, Life. *Victory and Life* — it is the creed of Nuevah.'

I took the knife from him and slid it into the sheath. 'Do all Vahian weapons have the creed on them?'

'Yes. All have a creed, though not necessarily the same one. We,' he said indicating the others, 'are from the southern section of the land, the province of Purusmayo. *Victory and Life* is our creed.'

'How can you have victory and life? Today we won but many died!' I asked.

'When we say life, we mean the life of us or our people. Today we won. Our enemies were defeated and we did not lose one man,' he answered.

'What happens if you have to die to gain victory?'

He smiled and leaned back slightly. 'Many people have asked me about that. If I were to die then the victory would not be complete. The side I had fought on may have won, but I would have lost. If too many were to die to attain a victory, then it would not be a victory at all.'

I was about to ask another question when Mikal called out. 'This may be educational for you but it is doing nothing for our meal.'

A quick look showed me the birds were almost burnt. I pulled our supper from the skillet, burning my fingers in the process. The others joined us, and soon the only noise to be heard was the crunching of small bones, as we all ate our fill.

After the meal Roebert took the first watch and the others turned in. I lay there thinking for some time, with the knife gripped in my hands, but sleep eluded me. I eventually rose and, with a blanket around my shoulders, moved over to where Roebert was sitting.

'What can I do for you?' he asked.

I had not had much to do with Roebert, but I felt, as the oldest of the companions, he would be the best to answer my questions.

'I was talking to Tomas before and I'm not sure I understand what he was telling me.'

'All right, sit down. What were you discussing?' he asked.

'The creed of Nuevah,' I answered.

'What did he tell you our creed was? *Victory and Life?*' he said.

I nodded.

'To be truthful, the creed reads, *Victory with Life*. To have victory you must be alive. When the Vahians first settled in the lands to the north of the Erg, they fought continually with the tribes who lived there. Many of the battles were won by the Vahians, but at an incredible cost of life. We have never been a prolific race and if this continued we would soon have died out. Our leaders at the time came up with the creed. We must win, but we must also live. Can you understand that?'

'Yes,' I answered. The way Roebert explained it made more sense.

'The Vahians have survived by virtue of their fighting skills and stature. Thanks to the creed, we are now, to the vexation of our enemies, once again a growing race.'

'Tomas said there was more than one creed; is that right?' I asked.

'There is only one true creed; the others are variations of it. The province of Ferrope's creed is *Victory through Peace*. And the creed of the Hollucho province is *Victory in Death*. The new Regent is of the Hollucho province. His Wolves, when confronted, will fight to the death, no quarter asked or given. They are as totally loyal to their Lords and creed as we are to ours.'

'Do all the different groups get on well together?' I asked.

'We call them factions. Yes, they all work together for the growth of our race. As you may have noticed all the creeds begin with victory for our people before the method of its accomplishment.'

'How could you tell some of the attackers were Jackals?'

'To any member of the Wolves, or Jackals, as Raimend's soldiers are sometimes called, loss means death. Only the winners survive. This means any Jackal you meet will have been undefeated in battle. They take great pride in this, and each year they are awarded a scar. The more scars, the longer they have served, and the longer they have served the more dangerous they are.'

'Are the scars the only way?'

'No, beneath the robes or cloaks, they would be wearing the tabard with the crest of their Province and rank.' As he said this he drew open his cloak to show me his tabard. It was white with a large green tree which took up most of the chest. The right shoulder showed a striking snake, and the other shoulder bore a golden four-pointed star, his badge of rank.

'What faction did the Prince belong to?'

'He will follow his father's way — that of the Ferropeans.'

'How is that possible? Surely the Prince and the Regent would be of the same province?' I asked.

'It's common for the King to take a bride from either one of the northern or southern provinces,' he explained. 'Raimend grew up in the Ferropean province, but once he had finished his training at the Collegium, he made his home in the northern province of Hollucho, the birthplace of his mother . . . Now it is time for me to wake Tomas for his watch. I suggest you get some rest.'

I rolled myself up in my blankets. I lay there for some

time, my mind turning the things I had heard over and over. With the blankets wrapped tightly around me, and clutching the knife firmly in my right hand, I thought about the journey ahead, and of the new and strange things I would see.

I felt myself being shaken, and I realised the night had passed and the sun was climbing into the eastern sky, throwing long shadows across the camp.

'No fire this morning. We'll leave as soon as the ponies are saddled. We must reach Beestrone and get passage to the coast as soon as possible,' Roebert told us.

We rode and finally came to the ferry. We paid our fares and crossed the West Wyernt River. I would have preferred to have crossed the Wyernt the same way, but at the time we did not have much choice. At least we didn't have to swim that one as well.

Once off the ferry we turned south, and in less than an hour, we crested a small ridge and looked down on the town of Beestrone. It was much larger than Dienall, and was built on the western bank of the junction of the Wyernt and the West Wyernt. The main business of the town was trading. The merchants of the town would buy or sell anything.

Beestrone was a town which had grown in uncontrolled spurts. As its trade had increased, new sections of the town mushroomed with little regard for planning. The narrow, twisting streets which snaked their way between prospering businesses sometimes turned back on themselves, ending suddenly at the rear of one of its own establishments. Newcomers to the town were often forced to travel the maddening streets for hours before they reached their destinations.

The mountain ranges to the north were full of miners and trappers who brought in their finds and catches to the town to deal with the merchants. Not many of the mountain people ever struck it rich, but they made sufficient to allow them to live their lives in the mountains away from what they call the 'madness' of the towns.

After the trading was finished, the goods were sent downriver, where they could go from treble to ten times their purchase price. The merchants of Beestrone had this trade tied up; they were the only ones who operated the river trade. We rode down from the ridge into the town.

We took lodgings at an inn four or five streets back from the waterfront. While Roebert and Tomas went to arrange passage south for us and our mounts, Mikal and Danel looked for stores to replace those we had used. I was left to tend to the mounts. Mikal had given me a small purse full of coppers. I counted them and found it contained twenty of the small copper coins of the Plains. Coins of the Plains were either copper, silver or gold and were small and square. I could not believe I was holding so much wealth in my hands.

I felt like a king as I strode across the street to the livery. The purse jingled on one hip, while the knife slapped at my thigh. I entered the livery, and instantly the owner was at my side. The way I walked in, and the sound of the coins, had attracted him like a moth to a flame.

'How can I be of service, young Lord?' he asked.

I was still wearing the travelling cloak Mikal had given me. The owner bowed as he spoke to me. I had bowed that way myself many times while working at Harnet's tavern.

'My apologies, Lord. Of course you wish the animals to be tended,' he said bowing even deeper. He turned and called for his son and helper. They relieved me of the reins of the mounts and were soon leading them to stalls at the rear of the building.

I had done this task many times in the past. Often the traveller would throw me a small coin which I would take to Harnet. I slipped my fingers into the pouch at my hip, and drew out some coins. I counted out five. Three I dropped into the owner's hand; one each I tossed to the other two. They thanked me as I left the livery.

Entering the inn where we had our lodgings, I walked into the tap room and began to look about. It was larger than Harnet's, but that was the only difference. As I was standing there, I was approached by a small chubby man. He was busily wiping his hands on a large apron tied around his ample middle.

'May I help you, Lord?' he asked.

Again I was taken aback by the fact that somebody took me for a person of station.

He obviously took my startled look to mean something else.

'Of course, Lord. This way.' He led me to a chair by the fire. 'Please, if you will be seated, I will bring you some refreshments.' He slipped from my side and disappeared into the dark recesses of the kitchen. He soon returned with a mug of ale and a platter of fine-smelling cheese. He placed these by my side and again disappeared.

I settled myself by the fire, placing my feet on the edge of the fireguard. I helped myself to the cheese, and sipped at the ale. Both were pleasant-tasting and refreshing. I finished the mug and turned to order another, but before I could call, a girl appeared at my side with a full mug.

From over my shoulder a voice said, 'Do you think we may join you, young Sir?'

I waved to the vacant seats nearby, indicating they could seat themselves. For the first time in days I was warm and relaxed. I turned my head slightly to look at the speaker. I nearly spilt my drink when I saw the ones seating themselves were in fact my travelling companions.

Seeing my surprise, the others began to laugh. Tomas moved to the fire and warmed his hands. 'The passage downriver is booked, supplies are bought and equipment is ordered. Everyone has been exceedingly busy. But the busiest of all, it seems, is our companion here.' Tomas nodded at me, then the crackling fire and the nearly empty cheese platter. 'Perhaps we should help our friend in his labours?'

Danel signalled for a round of drinks while the rest of the group brought their seats in closer to the fire. As I sat there and listened to them tell stories and joke with each other, I felt a companionship I had never felt before.

We stayed at the fire for hours, singing songs from their homeland, and, even though some of the words were still strange to me, I found myself singing with them. As I sang I seemed to pick up the meaning of the songs.

The next morning at breakfast, of which I ate very little, I heard my companions discussing the coming journey downriver. It seemed that the only passage that could be had at present was a large raft going downriver in seven days. There were several other barges and rafts leaving Beestrone, but all were cargo carriers and were full. No amount of talk would convince the merchants to leave a small portion of their cargo behind and carry us instead. If we paid the sum that the cargo left behind would bring, we would be more than welcome, but the amounts quoted were exorbitant.

My companions were disturbed by the news, as this would allow the merchant, Geerge of Lyram, to realise that his first message had not been received and that a second would need to be sent. The longer we delayed here, the closer the Regent would be to learning of the possibility of the Prince's existence.

I, on the other hand, found the news welcome. On hearing it, I immediately left my companions to their meal and went upstairs to my bed. The cheese which was matured in this area must have been of a very strong type. It seemed to have given me a headache, and had left me feeling quite quite ill.

5

JON

I WOKE and climbed from the bed, feeling much better for the extra sleep. I crossed to the window and looked out on the town. The sun was high, showing it was a little after noon. I turned to the chair for my clothes and found they were gone. A brief search revealed some clothes hanging by the door. They were my size and cut in the style favoured by Vahians. I dressed quickly. The clothes were the finest I had ever worn, they felt soft against my skin and were smooth to touch. I threw the cloak around my shoulders. Touching the purse and settling the knife in a better position on my hip, I left the room.

I went down to the tap room but the others were not there. The innkeeper hurried over to my side.

'Your men have not returned yet, Lord. Would you be wanting something — food or drink?' he asked, again rigorously rubbing his hands on his apron.

'No,' I answered. 'I am going for a walk. When my . . .' I paused and thought about what he had said, 'men return, tell them I will be back shortly.' With that I left the inn.

Once out of the inn, I began to wander the streets absorbing the sights, sounds and smells of the city. All the sounds and smells were new to me. Dienall was never like this. Everywhere I looked there were women in strange clothes and armed men. Traders were calling out their wares in the hope of attracting the attention of a buyer.

Paying no particular attention to the direction I took, I soon found myself at the riverfront. There were barges and rafts of all sizes and shapes. There were only a few boats, but this was because they were expensive, or so I was told by one of the workers. He also explained to me that rafts and barges were profitable as the lower plains had very few trees, and the timber from the vessels was sold for additional profits.

I got to know the worker well. His name was Jon. The next day I met him at the docks, and I did the same the following day as well. The stories he told me were wonderful, and he almost made me believe that they were true. On the third day of our stay in Beestrone, we were sitting talking, when he told me he was leaving the next day on a barge going downriver.

The news was distressing, as I had hoped we would be able to share the time I had left to wait till our barge south was ready to leave.

'Do you have to go?' I asked.

'I'm sorry, Teal,' he said, 'but I've no choice in the matter. By last light today the barge will be loaded and after one last night on the town, I'll be away.'

I was about to speak, when I noticed a small sailing vessel angling across towards the docks. It was full of armed men; they were wearing cloaks of deep red, almost the colour of blood. Their hoods were thrown back and I could see they were wearing metal helmets with a long red crest starting over the nose and running over the head to the nape of the neck.

59

The boat touched the dock with a thump, and the soldiers climbed from the vessel and began to move among the crowd. As one soldier moved, his cloak parted and I could see a red tabard with a green tree in a white circle displayed centrally on his chest: the tabard of the Hollucho Province of northern Nuevah.

I began to get to my feet, but Jon stopped me, placing a restraining arm on my shoulder.

'From the look on your face,' he said, 'they don't seem to be friends of yours.'

I believed I could trust him. 'They're not,' I told him. 'They, or others of their kind, have been following and attacking my companions and I for some time.'

'Then hold fast till they're gone or you'll be giving yourself away.'

Willing hands secured the small vessel, while the soldiers moved through the crowd asking questions. All the people they asked shook their heads in response to their questions. The soldiers were working their way through the crowd, getting closer to where Jon and I were sitting. I pulled the cloak tighter about me to hide the Vahian style clothing I was wearing.

As they came closer, I heard one of the soldiers asking a dockworker if he had seen a party of five Vahians; one of them a youth. I caught my breath — they were describing me as a young Vahian.

One of the soldiers stopped in front of me. He leaned forward and asked, 'Have you seen five Vahians travelling south; possibly looking for passage on a barge?' His cloak had been thrown back behind his shoulders, and I could clearly see the wolfhead emblem adorning the right shoulder.

I just shook my head. He seemed about to ask me again, but Jon cut in.

'It is possible I have seen the ones you are after. But

where they are at present seems to have escaped me,' he said and scratched his head in a thoughtful way.

I must admit my first thought was that he was going to betray us, but when I looked up at him he winked and smiled. The soldier turned and called to another of the armoured men, who shouldered his way through the crowd towards us. He was a head taller than all the others. As he had removed his helmet, I saw that his face was covered in scars, so many, in fact, that there was not a place another scar could go. As he threateningly leant over Jon, I could see there were even scars on his neck.

'You have seen the ones we seek?' he demanded.

'It is possible I have, but it is difficult to remember,' Jon answered.

'What will help you to remember, friend?' the large scar-faced man asked.

'If I knew I had the price for a jack of grog after my day's work is done, it would relieve my mind, and I'm sure it would help me to remember,' Jon answered, as he again scratched his tangled hair in thought.

A coin was thrown on the ground at Jon's feet. He stooped, picked it up, bit it and had it away before I could even see the size of it. He licked his lips, and said. 'About two days ago, as near as I can remember, five Vahians like the ones you described, tried to book passage to Lyram. They were told the next barge wasn't for seven days. The last I saw of them, they were mounted, with maybe five pack animals in tow.'

'Which way?' Jon scratched his head in thought until another coin landed at his feet. He stooped and went through the same routine as before. Once the coin was out of sight he said, 'Northwest'.

The smaller Wolf turned to the heavily scarred one and said, 'Carnnoc!' They turned, and moved quickly to the livery behind the docks.

'Why?' I asked.

'A man has to make a living where he can. 'Sides, I never did have any time for those Jackals.' After saying this, he spat on the ground. 'I'll be gone by the time they find I've steered them wrong.'

'Gone?' I asked.

'Remember, I leave at first light tomorrow.'

I turned and looked to where the Wolves had disappeared and then I looked down at the barge nestled into the dock. Finally I looked up at Jon. A large smile came to my face.

'All right,' he said. 'But you'll have to be here at first light, and no horses. I'll have to get rid of some of the load as it is just to accommodate you and your friends.'

'We'll be here,' I told him.

'Right, dawn tomorrow,' he said. 'I'll see you then.'

He turned back to his work, and I started to walk back to the inn. On the way an idea came to me. I stopped and turned back towards the docks. At the livery into which the Wolves had disappeared I crossed the street and waited in the deep shadows of an alley. After a short time, the scarred Wolf and three others came out into the street. They were leading eight horses which were saddled and had blankets and waterbags tied to the saddles.

They led the horses a few hundred yards up the street. Once outside a large building they met up with the other five of their party. These five were busy loading supplies onto six pack horses.

Drawing the cloak about me, I left the alley and strolled along the opposite side of the street till I drew abreast of the eight men. As I passed them, they finished packing the last of the supplies. They mounted and rode towards the northern gate, leading the pack horses. I watched them disappear round a corner, then I ran after them. I kept after them until eventually I saw them at the northern gate waiting for one of the guards to pass them through.

I ran back to the inn. As I approached the front door, I forced myself to slow to a walk. I headed straight for the tap room. My travelling companions were there, seated around a table in the far corner. They were talking and gesturing as I approached them.

'There were five of them and they were buying supplies at that big place down on the riverfront,' Tomas was saying.

'How many pack animals?' Danel asked.

'Six, but I saw no mounts. There could have been more of them seeing to the horses,' Tomas added.

'They obviously heard we could not book passage,' Roebert said, 'so they believe we left and travelled south on horseback. With them in front of us, it is going to make things very difficult.'

I was noticed for the first time. 'Teal,' Mikal said, 'you'll have to stay in for a while — there are Jackals in the city.'

I nodded. 'Yes I know,' I answered. 'I saw them.'

Roebert turned from the table to look at me. 'Did they see you?' he asked.

I nodded again. Mikal stood and Danel's hand dropped to the hilt of his sword. Tomas turned to Roebert. 'Do you think they recognised him?' he asked.

'They have no idea what the fifth member of our party looks like,' Roebert answered. 'But they would have recognised the style of clothing.' He turned back to me. 'Do you think you were followed?'

'No. They seemed to pay hardly any attention to me. Besides they're gone now, so we have nothing to worry about,' I answered.

'How do you know they're gone?' Roebert enquired.

'I followed them to the gate and watched them leave. There were eight of them.'

'Which way did they go?' All of them were standing now.

'North. They think we are trying for a place called Carnnoc. Well, that's what one of them said, anyway.'

'How did you hear that?' Roebert asked.

'They asked me if I'd . . . ' I never finished.

'Asked you!' Roebert said, grabbing me by the shoulders. 'What do you mean, they asked you?'

'I was at the docks with Jon when this boatload of Wolves arrived. They asked everyone, including me, if we'd seen you. Jon said he had, and that you had left the city heading northwest. That was when I heard one of them say "Carnnoc".'

Roebert looked at me. He could see I had not told all. 'And,' he said, 'keep going . . . '

'Well, they bought horses and supplies and left the city. I followed them right up to the gate, but they were moving fast and didn't even look back.'

'This friend of yours, Jon. What made him tell them we were going northwest?' Mikal asked.

'He said he did not like them,' I answered.

'Very well,' Roebert said. 'The first Waystation is about two days' ride from town. By the time they reach there, and find we haven't passed they'll know they were given a false lead. It will take another two days for them to return. This gives us four days to get out of Beestrone and as far away as possible.'

'We could,' I told them, 'be in Lyram in five days, if we get a barge downriver.'

'But there are no barges,' Mikal said.

Roebert saw me smile, and said, 'Perhaps there is a barge.'

The others faced him, then all turned to me. 'What else have you been up to this morning?' he asked.

'Jon is leaving tomorrow on a large barge heading for

Lyram.' This got their attention. 'If we are at the docks by first light we will be able to travel with him, but no horses — he hasn't the room.'

'You have certainly been busy this morning, Teal. What you have done has helped us a great deal. But in the future I want you to get one of us before you attempt what you did this morning. It would have been so easy for them to see you following them. If they did and they followed you here, all would have been lost. Understand?' Roebert said, and smiled.

'Yes.'

We all left the tap room. Roebert and Danel went to arrange for the sale of the ponies and pack horses. The rest of us went upstairs to pack our gear. I was looking forward to tomorrow — I had never been on a barge before.

6

THE WYERNT RIVER

I AWOKE. Mikal was gently shaking my shoulder. 'It's time to go,' he told me.

After throwing off the covers, I climbed out of bed and sleepily began to dress — not in the new Vahian clothes I had been given, but in well-worn travelling clothes which I had bought yesterday.

Roebert had settled our debt with the innkeeper the night before, so there was nothing we needed to do that morning, but pick up our equipment, and leave the inn by the rear door, to make our way to the docks as quietly as possible. The rising sun could not reach between the tall buildings, so the streets were still dark, and there was no sound as we travelled the streets to the docks. It was eerie; I was looking over my shoulder continuously.

The docks were bathed in the red glow of the rising sun and looked deserted. A short sharp whistle suddenly came from our right, and we turned and made our way in that direction. Jon was sitting on the edge of the dock overlooking the barge on which we would be travelling.

I was about to greet him when he placed a finger to his

lips to silence me. He jumped down to the barge and signalled for us to throw our gear down to him. We did, and then boarded the barge ourselves. After the gear had been stowed away, he released the lines holding us to the dock and we began to drift out and pick up speed. Jon took up a long pole and began to steer us out further from the docks. The further we got, the faster we went. We were soon moving at what I judged to be a fast walk.

'How long will it take us to get to Lyram?' Roebert asked, as he looked at the passing riverbank.

'Five days travelling,' Jon answered. 'We will have to stop at Liechen, Boarric and Merbah.' All the time he was talking, he was at the rear of the barge, using the steering pole to keep the barge in the centre of the river. 'The current is faster away from the banks,' he explained to us. 'It's also much safer out here.' He didn't elaborate about the last statement, and no one asked, as all of us were settling on and around the cargo trying to catch up on some sleep.

The ride downriver was somewhat of a disappointment. We reached Liechen and then travelled on to Boarric. At each of the stops, cargo was unloaded and some items were added. We finally reached Merbah. There the entire cargo was off-loaded and replaced by a different one. The previous load had been boxes and crates. This one was made up of kegs and casks.

We were again on our way. Each night we made for the riverbank and tied up. With one sentry, the rest of us got a good night's sleep. However, on the last night before we reached Lyram, Jon had us hold position out in the centre of the river, using as an anchor a large stone he took on in Merbah. The current was not strong enough to drag the anchor so we were secure for the night. That night we had two sentries at each watch.

'Do you expect trouble?' Roebert asked.

'Yes,' Jon answered. 'This section of the river is notorious for scavengers. If we keep to the centre of the river with a double sentry, we should be safe.'

'What shall I do about the evening meal?' I asked him. 'With no fire, I won't be able to prepare something hot. We'll need something to keep the cold out.'

'You'll find cold meat, a spicy cheese, and some bread up forward by the small cask. Bring the cask as well,' he added. 'I picked this up while we were in Boarric. The meal should do us till we are in Lyram tomorrow, and the cask contains a beverage which will not only keep out the cold, but also keep us awake. It will do so for several days if too much is drunk.'

We ate, and Roebert and Mikal drank a small portion from Jon's cask. The rest of us turned in. There was a chill wind blowing from downriver. The barge was still and the only noise was that of the water as it moved between the logs of the barge.

Jon and I were woken for the second watch. I sat up and rubbed the sleep from my eyes. The chill wind was still blowing, so I kept the blankets wrapped around my shoulders as I crawled over to Jon.

'Here,' he said, offering me a full mug poured from the small cask. 'This will get the chill from your bones.'

I sipped at the beverage. 'Jon, what will happen to you when you return to Beestrone?' I asked. At every opportunity I had questioned Jon about the things he had done and the places he had seen. 'Those Jackals are not going to be too happy with you. You have cost them at least four days.'

'I won't be going back,' he answered. 'I have decided this will be my last trip downriver.'

'Why? Don't you like the river?' I asked.

'I don't mind the river; in some ways it reminds me of the sea. I love the sea.'

'Why are you here then?' I asked.

'Years ago the sea was a place of beauty, but now the Corsairs keep all the shipping to the coastal waters. Galleys and galleasses have replaced the sailing ships of old.'

'What about the Great Western Ocean? The Corsairs can't control that as well?' I enquired. The great ocean to the west was enormous. I had never seen it. As a matter of fact, until I met Jon I had never met anyone who had seen it.

'The Great Western Ocean is like the Uskery Sea,' Jon said. 'Once shipping covered it to the horizon and beyond, though not too far beyond. The monsters were few, and Corsairs were unknown. In those days, a man could sail from any port, on any type of vessel. But a few years ago the monsters began to increase in number.'

'Monsters?' I asked.

'Yes, monsters!' he answered. 'Creatures which, once seen, could never be forgotten, huge fish which could swallow a vessel whole, spitting out the crushed timbers once the delicate morsels had been separated. Other beasts have arms like mooring cables which they wrap round the vessel, slowly tightening their grip until the crew are forced into the turbulent waters, easy prey for the waiting young.'

'Where did they come from?'

'They had always been there, but if you steered clear of them they would do you no harm. But as their numbers increased they would attack ships without reason. Soon no shipping could venture out of sight of land without being destroyed. Shipping began to hug the coast, much the same as they are forced to do in the Uskery Sea now. But then other dangers began to arise.'

'There are creatures called Plastrons living in the shallow tidal waters of the western coast. They are man-like in shape, but that is where the resemblance ends. Half again as tall as a man, they are scaled like fish. Their feet and

69

hands are much like humans,' although they are webbed, and have six fingers. The mouth is a long slash across the face holding dozens of razor-like teeth. They have a short, flat tail which propels them through the water, and balances them on land.

'The Plastrons, like the monsters of the deeper water, generally left the shipping alone, and in return they were left alone. But with the monsters roaming in close to the coasts, the Plastrons were forced to hunt closer to home. At first they kept to the tidal waters, but it became evident they would soon die out if they continued. Then they began to raid the coastal villages; only the smallest villages were attacked, but even so, the villagers outnumbered the Plastrons and were usually able to drive them off using fire.

'As shipping was forced closer inshore many ships began to run foul of the shoals which are in abundance along the coastline. The Plastrons found they could plunder the wrecks and get all the food they needed. The next step was the attacking of ships as they travelled the shallow waters.

'The Plastrons live in small family groups, usually five or six males with three times the number of females and dozens of young. The males climb the sides of the vessels and wreak havoc on the crew, while the females and young stay in the water and attack any who try to flee.

'The Plastrons have large plate-like scales on their chests, shoulders, and sides. These are like breastplates and will stop even the strongest stroke. The scales on the arms and legs are not as thick, but deflect many a stroke which is not well aimed. The top of the head is covered in a thick bony plate. Against this natural armour, the sailor's weapons are ineffective. There are only a few places that the creatures are vulnerable. One is under the arm, where a good strike could penetrate one of the two hearts. The other is the eyes. A good archer might be able to place an arrow in one of the eyes. This will enter the brain, killing the creature immediately. The third and last place is the groin. Unfortunately, this entails lying on the floor and stabbing up at the groin as the creature steps over you. This, however, is not a death blow and the attacker is usually torn to pieces by the Plastron before it dies.

'So, there is no more life on the ocean for me. And, until the Corsairs are gone, there is no life on the Uskery Sea either. I think I might try one of the great rivers to the east once I leave here.'

Jon continued to talk throughout the entire watch. I was enthralled — I never believed it possible one person could have done, or seen, so much in one lifetime. Eventually our watch ended and I crawled back to my sleeping position. Curled in my blankets, I tried to will myself to sleep.

Once asleep, I dreamed. I saw the flashing oars of a trim corsair as it cut through the swell chasing a fat merchantman. The side rails of the corsair were lined with shields, protecting the armed crew who waited their chance to board the lightly-protected merchant vessel. I also saw grey-scaled Plastrons as they swarmed over the rail of a wrecked carrick, slashing the crew to pieces in their lust for battle, and later in a feeding frenzy.

Further from the hazy coast, I saw large creatures driving through the ocean waves as they closed in on a fleeing trading vessel. Smooth bodies flashed through the water as their spiked heads rose ready to strike the slow quarry. With a crashing of timber, the hull was breached; water poured in through the hole, causing the stricken vessel to slow and settle in the water.

I also pictured the southern sky lit by dancing lights, as towns were put to the torch by raiding Navealozan slavers. Women screamed as the raiders strode through the streets, their clubs rising and falling as they gathered more victims.

71

More and more scenes filled my dreams until I was at last woken by Mikal.

Jon hauled in the rope and cut it close to the stone. 'There's no need to take the stone with us, but it is a shame to waste good rope,' he said. He stowed the rope away with the rest of the cargo, and, taking up his steering pole, began to steer us once again downriver.

Several hours later, we rounded a small bend. I heard Jon give an angry curse and saw him leap to his feet. Someone had strung several thick cables across the river ahead of us. They were stretched across the river at an angle, so when a raft or barge struck them they would be driven into the bank on the right. There, in plain view, were many armed men. They were wearing a strange collection of mismatched armour and carrying assorted weapons. My companions had removed their armour and had it packed away in our gear — the armour might be light, but it was heavy enough to pull a tired man to the bottom, should he fall into the river.

'Scavengers!' Jon called. 'If they get us close enough to the bank, they'll board us.'

'Can we cut through the cables out here in the centre of the river?' Roebert shouted from the bow.

'The cables can be cut, with effort, but they will be greased so we will not be able to use them to keep us in centre stream.' Jon pushed his pole over the side till his hands touched the water. 'The water is too deep to use the pole as an anchor.'

'It's a pity we did not keep the stone we used last night,' I said quietly from the stern. I looked towards the bank to see if the scavengers had boats. I shouted to the others, 'They've got archers!' Then I threw myself to the far side of the cargo as a flight of arrows arched towards us.

From behind the cargo, Mikal lifted his large shield and covered Tomas, who was stringing his bow. The rest of the arrows struck the cargo harmlessly. Tomas stepped up from behind the cargo and the shield, and let an arrow fly at the scavengers. He grinned with satisfaction as it took one of the archers in the chest.

Mikal lifted his shield to block another flight of arrows. Tomas tried to repeat his previous shot, but this time the scavengers were ready for him. Only half fired at the barge, the rest held their shots until Tomas appeared. Realising the scavengers' plan, Tomas dropped back down behind the cargo just as the arrows struck.

Danel had leapt to the bow of the barge and was wrestling with one of the thick cables, which was proving difficult, as he had to stay behind the cover of the heaped cargo. The grease made it nearly impossible to get a firm grip on the cable, but he eventually managed to get it over a keg. Then, with one great blow from his glaive, he severed the cable, smashing the keg.

All this time, we were drifting closer to the bank and the waiting scavengers. Roebert and Jon were waiting, ready to try to repel the coming attack.

The current had swung us around. We were now broadside to the cable, with the stern moving closer to the riverbank. Danel cut a second cable; only two were left.

As the barge touched the riverbank, the scavengers swarmed aboard. The sheer number of them forced Roebert and Jon back. Jon used the steering pole to push scavengers into the water, until it broke. He threw the remainder of the pole at another scavenger and drew his cutlass. Roebert was swinging his flail in a deadly pattern before him. No one could approach him without being smashed to the deck or thrown overboard.

But by now the advantage was with Tomas, as the scavengers' own numbers hampered their archers. Tomas did not have this problem, and was systematically dropping the archers on the bank.

Danel cut the third cable. I saw a lot of people run from the cover of the trees nearby. At first I thought they were coming to our aid. Then I saw that they were more scavengers. I called out to Tomas, who, having discouraged most of the archers on the bank, now turned his attention to the new threat.

I heard a gasp from behind me, and turning, I saw Danel had dropped his glaive and was bending forward holding the shaft of an arrow protruding from his right shoulder. There was a look of surprise and shock on his face as he slowly folded to the deck of the barge. The last of the cables was still intact and holding us against the bank.

Mikal had gone to the aid of Roebert and Jon. Between the three of them, they were keeping the scavengers at bay.

I drew the gladius from Mikal's saddle sheath, and climbed to the far side of the barge. If I could cut the last cable, the river's current would carry us away from the scavengers. I put the gladius down and began to work at the last cable. I almost had it over a keg when I noticed several small boats coming from the far side of the river.

The others were all busy, so I left the cable and moved to the side of the barge. Danel had been giving me lessons, but at present I had added little to what he had taught me previously of the stance and grip of the weapon. It was going to have to do, as the first of the attackers reached the barge and attempted to climb on board. I swung wildly and it caught him across the forehead, pitching him back into his companions. This gave me a minute to think. Danel had drawn his dagger and was beginning to cut through the remaining cable. If I could hold the attackers in the boats for a short time, we could be away.

I aimed a straight cut at the next attacker and took him across the throat. Danel had his dagger in his left hand and was sawing at the last cable. My downward slash at the next boarder again brought results as he fell from the barge into the water, and was carried away by the current. By this stage, the next attacker had gained a footing on the barge. The ringing of steel on steel drew the attention of the others.

Jon swung his cutlass wildly, and drove two attackers into the river, then turned and joined me at the edge of the barge. Danel finally cut through the last cable, and we were free of the riverbank.

The scavengers in the last four boats saw that their prize was escaping. They attacked in one last effort to overcome us. Jon forced two into the river as they tried to climb aboard, while I blocked the strike of the next and, with a kick, sent him over the side. The next scavenger ignored me and turned to attack Jon, who was busy keeping three more attackers from gaining the barge. I cried out, and leapt at him.

He flicked his sword out at me. I avoided it by stepping to the side, and bringing the flat of my blade down across his wrist. He dropped his sword. I thrust my sword at his face, driving him back towards the edge of the barge. Finally he stepped off into nothing and, flailing his arms madly, fell into the river, and was pulled away from the barge by the current.

The scavengers' boats were left behind as the current took us downriver. Tomas moved to his brother's side, while Jon grabbed the small pouch of medical supplies. Mikàl and Roebert were sitting in the middle of the barge watching back upriver to make sure we were not being followed.

7

THE MERCHANT ARDEMUS

'ARE they always that persistent?' Mikal asked.

'Not usually,' Jon answered. 'When the cost looks to be too excessive, they usually give up and let you pass.' He was still helping Tomas with Danel's wound.

'Well, they were certainly interested today. It was as if they knew the cargo was worth the trouble,' Roebert said.

'Yes,' Jon said, scratching the stubble on his chin.

Danel was sitting up and he looked much better; either because the arrow had been removed, or because of the liquid he was drinking from another of Jon's small casks. 'Did you see the way Teal used the gladius?' Danel beamed. His voice was slightly slurred and he seemed to be having trouble keeping himself upright. 'I tell you, Tomas, it would make Father happy to see there is someone else who can use the gladius with such skill. I remember Father was annoyed when you chose the bow.'

'I also remember,' Tomas added, 'what Father was like when he found you had picked the glaive rather than the short sword.'

'The lad's a natural,' Danel continued. 'The way he worked the sword, those Jackals had to have been right about him. He must be Vahian. No one else could pick up the handling of the weapon so quickly.' Danel relaxed. He closed his eyes and leant back against a large keg.

'He'll be okay, won't he?' I asked, as Tomas passed me on his way to the bow.

'He'll be fine. He'll wake up with a head worse from the drink than it will be from the wound.'

I slipped Mikal's sword back into its sheath, and lay down to think about what had happened, and what had been said that morning. The effort of the fight and the excitement had exhausted me, and I fell asleep.

This time my dream was full of swords and blood. I stood on a large timber deck. Men lay about my feet, each with a grievous wound. A short sword in my right hand was covered in blood. As I studied the bodies, I noticed that none of them seemed to have faces. I could not recognise them, and I didn't really care. It was as if their deaths meant nothing to me in any way, and in a way, this thought disturbed me more than the dream itself.

I awoke to the sounds of strange voices talking fast and close by.

I sat up quickly and looked around. There were people everywhere. They were beginning to unload the cargo. At first I reached for the sword, only to find Mikal's gear was not there. Looking around, I saw none of our gear was on board.

'Up here, Teal,' someone called. I looked at the riverbank and saw Roebert and Mikal, beckoning to me to join them.

'This is as far as we travel by river, but hopefully we will be able to get a ride into town on one of the wagons,' Mikal said.

I noticed the wagons for the first time; there were seven of them. They were low, and if the size of the springs was any indication, they had been made to carry considerable loads.

Roebert turned to Jon as he approached. 'Is it customary to unload the barges outside the city?' Roebert asked.

Jon smiled. 'Sometimes it's wiser to,' he answered.

Roebert started to laugh and was soon joined by the others. I had no idea what they were laughing about. Even some of the workers began to laugh, but they soon stopped when a large portly man wearing rich brocade robes appeared.

'My friends,' Jon said. 'This is the merchant Ardemus of Lyram. It was his cargo you helped to protect.'

'Protect!' the merchant cried. 'What has happened?'

'Scavengers,' Jon answered.

'Oh,' answered the merchant, 'is that all.' He seemed to relax somewhat. 'I'm sure with the number of you on the barge it should have been no problem to chase a few scavengers off.'

'Quite true,' answered Jon. 'I would, however, have been hard pressed to defend the cargo on my own.'

'Oh? Why? How many were there?' the merchant asked in what seemed a completely disinterested tone.

'I would say at least sixty,' Jon answered. 'Probably more if we count the ones in the boats as well. Would you say that was about right?' he asked Roebert.

'Easily sixty,' Roebert answered.

At first I didn't think the merchant believed them, but when the expression on Roebert and Jon's faces did not change, he licked his lips and asked, 'How far upriver did this attack take place?'

Jon thought for a while. 'Six or seven miles, I'd say.'

The merchant looked around nervously. 'So close and so many, it would seem to me they knew of our cargo. I must have my steward travel to Merbah and pay his respects to our mutual friend there. He seems to be getting rather lax with the information about my shipments.'

Only now did Ardemus notice one of our party had been injured. 'Please, gentlemen, I had no idea one of you had been wounded. I will have my wagon brought over immediately, and have your companion taken to my personal physician at once.'

Tomas was kneeling at Danel's side. Roebert and Mikal were standing behind one of the wagons. They left the shelter of the wagon, as Tomas stood to thank the merchant for his offer.

'Vahians!' Ardemus exclaimed. 'I should have realised Jon would not tell me falsehoods. But I was hard put to believe the six of you could fend off so many attackers. My apologies. If you have no lodgings in Lyram, I would take it as an honour if you would consent to stay at my small, but comfortable lodgings.'

'We would be honoured to accept your offer,' Roebert answered.

'Good, good,' he answered. 'I don't suppose you are in need of work?' he then asked.

'I am unable to answer you at the present moment, but if you were to keep the offer open, I could have an answer for you in a short time after we've entered Lyram,' Roebert told him.

'Good, good,' Ardemus answered, rubbing his hands. 'I will have your friend placed on my wagon, and personally see him into the care of my physician.'

With this, he turned, and called several orders. Many men ran towards Danel, and lifted him from the ground, and began to carry him towards the smallest of the wagons. Another man appeared beside Ardemus. He was the biggest man I had ever seen. Taller than Mikal by a head, he was even several hands across the shoulders broader than Danel. Ardemus barely came up to the man's chest.

The giant was wearing ring mail and a helmet which covered all his face, save his eyes. Held in both hands across his chest, was an enormous axe. It was double-headed and had a haft at least five foot long. Ardemus was explaining something to him. The giant was nodding and occasionally looking upriver. At last, he departed with a dozen or so followers; they moved over to a group of horses, mounted, and rode away to the north.

'Who was that?' I asked Jon.

'The men are some of Ardemus' personal guard. The large one is Ardemus' steward,' he answered.

'I thought a steward looked after someone's house and goods?' I asked.

'That's right. However in this case Kevyn, that's the steward's name, looks after his Master's affairs further afield.'

Ardemus again turned his attention to us. 'I must leave now — your companion is aboard,' he said.

'I would like to thank you,' Roebert said. 'And if I could impose on you again . . . ?'

'Anything,' Ardemus said.

'Could Teal here accompany Danel? The rest of us will wait and ride in with the wagons,' Roebert asked.

'Certainly, certainly,' Ardemus answered, and again rubbed his hands together. Three Vahians riding with his wagons should safeguard them to the city walls.

Ardemus then bowed and climbed up to his seat in the wagon. The driver flicked the reins, and we were off. The wagon had a bright canvas cover, with red, yellow and green stripes. The sun seemed to light it up and make the wagon feel bright and cheerful.

Danel was leaning back with his eyes closed, but he seemed to sense my eyes on him. His eyes opened, and he straightened. This brought a slight grimace to his face.

'What's your problem, Teal?' he asked.

'How are you feeling?' I asked, though I could see he was squinting because of the bright light coming through the canopy.

'Pretty good, considering. Though my head aches something fierce,' he answered.

'Tomas said your head would ache from the drink.'

'Rubbish. Obviously I struck my head when I fell,' Danel said.

'If you say so. I didn't see you hit your head though. What was it you were drinking, anyway?'

'Coal oil, if the taste left in my mouth is any indication,' he said, this time not trying to hide the grimace, as he ran his tongue around the inside of his mouth. 'What was it you wanted?'

'I was just wondering if you were up to telling me more about Nuevah, and why you think I could be Vahian.'

He leaned back and closed his eyes. It looked like he was going to go to sleep, but after a short time he began to talk.

'Generations ago, my, ... our ancestors came to the land north of the Erg. They had travelled there, so the story goes, in seven great vessels, sailing ships of immense size. Where our original homeland was, is lost in time. Even the direction they had sailed to reach the new land is lost.

'One of the great vessels was lost, crossing some huge ocean. The six remaining ones reached land at Journey's End, a bay located in the northwest corner of Nuevah. Here the people of three of the vessels decided to stay. The other three vessels sailed away, and nothing has ever been heard of them.

'The three boat loads of people who remained began to settle down and spread out. As time progressed, another

81

race of people were found. The Ferropeons gained a shaky peace with them, and they and our ancestors lived side by side for many years. There were small incidents at first, but soon they began to grow and become more numerous. Finally, both peoples were at war.

'At first both sides were evenly matched. The tribes were numerous, but the Vahians were better fighters and better armed. Eventually the tide turned in our favour. The tribes were pushed south into the Erg — a vast desert — and the Vahians settled in the lands once owned by the vanquished tribes.

'The Ferropeons stayed where the ships had landed. The Purusmayons moved to the southern edge of our new land. It would be their role to ensure that the tribes now living in the Erg did not return. The Holluchons then began a period of extermination. They believed that all people not of the Vahian race should be killed. Many of the defeated people fled to the land of the Ferropeons and Purusmayons where they were taken in and taught skills, and given land to farm. This freed more Vahians to help keep the borders safe.

'Seeing this, the Vahians of the Holluchon province changed their ways and began to round up the fleeing people. They were then placed in large settlements, where they were allowed to breed, and grow food. It was then that the creed first appeared. Do you know about the creed?'

'Yes, Roebert and Tomas have told me about it,' I answered.

'Well, with the coming of the creed, our people settled down to a time of great prosperity. As they were freed from the troubles at the border by the new soldiers they had trained from the defeated tribes, they were able to concentrate on other problems.

'From the time of the first landing, our race has been

plagued by a small population. Even now, tens of generations after the arrival, we are still troubled by this. Each
female may bear only three children before childbirth
becomes impossible.'

'But that's sufficient, surely?' I asked.

'It would be, except for one thing. There is only one
female born out of every ten births. There is one other
problem. Vahians cannot have children with people of
other lands. So even though it sounds like a sufficient
quantity of children are born each year, we are still only
just holding our own.'

He stopped talking and simply lay there looking up at
the sun shining through the canopy. Only one female in
ten. No wonder they held life over all else. One war could
have crippled them as a nation and allowed the tribes of
the Erg to sweep back into the north.

He opened his eyes again. 'There is another way in
which we are different. At birth our children are the same
as others of different lands. They pick up several words
and learn to walk as they progress. But when they reach
the age of five, they begin to learn at an unsurpassed rate.
The language of our people is in the mind of all children
from birth and only awaits the right time to show itself. At
five they are sent to a school where they are educated. At
eight years of age, they return home till they reach ten.
Then they are sent to the Collegium where they are taught
the laws and history of our people.

'It is at this age that they begin to use weapons. Again
all Vahians are endowed with the knowledge of weapon
handling from birth, but simply need the right motivation
to bring it to the surface. At sixteen, they are returned to
their families to study under fathers or older brothers till
they come of age. It is at this time that they choose the
weapon in which they will specialise. At the Collegium
they are taught the handling of all weapons.

'This is why you were able to pick up the use of the sword so quickly. Your training should have started years ago. When next I see . . .' he stopped and gave me a strange look and then shook his head.

By now we had swung out onto a busy road, and I could see the city walls ahead.

8

ELRED

DANEL had fallen asleep. This gave me time to think over all he had said. I still found it hard to believe I was of Vahian descent. For a race that needed children so desperately — where a child, whether male or female, could make a difference — to lose a child seemed impossible. Though it would explain why I had learnt how to use a weapon so quickly and why I could understand much of the Vahian language without having heard it before.

We crested a small ridge, and the walls of the city again came into view. This time the gates were visible. There was a long line of wagons drawn up at the entrance to the city, and more were joining the line as we got closer.

Ardemus was looking around at the amount of traffic and at the confusion at the city gates. 'Good, good,' he kept saying to himself, in a voice barely above a whisper.

I couldn't see what was so good about it. It would be dark by the time we entered the city. Danel seemed okay, but the sooner the wound was treated, the sooner it would begin to heal.

There were armed men at the gate; they were searching the wagons. Ardemus ordered his driver to swing the wagon into the outbound lane. A soldier strolled over to the wagon and told us to get back in line like everyone else and wait our turn. An officer interceded, and the soldier retreated to his post, mumbling something about the union of a pig and an animal I had never heard of before.

Ardemus bent down and passed the officer a small purse, then straightened and pointed in the direction from which we had just travelled. I supposed he must have told him about the scavengers. The officer took the purse and nodded. The purse was out of sight by the time he turned and told the soldiers to let us pass. Ardemus' driver started the team moving, while Ardemus craned around in his seat to watch the gate.

'Perfect,' he said, rubbing his hands. 'Perfect.'

Danel had woken. 'We are almost there,' I told him. I also told him what happened at the gate to the city. He too smiled and looked about. I seemed to be the only one who did not find the traffic amusing.

I could not describe the sights I saw around me. Never had I experienced anything like this. The colours and the sounds were incredible. The people were all so different, yet at the same time all the same. Everywhere I looked, I saw armed and armoured men. There were also all manners of goods to be found. How the driver could steer the team through the crowds of people was also beyond me, but somehow he managed to. At last he turned the wagon into a large flagstoned courtyard. At the sight of us, there was a great deal of activity, as servants ran from everywhere to help Ardemus to the ground, to hold the horses, to unload the wagons, and, at orders from our host, to remove Danel from the wagon and have him carried inside.

Ardemus' 'small, modest home' was a white stone

multi-storey structure. Gardens were at the base of every wall and dotted the courtyard.

I jumped down and followed Danel into the main building. The lamps were shaded by coloured cloths, throwing a marvellous rainbow across the white walls of the room. The colours were the same as the ones on the canopy of the wagon. I kept after the cluster of people around my wounded companion. They climbed several flights of stairs, and at last entered a spacious room where Danel was placed on a large bed.

'The Master's physician will be with you shortly, Lords. If there is anything you need while you wait, it is my role to serve you.' The young man who looked about my age, bowed low as he spoke. He was dressed in flowing robes of pastel colours, tied at the waist by a red sash.

Danel raised his arm and waved towards the door. The bowing servant backed from the room without moving his gaze from the floor.

Once he was gone, and the door was closed, I asked Danel how he felt.

'Not bad, Teal, not bad,' he answered.

'Ardemus certainly has a lot of people working for him,' I said. Harnet once told me the best thing to do for a wounded man was to let him sleep. If he couldn't sleep then keep up a conversation with him to keep his mind from the wound.

'They're not employees or servants, Teal. They're slaves.'

Slaves! I was shocked. I did not think civilised people kept slaves. I had thought that only the savages of the southern lands were capable of such barbarism.

'Surely not all are slaves?' I asked.

'All save the men at arms. They will be free men in bonded service, but I'm afraid, the rest are all slaves. You must remember we are in the southern region of the

Plains. Here they follow the way of their southern neighbours, where slavery has been a way of life for generations,' he said.

'It was just Ardemus seemed so . . .'

Danel cut in. 'Nice. Of course he seems nice, there's no reason why he shouldn't be. Just because he has slaves, doesn't make him an evil man or a monster. I have seen slaves treated better than some of the northern bond servants. Ardemus probably has slaves because it is the done thing. If slaves were to go out of fashion, he would free his and keep them on as servants. Loyal people are hard to find these days.'

That at least made me feel slightly better. The physician arrived and I was ushered from the room. I began to wander the corridors out of curiosity. After looking into three or four rooms, and investigating several more, I found something of great interest.

It was a large circular room, with a high domed ceiling. On the walls was the greatest collection of weapons I had ever seen. Some I recognised, but most were foreign to me. I strolled around the room, lost in my examination of the weapons.

I heard a discreet cough from behind me, and spun around to find the same young man who had offered his services earlier.

'Yes?' I asked.

'The Lord Danel's wound has been dressed, and he wishes to see you when you are free,' he said. As he spoke, his eyes were lowered to the floor.

'Thank you. What is your name?' I added.

'Elred, Lord,' he answered.

'Do you ever use this room?' I asked.

'On occasions some of the soldiers will want someone to train with when they do not want the others to know they are doing extra work on their weapon handling,' he said.

'Are all the soldiers allowed to use the training hall?'

'No, only Kevyn and a few of the Master's personal guards.'

'Thank you. Can you show me where my companion's room is? I would appreciate it,' I said.

'Certainly Lord, this way,' he said, and led me from the room.

Danel was sitting in the bed with a heavy bandage on his shoulder. His entire right arm was bandaged to his side. Even with all the bandages, he still looked much better.

'How was your exploration?' he asked.

'Fine. I found a great training room. I hope we will be able to use it.'

'I doubt if I'll be able to use it for several weeks,' he answered, looking down at the heavily bandaged arm and shoulder.

Roebert returned from the Vahian Ambassador's residence with news that the merchant Geerge was out of the city, and was not expected to return for five or six days. To stay at the Ambassador's residence would draw attention to ourselves. So Roebert took up Ardemus' offer of employment. Roebert, Mikal and Tomas signed on as guards for several caravans which were leaving the city in the next few days. Each caravan re-entered the city within hours of its departure, though always through a different gate and with a different appearance.

I had only just worked out the type of business our host conducted. He was a smuggler. Each time a cargo appeared in the courtyard it was spirited out of sight within minutes.

Geerge returned after seven days, and an appointment was

made for the following day. We left Ardemus' residence in a shower of gifts. On hearing he had three Vahians as part of his caravan guard, many merchants used his facilities and caravans, at a great profit to Ardemus.

Each of us was given six silver pieces for services rendered, as well as gifts. Mounts were provided for us, as well as stores and equipment. Tomas was supplied with two quivers of arrows. Roebert was given a detailed map of the coastal waters. Mikal received two beautiful throwing knives. Danel was given a small buckler to wear on his injured arm, while using his steel glove as a weapon. I was wondering what I would be given, but it seemed Elred had had a hand in this.

While the others had been busy protecting the caravans, he and I had taken the opportunity to use the training room. I tried as many as possible of the weapons which had taken my interest. My favourite was a matching set of short swords — only eighteen inches in length and narrower than the usual Vahian gladius. Their weight suited me perfectly.

My gift was the matched set of swords from the training room. As well as the weapons, there was a leather harness to carry them. I thanked Ardemus most sincerely, and carefully rewrapped the gift. I then placed it in my pack, which was secured to one of the pack animals. I had wanted to give Elred a parting gift, but Mikal had explained that Elred, being a slave, would have nothing to give me in return, and he might feel embarrassed. It seemed that slaves were not permitted to own anything, though in our training sessions, I had noticed a thin ring on a finger of Elred's right hand.

We mounted and rode from the compound amidst many farewells. The streets were still as crowded as they were when we first entered but now they did not seem as

daunting. Roebert led the way to the Ambassador's residence. The ride was only a short one, and soon we were
dismounting in the forecourt before the Ambassador and
several other Vahians.

From what I could see of the Ambassador's residence, it
differed little from all the others we had passed, multi-
storeyed, with an open architecture, full of arches and
windows.

I was surprised when Tomas stepped forward and
began the introductions. 'Companions, I would like to
introduce to you the Vahian Ambassador to Lyram.'

The Ambassador was a typical Vahian in all aspects,
except he wore only a dagger on his weapon belt. He
bowed and stepped forward.

'Honoured Guests, I would like to introduce you to my
other guests.' He indicated first to the right, then the left.
'My grandson Kyle, and his brother Kryss, and a travelling
companion of theirs, Rychard.'

Kryss and Kyle were alike in most aspects, but it was
easier to see that Kryss was older. Both wore their hair
long and held back by braided leather bands. Kryss had an
open smile, while Kyle seemed more reserved, unwilling to
commit his friendship so soon. Kryss wore a broadsword
of medium length, about two-and-a-half feet, while his
brother had a short sword similar to the one Mikal carried
on his saddle. Rychard had a short-handled double-bladed
axe slung from his weapon belt. His hair was worn shorter
than the normal Vahian style. His eyes were quick, and
moved continuously, searching out all aspects of the room.

Tomas then introduced us. Once the formalities of
introduction were over, the two groups converged and
began to slap one another on the back. All of them were
talking at once. I stayed close to Mikal while this was
going on. He saw my surprise and said. 'Rychard and
Roebert are cousins, and while the Ambassador is grand-

father to Kryss and Kyle, he is also Tomas and Danel's grandfather. It seems you and I are the only ones who are going to get any sleep tonight.'

Mikal and I were left to ourselves, as the others asked questions about people and places. After several hours of this, the Ambassador told all present it was time to get down to business.

He led us into a large meeting hall. There was a long table down the centre of the room. Servants wearing the sign of bondsmen showed us to our seats. Food and drink were brought and the servants were dismissed. I was glad there were no slaves here.

'Gentlemen, it is time we get down to the problem at hand — the freeing of the Prince.' All those around the table nodded, and several suggestions were made. Rychard had his hand on the haft of his axe and was drumming his fingers rapidly on the leather binding of the grip.

'There have been several suggestions,' the Ambassador said, looking around the table and stopping at Rychard. 'Some of these are quite extreme.' This brought a ripple of laughter from those seated, and caused Rychard to drum even harder. 'But, I believe we have come up with the best solution possible.

'All of you, wearing Holluchon tabards, present yourselves tomorrow at the holdings of the merchant Geerge of Lyram. There you will pay the set sum of five thousand gold pieces and receive into your custody the Prince. Then, leaving the city by the north gate, you will ride till out of sight. Then Rychard, Kryss, Kyle and the retainers I have supplied will continue north.

'The rest of you, along with the Prince, will turn west and circle the city out of sight, and enter through the western gate. Once in the city you are to go directly to the waterfront where you will find a galley, the *Uskery Kestrel*, waiting for you. The captain is a good friend who has done many favours for me over the years I have been here. He has been told to take the party anywhere they wish to go and to charge all expenses to me.

'At the same time you put to sea, another party of Vahians will leave the city through the western gate and again strike out to the north.' Roebert was about to speak, but the Ambassador held up both hands and continued. 'Once you put to sea, you are on your own. I don't wish to know of your plans, and I think it best you tell no one else. Agreed?'

Everyone nodded.

'Good then, we are ready. I suggest we spend the rest of the time with old friends. I, on the other hand, am interested in meeting this previously unknown Vahian. I admit I am a little sceptical a Vahian child could disappear and I not hear of it, but stranger things have happened.'

Everyone rose and left the room. The Ambassador and I were the only ones left.

The Ambassador walked from the room and I followed. I found myself in a small circular garden. There were many plants; most were in bloom and filled the small area with a scent which was almost overpowering. The Ambassador moved to the centre of the garden and seated himself on a stone bench beneath a large tree.

'Here, Teal, sit by me,' he said, and patted the seat beside him.

I sat down with my hands on my knees. I was not sure what to do or say. Even though he was the brothers' grandfather, he seemed no older than Harnet. There was no sign of wrinkles or the advanced ageing one would expect of a grandfather.

'Danel tells me you are good with a short sword,' he said.

I nodded.

'I also hear that you now possess a matched pair of blades. It is good to see you are taking an interest in weapon skills, but don't be too quick to choose your weapon. Try as many as possible. You will find one day a weapon will come to you which seems perfect in all ways. When it happens, that is the weapon you should master. But, as I said, in the meantime try as many as possible.'

'Have you found your weapon yet?' I asked.

'Great Krodil, yes. Years ago; more than I'd really care to remember,' he answered.

'Is it the knife?' I asked.

He threw back his head and laughed. 'No, Teal. Come with me and I'll show you my chosen weapon.'

He rose and left the garden with me on his heels. We passed through several rooms, each of which had a heavy timbered iron-banded door. The further we went into the building, the more I noticed the material used in its construction was changing. Now all the walls were stone, as were the floors and ceilings.

'Outside, this building matches all the others in the street, but it is always safer to have a place where you can go when trouble threatens. The inside of this building is defendable by only a small number of people. Should trouble ever arise, my staff and myself could hold out here indefinitely,' he said.

We passed through a large door and I found myself in a small room. The floors were covered in thick carpets and the walls were full of niches. Each niche contained kegs, bales and boxes of all sizes. There, suspended from the wall on large hooks, was an enormous sword.

The blade was six foot long and at least six inches wide. The Ambassador reached up and lifted it down effortlessly from the wall. With the sword held in his left hand, the blade resting on his right forearm, he turned and walked across the room towards me.

'This is my chosen weapon,' he said. 'You can see it would be awkward to carry it about.' He flipped the blade from his arm, and grabbed the hilt in both hands. Holding the weapon aloft, he let his eyes travel the length of the blade. His eyes were alive with light as they took in the length and beauty of the weapon.

The blade was like a mirror. From where I stood, I could see the Ambassador's face reflected in the blade. There was a look in his eyes which seemed to make him look even younger. His face was full of life and I could sense the joy radiating from him.

He held the blade almost lovingly in his arms as he crossed the floor, then he reached up and returned the sword to the wall and stepped back.

We walked in silence and soon joined the others who had returned to the meeting hall.

The next day, after the morning meal, we were taken to a room full of weapons and armour. Here I was outfitted with scale mail, and all of us were given red tabards to wear. Each had the Vahian tree in the centre. The right shoulders also bore the emblem of Raimend, the Vahian Regent: the head of a Wolf, with jaws parted as if ready to attack.

The scale mail was made of overlapping metal scales. It was split at the ankles to allow it to go over the high boots which were worn with it. The boots were leather covered in metal studs, with steel plates in the soles.

The mail was in one piece, which was open down the front. There were two flaps at the front, one hanging to either side. The right was folded across the chest and was tied at left hip, chest and shoulder. The left flap was then folded over the right and was secured in the same fashion, right hip, chest and shoulder. The hood was then pulled up over the head and covered by the helmet.

The armour was then covered with the tabard, which was slipped over the head and secured at the waist by the weapon belt. Last of all were the gloves. These were made of a thinner, more supple leather than the boots, with the back of the hand and fingers reinforced with metal scales.

The double layer of mail over the chest saved having to wear a breastplate and therefore cut down the weight of the armour needed to be worn.

Once dressed, we met in the courtyard. The horses were already saddled, and without wasting any time, we mounted and prepared to ride out.

'Remember, you are Wolves. Do not remove your helmets for any reason at all. If a spokesman is needed, then let it be Danel. The one scar he has may be sufficient to convince them he is a Wolf, though of low rank,' the Ambassador told us.

We rode through the streets three abreast: Kyle, Kryss and Rychard in the lead, with Mikal, Roebert and Tomas at the rear. Danel and I were in the centre, with three retainers in front and another three behind us.

Rychard and the others played their parts well. Riding through the streets they gave way to no one. Even a squad of the city guard was forced to give way before our party.

At last we reached the holdings of the merchant Geerge. We were met at the entrance by slaves waiting to hold our horses, but we halted and made no attempt to dismount. One of the slaves approached our party.

'If you would care to dismount and follow me, I will conduct you to the presence of my Master,' he said.

Danel nudged his horse forward, making the slave jump back or be trampled. 'Tell your Master we are here for business. We have here what he wants.' Danel indicated the chest tied to the spare horse beside me. 'We are, naturally, in a hurry, so if he will bring forth the merchandise, we will conclude our business and be on our way.'

The slave disappeared inside and returned with a small man, dressed in silk robes. The man's fingers were laden with rings and around his neck hung many gold chains.

'This is my Master,' the slave said, and backed away.

Geerge looked up at us. 'I had hoped you would share some refreshments with me, but I see you are indeed in great haste, which is a pity.' He raised his right hand and the gold rings caught the sun, making his fingers appear to be on fire. This was obviously a signal because a slave appeared leading a man dressed in the style of a Vahian Lord.

Danel dismounted and led the man aside and had several words with him. They returned and Danel nodded to Roebert. The chest was passed to waiting hands and the key was given to the merchant. Having assured himself the amount of money discussed was indeed in the chest, he stood and bade us farewell.

The Prince was shown to the spare mount. The three retainers who were supplied by the merchant, also mounted up, on horses provided for them by their previous Master.

We wheeled our mounts, and rode out into the street. In a short time, we were at the northern gate, and were being waved through by the city guards.

Spurring the mounts, we rode away from the city, anxious to get out of sight as soon as possible. Once out of sight, we parted company. No farewells were needed, as all had been said before we left the Ambassador's lodgings.

I watched them ride out of sight, and silently wished them luck. We discarded the tabards of the Wolves and donned travelling cloaks, and rode hard for the western gate of the city. As the sun was setting, we entered the gates and quickly passed through the city to the docks.

By the time we reached the docks the lanterns had been

lit. In the halflight of the lanterns, the vessel was hard to make out. Roebert ordered the halt and we swung down from the saddles, gathered our gear, and made for the vessel. As soon as we boarded, the Captain gave orders to get under way. We were shown to cabins where I threw myself onto a bunk and fell into a deep sleep.

9

THE BLACK SHIP

FOR the first time in days, I was truly alone. I was lying on my back on a bunk. The sun had only just cleared the horizon, and seemed to be streaming straight through the port into my cabin. I could hear the voices of the officers above me calling orders to the crew. The sounds were muffled by the thickness of the deck.

Forward of my cabin I could hear the creaking of the oars; their rhythmic sound was almost enough to put me to sleep again. There was only a faint rolling of the vessel, so I had not suffered from sea sickness, as I had feared I would.

My curtain was flung open and the Prince's steward stepped in. I did not like the man. He had the face of a weasel whose eyes were never still. Around the Prince he smiled and bowed, but as soon as the Prince was not around, he was arrogant, and bullied the younger two retainers, who were scared to death of him.

He sneered down at me lying on the bunk and then examined the room. 'The quarters they have placed me in are far too small for me and those other two. So I have arranged for my things to be moved in here.'

I sat up on the bed. I still didn't like him but there were two bunks in this cabin. 'Certainly,' I answered. 'The top bunk is free.'

'It would seem you have misunderstood me,' he said, giving me one of the sickly smiles he was always wearing around the Prince. 'I am sure there is no need to keep up the masquerade now we are safely at sea.'

'And what masquerade is that?' I asked, trying very hard to keep from throwing myself at the wretch.

'You know exactly what I mean. I'm sure there was a logical reason behind disguising you as a Vahian, but, as of now, I believe you can best serve your Masters from another cabin.'

I climbed slowly to my feet. I looked him in the eyes as I took one step towards him and then another. His eyes were holding mine, but he was beginning to sweat profusely.

He tried one last time to exert his authority. He reached out and took me by the collar, and began to draw me towards him.

I let his fingers curl around my collar and stepped forward as he pulled. His eyes opened wide and the perspiration began to pour from him. He slowly lowered his eyes till they were on the knife I had drawn and laid alongside his wrist. He once more looked into my eyes, but this time I saw fear in them.

I reached up, and with my free hand, I uncurled his fingers from my clothing and then, placing my open hand against his chest, I gave a good shove. He left my cabin almost as fast as he had entered, though this time he was going backwards. His heel caught on something, and he ended up sprawled in the passageway, hitting his head hard against the opposite wall.

The commotion caused Roebert to glance out into the passageway. He took one look at the situation and withdrew his head. I stepped back into my cabin.

I replaced the knife in its sheath and was about to sit down when there was a soft voice at the curtain.

'Enter,' I called.

The younger of the Prince's retainers drew aside the curtain and timidly peered in. He had a bundle of clothes which looked like they had been thrown together rather hastily.

'What can I do for you?' I asked, knowing full well what the answer was going to be.

'I have been told by the steward Percyl that I am to share this room with you, Lord,' he said. He was very nervous; obviously he knew what had happened to the steward and feared he would get the same treatment.

'Of course, lad. You take the upper bunk. I'm comfortable where I am,' I answered him.

'Thank you, Lord,' he answered, and closed the curtain as he entered the cabin.

'What is your name?' I asked.

'Rafe, my Lord.'

'How old are you?'

'Fifteen, Lord,' he answered.

'Well, Rafe, I'm going up on deck should anyone be after me,' I told him, and left the cabin.

Up on deck, there was a good wind blowing from astern. A look around the horizon revealed nothing but clear sky. I walked over to the rail and looked down at the water as it raced past the hull of the vessel. I was surprised to see there were strange creatures in the water keeping pace with the *Kestrel*. They were slipping in and out of the water as they swam parallel to us.

The bodies of the creatures looked smooth, and their tails were driving them through the water with what appeared to be easy strokes. As I watched, more and more joined in the race. Without warning they were gone. I looked about for some sign of them but there was no trace.

A voice from behind startled me. 'Probably one of the smaller monsters is about. The Swimmers can sense their presence and will avoid them where possible.'

On hearing the voice, I spun around and found myself confronted by a man of many years, if the wrinkles on his face were a true measure of age. His skin was dark, the colour of treated leather, and his hair was a light colour, as though it had been faded by the sun and salt.

'They have a great deal of ken, these local sea beasties. Many a time I have avoided disaster by following the example of those creatures.' With that statement he shouted an order to the helmsmen and the vessel slowly altered course.

'Why are the rowers idle?' I asked.

'The rowers have been allowed to rest while the wind is favourable. It is only when we are forced to take refuge in the shallow waters that they are really needed,' he answered.

I learnt he was the Captain of the vessel, who hoped one day to be the owner of it. He claimed the *Kestrel* was the fastest vessel in these parts, except for perhaps one or two Corsairs which had just started to operate in the area.

After five days' sailing we were in sight of Esherweld. On several occasions, sails were seen on the horizon, but the Captain ordered a change of course and the *Kestrel's* superior speed would soon have us alone on the water again.

We passed the entrance to the harbour and continued east towards our destination, the Capital, Tharrac.

Three days on from Esherweld, a sail was sighted well astern. The Captain ordered the change of course, and the vessel was gone from my mind, till later, I happened to glance around. To my surprise not only was the sail still there, but it was now noticeably larger. All day long the chase continued, with the vessel behind slowly overhauling us.

All my companions were on deck.

'How long?' Roebert asked the Captain.

'If this wind holds, he will be within bow shot by first light.'

'Is there any chance of losing him in the night?' Mikal asked.

'If I were to alter away to starboard, I would be able to lose him in the darkness. But that would put him ahead of us. If you are willing to turn back to Esherweld, then, once behind him, we may be able to beat him back to port. But to continue on to Tharrac with him waiting ahead would be suicide,' the Captain answered.

As the evening wore on, the vessel became clearer. She was similar to the *Kestrel* in all details, save colour. She was totally black.

'She must be stripped down to the bare minimum to get speed like that out of this wind,' the Captain said almost enviously. He explained that the ship pursuing us was called a galleass, a heavy, low-built warship larger than a galley, powered by both sails and oars.

That night there was not much sleeping done. Any minute I expected to hear the sound of timber against timber, as the two vessels touched, but there was no sound apart from the slapping of the sea and the beating of the canvas as the wind lifted and dropped.

We were all on deck before the sun rose. The crew was armed and we wore our armour. The red tabards of the Wolves had been disposed of north of Lyram. The white tabards of Purusmayo lay folded in our cabins. The Prince had at first insisted that he should wear the green of

Ferrope, but Roebert managed to convince him we should not yet show our hand, and reveal to the Corsairs who we were. At last the Prince agreed, so we were wearing the blue tabards of Free Vahians — loyal to the country but having no alliance to any province.

As the trailing vessel neared, a single arrow arched over the gap between us, and then plunged into the sea, yards short. Tomas stepped to the rail at the stern and nocked an arrow. He drew the shaft towards him till his left arm was straight, then he released it. The long shaft climbed high into the morning sky, then, when it seemed the arrow would be lost, it began to angle downward.

The archer at the bow of the galleass staggered back, clawing feebly at the shaft protruding from his chest. The other archers who were waiting for the range to close ducked back behind for cover. The crew of the *Kestrel* sent up a cheer which was heard across the intervening waters.

After the cheering had died down, I turned my attention back to the closing vessel. The bow of the galleass was now full of wicker shields, obviously brought up to protect their archers.

Standing beside Tomas was the Prince's steward and the older of the retainers. Behind them was Rafe, who was carrying quivers of arrows for their short curved bows.

A few of the Corsairs' arrows were reaching the *Kestrel*. Tomas turned and said something to Rafe, who dropped his load and raced below decks. He returned carrying a small brazier and a bundle of rags. He also had a small flask. Wrapping a piece of rag around the head of his arrow, Tomas poured some of the liquid from the flask over it, careful not to spill any on the timber deck. He nocked the arrow and lit the rag from the brazier. Again drawing the shaft back to its full extent, he released it. Cries could be heard from the black vessel as the arrow, with its trail of smoke, was seen curving through the sky towards them.

The arrow struck one of the wicker shields which instantly burst into flames. Some of the hidden Corsairs threw the shield over the side. This did not give the flames time to reach the other shields, but it did give Tomas and the Prince's steward several open targets. Two of the Corsairs were hit, and dropped screaming to the deck. One held a bloodied thigh, the other had both hands pressed tightly against his stomach, trying to stop the flow of blood which oozed from between his white fingers.

As the vessels closed, flights of arrows flashed between the two groups of archers. Many crewmen on both sides were struck, and the Captain ordered some of his crew to take the wounded below decks. At last the two galleys ground together. Grapples were thrown over the rails which the Corsairs attempted to make fast as the crew of the *Kestrel* cut as many of them as they could. Mikal and Roebert were on the lower deck to aid the crew in an attempt to separate the two vessels. Tomas was beside the Prince. Danel was wearing his steel glove and sleeve but was only carrying a short sword. Even though his wound had healed sufficiently to allow him the use of his arm, he did not think it was strong enough to wield the heavy weapon for any long period of time.

The first wave of Corsairs swarmed over the rail and engaged the crew. The *Kestrel*'s crew were hard, strong men, but they were no match for the barbaric Corsairs who were wearing hardly any armour, yet gave no thought to throwing themselves against greater odds or at the armoured men who made up the main defence of the *Kestrel*.

A second wave followed the first. Mikal and Roebert were forward, cut off from us by the second wave which seemed intent on taking the stern of the vessel. Danel and

Tomas, now also carrying a short sword, positioned them-selves on either side of the raised stern to deny the Cor-sairs the use of the stairs from the lower deck. The Prince and I, with the steward and the two retainers, were well to the stern of the vessel.

Roebert and Mikal were being forced towards the bow of the vessel. Many of the *Kestrel*'s crew were dead or wounded. The second wave was attempting, yet again, to gain a foothold on the raised stern. So far Mikal and Tomas had been able to hold them, but, as the *Kestrel*'s crew fell beneath the flashing cutlasses of the Corsairs, more and more attackers were freed to help the assault on the stern.

A third wave boarded our stricken vessel, and with them to swell the numbers of the attackers, they managed to reach our position. The Captain, the Prince's steward and the two retainers threw themselves at the attackers. Danel was down, not moving — I feared he might be dead. Tomas was trying to fight his way to his brother's side, but the attackers were just too many. The older retainer was down, his throat torn open by a slashing stroke of a cutlass.

The steward took a blow to the head from a heavy club and was thrown to the deck. Another Corsair bent to finish him off with a sword thrust, and was set upon by Rafe. The youth had armed himself with a dagger and had wrap-ped himself around the attacker, repeatedly striking at his body. Rafe's dagger and right hand were covered in blood by the time the Corsair fell. Rafe turned to help the stew-ard but was run through from behind. The cutlass had taken him through the small of the back, slightly right of centre and the blade was protruding from his stomach.

The Captain and Tomas were fighting back to back; both were bleeding from many wounds. The only other Corsairs alive turned towards the Prince and I. They were smiling, obviously believing we were easy targets.

I screamed out the battle cry I had heard Danel use on many occasions and leapt at the closest Corsair. He was caught unprepared by my sudden attack, and fell to a straight thrust to the throat. Without giving them a chance to think, I threw myself at the next attacker, who blocked my right blow, only to find himself impaled on my left sword. I withdrew the sword and spun around in time to block the attack of another Corsair. We struggled back and forth, trading blows for several minutes, before he left himself open, allowing me to slip one of my blades between his ribs.

He folded and fell to the deck, sliding from my sword as he did so. There were no other Corsairs standing on the stern. Tomas and the Captain were driving the last of the attackers down the stairs to the lower deck. The clashing of swords could be heard from forward. So there were more of us still alive, though how many I could not guess. I was still surprised at the ease with which I was able to despatch my enemies, and how, after a fight, there was no feeling of remorse for the fallen. My only concern was for Mikal.

As I watched the lower deck, I saw three men climb over the rail from the other vessel. One was dressed much the same as the merchants I had seen, in a flowing robe of rich fabrics and bright colours, while the other two were wearing heavy, dark cloaks.

The man wearing the merchant's robe said something to the smaller of the two men with him, who stepped forward and threw off his cloak. Beneath the covering he was wearing scale mail armour and a red tabard with a small tree in the centre, smaller than the one on mine. This meant he was a Wolf of the Holluchon Province. He took a long-handled axe from his belt and began to cross the deck towards me. The axe was single-bladed, but this was of no great comfort to me, as I had never faced an axeman before.

He climbed the stairs to the stern. The Captain and Tomas were unable to free themselves to stop him. He stopped several paces from me, as if waiting for me to make the first move. I had no intention of doing that. The longer he waited, the more chance I had of getting aid from my companions, if any were still alive to offer it.

The merchant shouted out an order; the Wolf nodded his head and began to advance on me once more. His axe flashed out at my head. I raised my left sword to divert the blow. But, in midswing he changed direction and sent the axe towards my side. My mail would not protect me from such a blow. I had only one choice open to me. Stepping in close, inside the swing of the axe, I dropped my left sword and grabbed his wrist, slowing the blow down sufficiently so the haft of the axe struck my side with only enough force to push me aside.

I did not release the axe hand of my attacker, and I was in too close to use my remaining sword. I could only cut with it at this range, and his armour would protect him. I straightened my right arm, raising my sword as high as I could, then I brought the pommel down hard on the collarbone of my assailant. There was a distinct snap as the bone broke. His left arm dropped to his side, and he jumped back, shaking my grip off as he did. We were again several paces apart. His left arm was at his side and there was perspiration on his brow.

I attacked, changing the sword to my left hand. He blocked my blow with his axe. I slammed my fist into his broken collarbone. He cried out and staggered back. I followed with another right to the same place. This time he dropped his axe and brought his right arm up to protect his shoulder. This let me bring the flat of my blade down across the side of his head. His eyes rolled back, and he crashed to the deck at my feet.

The other cloaked figure stepped forward and threw off his cloak. Again I saw the red tabard of a Holluchon, but the tree was large and the Wolf emblem on his right shoulder showed this time I faced a Vahian Lord, one of Raimend's . . .

I had no doubt that, against the people of the Plain and other similar people I could hold my own, and my armour gave me an advantage, but against a fully-trained and armed Vahian Lord I had no chance.

He drew a mace from his weapon belt. This weapon was similar to Roebert's. It was a steel ball covered in spikes mounted on a handle about eighteen inches long. I had seen the damage which could be done with such a formidable weapon and I knew that I had no hope of surviving this contest.

I stooped and picked up the axe which was at my feet and faced the advancing figure. Suddenly there was movement beside me. The Prince stepped from behind and stood at my side. His sword was drawn and in his left hand. The sight of two foes did not stop the advancing Wolf Lord, until the Prince reached up with his right hand and tore the cloak from his shoulders.

The eyes of the Wolf Lord widened in surprise; then terror; but almost instantly they regained their emotionless gaze. He had, however, stopped his advance, and as I watched, began to retrace his steps towards the other vessel. He growled out an order to the merchant at the rails. Then both climbed back to their vessel. The sounds of combat had ceased and the remaining Corsairs were making their way back to their vessel. All were wounded and many carried fallen comrades. Soon all were aboard the galleass and the ropes were cut. As the distance between the vessels widened I could still see the Wolf Lord watching me. At last, the wind filled their sails and they began to draw away.

I turned to the Prince to thank him for his timely intervention. I noticed a gold chain around his neck holding the emblem of a tree on a silver background: the sign of Vahian royalty. No wonder the Wolf Lord had turned and fled.

The Captain began an inspection of his vessel and remaining crew. The dead were thrown over the side. The Captain had some skill in healing, and saw to the wounded, including Danel. He had been laid low by a blow to the temple. He had a large bruise and a headache, and his eyes were glazed.

'How are things, Captain?' Roebert asked. His tabard was slashed and bloody, though most of the blood did not seem to be his own. He had a cut over his right eye and his buckler was dented in many places. 'Will we be able to get under way?'

'I don't have the crew to man the sweeps and there isn't enough breeze to ruffle my hair, much less fill the sail. Unless a wind picks up we are here till help arrives,' the Captain answered.

'Is that likely?' Tomas asked. The worried look had left his face now he knew his brother was all right.

'This area is on the main shipping route. We should not have too long to wait before another vessel happens along.'

'Yes,' I said, 'but will they be friendly, or another galleass?'

All eyes swung toward me. The few crew who were left began to watch the horizon.

'Regardless of who appears on the horizon next, we must be prepared,' Roebert said. 'Tomas, gather what arrows you can; Mikal, collect all the other weapons you can find. Take several of the crew to aid you.' He turned to the Captain. 'Is there any way we can anchor? I don't fancy running aground and drowning after all we have been through.'

The Captain nodded and called orders to the remaining crew. Soon lead lines were over the side and once the depth was found to be only a few fathoms, the anchor followed.

For five days we laid at anchor. The water was beginning to run low, and three more of the crew had died, due to the seriousness of their wounds. Rafe was still alive, the Captain had done all he could for him, and was amazed he still lived. Percyl, the Prince's steward, was all for throwing him over the side with the dead, but I would not have that.

'While there is life in his body we will do all we can to save him. Remember he was injured while protecting you,' I told him. From that time on one of us was with Rafe at all times.

Roebert and the Captain spent a great deal of time together. They had several charts brought to the Captain's cabin, as well as one of the crew who came from a fishing village near our anchorage.

At last Roebert appeared on deck. He beckoned for us to join him. 'If the activities of the Corsairs have increased along this section of coast, then it could be days, possibly weeks, before another vessel arrives. Because the Prince is known to be on board, we cannot afford to wait any longer. First thing tomorrow, we will take one of the longboats and attempt to reach a fishing village, which should be only a day's journey west along the coast. We will have one of the crew along as a guide. The Prince, Percyl and Rafe will accompany us. Rafe will have more of a chance if we can get him to the village. One of the crew has told me they have a good healer.

'The Captain,' Roebert continued, 'will remain here

with his vessel and crew, and, if possible, we are to send some of the villagers back to help them get under way. I also hope we will be able to buy horses at this village. We will not take any water with us, as all will be needed here. Our guide assures us there is plenty of water to be found all along the coast.'

10

THE SEARCH ENDS

AT first light the next morning we were on deck ready to leave. The longboat had been loaded with as many supplies as could be spared. All our gear, including armour, had been packed in waterproof skins and stowed away in the boat. We said our farewells to the Captain and crew, telling them we would send help as soon as we could.

We climbed into the longboat and took our positions. Our crewman-cum-guide was in the bow, with the Prince. Roebert, Tomas, Mikal, and myself were at the oars. Danel and the injured Rafe were in the stern, and Percyl was on the tiller. The guide was to call out any change of course that would need to be made, and Percyl would move the tiller accordingly.

Our guide seemed preoccupied and nervous. Several times the Prince had to point out shoals or sandbanks, and order a change of course.

It was mid-afternoon when Roebert told Percyl to make for the shore. The longboat slipped in between the sand bars and struck the sandy beach with a shudder. Our guide was first over the side. Roebert and I followed; between us we pulled the boat up onto the beach.

We emptied the boat and dragged it further from the water. Mikal and Percyl gathered wood for a fire, while Roebert and our guide walked off inland for a short distance to study the terrain. By the time they returned, a fire was blazing and the evening meal was on. Tomas and I were given the first watch. We walked out some distance from the camp and separated. Each of us found a spot and settled down for the watch.

I was relieved four hours later by Danel. It was quite easy to find my way back to the camp as the moon was full. The sight of the moon, and the sound of the waves reminded me of one of Jon's stories.

It seemed Plastrons always attacked the coastal villages on or around the full of the moon. Jon said it had something to do with the height of the water allowing them to swim in closer to the shore.

At once, I realised what the guide had been so nervous about. The shallow, shoal-filled area we had been moving through all day had the type of conditions Plastrons preferred. I looked up again at the full moon. If there were any of the creatures to be found in the waters just offshore, then tonight would be the time they ventured up onto the land in search of food. This beach was the perfect place for them to emerge from the water — it had a gentle slope and with the high tide tonight the creatures would be able to get almost to the tree line before having to leave the safety of the water.

I ran the rest of the way to the camp. My crashing through the underbrush had woken everyone, so by the time I got to the beach they were all up arming themselves. I caught my breath and told them about Jon's tale. Percyl was sent to wake up the guide, but soon returned telling us he was nowhere to be found, and some of the stores were missing.

Roebert had the sentries brought in, and then had the camp moved inland away from the open sandy area. We set up our new camp in a cluster of rocks, not as comfortable as the first camp, but more easily defended.

The rest of the night passed without incident, and first light found us finishing our early meal. Roebert dispatched Mikal and Tomas to the shore to ready the boat. He also had Danel and Percyl make a wide sweep of the area to see if there were any signs of our runaway guide.

Tomas returned with the news that the boat was unharmed and ready — and that there were many prints in the wet sand around it. He had not seen the like before but a brief description brought to mind the type of feet Jon had described when talking about Plastrons.

The others returned. They, too, had seen no sign of our guide.

'If the creatures offshore know we are here,' I explained, 'it will be quite easy for them to wait and when we are a suitable distance from dry land, attack us. From what I have been told, it will only take two of the creatures to overturn us and throw us all into the water. Once there, we are at their mercy.'

'Why would they attack us? There are enough fish in the sea, and no large monsters hereabouts to drive them onto the land,' Percyl said. He looked around at the rest of the party, waiting for someone to agree or disagree with him. When no one said anything he continued. 'Why would a creature of the oceans leave the open expanses of water and empty coastlines and move to this particular area of the Uskery Sea?'

'A good friend of ours, Jon, who knows the habits of these creatures, told me there is a breed of Plastron living along the shore and in the swamp to the south of the

115

Uskery Sea. If they live there, why not here?' I told him.

'If that is the case,' Percyl said, 'we should forget about the sea and carry on to this village on foot. It can't be much further, and we should not endanger the life of the Prince needlessly.' As he spoke, he moved closer to the Prince.

'I agree,' the Prince said. These were the first words the Prince had said to any of our party apart from his steward, and Danel.

'All right,' said Roebert. 'Mikal, you and Teal tear up some of the blankets so each of us can carry his own gear.'

It did not take long to make up crude backpacks, and a litter for Rafe. Once these things were done, we collected our gear and began our trek westward. As we travelled, the land slowly rose.

We sighted the village just after noon, nestled in a cove at the base of a long line of low cliffs. It took us an hour to wind our way down to it.

I don't think the villagers were too happy to see us when we first arrived. They had been raided by Corsairs several days ago and did not have much food to spare. When they found we were carrying our own supplies they were quite willing to find us a place to rest. When word spread we were fighters and we carried armour and weapons, the Headman himself made us welcome. We told them about the longboat, and several men were sent to fetch it. Roebert explained to the Headman they could keep the longboat as payment for their hospitality. It would replace the boat the Corsairs had destroyed when they found out that the village was so poor.

Rafe was taken into the hut of an old woman who was supposed to have great skills in the art of healing. The rest of us sat around the fire and shared a meal with the Elders of the village. We asked them about the Corsair attack and the Plastrons. They told us the vessel was totally black and it came in close to shore during the night. The Corsairs were few in number and many were carrying fresh wounds. They were extremely angry at the lack of food in the village, and in their anger they destroyed the only boat and several of the larger huts. They told us that the possibility of Plastrons attacking was quite rare, as only the weak and old had moved from the great oceans into the Uskery. These were easy to drive off, as they were afraid of fire. As long as a watch was kept at all times, so the village was not surprised, they were no real threat.

We paid the Headman a small sum of gold. For this he would supply us with some men to take us by boat to Esherweld. He would also send word to the nearest town about the plight of the *Kestrel.*

I gave the old woman three gold pieces for the treatment of Rafe. At first I was not too sure about leaving him in the hands of the old woman, but there was something about her which seemed to fill me with confidence each time I was near her. She assured me he would live, and I believed her. But he would be weak for a long time, she said, and would not be able to be moved from the village.

We stayed at the village for the rest of the day, and as it began to grow dark and the longboat had not arrived, we decided to stay the night. Because of the damage done by the Corsairs, we were forced to sleep on the beach. No one seemed to mind this too much — except, perhaps, Percyl.

The following morning I went to say goodbye to Rafe, having been assured by the Headman that the longboat would arrive before noon. The old woman was not in her hut, but Rafe was at the rear lying on a pallet. He was pale and his eyes seemed to have sunk into his head. He did not seem to be in pain; at least the old woman had accomplished that much. He smiled when he saw me and patted the pallet on which he was lying.

I sat down beside him. 'You look much better,' I told

him. 'We are leaving now. I will send someone back for you. The old woman says you will live, but you must rest.' I took his hand; he tried to close his fingers but had no strength. 'You'll be back in the service of the Prince soon enough.'

'He's not . . . ,' he said.

'I understand,' I said. 'I don't think he's much of a Prince either, but he is the only one we have. Without him Nuevah will fall into the hands of Raimend.'

Rafe was trying to say something else, but no sound emerged from his open mouth. Slowly his head lowered to the straw pillow and his mouth closed.

'He is asleep,' I heard from behind me. 'He will need all the rest he can get if he is to be well again. His youth will help him to overcome a great deal of the hurt, but it is lucky you chose to bring him here.'

I looked behind me at the speaker. It was the old woman. She was short and bent, with hands like claws, and her voice was rough. Each time I saw her, I was amazed that anyone could be so old. She had a bundle of herbs and local vegetables in her arms.

'You'd best be going now. Leave him to sleep,' she said, moving across the hut to her small fire. On a small block of wood beside the fire, she began to peel and cut the herbs and vegetables. As she finished with each one, she dropped it into a small pot suspended over the fire.

The longboat did not arrive by midday, and again it grew dark without it being sighted. We were forced to spend another night in the fishing village. During the night the longboat arrived. The villagers had seen no sign of Plastrons, which was good news. The Plastrons' aversion to fire isn't exactly something you can turn to your advantage when you are facing a starving nine-foot creature, especially if you are in a small boat several miles offshore.

The wind was strong and before long we were cutting through the water. The spray was bursting against the bow, and was being thrown back at us, cool and refreshing. The villagers fished as we travelled, and each night we dined on an assortment of seafoods. Each night we carried the boat well up from the water and slept close by it. Small fires were lit as a protection from animals, but they were kept low and well-covered so as not to be seen any distance away.

I couldn't think of the last time I had enjoyed myself so much. At times I had even forgotten the reason we were there. I decided that when this was over I would buy a boat — not that size, of course; one considerably larger — and would sail around the Uskery, stopping only to fish and swim.

After six glorious days, Esherweld came into sight. Roebert suggested that the villagers put us ashore out of the city. They were happy to do this — for some reason they did not seem eager to enter Esherweld.

Soon we were walking again. It was an effort to stay in a straight line, and took us all considerable time to work the stiffness out of our legs.

The gates of Esherweld were similar to those at Lyram, not in design or construction, but in the fact that there were armed men stopping all who entered and searching them.

We walked to the gate. The guards asked our business. Roebert explained that our vessel had run aground down the coast and we were only intending to stay as long as it took to arrange passage east. As he told the tale, he dropped a large purse into the man's waiting hand.

The guard waved us on, informing us the best place for lodging was at the Black Eel. Roebert thanked him and we moved on.

'Let us thank the God of Corruption. If not for him we would find it difficult to travel anywhere in this suspicious land,' Mikal said, once out of earshot of the gate.

The city's buildings were constructed from large rough-cut stones, light grey in colour. Each roof was red-tiled, and had wide eaves which threw a continuous shadow over the street.

Esherweld was smaller than Lyram, not only in actual size, but in the width of the streets as well. The going was slow, as around each corner another stalled wagon or group of pedestrians was found. If we had been mounted we could have forced our way through, but on foot, and carrying all our equipment, there was not much we could do.

We found the Black Eel, a sprawling timber building which looked slightly the worse for wear, and booked three rooms. I bathed and dressed, then went downstairs to find the others. They were in the tap room as I expected. After a good meal and some liquid refreshments, Tomas and I decided to have a look around the city.

We left the inn and began to explore the city. After many turns we came to a section of the city which was full of stalls. We passed between the stalls, listening to the hawkers as they tried to sell their wares. Tomas stopped at a fletcher's stall and looked over the merchandise. He chose several items, and haggled with the owner over the price of them.

We stopped at several more stalls, and picked up a few items which we thought might be of use in our travels.

Back at the inn, Tomas pulled out the items he had purchased at the fletcher's stall. He gave Roebert the buckler he had bought to replace the one damaged in the Corsair attack. He then took several of his arrows and began to examine them closely. A couple of the flights were loose, and one of the nocks was broken. With the replacements he had bought that morning, he began to repair his arrows.

Mikal and Danel were sitting with the Prince.

Percyl emerged from the kitchen carrying a large cheese which had taken his fancy at the midday meal. Without warning he screamed and dropped to the ground. He was writhing on the floor, both hands wrapped around a shaft protruding from his right thigh.

'Down,' cried Danel, pushing the Prince from his seat as he did so. Mikal rolled from his seat and onto his feet in one fluid motion. He ran across the room towards the rear door of the tap room.

Tomas followed him, grabbing his bow from beside the door as he ran. Once safe from possible attack he strung his bow and waited for his chance to attack our assailants.

I dropped to the floor and crawled under the closest table. Percyl was still rolling about crying in pain. I began to slide across the floor towards him. I reached his side, and examined the wound. A quarrel was lodged deep in the fleshy part of his thigh, but it had missed the bone. I removed Percyl's belt and tied it around his thigh to help slow the bleeding.

'We're too open here,' Roebert said from behind an overturned table. 'We have to get upstairs, away from all these windows.'

Danel picked up Mikal's shield from where it dropped when Mikal made his dash for the door, and holding it in one hand, he grabbed the Prince and began to lead him across the room towards the stairs. Roebert lifted the table he was behind and, using it as his shield, made his way over to where Percyl and I were lying.

'Teal, get Percyl on his feet,' Roebert shouted as he neared us. 'Make sure you keep the table between you and the front windows,' he added.

Once Roebert was in position I helped Percyl stand. His right hand still grasped the quarrel, and his left arm was over my shoulder. Suddenly a shaft struck the table. Tomas stepped around the corner and replied with an arrow of his own. His shot must have been successful, as we heard a loud grunt, followed by a thud.

The cover given us by Roebert's table got us to the base of the stairs. The table was too awkward to manhandle up the stairs so we were going to have to climb without cover. Tomas began to send arrows through the front windows as quickly as he could. Roebert and I literally dragged Percyl from the cover of the table and climbed the stairs. Only two quarrels came near us as we climbed. Both of these were wide of their targets, thanks to Tomas' covering fire. We reached the top of the stairs and called for Tomas to follow. He leapt from cover and raced across the room. He was moving too fast for the crossbowmen to get a good shot at him, though several quarrels flashed passed him. Danel followed, using Mikal's shield as cover.

We urged the Prince on and were soon descending the rear stairs. I expected to come under fire as soon as we left the cover of the inn, but we reached the compound behind the inn safely.

'This way.' We turned towards the sound of the voice and saw Mikal waving to us from the corner of the inn. Roebert and I were still carrying Percyl, so the rear guard position was left to Danel. 'This way — keep close to the edge of the building,' Mikal said.

As we followed him we passed the bodies of three crossbowmen. They were stretched out alongside the building. This explained why we were able to descend from the inn's upper level without being attacked. Mikal had found the sentries, and dealt with them.

Mikal peered around a corner. Turning back to us he whispered. 'Their horses are tied across the street. There are four guards.'

The others nodded. Tomas drew an arrow from his

quiver and readied it. Danel passed Mikal's shield back to him and loosened his glaive in the scabbard.

'Mikal, you stay with the Prince. Teal, you see Percyl crosses as quickly as possible. Tomas, you take the two on the right. Danel and I will take the two on the left,' he looked at Danel. 'One each?'

He and Danel then slipped around the corner, and ran across the street towards the unsuspecting guards. They were watching the front of the building; the attack on the inn was supposed to have caught us in the tap room. Should we escape the quarrels, the front of the inn was the only way we could escape without exposing ourselves to the shots of the enemy crossbowmen. So apart from the few sentries Mikal had taken care of at the rear, the main force was situated at the front of the building waiting for us to break from the cover of the inn. I looked around the corner just in time to see Roebert and Danel reach the guards. Tomas stepped out beside me and dropped one of the right hand guards with a shot to the chest. He quickly nocked another arrow and took the second guard in the throat.

Roebert and Danel had taken care of the other two. I ran across the street with Percyl over one shoulder. I could hear Tomas behind me, urging the Prince to greater speed. If the dead men in the alley were found, then the warning would go out and we would be trapped in the open.

I pushed Percyl up into a saddle and then chose a horse for myself. All the others were mounted except for Mikal who was moving among the remaining horses, whispering calming words to them as he cut through the cinch straps.

Once this was done, he mounted, and we turned and kicked our horses into a run. We could hear shouts behind us. It would not be long before we were pursued. It was almost sunset: the gates from the city would be closed, as the inhabitants feared attack at night by brigands. By the time the gates were opened to us, our attackers would have had time to find new mounts and cut our lead by a considerable amount.

We raced through the streets of Esherweld, Tomas at the rear. At last we came to the gates — as we expected, they were closed. Roebert brought his horse to a sliding stop and dismounted. He began to open one of the large gates and nearly had it wide enough for us to ride through, when there was a call from a small building on our left. A man raced over; several others began to tumble from the building in his wake.

'Here! Stop that! You can't open the gate at this time of day,' he called.

He stopped before Roebert, who calmly lifted his flail from his weapons' belt and struck him over the head with the handle. The man fell unconscious to the ground. Tomas shot an arrow into the ground in front of the other guards, which caused them to stop. Roebert finally had the gate open sufficiently for us to ride through. We could hear the sounds of pursuit behind us now. We rode from the city. Roebert began to swing the gate closed behind us, but a noise caused him to look up. Riding hard towards the gate were a dozen or so horsemen. The sight of them bearing down upon him had him leaping for his mount. Swinging the horse's head around with a sharp cry, he spurred his mount after us.

Several times they came close enough for quarrels to whizz past our ears. But each time that happened we swung our mounts, and the change of direction threw them off momentarily. It took us several hours to lose our pursuers, and only then due to the encroaching darkness.

We were holed up in a small creek bed. We had heard no sound of pursuit for twenty minutes or more. Roebert and Tomas had crawled up the creek bank and were watching for any sign of our pursuers. Mikal had lifted the wounded and cursing Percyl from his horse, and was about to remove the shaft from his thigh. The Prince was off to one side, seemingly undisturbed by his steward's plight. He was leaning forward in the saddle the same as I was. It was the only way I was able to keep myself mounted. I seemed to have lost all feeling in my legs. Roebert slipped down the bank.

'Tomas will watch for a while. We will stay here for a couple of hours to rest the horses, then we will ride north. That was the last town we will stop in, from now on we will stay out of sight,' he indicated towards Esherweld. 'From now on, we eat what we catch, or we go hungry. They were on to us faster than I had anticipated. We can't take the chance again. The next time we may not be so lucky.'

Mikal pulled the shaft from Percyl's thigh. All the time Percyl had been cursing just loud enough for me to hear. 'Bastards,' he said again, this time louder. 'They'll pay for this.'

Roebert looked up at the Prince. A strange expression came to his face, and I turned just in time to see the Prince topple from the saddle, a shaft protruding from his back. Roebert was the first to reach the Prince's side. There was a dried circle of blood around the wound.

I feared the worst.

11

THE TRUTH

ROEBERT lifted the Prince and carried him over to the edge of the creek. He laid him down, and grabbed the Prince's wrist. Then he placed a finger on the Prince's neck.

'He's dead,' Roebert said. He was staring down at the body in disbelief. 'He must have been hit soon after we left town. I wonder why he didn't call out?'

'Even if he had,' Danel said, 'we would not have been able to stop. Those riders were right on our tail. Perhaps he knew we could not help him until we lost them.'

In every attack, I had worried about myself or one of the others being killed, but never once did I think the Prince would be the one to die. The moment we rode from Lyram, I thought the search was over. All we had to do was ride north to Nuevah and place the Prince on the throne.

I realised the way would be dangerous, and there would be opposition, but I always believed we would succeed. Without the Prince, there was nothing we could do to stop the Regent from gaining the throne.

'Do we bury him here?' Mikal asked.

'We might as well; there's no use taking him any further,' Roebert said. There were tears in Roebert's eyes as he covered the Prince with a blanket which had initially been brought over for the Prince's comfort.

A shallow grave was dug and marked. 'One day,' he said, 'we will return, and mark the grave as befits a Vahian noble.'

'What about me?' Percyl asked.

'We will return you to Lyram; we must tell the Ambassador what has happened,' Roebert said.

'I can't return to Lyram. Take me to Nuevah with you,' Percyl pleaded.

'We are hunted,' Roebert continued. 'We can't return home. You would be best to return to Lyram — it is not your fault the Prince was killed. You have no need to return to Geerge's employment. I'm sure the Ambassador can find a position for you.'

Roebert signalled for Mikal to help him with Percyl. They lifted him and tied him to his horse. All the time he was protesting and cursing. Tomas was called down from his sentry position for the burial. It was as if the death of the Prince had drained all the life from my four companions.

We rode in silence, only stopping long enough to snatch quick meals, then we were on our way again. The days blurred, and I lost all sense of time. Percyl's injury worsened, but there was not much we could do for him except get him to a physician as quickly as possible. Finally, through tired eyes, I saw the walls of Lyram before us. Our horses had barely enough strength to continue, but brought us finally to the residence of the Ambassador.

There was a great deal of activity when we arrived; retainers and servants were sent in all directions. We were taken inside and fed, then we bathed and changed. Once this was done, we told our story. Then we dragged ourselves off to bed, where we slept for the rest of the day.

Percyl had been taken to the Ambassador's physician. During the journey, we were unable to treat his wound properly. His leg was now inflamed and there was a terrible red colouring around the wound. Most of the time he had been unconscious and it was only because he was tied to his saddle, that he was prevented from falling.

The news of the Prince's death affected the Ambassador and his staff in the same way it had my companions. The house was quiet, and the servants went about their business with none of the smiles and friendly exchange which had been present on our earlier visit.

Later that day, the Ambassador called for Roebert.

'It seems the quarrel which wounded Percyl must have had some form of poison on it,' he said. 'My physician tells me his patient's condition is deteriorating and he will not see tomorrow. He has just regained consciousness and has asked to speak with you.' The Ambassador looked up, 'All of you.'

We crowded into the room. Percyl was lying on the bed, white-faced and trembling. He had lost a great deal of weight. As we entered, his eyes turned towards us and his mouth opened and closed several times, before a soft croaking sound escaped from between his clenched teeth.

'About three years ago Geerge bought a score of slaves from a trader who claimed they were captives from some northern skirmish. He held the slaves for several days, and then sold most of them. He kept the four best to toil as oarsmen on one of his new galleys. A couple of months after this, the vessel was attacked by Corsairs. The crew was slain and the slaves taken.'

Percyl's eyes slowly closed, and his body relaxed. No one in the room spoke as all waited for Percyl to continue.

Slowly his eyes fluttered open and his croaking voice broke the silence once more.

'Nothing more was thought of the incident until nearly two years later. During one of his trips, Geerge found out that a Prince of the Vahian Royal Family had been lost in a skirmish about the time he had bought the captives. When he returned to Lyram he had a detailed description of the missing Prince sent to him by one of his agents. Then he went through his records and found that the description matched one of the slaves he had bought. His records showed he had sent the slave to one of his galleys — the one which was later attacked by Corsairs.'

As he spoke, Percyl slowly raised his head from where it rested on his sweat-stained pillow. His urgency was infectious: all those standing around the bed took a step closer to the dying man.

'Geerge tried to find out what had become of the slaves from his vessel, but there was no trace, as the Corsairs in question had in turn been attacked, their vessel sunk, and the survivors hunted down. No matter where he had his agents search, or how much he offered for information, the whereabouts of the Prince remained a mystery. Geerge then came up with the ploy of offering up a false Prince.'

At this statement, all eyes opened wide. Everyone was staring at the emaciated body on the bed. Percyl paid them no attention, but continued his story.

'He found a Vahian slave who had served with a noble in Tharrac. He had been a Runner years earlier, and had little reason to escape and return home. Then he sent the message to the Regent. The slave could speak Vahian, and knew the customs well enough to get by with the masquerade, but once we were near Nuevah, I was to kill him and flee. Geerge had hoped you might kill the Prince as soon as he came into your possession, but you didn't.'

'What did the imposter think of the idea of dying for the merchant's profit?' Roebert asked.

'He had no idea of that part of the plan,' Percyl croaked. 'When the Vahian border was in sight, we were to kill the other two retainers and flee south, to Lyram. Geerge had told him he would be paid a quarter of the ransom, and then taken to any city of his choice outside of the Plains.'

'So what happened to the real Prince; if it was the Prince?' Mikal asked.

'Oh, it was the Prince all right. The description matched perfectly,' Percyl told him. 'As I said, there was no trace of him or the Corsairs who attacked the vessel on which he was a slave.'

Roebert stood, and walked several paces away. 'So, there is still a chance we may find the Prince. All we have to do is find information on those Corsairs.'

'But,' I asked, 'if the merchant could not find any clues to his whereabouts, how can we?'

'I don't know, Teal. The first thing we have to do, is to pay a return visit to our friend Geerge. He may have found some new information,' Danel said.

'I do not like people who sell Vahians into slavery,' Roebert said angrily.

'And I would like to retrieve my five thousand gold pieces. We may have need of them to buy information,' the Ambassador said.

I looked down at the bed. Percyl's eyes were closed and his chest no longer moved. He was dead.

We left the room and went to the main hall to plan the rescue of the Prince.

'If the Prince is indeed still alive, then he was probably sold by the Corsairs, before they were attacked themselves. We must find out all we can about the particular band of Corsairs. There has to be some of them still alive, and possibly operating with other Corsairs. Or, perhaps they have left the risky business of raiding vessels, and have taken up a different occupation — one less hazardous to their health,' the Ambassador said.

The Ambassador then assigned each of us a different task. We rose and left the room. First, I would accomplish my given task, then I would look up an old friend, one who might be able to shed some light on our problem.

12

A FRIENDSHIP RENEWED

IT took me quite a few days to accomplish the task I had been set. Once finished I made straight for the holdings of Ardemus the merchant. I hoped that with his help I would be able to find the whereabouts of Jon.

On our travels south, Jon and I had talked at great length. He had sailed the Great Western Ocean and the Uskery Sea for many years. I hoped he might know something of use concerning the habits of the Corsairs. If the Corsairs responsible for the capture of the Prince were attacked and dispersed, as Geerge had been informed, then Jon might know whether they would still have the captives or whether they would have sold them.

I was lucky. Jon was still in Lyram and Elred was able to take me to where he was staying. It was a small place down near the docks. The building was old and run down, and I would not have thought to look for my friend here.

The tap room was dark and full of a foul-smelling smoke. The sounds of arguments, both verbal and physical could be heard from all corners. Elred and I were both wearing heavy cloaks, and were armed. We moved quickly across the room towards the stairs which led up to the next floor where Jon was supposed to be staying.

Before we reached the stairs, we were intercepted by a big man in a greasy apron. His girth was enormous, and his arms were covered with thick, dark hair. His hair was black and matted, and he reminded me more of a bear than an innkeeper.

'Can I be of service, young Lords?' he said, with a laugh. 'Would you be interested in a drink, or a bit of female company?' On hearing this, several of the closer patrons also began to laugh. It was obvious he intended to have a bit of sport with us.

My right hand dropped, and disappeared into my cloak to rest on the hilt of one of my swords. I had transferred my swords from my usual shoulder harness while I was wearing the cloak. I had no chance to draw the sword before Elred stepped forward and slapped the man's face. The slap was hard, and caused the innkeeper to step back to keep his balance.

'My companion and I,' said Elred sharply, 'are not here to be the brunt of your jokes. So if you would be so good as to step aside, we will continue with our business.' His tone was commanding, and he left no doubt in the minds of those watching that he was more than a youth out for a night of entertainment.

The burly innkeeper stepped aside and allowed us to pass. His face was full of anger as he watched us.

'He will do nothing,' Elred whispered to me. 'At least, not in public. When we leave here tonight, we will have to be careful, but while there are people about, we are safe.'

We climbed the stairs to the first floor and looked for the room Elred was told Jon rented. Elred knocked twice and we waited. The noise of movement could be heard from inside. Elred knocked again.

'Jon, it's me, Elred,' he called. 'I want to speak with you. I have an old friend of yours with me; he wants to ask you for your help in a matter of extreme importance.' He winked at me while he spoke. He did not know the true reason for my wanting to find Jon, but what he had just said was, unbeknownst to him, the truth.

The door opened slowly, and the thin face of a man was thrust out.

'What do you want? There is no one here by that name. Go away!' he said, and made to close the door.

Elred produced a small full purse; and shook it in front of the man's sharp nose.

'Are you quite sure my friend is not there? I have something for him I think he will find interesting — and extremely rewarding.' With that, the purse disappeared out of sight beneath the folds of his cloak.

I heard a familiar voice, 'It's all right — show them in.'

The thin-faced man stepped aside, and opened the door wider. Elred entered the room, giving him a knowing smile. I entered next, but my attention was held by the room rather than the man who was closing the door behind us. The room was filthy, and smelled of week-old rubbish. The only furniture in the room was a small table, a lamp, and a chair. The latter was occupied by a richly-clothed man, who rose as we entered.

'Elred, old friend. How are you?' Jon asked.

'It is good to see you again, Jon. You are slightly better dressed than usual, but I see your surroundings are the same as always,' Elred said as he surveyed the room.

'I had a small piece of good fortune,' Jon answered, brushing imaginary dust from his clothes, 'which has unfortunately gone bad on me,' he said, and waved both hands in the air to indicate the room.

'We have a proposition to put to you,' Elred said.

Jon turned towards me and smiled. 'I see I am not the

only one to have come upon good times. Now, what is it I can do for you two young sirs?'

I glanced over my shoulder at the thin-faced man who was still standing to one side of the door. His arms were folded across his chest in a peculiar way. Since we entered the room, he had not moved, nor did he seem to be interested in the conversation taking place.

'You may speak freely. Not a word you say will be repeated outside this room,' said Jon.

I had already told him about how I had met my four companions and how the village of Dienall had been attacked and destroyed by Wolves in the hope of capturing or killing my companions. I told him what had happened since we parted company. As my story unfolded, Jon rose and began to pace back and forth across the room. The mention of the black galleass stopped his pacing and he made me give him every detail about the vessel and the merchant who commanded it. Once this was done, he carried on pacing. I told him of the Prince's death, and how later we learnt the Prince was a fake and the real Crown Prince had survived the battle in the Erg, only to be sold into slavery.

'Where he is now is not known to anyone, except the Corsair crew who took him from the galley on which he had been serving,' I told him.

When I finished talking, Jon stopped his pacing and stood by the dirty window which looked out over the alley at the rear of the building. For some time he did not move or say anything. Then finally he turned and faced us.

'What you are asking me to do will be next to impossible — the trail is three years old, and the ways of the Corsairs are known by few. But, I will see what can be done. I promise nothing. If I find anything, I will give it to Elred and he can pass it on to you. I do not wish to know where you are staying. There are too many people who have taken an interest in your friends' whereabouts. The Regent's Wolves are after you for what you know about the death of the King and his son. The merchant Geerge is after you to try to silence you about the false Prince he was trying to sell to the Regent — and be sure, he will not have given up on finding the true Prince himself.'

With these words in our ears, Elred and I were shown from the room by the thin-faced man. Rather than pass through the tap room, as we had done when we had entered the inn, we used the back stairs, which Jon told us about as he ushered us towards the door of his room.

'There's no need to take unnecessary risks,' he said. 'It is quite possible that the innkeeper and a few of his friends may be waiting for you to leave.'

We slipped down a side alley and were soon back in the main street. Jon was to contact Elred if he found anything of use, so I parted company with my friend, telling him that I hoped I would be seeing him again soon.

It did not take me long to reach the Ambassador's residence. Once there I told my companions of the arrangements I made with Jon. They agreed that Jon's knowledge of the Great Western Ocean and the Uskery Sea could be of great use to us.

'This time,' Roebert said, 'if we have to travel by sea, we should see if Jon is free for hiring. It is just possible that his skills and connections may have saved us from some of the difficulties we encountered on our previous voyage.'

Even though I had hoped to hear from Elred soon with a message from Jon, it was closer to three months before word reached me that Elred had news. In those three months, I continued to increase my fighting skills under Danel's tutelage. The Ambassador also instructed me in the responsibilities expected of a Vahian Lord.

One day, a message was brought to me during my morning meal. It said Elred had news from a close friend and wished me to meet him at the Brown Sow, and that I would find what he had to tell me of great interest.

Mikal had joined me for the meal, and when he heard the news he leapt to his feet, knocking over the bench he had been sitting on.

'We will meet him,' he said to the messenger.

Once the servant left, he turned to me. 'This is great news. Elred would only send for you if Jon has found something of interest.'

'He may also want to see me,' I told him, 'to tell me he has been unable to find anything of value.'

'That is quite true, but it does not hurt to look on the bright side of things rather than the dark side.'

'You're right. Shall we tell the others? Or will we find out what the answer is first?' I asked.

'I think it would be better to tell them when we know exactly what the full story is about this meeting. Agreed?'

Mikal and I arrived at the Brown Sow at the specified time. I took Mikal via the rear alley and stairs, rather than chance the innkeeper's memory. Mikal kept a sharp watch down the hallway, while I knocked quietly on the door of the room where I had met with Jon three months ago.

The door slowly opened and the thin-faced man peered out. He gave Mikal a good long look, then glanced quickly at me before stepping back into the room and opening the door wide.

Elred was already seated at the table, and Jon stood by the closed window. 'The Corsairs who attacked the galley the Prince was interned on, were from the vessel *Pegasus*,' Elred said. 'The Captain had a full crew so none of the slaves were freed. Some months later the *Pegasus* herself was sent to the bottom by vessels from the Capital. They had been patrolling off the Lyram coast and happened upon the *Pegasus*. Any crew who survived the attack were taken on board one of the war vessels and hung. No slaves were found.'

This last piece of news was bad, especially for Mikal. I could see the news had hit him hard. He had been so confident the real Prince had been found. Jon had maintained his watch at the window, and the thin-faced man was listening hard at the door for any noises from the hallway beyond.

Elred reached for a piece of paper and held it up for us to see. 'This is a Bill of Sale for seven slaves, sold by the Captain of the *Pegasus* some time before his demise. It seems the seven slaves were sold to a merchant in Wirralac. Four of the slaves were of large stature, which means one of them could have been the Prince.'

13

RAFE

MIKAL and I hurried back to the Ambassador's residence with the new information. Mikal called all concerned to the audience hall, where he passed on the information. There were cries of joy from all present as weapons were drawn and brandished in the air. Almost at once, plans were formulated.

The following day the exact plans were revealed. We were to take ship to Wirralac. This time there were to be five vessels. Three would be fighting vessels, privateers. The Ambassador had hired them for an indefinite length of time. The fourth vessel would carry horses, in case the trail led over land. The last one would carry the searchers themselves.

The group would consist of myself, my four companions and others. Elred was allowed to accompany us: his knowledge of languages would be of great use if the trail led far. Jon and his thin-faced associate, Tryell, were also to travel with us. Jon said some of his questions had drawn too much interest, and it would be a good thing if he were to disappear for a short time. Kryss and Kyle would come along as well. I was particularly happy about this, as they were bringing fifty fighting men with them. The fifty were Janissaire of the Purusmayo Province. They had been trained by Vahians, and had ridden in Kryss' and Kyle's battle companies for many years.

With the three fighting ships as escort, we left Lyram and immediately made for deep water. Three fighting vessels as escort would usually signify rich cargoes on the protected vessel or vessels. This could have the effect of drawing Corsairs, rather than keeping them away. However, word that the vessels carried only fighting men and their equipment would, regardless of the short time involved, have reached the Corsairs. Their spy system ashore worked with incredible speed and accuracy. For once that system might work in someone else's favour.

With the shallows no longer a hazard we made good time. The sea was calm, though I had been told this could change at any second as this was the time of year storms swept the sea from the west. But the weather held, and we were soon passing Esherweld. All we saw of the city was the smoke haze of its many chimneys resting just above the horizon.

Two days later I had a strange dream. In my dream, I saw two people standing on a sloping beach. The figures seemed to move closer and I saw they were Rafe and the old healer. Rafe was smiling and waving. It was as if they saw me and were waving for me to come closer. I woke from my dream, and found myself standing at the drawn curtain separating my sleeping quarters from the others around me.

The dream was so realistic. If I had reached out, I swore I could have touched them. I went up on deck to let the wind clear my head. Elred saw me and crossed the deck to stand beside me at the rail.

'Are you all right?' he asked.

'I'm fine. Just need a breath of fresh air.'

'You look strange is all,' Elred said. 'The weather is beginning to get up — I thought you might have been starting to feel seasick.'

'No, I'm fine. I just had a strange dream, and it disturbed me with its clarity.'

'Where I come from,' Elred said, leaning against the rail and looking down at the passing water, 'dreams are used to see into the future.'

'The future! From dreams?'

'Yes. We are taught all dreams are linked to reality, and what you dream may come to pass either for you or for someone close. Funny you should mention dreams. I've been having the same dream since we left Lyram. I see two people standing on a beach and they are motioning for me to come nearer. Each time I go closer, but the two are strangers to me.'

'But that's . . . '

'The same dream you had! I thought as much. When I tried to reach them this time, I sensed someone else near. The instant before I woke I thought I saw you standing on the beach,' he explained.

'But that's impossible,' I told him. 'You don't honestly expect me to believe we shared a dream?'

'Believe what you like,' he said. 'I just described your dream to you. If I wasn't there, how could I have known about it?'

'True,' but before I could continue Danel appeared on deck.

'You two are up early this morning,' he said, and looked around the horizon. 'The weather doesn't look too promising. I hope we are not in for a storm.'

'Danel,' Elred asked, 'what do the Vahians think about dreams?'

Danel thought for a second and then answered. 'Personally I think dreams are harmless. Some believe the future can be told from them, and others I have heard say dreams are a type of communication, like talking, only done in your sleep. I have even heard some folks say they can talk to others in their sleep over great distances. But when questioned closely, they are never actually able to prove this.' He looked up at the approaching clouds, and then back at us. 'Why the interest in dreams?'

'No reason in particular,' Elred answered.

'Is Roebert up yet?' I asked, trying to change the subject.

'Yes, he should be up on deck soon.' Danel replied.

'Good. I thought I might ask him if we could stop in at the fishing village where we left Rafe. It has been a considerable time, and I'd like to know if he is all right.'

'I don't see why not — we aren't on a schedule. I wonder how the young fellow is. You know, that might not be a bad idea at that. I think I'll go and find Roebert.' Danel turned, and strode off across the deck.

'This friend of yours, Rafe — is he the one in the dream?' Elred asked.

'Yes, and the old woman is the healer we left him with,' I answered.

The Captain agreed to stop at the village. He did not like the look of the storm coming up from astern, and when he was told that the village had a sheltered bay, he was quite pleased. He signalled the other vessels of his intentions and immediately ordered a change of course.

By nightfall, all five vessels were straining at their anchors in the small protected bay, as a fierce storm swept in from the west. The storm had seemed to follow us as we altered course towards the coast. It was only when we were about to enter the sheltered bay, that the storm leaped forward, throwing itself brutally at the coast. Even sheltered as we were, it was difficult to believe that the storm could get worse, but one look at the mountainous waves beyond the bay soon changed my opinion.

'It's lucky you mentioned this bay,' the Captain told us, shortly after anchoring. 'I would not have thought the storm could have reached this intensity so quickly. I had every intention of running before the weather. But this is the worst storm I have ever encountered, and I doubt we would have passed the night without some serious incident.'

This made me think again about my dream. If what Elred said was true, then perhaps Rafe was calling to one of us, not because he was well and wished to see me, but because he knew the storm was coming. The first chance I got, I would look into this dream business — perhaps there was something to it after all.

As the night progressed, the storm worsened. Even at anchor in this sheltered bay, the vessels were in danger of being damaged by the severity of the storm. The crew was kept continually busy all night, and even on the shore the strength of the storm was felt, as huts were flattened and the crops carried away. The wind screamed in from the sea, making any conversation on deck impossible. There was little sleep for anyone that night.

The storm blew all the next day and into the following night. The Captain was certain that most, if not all, of the vessels would have been lost if we had not sought the protection of this bay. As the storm cleared on the third day, I began to make out the much changed outline of the coast. The trees which had protected the village were gone, as was the village itself. A large strip of the beach had been washed away, leaving a ragged edge like an open wound.

There, standing on the remaining beach, was Rafe. Beside him was the old healer, exactly as my dream had showed me.

Rafe and I were alone. We were sitting on my bunk on board the *Myranda*. Our small convoy was three hours east of the sheltered bay, again making good time.

'How is it possible?' I asked.

'Once my wounds were healed, Trycee began to teach me things I had thought were impossible. Trycee is not originally from this village. She was found on the shore one morning after a terrible storm, similar to the one we have just witnessed. She was in her early twenties, but had no knowledge of her past. The Headman allowed her to stay with the village. As time passed they found she was skilled in the ways of healing and she became a person of great power.'

He raised his right hand, and pointed to his middle finger. At first, I could not see what he was showing me. Suddenly, I saw a thin band of metal around the finger. It must have been there before, but I did not notice it. The ring was made of a reddish metal which seemed dull, and yet bright at the same time. The more I looked at the piece of jewellery, the more obvious it became, until I wondered how I missed seeing it.

He lowered his hand and continued. 'The villagers did not want her to leave. She explained to them that a great storm had brought her and a great storm will take her away. The last storm was such a storm.'

'But what will happen to the villagers now if they fall sick, or are injured?'

'She has trained eight women to replace her over the years. The most recently trained are a young girl of great skill, and a mother of six who has great potential.'

'What happened to the others?' I asked.

'They are dead.'

'How?'

'Old age. Each lived to a great age and died shortly after a younger woman was trained,' he answered.

'You mean each woman was trained just before the other died? That is impossible! If this were true, then Trycee would be ancient rather than old.'

'No one knows for certain. She has been in the village six generations,' Rafe answered. 'She gave me this ring, and since that day, I have had strange dreams. I saw you and your four companions riding with another who was hurt. I saw you practising your weapon handling in a large circular hall, and I saw you take ship. Four days ago I saw the storm appear as if from nowhere and I watched it get closer to you at an alarming speed. That was when I dreamt to Elred and called. You overheard. I hoped to bring you into the shelter of the bay before the storm struck.'

'How is it all possible?' I asked, not quite believing what he was telling me, yet knowing it had to be true. I had the dream and so did Elred. And Rafe's recovery in the four months since we left him had been miraculous. He seemed fitter than he was when I first met him.

'Trycee says it has something to do with the metal of this ring, but that is all she has told me. She says she will travel with us for a short time only and then she has to leave us. She is old, and she saved my life — if she leaves, then I will go with her, if she permits.'

'I understand, Rafe, but we are heading for Wirralac. There is not much there but the Uskery Sea and the Todismal Forest.'

'I know, but she is determined to leave us. She used a great deal of time and energy to help me. Once I was able to move around, I could see how the effort had weakened her.'

He was right. Since coming on board, Trycee had not left her bunk, and Myryca had not left her side. At least the young healer was helping Trycee to rest. If Trycee had come alone, I doubt that she would have seen out the voyage.

Myryca was about seventeen. She was quiet and tried to keep out of sight. When they were bringing her and her teacher from the beach in one of the longboats, she had remained at Trycee's side, wrapped in a large cloak, with a huge hood under which she would occasionally peek. Rafe told me about her, while we watched the longboat cut through the swell towards the *Myranda*.

'Myryca's mother died when she was born. She was brought up by the entire village. She is supposedly slow-witted and mute. I have never heard her utter a word, yet she takes in the lessons she is taught with enormous speed. She is forever studying or watching Trycee, trying to learn something new. The villagers were also surprised at the speed at which she seemed to learn. I think it frightened them somewhat, and that was why they allowed her to accompany Trycee.'

The fine weather held for the remainder of the voyage. It was as if the sea, having thrown all it could against us, was resting. We did not put into Tharrac, but continued eastward, and at last reached the coast and followed it south to Wirralac. Our small convoy anchored in an isolated part of the harbour, and all leave on the five vessels was withheld. The fewer people who knew of our mission the better.

Jon and Roebert went ashore to find the merchant who had bought the slaves from the Corsair Captain. Kryss argued that they should take some of the men along with them in case something unexpected happened. Roebert disagreed, but said if they were not back in twenty-four hours, then Kryss and Kyle and a number of their Janissaire could come ashore to find them.

This proved unnecessary, as the party returned within the stated time.

'What news, Roebert?' Mikal asked.

'We found the merchant in question. He bought the slaves, but he has since sold them. His records are, however, quite good, and Jon and I soon found reference to the ones we were after. Of the seven slaves, only four could possibly have been Vahian. Two were sold to a trader from Velliach, and one to a caravan owner from Murztal. The fourth was bought by a Captain as a replacement crewman for his vessel. The Captain's next port of call was Hocheken.'

Roebert looked around the group. 'The problem is, the first three travelled by land. If we are to keep track of them, then we should also travel by land.'

'This means we will have to split into three groups, doesn't it?' I asked.

'That's right,' Roebert said. 'Kryss, Jon and myself will work out the groups. Until then, I suggest you all get all the rest you can. With the size of the party split, there will be more work for each of you, so this could be the last time you will find yourselves with time on your hands.'

As we turned to leave, Trycee approached us. 'It is time we parted,' she said. 'Myryca is gathering our possessions and as soon as she is finished we leave. You must stay here. Rafe: you have much to learn. Be sure you keep your mind open for new ways.' She placed her hands on his shoulders. 'This one,' she said and looked at me, 'keep with this one and you will learn much.'

Just then Myryca came up on deck carrying two bundles. Trycee took one and crossed the deck towards the rope ladder she would descend to the waiting longboat.

'We will not meet again,' she said, and disappeared from sight.

Rafe and I walked over to the rail, and watched the longboat pull towards the shore.

'Is she right, do you think? Will we ever see her again?'
I asked.

'I have a feeling she's right. This is the last we will see
of her, but I don't think it is the last we will hear of her,'
Rafe answered.

14

THE OSSEAUX SWAMP

ROEBERT and the others came back on deck after several hours of planning. 'Gather round and I will tell you what has been decided.'

He waited while everyone moved closer to where he was standing. 'We'll be splitting into three groups. Myself, Mikal and fifteen men will ride to Velliach. We will take the coast road. Sergeant Dalzyl will come with us.

'The second land party will be Kryss, Kyle and another fifteen of the men. Sergeant Zeebah will be with that group.' He turned to Kyle. 'You will take the inland route and make for Murztal.

'The third group will stay with the vessels and travel on to Hocheken. Whether the Prince is found at your destination or not, all groups will meet at Hocheken. Remember we are still at least two years behind the Prince's movements. There is every chance he will be at none of the places. But I must make this very clear: no group is to go off by themselves if they pick up a lead on the Prince's whereabouts. The few days it takes to ride to Hocheken and get the rest of the party will make absolutely no difference to whether or not we catch up with the Prince. After three years, a few days won't hurt.'

It took the best part of two days to unload the horses and buy food and stores for the two groups. At last everything was ready. They mounted up and at a signal from Roebert rode south, out of town. Just outside of town, the two parties would split.

Because of a favourable tide the convoy sailed immediately. We had further to travel than the distance we had already covered. However, this time we would pass no towns or villages. The coast was completely devoid of habitation.

Stretching four hundred miles east from the coast was the Todismal Forest. The forest ran north for one hundred miles and south for six hundred miles. It was crisscrossed by trade roads. Because of the isolation along the coast, most trade passed through the forest. At regular intervals there were Waystations. There were occasions when trade caravans were forced to spend the night out under the leafy canopy of the forest, but this only happened when a caravan was delayed by an accident or the like. No one intentionally stayed in the forest at night, and if they did, they never did it again.

The two roads the other parties would be taking were well-travelled. It was our party which would be alone through the length of its journey. Once past the forest, there was the Osseaux Swamp. It would be safe to stop only when we had passed this natural obstacle.

We were having to battle against strong headwinds, and the storms were becoming more frequent. Already one of the privateers had been forced to turn back. She sustained heavy damage to her sails on the second day out from Wirralac. By the sixth day, the coastline was hidden from view by the worst storm yet. The other vessels were nowhere in sight. Three of the crew had been swept overboard, while the rest of us were kept busy at the pumps.

Storm lines had been rigged, but even so, to venture on deck was to literally take your life in your hands.

I was working with several of the crew at one of the pumps when a crash was heard above the roar of the wind. A naked crewman, soaking wet, raced past and shouted, 'The main mast is down!'

A few of the men were ready to run, but in a loud voice, which surprised even me, I called them back to the pumps. The vessel was not military, but the discipline was good, and the hands returned to their work.

By midnight the storm had eased and there was no longer any need for all the pumps to be manned. I was on deck with Tomas and the Captain. The stars were still hidden by clouds, so it was impossible to tell exactly where we were, but, with the main mast gone, and most of the sails in tatters, we wouldn't be going anywhere but where the wind wanted to take us.

'How far are we from the coast, Captain?' I asked.

'I don't know exactly, and I won't be able to find out till the sun rises. That should be in about four and a half hours,' he answered.

Suddenly, there was a loud tearing sound and the deck rose beneath my feet. Spars and lengths of rope fell about the deck. The bow rose higher and higher, as we were flung across the deck by the force of the blow.

There were screams from below decks and the cracking of timbers could be heard. Some of the crew were in the water, having been thrown from the rigging when the vessel struck. The deck was tilted at a steep angle, and more rigging was falling.

'We've struck a reef!' the Captain called, climbing to his feet. 'Get men forward with lead lines. I want to know how far up we are, and get some men to check on the damage

151

to the hull.' The last was shouted to the First Officer, who disappeared below deck yelling orders as he went.

'Get a line to those men in the water,' the Captain called down to the men climbing to their feet on deck. He turned to us. 'It might be an idea if you were to bring any possessions on deck. There's no telling how badly we are damaged.'

Tomas and I clambered along the sloped deck. We met Danel and Jon on the way. Jon was bleeding from a nasty gash over his left eye and was being supported by Danel.

'The Captain says to get whatever gear we want on deck, just to be safe,' I told them.

The damage was about as bad as it could be. The vessel was holed in three places, and it was only the angle of the bow which stopped the hull from filling with water.

'There's no hope of repair; we'll have to take what we can and make for the shore,' the Captain told us. 'We are quite safe at the present, however, as the vessel is well and truly caught. Only another storm will free the *Myranda*.'

The task of ferrying all the usable material and stores to the shore started. Once the sun rose, we were able to make out the coastline. It was a long strip of brown against the green background of the swamp's vegetation. Trip after trip was made, and the sun was setting as I finally made it ashore, though as soon as my foot hit ground, I wished I had stayed on the *Myranda*.

Stepping from the boat, my foot sunk into brown mud. I drew it from the mud, and saw that most of the sticky substance was still clinging to my boot, and what was worse was the sickly decaying smell released by my actions. I looked about the landing site and saw it was the same everywhere. Nowhere seemed to be free of the vile-smelling mud.

Palm fronds and other large pieces of vegetation had been laid out like a walkway, but the amount of traffic had churned them into the mud and made them quite useless. With a loud sucking noise, I dragged my feet from the sticky mud, as I made my way across the mud flats, towards the trees.

By the time I reached the tree line, I was exhausted, and covered to the knees in the foul-smelling stuff. All the salvaged equipment was stacked well back from the mud on a hastily constructed platform. A small walkway, constructed of young trees, zig-zagged its way into the swamp.

As I followed the walkway, I met Tryell. He was standing waist-deep in a pool of black water, scrubbing the mud from his body.

The thought of entering the pool sent a shiver through my body. Tryell noticed this and stopped his washing. 'It might look bad,' he said, 'but it's better than stinking of that stuff.' He laughed, and pointed to the mud which was quickly drying on my boots and legs. 'Ease yourself down here beside me, and wash the stuff off before it dries completely.'

I slipped slowly into the black water, not knowing what I might find in its hidden depths. The water was warm, and a smell of putrefaction rose from it once it was disturbed. I glanced about nervously and began to scrub myself clean. Each time I bent to wash mud from my boots my face was brought closer to the water and the stench became almost overpowering.

Finally I climbed up to the walkway, cleaner, and happier to be out of the water. The whole time I was washing myself, I had an uncomfortable feeling something was wrong.

Tryell finished before me but waited on the walkway for me. 'All right, we're finished now. Thanks for the help,' he called softly.

Looking around, I noticed one of the Janissaire standing a short distance back from the dark pool's edge. He had a cocked crossbow in his hands. I turned back to Tryell, a question on my lips. Tryell held up a hand, and then pointed to the far side of the small pool we just left. I could not see what he was showing me at first, but finally I saw it sitting in amongst the low foliage. It was the long snout of a creature; the rest of its body was hidden, but the mouth, full of needle-like teeth, was quite visible and sent another shiver down my spine.

'I figured what you didn't know wouldn't hurt you,' Tryell said with a smile. Then turned and disappeared along the walkway. The sentry with the crossbow smiled as he passed me, and then he too disappeared along the walkway. As I stood there, I heard the sound of laughter from ahead of me.

I followed the sound of the laughter, searching to either side of the rough-hewn path as I did so. Only then did I notice more of the long-snouted creatures lurking in the shadows of the foliage. I quickened my pace until I was nearly running.

The camp site was a large area cleared of many of its trees. Those which had been cut down had been lashed to those still standing to form a framework for a large plat-form. All the stores were eventually moved here from the muddy water's edge, and stacked on a smaller platform of logs to one side of the main platform. Most of us would sleep in hammocks, so the platformed area was mainly to be used for cooking, eating and traffic.

'Don't you think we are getting a bit elaborate, consid-ering we may only be here for a few days?' I asked. 'The other vessels are sure to continue the voyage to Hocheken, and as they pass we have only to signal them.' I was talking to Danel, but Tomas came over with Jon to join in the conversation.

'True,' Tomas answered, 'but would you like to spend two or three days in the mud by the water's edge?'

'No, not really,' I answered.

'What if the vessels are delayed, or worse yet forced ashore like we were? What are we to do then? When would you suggest we stop waiting and start thinking about survival?' Tomas added.

'You're right. I hadn't really thought that far in advance,' I answered.

15

AMBUSH

THE chiggers nearly drove us mad the first night. The only way to protect yourself from their stinging bites was to cover yourself completely with a blanket or piece of canvas. The problem with this was the weather. It was so hot that after ten minutes of being covered in this fashion you were sweating profusely. And after half an hour, you had to unwrap yourself to allow your body to cool. Of course, as soon as this was done, the chiggers returned in even greater numbers, with greater appetites.

I awoke covered in bites. There was dried blood all over my arms and hands, where I had killed chiggers as they fed on me. If it was going to be like this each night, it would not be long before we would all be dead on our feet from exhaustion; or worse yet, driven out of our minds by the intolerable itching.

After eating, half of us set about salvaging what we could from the remains of the wreck, while the rest finished off the walkways and sleeping platform. Several of the men under Sergeant Ransyn were assigned the task of finding food. There was plenty of water on board the *Myranda*, and the barrels were not damaged when we ran aground. There was also plenty of salt pork. Some of the water and salt pork had been brought ashore the previous day. We had no idea how long we would be marooned here, so it had been decided we would live off the land if possible, and save our stores in case we were forced to find our own way out of this malodorous swamp.

The most prolific animals found so far were birds. There were hundreds of them of all descriptions, plus monkeys and the swamp creatures. The long-snouted creatures were called gavials. Sergeant Ransyn said they ate fish or other small creatures which fell into the water from the overhanging foliage. I was sure he was right, but I had no intention of bathing in any of the gavial-inhabited pools again to prove the point.

The birds were easy to bring down, as were the monkeys. The gavials proved to be somewhat more difficult to kill. Crossbow bolts bounced off the thick-plated upper body, and only an eye shot could stop the creatures. Sergeant Ransyn had been right so far: the creatures had made no attempt to attack us, unless provoked — so we were going to cross them off our diet and give them a wide berth.

For five days, we sat in that infernal place. The foul-smelling mud on the shore was the only thing which kept the chiggers away. So each evening, a large bucket was brought up and we all covered our exposed parts with the brown ooze. With the chiggers kept at bay, and plenty of water and food, we had no immediate problems, but it was obvious we could not sit here indefinitely. The men were already beginning to get restless, and there had been four incidents of fighting between the remaining crew of the

Myranda and the Janissaire who were with us from Kryss' battle company.

It was obvious by then that the other vessels had probably suffered a fate similar to or worse than ours. It was up to us to get ourselves out of this infernal place. The Captain had volunteered to take most of the crew and three of the longboats, and to sail to the nearest fishing village. They would have to travel west, as east would only take them back to the Todismal Forest. Water, and other supplies were loaded, and Jon offered to go along as well, but the Captain said that if they failed, Jon would be needed to take the remaining boat and attempt to get help elsewhere.

The seventh day in the mud hole saw the Captain and his party put to sea. They rowed out against the swell and passed the wreck of the *Myranda*. Once safe in deep water, they hoisted their sails, and with the wind blowing gustily from the west, struck out for help. The going was slow. It took the rest of the day for them to disappear from sight over the horizon.

'With this wind,' the Captain told us before he left, 'it will take us at least eight days to reach the closest village. With another eight to get back, and four in case of trouble, you should expect us in about twenty days. If there is no sign of us by then, you will know we have failed. It will then be up to you to decide what should be done. May the Goddess of Good Fortune be with you.' I hoped for our sakes she was with him as well.

There was nothing more we could do. Sergeant Ransyn and a party of six were out hunting. Jon, with the remaining seven crewmen of the *Myranda*, was busily engaged in making fish traps. Danel, Tomas and Tryell were sitting off to one side speaking in whispers. The other Janissaire were either on sentry duty or half-heartedly rolling dice.

158

Elred and I were sitting on the edge of the platform watching three small gavials fight over a small fish one of them had caught. We had constructed a large fire in case a vessel was seen, but the fire would probably not be needed as the *Myranda* was still high on the reef for all to see.

Each day we hunted and fished. Sentries were set to watch for passing ships. But none were seen. Jon and Tomas tried to keep us as busy as possible; they did not want us to think about what would happen if the Captain were not to return. There were too many of us for the one remaining longboat, and if the Captain with his experienced crew could not make it, how could we?

It was the morning of the eleventh day, and I was on sentry to the south of our camp. That position was mainly used to keep us occupied. There couldn't be anything south of us — there was just mile after mile of swamp.

I'd been perched in a tree for about an hour when I saw something moving through the trees in short staggering runs. As the figure drew closer, I saw it was one of the *Myranda's* crew. He had been assigned to Tryell for the day's hunt. As he approached the tree, I dropped down and confronted him.

At first he didn't seem to recognise me. Then he began to wave in the direction from which he had just come. 'They're all dead!' he cried. 'They're all dead!'

'Who are dead? The hunting party?'

'We have to tell the others! We can't let them surprise us as well,' he shouted hysterically. 'We have to warn the others!'

With these words, he darted past me and began a stumbling run through the mud towards the camp. It would be useless to follow him through the mud, so I climbed back up into the tree and dropped down on the other side. There was a small walkway built for the sentries' use.

Even with his headstart, we reached the camp site together. He dropped to the timber platform, and curled up into a gibbering ball. Everyone crowded about trying to find out what was going on.

'What is it, Teal?' Danel asked.

'He came stumbling through the swamp, and when I asked him what was wrong he began to shout, "They are all dead!" Over and over, that's all he says.'

'They're all dead!' he said again, just to prove me right. 'They surprised us from the trees. We weren't expecting trouble to come from there, so we didn't look for it till it was too late. One minute we were standing there looking down at a kill, then, suddenly they were dropping down around us, dozens of them.'

He seemed to have calmed down since reaching the platform. He was given a drink by one of his shipmates, then he looked around at all those present.

'They never had a chance. Two went down almost immediately; the rest were swarmed over. I was the furthest from the kill, so, when I saw the others go down I turned and ran. Several of the things came at me, but I just kept going. I don't even remember whether I fought them off, or just outran them.'

'Are you sure the others are dead? They may just have been knocked unconscious,' Jon asked.

'Dead! Dead! Those things were everywhere; how could they be alive?'

'All right, there's nothing we can do about it now. It will be dark in an hour. There's no sense in stumbling around in the dark. We may only lose more of us,' Tomas said.

'They mightn't be dead,' Jon said angrily. 'This fellow has no idea what happened. They may all be alive out there waiting for us.'

'Then they will have to wait till morning. To go out now would be suicidal.' Tomas turned from Jon, and addressed

Sergeant Ransyn. 'I want all the men on sentry tonight in three shifts. They are to be paired off — no one is to be alone. All those not on duty are to keep their weapons handy. Once the meal is over, the fire will be extinguished; there's no need to advertise our position.'

'Yes, Lord. What about the longboat? Will I have sentries placed there as well? There's no chance of us getting it closer to the camp.'

'No, Sergeant. The longboat will stay where it is. Hopefully they will not be able to find it in the dark,' Tomas answered.

'They, Lord?' Ransyn asked.

Tomas glanced over to where Jon and the now-calmed crewman were talking. 'I have no idea. Hopefully, we will soon know what we are up against. Once my orders are carried out report back to me.'

'Yes, Lord,' Ransyn answered, and turned to his work.

Tomas crossed over to beside Jon, who had continued to question the terrified crewman. 'Well, who was it who attacked them, Jon?'

Jon rose, and, taking Tomas by the arm, steered him away from the crewman, towards where I was standing.

'I believe, from his description, the party was attacked by Plastrals. They are a smaller type of Plastron. I have heard they prefer the coastal region near this godforsaken swamp, but I had no idea they were actually living in the swamp,' Jon answered.

'Will there be many of them?' Tomas asked.

'I shouldn't think so. The Plastrons were never large in number, so I don't see why their smaller cousins should be any different.'

'I suppose that's something,' Tomas said, with a shrug. He turned towards me. 'What watch did you end up with, Teal?'

'Last. Tomas, are we all going to look for the hunting party in the morning?' I asked.

'No. Jon is going to remain here with the sailors and three of the Janissaire. We have to have someone here to tell our rescuers what has happened to us.'

'Let someone else stay. I'll be going with you tomorrow,' Jon said sharply. 'I'll not leave Tryell in the hands of those creatures.'

'We don't intend to leave anybody anywhere. These sailors are not trained to fight, and you've seen the way they travel through this country. No, they'll have to stay behind, but I'll not abandon them, they have to have a way out. That way is you, Jon. You're the only one who can navigate on the open sea. With you in command of that longboat, they will at least stand a chance of getting out of here.'

'I suppose you are right,' Jon answered begrudgingly. He didn't sound too sure, but I believed he had realised that Tomas had to think of the group as a whole.

I walked back to where my sleeping gear was laid out. I doubted sleep would come to me but I had to try. Lying on my back, I listened to the sounds around me: the clink of weapons as the sentries positioned themselves, and the snoring of those already asleep.

The first sentries were already in place. They would not be walking back and forth, because in the inky blackness of the swamp, sound was what gave you away. Nothing could be seen until you were literally on top of it. But anything trying to move out there would make considerable noise. Even if the creatures did live in this smelly bog, they would not be able to move about without disturbing other creatures or splashing through the mud. All our sentries had to do was get comfortable and remain alert.

At last I managed to fall asleep, and as soon as I did, I began to dream.

I saw Rafe and Tryell. They were lying on a rough platform of large branches. I could also see three other figures lying nearby. Rafe raised his eyes to me and smiled. His face was covered in mud and there was a large welt on his forehead. He lifted his hands and showed me they were bound, then indicated to the surrounding area.

All around the small group of captives, I saw the prone figures of creatures. A close look at one showed it resembled the description of a Plastron given to me by Jon so many months ago. However, there was a difference. These creatures were smaller, and they were wearing a girdle around their waists. From this girdle, hung a short kilt and a wicked-looking short sword of a type I had not seen previously. There was also a small dagger of the same type worn on the opposite hip. Lying on the ground beside some of the creatures were strange-looking spears.

I found myself moving, swinging around and behind the sleeping figures. Even as I did this there was no sense of motion. I just seemed to be there. I still did not understand this dreaming, but at least I now knew all but one of the party were still alive.

I woke up and found I was in a sitting position looking out into the swamp. I looked around and saw Elred sitting across the platform. I moved over beside him. Tomas and Jon were already there.

'Well, they're definitely alive,' Elred said. 'They are tired and well-guarded but they are not seriously injured.'

'How many did you see?' Tomas asked.

'All but two. With the one who escaped it means only one is missing,' Elred answered. 'Is that what you saw, Teal?'

'Yes, they seemed well enough. I don't think they are far away. I got the impression of nearness.'

'Which direction?' Tomas asked.

'That way,' Elred said, and pointed in the direction I had been facing when I woke.

'You dreamt this as well, Teal?' Jon asked.

'Yes.'

'When you leave tomorrow,' Jon said. 'I think Elred should stay with me. There seems to be something to this dreaming, and with Elred here, and Teal with you, we may be able to keep track of each other's movements.'

'I can't say I understand this dream-talking, but it proved to be correct once, so we may as well do as you suggest,' Tomas said. 'Do you think you will be able to communicate with each other as Jon suggests?'

Elred and I looked at each other. 'We don't actually communicate. We simply share a dream, but I don't see why it won't work,' he answered.

'Good. Get some sleep. You'll need it tomorrow,' Tomas said.

'There's one more thing,' I told them. 'There are a great number of the creatures, and they are similar to Plastrons, but smaller. They are also clothed and armed, and are carrying strange swords with undulated blades and daggers to match. Many are also carrying strange triple-headed spears.'

16

THE ANCIENT CITY

EVERY step was a great effort, as the mud's hold was hard to break. We had been travelling for three days, each day like the one before. Despite our efforts, there looked to be no end to this malodorous swamp, just miles of mud, chiggers and more mud. Most of the men were about finished. If not for the fact we were gaining on our captured friends, I was sure the pace would have slowed.

Shortly after leaving our camp we came across the site of the ambush. We found the body of one of the hunting party, and over twenty dead Plastrals. The bodies of the creatures were stripped of all weapons, as was the body of our man. With the discovery of the body, we learnt the Pastrals were not after food, but captives. Not much information was gained from the details at the ambush site, as the mud hid everything that happened in this accursed place.

My dream the first night after leaving the camp was similar to the night before except it seemed stronger. The next night's dream was stronger still. We were closing the gap between us and our quarry. The problem was, were we moving faster, or were they slowing down to allow us to catch up?

From my dreams, I found the Plastrals numbered slightly more than sixty. At first this alarmed me, but then I remembered that our hunting party, though surprised and greatly outnumbered, had killed over twenty of the scaly creatures. They were obviously not fighters like their ocean-going cousins.

By the afternoon of the third day, we found ourselves standing on firm ground. It had risen from nowhere and was a much welcome relief. With only an hour or so till last light we should have stopped for the night, but Tomas was eager to get as far away from the chiggers and mud as possible.

That night the dream was even stronger. I could almost sense my friends just out of sight. When I woke, it was still many hours till first light, but I woke Tomas and told him about my dream and how I believed our friends were close. Because of this, he had us up well before first light, and we were miles from our night's resting place by the time the sun had risen above the trees. Not long after sunrise, we came across the first sign of our missing friends.

We found evidence of a large number of beings having spent the night. There was no sign of a fire. The Plastrals probably feared fire as much as the Plastrons.

Sergeant Ransyn appeared out of the vegetation. 'They are about half a mile ahead of us,' he said, glancing over his shoulder at the thick vegetation behind him. 'There are no scouts or sentries out, so I doubt they are expecting trouble. In fact, I don't think they know of our presence,' he said with a grin.

'Can we get around them, Sergeant?' Tomas inquired.

'No, Lord, the solid ground is beginning to narrow, and

there is no way we could pass them if forced to enter the swamp again,' Ransyn licked his lips and continued. 'If I could make a suggestion, Lord?'

Tomas signalled for him to go on. He was beginning to realise how much experience the Sergeant had.

'Well, Lord, as I said, there is no way we can pass them. But I don't feel there is a need to get ahead of them. They are beginning to increase their speed, and our men are beginning to tire. If we were to put in one last burst of speed, we should be able to reach them before they increase their lead. Then, we just keep going, and roll right over them. If Lord Teal's information is correct,' he said, as he made the sign to ward off evil, 'then we should be more than a match for them, even in our tired condition.'

Tomas and Danel talked quietly for several minutes. 'All right, Sergeant, we will do as you suggest. Have all those carrying supplies moved to the rear, and then get the men moving.'

The pace was murder. We were almost running, but the men sensed that this was the last chance we had of catching up with our captured friends.

Suddenly, from ahead, there came the clashing of steel and the cries of battle. I drew my weapons and tried to get a little more speed from my tired legs, but they were numb and refused to move any faster. As I broke through a thick clump of bushes, I saw the battle ahead. Everywhere I looked, I saw men, and the grey creatures from my dreams, struggling back and forth.

I rushed forward, and began to look for Rafe and the others. After despatching several Plastrals — they were not very good fighters at all — I finally saw my friends off to one side of the fight. Several of the Janissaire were protecting them as the fight swirled around them. I staggered over and lent my swords to the fight.

I couldn't say the fight was easy, but, at last, all the

creatures were dead. None tried to flee, nor was any quarter asked. After a quick check, we found only one of our number was dead. There were, however, five wounded, one seriously.

We freed our friends, and with the body of the dead Janissaire and the wounded, we moved away from the scene of the battle. Tomas refused to leave the body of the dead Janissaire behind. He explained that, as a loyal follower, he deserved better than to be left in this stinking place. Once we were far enough away, we set up camp, and the Janissaire was buried with great ceremony. Though hours till dark, our men could not go any further, and our wounded needed treatment. Tomas and Danel seemed upset by the loss of the Janissaire, though I thought the cost was slight, compared to the victory, but Tomas said the price had still been too high.

Our scouts reported that they had found a stream not far away, which would supply us with fresh water to replace what we had used in our chase. Rafe began to treat the wounded. He told Tomas it would be best if we were to rest here for several days. We now had plenty of water, and there was lots of game in the area. None of the Plastrals had escaped, so after several minutes with Sergeant Ransyn and Danel, Tomas told us we would remain here for three days. Then we would strike out in an attempt to be free of that place.

Two days after the rescue, the longboat appeared. Rafe had dreamt to Elred about our freeing the captives. He also showed him the stream. Jon's group had set out the day we had left, and they had passed a stream on the fourth day. He ordered the boat about and headed back to the stream. Once they found it, they struck out upstream in an attempt to find us before we moved on. Elred and Rafe had kept in contact with each other at night to show each group's progress.

'Why didn't I have the dreams?' I asked them.

'We did not know if there were any others in the area who might pick up our communication, so we linked directly, because I knew roughly where Rafe was. You could not have joined in this time. Because on the other occasions the dreams have been general, any Usare could have intercepted and shared them,' Elred answered.

'Usare?' I asked.

Elred lifted his right hand, and asked me what I saw on the middle finger. I looked closely but there was nothing to be seen, though I sensed there was something there, something hiding from view. He made a fist and then opened his hand and asked me again. I looked and this time I saw a ring. On the middle finger was a small ring, the same as Rafe's, so thin that, even when I knew it was there, I had trouble seeing it.

'This is how we are able to communicate through dreams,' Rafe said. 'Both Elred and I have a ring which allows us to link our minds while we are asleep. How you manage to join us, has got us both confused. At first, we thought you were a Usare as well, but then we learnt you could not receive or send a call, but you could join in a dream in progress.'

'But where did you get the ring from?' I asked Elred.

'My grandfather gave me mine,' Elred said. 'He told me his grandfather had given it to him. The ring has travelled through our family for years, missing every second generation.'

'Why's that?' I asked.

'Once the ring is upon the finger, it may not be removed until the wearer is dead. By the time my grandfather died, my father was too old for the ring,' Elred answered.

I turned to Rafe. 'But you said Trycee gave you your

ring. How is that possible? She was very much alive when she left us.'

'She did not take the ring from her finger. She had a small black bag on a chain around her neck. She gave it to me. When I touched the bag it felt like silk, but at the same time looked like velvet. I could feel the bag was empty. I smoothed the bag between my fingers, and I felt nothing inside. When I opened the bag, I saw that it was indeed empty, and thought this some type of elaborate joke. Trycee then told me to feel inside the bag. I cautiously felt inside. As my fingers entered, I felt a strange sensation and quickly pulled back. Then, looking down at my right hand, I saw there was a ring on my middle finger.'

'Did you try to take it off?' I asked.

'Yes, but it wouldn't move. Trycee explained to me what the ring could do, and how it would help me cure sick or injured people. I tested the ring, and found out this was so. I decided I wouldn't fight it, but use it to help people in need,' he answered.

We talked for several hours about the rings and how they could be used. When one of the scouts entered camp in a hurry, I crossed to where he was talking to Tomas. Danel and Jon joined me.

'Trouble?' Danel asked.

'Not really,' Tomas answered. 'The scouts have found a major Plastral village about eleven miles south of here. There are at least two hundred of the little grey devils, and what's more, there are hundreds of human slaves working at some kind of excavation.'

'Is there anything we can do?' I asked. 'We can't just leave them there. We must help.'

'I don't know. Sixty of these creatures is one thing, but two hundred ... ' Tomas said. 'There may even be more the scouts did not see.'

'All we have to do,' Danel said, 'is to create a large

enough disturbance so we can free the slaves. Then we will outnumber the Plastrals. The slaves won't be armed, but there must be digging tools of sorts there.'

'It might work,' Jon said. 'They will probably be weak, but the chance of freedom should lend them strength. It sounds all right.'

'Have Sergeant Ransyn send our scouts out wide of the camp,' Tomas said to Danel. 'We must be sure there are no more Plastrals in the area. If there are none, then we will attack as soon as it is suitable. The wounded will remain with the longboat and follow on behind. They and the crew are to stop short of the camp and not show themselves until sent for.'

We were creeping through some thick scrubby brush. The slave camp was just the other side of it. Our scouts had ranged out and found no sign of other Plastrals. Our small force was spread out north of the camp waiting for the signal to attack. Jon, Elred and Rafe were to the west, waiting to enter the camp during the confusion and free the slaves.

The slaves were kept in several small compounds with tall walls made of logs. The guards were few, and it was only their presence which must have kept the slaves from escaping, as the gates were only roped together, and a good blade would soon have had them free.

On the signal, we leapt from the cover of the bushes and ran screaming into the camp. Most of the creatures were unarmed, and though many fell before our blades, more arrived all the time.

Some of the slaves working outside their compounds threw themselves on their guards. We had reached the centre of the compound when we began to meet with fierce resistance. First we were stopped, and then forced slowly back in the direction we had come.

At last we heard cries of anger and saw slaves armed with picks and shovels running towards the creatures. There seemed to be very few of them. Perhaps the slave compounds were better guarded than we had first thought.

With the help of the freed slaves, we began to force the creatures back. At one point, I noticed Elred fighting at my side. He fought as if he were still in Ardemus' training room in Lyram; with calm efficiency, his thin sword striking out, and then returning as his opponent fell. We were parted for a time, but, eventually, we were again side by side.

'Where are the rest of the slaves?' I shouted. 'There are barely a handful of them fighting with our people?'

'That's all there are,' Elred answered. 'One of the compounds was full of mercenaries, not slaves. We lost three men before we realised what was happening. We finally overcame them, and rushed here to help, but by then, many of the slaves had either been killed or had fled.'

This was terrible news. The Plastrals were fighting harder than the previous group, and we were taking serious casualties.

'Teal!'

I swung around and saw Tryell forcing his way towards me. He was bleeding from several wounds to his lower legs, but they did not seem to affect him greatly.

'What is it?' I asked.

'One of the men we left at the boat has just arrived. He says a large number of mercenaries under the leadership of several strange-looking men are coming upriver by boat. The crew will hold them till we return with aid. The trouble is, there are not enough of us to divide our forces. Tomas sent the man back with orders that they are to fall back towards us. We have to finish off these creatures before their help arrives.'

He turned and disappeared back into the press of fighting figures. With one last push, we forced the creatures from the high ground into the swamp.

'To me,' I heard called. 'To me.'

The small band I was with turned, and we made our way slowly towards the summoning voice.

It was Jon. 'There is a large force of mercenaries coming upriver. We are not in any condition to meet them,' he said, 'but we have a plan.'

He was right — we could not meet this new threat. I could see most of our people, but there were very few slaves left standing. Tomas arrived, and began to wave us towards the excavation site. Danel, Rafe and Elred were already there with two of the slaves.

'We are in no condition to fight or run,' Tomas said. 'So we are going to hide.' There were a few murmurs from the men. 'Behind me,' Tomas continued, 'is the entrance to the tunnels where these men have been forced to work.' He pointed to the slaves who had gathered to one side. 'I have been informed the Plastrals will not venture underground. If this is true, it will help us considerably. There are many entrances, so the enemy will have to split its forces to watch them all. When we are rested, we will come out of one of these, and make our way towards the west and safety.'

There were nods of agreement from those present.

'Sergeant Ransyn,' Tomas continued. 'Collect some torches — this slave will show you from where — and take half our people into the tunnel system, and ensure the way is clear. This slave knows the tunnels and will accompany you.' Tomas indicated a slave standing near the entrance to the tunnels. He was a large man with a terrible wound across his throat.

'He cannot speak, so just follow his gesturing. Danel, I want you to take the rest of our force and bring up the rear.

173

Elred you stay by me. I may have need of your skills. Rafe, organise any slaves not injured to help with the wounded.'

All the time Tomas was speaking, the Janissaire and slaves kept looking over their shoulders, expecting any minute to see the enemy arrive.

'Jon, once Sergeant Ransyn has been given enough lead, you and Tryell follow with the freed slaves and the wounded. Teal, I want you to help this fellow. He is injured. It was his suggestion to enter the tunnels as a means of escape. He knows the exits, so keep him safe.'

The slave I was to help was thin and wasted. His left leg was bandaged and his right eye was swollen closed. I draped one of his arms over my shoulder, and began towards the entrance. As we were about to enter, the boat party arrived, or rather what was left of it.

One Janissaire and two crewmen, one wounded, staggered from the scrub. All were breathless, and only the Janissaire was armed.

'They are right behind us. The rest of our group is dead or taken; we are the last,' he said, as he fell into the arms of one of the slaves.

'Move!' Tomas called to them and waved to Danel. 'Keep close, don't let yourself get cut off from us.'

'Don't worry,' Danel called back. 'Just don't take too long up front, all right?' he said, and laughed.

The last of the slaves were in, and Tomas, Elred and I, supporting the wounded guide, entered the darkness.

Our torches threw strange dancing lights on the walls of the tunnel. The walls had been roughly dug from the solid rock which seemed to be the base for the dry ground now above us. As we got deeper into the tunnel the floor began to drop away quite noticeably. Most of the time the tunnels were dry, with only the tiniest trickle of water in some of the steeper areas. Considering we were under a swamp, the builders of these tunnels must have had great engineering abilities.

17

USARE

WE had descended to the second level. The tunnels were identical in all ways to those we had just left. Danel's rear guard had caught up to us.

'There's no sign of pursuit,' Danel said. 'How much deeper are we going to go?'

'As deep as we have to,' our guide answered.

'How many arrived?' Tomas asked.

'About a hundred, all mercenary humans. I'd say with those who escaped our attack, there might be as many as one hundred and fifty — one sixty if they're lucky, including Plastrals,' Danel answered.

Tomas turned to the injured guide. 'How many openings on this level?'

The injured man took his arm from around my shoulder and limped over to the closest wall, where he steadied himself before answering. 'There is one on this level, and one on the level above. The third level has two, and the fourth three. That's as far as any of the slaves have ventured,' he answered.

'So, our best bet would be to rest on the third or fourth level,' Tomas explained. 'That way, we will have the choice of five openings, and if our guide is right, Danel, they will have to split their forces, which will mean only thirty or so men per opening.'

'Sounds good. Anything wrong with that?' Danel asked the guide.

The guide shook his head; his leg injury must have been causing him a great deal of pain, as his uninjured eye was open wide and his face had lost all its colour.

'Danel,' Tomas said, turning again to his brother. 'Send one of the men forward and tell Ransyn he is to investigate the next level. If nothing suitable for a safe stop is found, he is to go down one more level, but no further.'

The man raced forward with the message, and we moved deeper into the strange tunnels.

The third level proved to be of no use, so we continued down to the next level. There, Sergeant Ransyn's men found several suitable rooms.

'I think it best, Lord,' the Sergeant said, 'if we keep to the one room. The larger would be best as it has four exits, although two are blocked by falls in the ceiling.'

'Is the room itself quite safe?' Jon asked.

'Yes. The rest of the ceiling seems solid enough.'

'Good, then it will do us,' Tomas said, and strode off with Sergeant Ransyn to the head of our small column. In a short time, we were settled into the room Ransyn found. It was enormous. The sheer size of it had me worried about the strength of the ceiling. With no central columns, what in Byldan's name was holding it up?

Tomas called us all over. 'Danel, our group will take watch at that door,' he said, pointing to the far side of the room. 'Sergeant, your people take the door we entered through. Place torches down the tunnels so we can see as far as possible. We don't want to be surprised.'

'Jon, you and Tryell help Rafe and Elred with the injured. I want all the food and water we have left divided equally between all here. Then find out how many torches we have left. Can anyone see any difficulties?'

'Do you think they will follow us down here?' Ransyn asked.

'The Plastrals won't,' our guide answered, 'but the mercenaries may — if properly coerced.'

'I suggest we all get some rest as soon as we find out just how we stand supply-wise. In the meantime, Teal and I will see if there is any way through the blocked passages.'

I was careful as I pulled rocks away. I didn't want to bring more of the ceiling down on my head. The more rocks I moved, the more it became clear it was hopeless. We would never be able to clear this blockage.

I was about to give up, when I noticed something in the rubble. I bent down to get a better look. In the poor torch light, I found a skeletal hand protruding from beneath the rocks. I cleared away some more of the blockage and found the top half of a human skeleton.

The right arm was extended, and the left was drawn up close to the body. In the left hand, held tight against the chest, was a small box about the size of my first. I reached into the rubble, and lifted the box from its resting place.

The box was made of metal, and the edges were rusted slightly. There were signs of rusting around the hinges and lock as well. It was very light, but the lock was quite sturdy.

Using my knife, I worked on the hinges until both were broken. Then I carefully removed the lid from the box. A close inspection revealed three small black bags. I lifted each small bag out. They seemed empty. Then I remembered the story Rafe told me about his ring.

I was about to place my fingers in the bag when I

remembered what he said about the ring placing itself on his finger, so instead I emptied one pouch out onto my hand.

The first was full of delicately cut gems, fourteen of them. There were diamonds and emeralds, red stones and several blue gems. All caught the torch light and sparkled brightly. As I looked at the stones, I realised I was holding my breath. Cupping my hand, I slipped the stones back into the pouch and slipped it inside my mail shirt.

The next pouch had an amulet in it — a crystal, about an inch long, and tapered, set in the centre of a gold disc. A golden chain hung from the amulet. Rather than put the amulet away, I slipped the chain over my head, and dropped the amulet inside my clothing. I slipped the empty bag in beside the gem-filled one.

I upended the last bag, but there seemed to be nothing in it. As I turned it over to see if anything was caught inside, I saw a small thin ring on the middle finger of my right hand — when I emptied the bag the ring had slipped straight onto my finger. Impossible, but the ring was there, and no matter what I did it wouldn't come off.

Slipping the empty bag into my pocket with the others, I fingered the ring. It looked like the type worn by Rafe and Elred, and the way it slipped onto my finger proved it was of the same type. What type? They said each ring had its own properties. What would this one have?

'Anything, Teal?'

'No, nothing,' I answered, sliding the small box back into the rubble. 'There's no way through this lot.'

'All right, come over here, I've found something,' Tomas called back. I was about to answer, when I was interrupted by a raised voice.

'One of the torches has gone out,' the cry was from one of the seamen at the furthest door. 'Could it be a wind?' Tomas asked.

'What wind?' asked Jon.

'There goes another one,' the same man called.

'Tryell,' Tomas called. 'Get everyone to the far side of the room, between the two rock slides. Ransyn and his men will remain where they are. Everyone else fall back.'

We placed the wounded in the corner, and had the crewmen watch over them. The Janissaire positioned themselves between the two piles of debris, and made ready to meet whatever threat might appear from the now-dark tunnel.

Suddenly, a man stepped into the room. He was short and his skin was totally white. His hair was silver and was held back by a band of gold. He was carrying a sword. I had never seen one like it, but I had seen drawings of similar swords. The weapon was an aor, a short, wide-bladed, double-edged sword. It was a weapon of great age. There were diagrams of several in Ardemus' training room, but he told me he knew of no one who had one in their possession.

The man was followed by two more who could be reflections of the first; they were so alike. All of them began to slowly move along the wall towards us. As I watched them, I noted the only clothing worn, apart from the headband, was a cuirass of what looked like coins, used to protect their bodies from neck to knees.

But there was something strange, not so much about the three, but in general. Then I realised what it was. Not one of the Janissaire had moved, or shown any sign of having seen the three. In fact, no one had turned their attention from the door. It was as if they were invisible to all but me.

Even as I watched, the three drew closer to the rock pile on our right. The first of the three was now only feet from the closest Janissaire. Slowly the attacker drew back his weapon to strike the unsuspecting man. Before he could do so, I cried out and leapt towards him.

My cry caught our party by surprise, to say the least. Men crouched, searching for an unseen enemy in the gloom.

I reached the closest of the three in one leap, and knocking aside a feeble blow, I slid a sword into his heart. He dropped to the floor, and I turned to face the others. To my surprise, they were running for the door, throwing terrified glances over their shoulders, as they did so. I bent to search the one I felled.

My companions were now truly confused. First I attacked nothing, and now I searched nothing. I took up the weapon, and turned it over in my hands. The balance was perfect, and the workmanship was magnificent.

The cuirass, as I thought, was made of coins of all sizes fastened to leather. As I rolled the man over, I noticed the thin ring on the middle finger of his right hand. I reached for the ring, then stopped, remembering my last encounter with a similar ring. Reaching into my armour, I brought out the empty black bag which had contained the ring that was now upon my finger.

Using the bag, I removed the ring from the dead man's finger. The ring vanished. There was no way to tell whether it was in the bag or not. There was a collective gasp from behind me as my friends saw the body for the first time. I rolled the sword and golden headband in the cuirass and bound it with the swordbelt.

'Where did he come from?' Tomas asked.

'I have no idea,' I answered. 'I was watching the door, when suddenly he and his two friends entered.'

'Friends?' several of them cried, some dropping to crouches, others redrawing weapons.

'They are gone,' I told them. 'They fled, when I slew this fellow. Perhaps they are used to killing intruders while they, themselves, remain unseen.'

'They do,' answered the guide. 'This is the lowest level

any of the workers have reached and returned from. All those who ventured to the next level stayed, except for myself and my self-proclaimed protector.' He pointed to the tall slave with the terrible throat wound. 'We have travelled to the lower levels and returned.'

'Were you alone?' I asked.

'There were thirty-six of us when we left this level, and only the two of us returned. We did not meet with any of these invisible ones, or perhaps we too would have met our end in the darkness below. What we did encounter were creatures that have not been seen for a thousand years.'

'How is that possible? How do they survive down there?' Tomas asked.

'I have no answer, but in a room four levels below this one, there is a wall covered with the writings of a people long dead.'

Elred stepped forward. 'Is it possible to get to this room from here, now?'

'Elred, your interest in languages will have to wait. We have no time now. If there are stranger creatures than the one we have just encountered, I suggest we leave here at once,' Tomas interrupted.

'I agree,' said the guide. 'From what little I was able to decipher before we were forced to leave, I gathered, somewhere deep below us is a room which holds something of immense power. That was all I could read, and it was only a small portion of one section. The story covered the entire wall of a room larger than this one. The only other thing I could gather was, the thing is well guarded.'

I placed my hand on Elred's shoulder. 'If it is possible, my friend, we will return to this place.'

18

THE TRUE PRINCE

'WHERE is the nearest opening to the surface?' Tomas asked.

'That way,' I answered, and pointed in the direction our recent visitors had left.

'How do you know?' Danel asked.

'I don't know, it just seems the right way to go.' I couldn't explain it to him. I just sensed it was the safest way out.

'He's right,' said our guide.

Before anything else was said, a call came from the chamber entrance being watched by Ransyn and his men.

'We have trouble,' called Ransyn. 'There are a large number of armed men moving into the far end of the tunnel. It looks like a group of the mercenaries. There's also seven tall strangers who seem to be giving the orders. Here they come!' The last was shouted, as he and his men stepped out into the tunnel to head off the attack.

'Can we . . . ?'

Tomas never had a chance to finish his question.

'This way!' I called, and moved towards the other opening. 'This way will take us longer, but it will still get us to the surface.' Again, I had the feeling I was right, and this was the only way out of our predicament.

I led the way with the guide and his protector beside me. The silent protector had an axe gripped firmly in both hands, and from the look on his face, I would have hated to be the one to come between him and freedom.

After many turns, and passing several small rooms, we reached a steep ramp heading up towards the surface. I waved for the two of them to start up. Then I waited and started to hurry the freed slaves after them. All the slaves, and most of the Janissaire had passed me when Jon stopped beside me.

'How's it going?' he asked me. 'What's the hold-up?'

'I don't know. They started up fast enough. They have probably reached the top, and are held up by whatever force has been sent to watch for us.'

'Well, Teal, they had better hurry. We can't hold this end of the tunnel for much longer,' he said.

I was stunned. The remaining Janissaire were among the best in Nuevah, and there were two Vahian Lords fighting beside them. What could possibly hold against them, let alone force them back?

'What's happening?' I asked.

'The mercenaries are regulars, good fighters but easily handled by our men. But the leaders are something else again. There are seven of them. Fortunately only two can fight in the tunnels at any one time, because only Tomas and Danel are able to stand against them. Tomas can just barely hold his own, and if not for Danel they would have swept the tunnels clear of us long ago.'

'I'll go back and help.'

'No, that's not what we need. What we want from you is something which will give us time to break the fighting, and open a gap between us and those following. Can you think of anything?'

'Yes, I can think of something. Tell them to hold until I signal, and then, they are to fall back as fast as they safely can.' I turned and got to work.

All the Janissaire had passed, save the rear guard with Sergeant Ransyn, when my preparations were completed. I could see Tomas and Danel slowly retreating towards me. Sergeant Ransyn and three Janissaire were also there.

'Ransyn! This way, quickly!' I shouted.

He ordered his men about, and they raced towards me.

'Get your men up the slope; you stay here with me. I have a small surprise for these people.'

As soon as Tomas and his brother started up the incline towards the surface, Ransyn and I began to throw lighted torches over the heads of Tomas and Danel at their attackers. This caused the strangers and their mercenaries to pause momentarily, giving the two rear guards a chance to turn and run. Seeing this, Ransyn and I pulled hard on a rope I had tied to one of the shaft supports of the sloping tunnel. Then we turned, and ran as well. Dirt and rocks were crashing down, on and around, the attackers.

When the dust cleared, the tunnel was completely blocked. By the time we reached the surface, the fight there was also over. Now I could see the reason why we were held up. There were at least sixty dead mercenaries as well as about thirty Plastrals. All but five of the freed slaves were dead, and only three Janissaire were still alive. Tryell was wounded, and was being tended by Rafe and Jon. Tomas and Danel were sitting on a log breathing in great gasps of much-needed air. Elred was bandaging a wound on the arm of the guide's silent protector. The guide, who had armed himself with a kris belonging to one of the dead Plastrals, was beside his wounded friend, but was looking towards me.

'Well, Sergeant, it doesn't look as if things went totally our way,' I said.

'We had best be moving, Lord. They can still reach us through the swamp, and we have already lost too many good companions,' he said.

'A costly victory,' our guide said softly, as he got to his feet.

'It was no victory,' Danel added, looking quickly at the few survivors gathered about him. 'Both sides lost too many to claim a victory.'

Tomas nodded at his brother's words, and for the first time, I understood the exact meaning of the Vahian creed.

Those who could, helped the wounded, as we again entered the evil-smelling swamp.

'We should be safe now,' our guide said, after we had travelled several miles. 'The Plastrals are slow moving through the swamp, and after the losses they have suffered, I doubt the mercenaries will be too quick to pick up the pursuit.'

'It's not them I'm worried about,' Danel said. 'It's those other ones. Who in Erebus' name are they? They fight almost as well as Vahians.'

'They are Eligere,' our guide answered, 'and I am Lyn. This is my minder Nels. We did not have much time for introductions before. The Eligere are the ones who have armed the Plastrals, and have been getting them to clear the tunnels. There is something of great value they want from Perdu, the subterranean city. The name of the city was engraved on the wall in the large chamber I told you of earlier. The thing they desire is of such importance that they are willing to arm those savages and stand with them against their own kind.'

'Where are the Eligere from?' I asked.

'From an island far to the south,' Lyn answered. 'They hate to travel, so they have not been seen often, which

186

shows even more the value they place on this object for. which they search. The ones who have been dealing with the Plastrals call themselves the Knights of the Great Forest. They are the Protectors of their people. They speak in a strange tongue I do not understand. All this I learnt from the Plastrals.'

'Do you know what they seek?' I asked.

'No, but from what I have heard, they have promised the Plastrals that when it is found, they will sweep the animals from the lands surrounding the Osseaux Swamp. We are the animals, by the way. The Eligere tend to believe all other races are savages and animals, fit only for slaves or death.'

'Nice people. You really know some charming characters,' Ransyn said.

'How was it you happened upon us in such a wretched place?' Lyn asked.

'We are searching for a Prince of Nuevah,' I answered.

Before I could continue, I felt a compelling presence. Turning slowly, I searched the faces of my companions until my eyes locked on those of Lyn's protector. His eyes held mine and I was immediately reminded of a similar happening before Harnet's inn in Dienall. Nels! Lyn had called his protector Nels. Even as I was thinking this, the protector slowly smiled as if he knew what I was thinking.

'It's you, isn't it?' I asked him. 'You are the Prince of Nuevah!'

Tomas and Danel studied the man's face for some time and then they knelt before him and pledged their loyalty. Sergeant Ransyn and myself followed suit, as did the three remaining Janissaire. The Prince raised his hand to motion to us to rise. Tomas and his brother were silent, tears were in their eyes.

The Prince had been found at last—soon he would be King. A fighting King. Now it was clear why he had such skill with the axe. He was a Vahian, and the axe was his chosen weapon. Now we would see how the Regent reacted when this news reached him.

There was no further pursuit. Keeping west as our general heading, we began to weave our way through the swamp. I scouted the trail, and was able to find solid ground most of the way. How I was able to do this was a mystery to me; it was as if I just knew the best route to take. Sometimes I made detours for no reason, other than believing I should. It was hard to explain the feeling.

As yet, I had not mentioned my ring to Elred and Rafe. Now I found I could see their rings at any time. I remembered when they first showed them to me, how I was unable to see them unless they allowed it. I had also made another startling discovery. Lyn also wore a ring. Sometimes I turned quickly, and caught him staring at me. My friends had not noticed this as they were telling the Prince all they knew of the assassination of his father and brother, and about our journey so far.

At last the swamp was behind us and, using one of the gems, I managed to get us passage to the coast on a local caravan. Hopefully the others would be waiting for us at Hocheken.

Rafe had been able to treat all the injuries on the march, even the damage done to the Prince's throat. It was still hard for him to speak, but this would pass in time.

On our first night free of the swamp, I approached Elred and Rafe about Lyn. As soon as I mentioned my discovery, they both looked at my right hand. I allowed the ring to appear.

'Where did you find it?' Rafe asked.

'In Perdu, along with the gems.'

'We thought something had happened, when you suddenly took over as scout and managed to lead us to the surface, and get us out of the swamp. Both are feats in their own right, when you consider you knew nothing of the area when we arrived,' Rafe said.

'As soon as you mentioned seeing the ring on Lyn's finger, when Rafe and I couldn't, we knew you were now a Usare, like Rafe and myself,' explained Elred. 'In fact, you are a Seeker.'

'A Seeker—what's that?' I asked.

'A Seeker is the only one who can see a ring when the wearer does not wish it to be seen. He is a finder of trails, and has a perfect sense of direction. Even though you may not have travelled the way before, you will never be lost, and will always know the safest route. Even though you did not realise it, you also used your new power to disguise our trail, while leaving the swamp. That explains why we were not followed,' Elred finished, thumping me on the shoulder. 'Now you are truly one of us,' he said.

19

A TASK OF GREAT IMPORTANCE

WE made the trip to Hocheken in what could only be described as luxury. The wagons were unsprung and rode rough, but a third class ride was better than a first class walk. By the time Hocheken was in sight all the wounds had been healed, save the one to the Prince's throat. He was able to speak, but only for short periods. Rafe claimed that, with care, the wound would heal completely.

The other two search parties, under Roebert and Kryss, were waiting in Hocheken. They were tired and dejected from their failure to find any trace of the Prince. Kryss' detachment found traces of a slave matching the description of the prince, but the caravan the slave was sold to failed to arrived at Murtzal. Kryss was going to backtrack the caravan, but remembered that, no matter what he found, he was to report his findings to the rest of the searchers at Hocheken.

Their mood changed when we told of our stroke of luck.

Roebert saw to the renting of a large keep on the edge of

town and without drawing undue attention to ourselves, we moved there at once.

The thirty Janissaire under Sergeants Zeebah and Dalzyl, sealed the keep. From the roof, a watch of the surrounding countryside was set to warn us if any attempt at approaching the keep was made. Plans had to be made for the Prince's return to Nuevah. In the meantime, all precautions needed to be taken to safeguard the Prince. It was hoped word of the discovery of the Prince would not reach any unfriendly ears, but this could not be counted on. So the Prince was to be guarded closely at all times.

The Prince, Roebert, Mikal, Tomas, Danel, Kryss and Kyle, locked themselves away from the rest of us to discuss the matter of returning home, and of the threat of the Eligere, a threat they believed was even greater than that of Raimend.

I spent as much time as I could with Elred, Rafe and Lyn. From Elred, I learnt more about the powers of a Seeker; what I could do and what to avoid.

'The one you killed in the chamber beneath the swamp was a Weaver, as would have been his two companions. He was not an Eligere, nor one of their mercenaries.'

'Then who are they?' I asked.

'I don't know,' Lyn answered. 'I have never seen their like before.'

'There's no way they could be Eligere?'

'No. The Eligere are a pure race, identical in many ways. The one you killed was just too different.'

'Do the Eligere have Weavers?' I asked.

'Yes.'

'And you.'

'I am a Weaver,' Lyn told us. 'With the ring's aid, I can change my outward appearance to anything I desire. Size or shape do not matter, as I do not actually change shape.

191

I simply project an illusion of the object I think of about my body.'

'I picture an object in my mind,' he continued, 'and then by concentrating on it, I transfer the thought from my mind to the ring. It is then projected about my body. It only affects my outward appearance; to the touch I am still the same.'

'I can only create this illusion about myself. No one else is affected. However, should someone stand close behind me, the illusion would hide them. It takes a great amount of energy to weave an illusion. Some are quite easy, for instance, a coin in the hand.'

With that, he opened his hand and a small gold coin was lying there. The coin looked to have substance, but I could see the palm of his hand through the coin.

'Is it real or illusion?' Rafe asked.

Lyn closed his hand, and when he opened it again, the coin was gone. My abilities as a Seeker had allowed me to see through the illusion. To Rafe and Elred, the coin would have appeared real.

'The larger illusions take a great deal more effort and preparation. A substantial Weaving can leave me exhausted, should I have to maintain the deception for any period of time. Once the illusion is dropped, I would be able to do very little physically, and I would require a long period of rest.

'That was why I could not use my skills to escape from the Plastrals. Even if I had enough strength to weave an illusion, I would have been too weak to travel once the illusion was dropped, and would have soon been recaptured. I had no intention of being taken again; I saw what they did to slaves who attempted to escape.

'Besides, once Nels . . . rather the Crown Prince, had saved my life, I could not leave him there, injured the way he was. And then, once his wounds had healed, I could not bring myself to abandon him,' Lyn said.

'Couldn't you have woven an illusion to hide you both, and then had the Prince help you, as you fled?' I asked.

'In a few more days, I would have been able to weave such an illusion. We had spoken of the possibility of escape several times, and would have tried it as soon as we were able. The work we were captured for was almost finished. Once it was completed, we were to be killed. They did not tell us this, but I learnt of it by listening to the conversations of the Plastrals.'

'Surely they would not have killed you all? There were over a hundred slaves. In these troubled times, they would bring a small fortune in the markets,' Elred said.

'To the Plastrals, maybe, but the Eligere do not seem interested in money. To them we were nothing. The Eligere are bred only to fight and serve the Order. They would snuff out our lives as we would a candle,' Lyn answered. 'They are completely different from any other race of people I have ever met. We rate as animals—intelligent, but still animals. We are here to be used and then disposed of.'

'But what of the mercenaries? They are not Eligere,' Rafe added.

'True,' Lyn continued. 'They are bought as child slaves from the Navealozans, the only people the Eligere will deal with. They are then trained in weapons and sold into the service of the Knights.'

'How is it you could understand them?' Elred asked. It was obvious his interest in languages had prompted the question.

'Many of the mercenaries spoke several languages. They used them when giving orders to the slaves. The rest of the time they spoke a language I had not heard before, and I have travelled a great deal and heard many languages.

They were very guarded about what they said when talking near the slaves, but the Plastrals were not as careful. They knew we were to die on the completion of the work, so they did not bother to guard their tongues.'

'What do you think the Prince will do now?' Rafe asked.

'Make straight for Lyram, I'd wager,' I answered. 'The Prince must be placed on the Throne as soon as possible. Once the Prince is crowned, the Regent will be made to pay for his crimes of regicide and murder. Then we will be able to deal with these Eligere.'

'What you have said is true—up to a point.' The voice was low and rough. We turned, and found the Prince standing at the door behind us.

'I will be returning to Nuevah, and the others will accompany me. But I have a different role for you to play, Teal,' he said. 'The Eligere are interested in Perdu, the buried city in the swamp. There is something there they want more than sanity itself. I must know what it is, and whether it is a danger to Nuevah and its surrounding lands.

'I must also learn more about these strangers from the south, the Eligere; what their plans are and where their land actually lies. I want you four to find these answers for me. Sergeant Ransyn and the three surviving Janissaire from the swamp have agreed to accompany you. I know I ask a lot of you, but I feel if any can enter the swamp for a second time and return, it will be you four. Lyn has explained your skills to me, and I believe they will be needed to carry out this important feat.

'Teal, I realise I am asking you to take on a role for which you have not been prepared. You have not had the benefit of the years of training at the Collegium, but I believe you are capable of commanding this small force. Sergeant Ransyn has years of experience—rely on him when you are unsure.'

He stopped, and moved closer to us. He was right—we had to find out more about these Eligere. 'Will you take the role I am offering you?' he asked us.

'I will go,' I told him.

'And I,' Rafe added.

'They will have need of me,' Lyn said.

Only Elred was silent. He looked around at us and then spoke. 'I am owned by the merchant, Ardemus. He released me for the search but now the search is over, and I am bound to return to him.'

'Elred,' the Prince said, 'I thank you for your aid. I cannot ask you to go further, but I tell you I will speak with Ardemus if you like. I am sure an agreement can be reached.'

Elred considered this for a time, then spoke. 'Yes, I will accompany you, but should I find Ardemus wishes me to return, then I will leave at once.'

'There won't be much chance of you getting word from your merchant in the middle of a swamp hundreds of feet below ground level, surrounded by Plastrals, mercenaries and Eligere. Will there?' Rafe added, with a faint smile on his lips.

'I suppose that's true,' Elred agreed, and then laughed.

'Then it's set. In three days we sail for Lyram. At the same time, you will begin the journey back to Perdu. You will need all your skills for this, so rest while you can. I will make all the necessary arrangements.' With that, the Prince turned and left the room, leaving us to our memories of the swamp.

Jon was to stay in Hocheken with Tryell to try to confuse any who might try to follow. During the next three days Lyn told me more about Usare, and how they were treated differently in each land. 'Many people do not know the full extent of the Usare powers,' Lyn explained. 'For a long time, they have passed off strange happenings as simple folk tales or drunkenness.

'We must be careful as we travel, as our powers can attract danger. In Nuevah we would be laughed at. Were we to show our powers, they would not be believed. For too long they have had nothing to believe in but themselves, so now they believe in nothing else.

'In the Land of the Plains, we would be tolerated. They know of the existence of people like us, and will suffer our presence amongst them, as long as we do not demonstrate our powers in public. Because then an explanation would be asked, and witchcraft would be the answer. Death would be the result.

'In Thay, though growing yearly in knowledge, they still believe in evil spirits and wraiths. If our powers should be discovered, they will kill us on the spot. To them we would be evil. Whether the person accused is royalty or peasant, native or stranger makes no difference. The penalty is death, so we must be careful.

'South of Thay is Navealoza. They are not savages, nor are they prejudiced. They will enslave any who take their fancy. They look down on all whites and treat them as escaped slaves, and will try to recapture us. They know of the rings, and in Navealoza you will see powers demonstrated in the streets. But remember the only way they can gain our powers is to take the rings from our fingers, after they have slain us.'

The three days passed quickly. Lyn told us more about his skills, and Elred told Rafe and I more of what we would be able to do once we mastered our rings. I also learnt that there were several types of Usare: Rafe's Healing abilities; and Elred's gift for languages, known as Speaking; my tracking and sense of direction, known as Seeking; and

Lyn's Weaving. The other types of Usare were: Stealth, Calling and Elemental Usare.

20

TALISMAN

AFTER many days of hard riding, we reached the capital of Thay, Thayik. Ransyn and I immediately set about asking questions at the various inns and taverns. When we finally returned to our lodgings at the Black Boar, we were both tired and pleased, because we had something firm to go on.

'The owner of one establishment,' I told my companions seated in one of our rooms, 'remembers a party of seven gentlemen and over a hundred armed followers passing through the city some time back. They paused long enough to leave a message with one of his guests, then they rode on. After their departure, the guest began to buy fresh horses and a considerable amount of supplies.'

'Well, that proves they came this way, and they may intend to leave the same way,' Elred said. 'Does this help us?'

'I believe they will return this way on their homeward journey, and if we make for Perdu we will be too late to stop the Eligere from obtaining whatever it is they are searching for. The only chance we have is to wait for them here, and, at the first opportunity that arises, ambush them and take the object.'

'You don't think they might mind us stealing this object they have worked so hard to find?' Rafe asked.

'It is possible they will mind, but many of their party were killed in the swamp and in the ensuing fighting in the tunnels beneath the swamp. There shouldn't be too great a problem stealing the object if we plan it right,' Lyn added.

'True, except for one small detail,' I told them.

'What detail?' asked Rafe.

'Five days ago,' I answered, 'fourteen more of the strangers passed through the city. They had a further two hundred fighting men with them.'

'That does complicate things slightly. What are you planning on doing?' Rafe asked.

'If we were to find employment in and around the tavern where the Eligere messenger is staying, we may be in a position to wrest the object from them and flee.' I looked around the room at the surprised faces. 'We'll start first thing in the morning.'

The next morning we began to search for work in the general area of the tavern. Rafe found a position with a local herbalist. He was not sure of the man's honesty, but the herbalist had seen a chance to make a quick profit and seemed willing to take a chance. I warned Rafe not to place too great a trust in the fellow, as he might sell Rafe to the Administrator of the city if things went wrong, or if the man saw a good profit in it.

Elred found employment with the city Administrator as a clerk. Hopefully this would forewarn us of any troubles coming our way.

Lyn used his Usare Weaving ability to disguise himself as a beggar, and he located himself at the main gate on the northern wall of the city so he could see each group of travellers who entered the city. Ransyn and the three

Janissaire teamed up with several of the locals, and foraged wide around the city in search of game for the tables of the many inns and other such establishments in Thayik.

I did not fare as well as my companions, until there was a lucky break. The third cook at the very tavern we were watching fell down the back stairs and very conveniently broke both his legs. Not too many people mourned the loss, as the man was not much of a cook, and had a tendency to be cruel with the tavern's animals and abrupt with the guests. Many saw the loss as a gain for the tavern.

The job required me to live on the premises, so I bade my friends farewell, and moved to my new lodgings. Lyn, in his guise as a beggar, was to be the messenger of the party, as he was able to move about the city unhampered.

In no time I proved myself to be a better cook then either of the two above me. The second cook complained, and was immediately dismissed. The chief cook, also the owner's brother-in-law, saw a way to make a name for the establishment. The business soon began to increase as people heard about the new cook and excellent meals at the Golden Fowl.

Once in a position of authority, I changed the inn's suppliers. All our meats were now bought from one small group of people, locals for the most part, but run by an outsider. They proved to be excellent suppliers.

'What do you have for me today?' I asked the stocky, black-haired man who had come to the back door of the tavern.

'I have a large variety. I'm sure you will find something to suit you, friend.' Ransyn answered.

I walked across the small yard to the wagon and examined the meats.

'Any word?' he asked quietly.

'None as yet,' I answered quietly.

'I'll take the fowls and the venison,' I said loudly, perhaps rather louder than normal, but this charade-playing was new to me.

'Good choice, friend. I'll see you again the day after tomorrow.' With this, he turned and signalled for the driver to start the wagon forward.

Over the next few weeks, the tavern's trade increased four-fold, and I had been offered employment at some of the larger eateries. I turned down all the offers, much to the surprise and gratitude of the Golden Fowl's owner. The landlord's wife was about to give birth to their seventh child, and was having a hard time. The extra money the tavern now brought in, would help to pay for a herbalist and midwife to help his wife with the difficult birth.

On several occasions I had mentioned the name of the herbalist who hired Rafe. I did not know a great deal about childbirth, but even I could see that the wife was in a bad way, possibly even beyond the help of a regular physician or herbalist.

After a particularly busy night, I decided to rise late. I was lying in my room, a much larger and better furnished one than I first had, when a strange feeling came over me. Suddenly I felt so alive. I sat up on the edge of the bed and looked about me. Everything seemed clearer, though nothing in the room had changed. I dressed and went downstairs.

Even as I walked downstairs I felt as though an enormous weight had been lifted from my shoulders. Everything I saw was clearer—and I felt so vital and dynamic.

Later that morning one of the assistants called that there was a beggar at the back door. I always put something small aside for beggars. The owner had not stopped this, as sometimes he handed out small portions of food to those who came to his door. I hurried to the back door.

There was a small wizened beggar leaning on a bent stick.

'Here you go,' I said, handing him a piece of bread and cheese wrapped in cloth.

'Thank you, Master,' he replied. As he did so, he raised his head. Though the body was old and emaciated, the eyes were alive.

He shuffled closer. 'What is happening?' he whispered.

'I have no idea. It's as if I have been asleep all my life and at last I have woken and come into my true self,' I answered.

'That's how it is with me. I feel so healthy and full of strength. I was sitting by the southern gate when suddenly I felt as if I'd been cured of some terrible, energy-sapping disease,' he said.

'You'd better go. Rafe will be here shortly. If the same thing has happened to him, I'll get word to you.'

The stooped beggar turned and left. As I closed the door, I heard voices on the steps behind me. It was Rafe and the herbalist. The owner was showing them upstairs. Yesterday his poor wife had grown progressively worse, and at first light this morning I heard the landlord send for the herbalist.

The landlord was soon downstairs again. He was distraught. He moved around the tap room trying to find something to occupy his mind. The herbalist and Rafe were with his wife for hours before the sound of a baby's cry was heard. The father raced for the stairs, and took them three at a time to the floor above.

The herbalist stayed with the proud parents, while Rafe came down to the kitchen to clean the paraphernalia used by the herbalist.

'It went well, I take it?' I asked.

'Not really,' he answered. 'The mother was too weak for a normal birth, and I tried to help us much as I could without being too obvious. But I eventually had to take over the birth completely. The mother and the child will be fine. I'm not too sure about me though.'

'Do you think he will report you?' I asked. 'Surely he would be better off putting your skills to good use. Not to mention the money he can make when word of your knowledge of herbal lore and healing skills is repeated.'

'I hope you're right, for my sake. The people of this area are so superstitious. Anything unnatural terrifies them.'

'But surely saving the child and the mother is not evil or unnatural?' I asked. I had never been able to understand the narrow-mindedness of certain people.

'Maybe not evil, but the herbalist knows the mother and child should have died, and he knows I did something which reversed that. He does not know how I did it, and that perhaps is the thing that really worries him the most—not knowing.'

Rafe finished washing the equipment, and after packing it away, went back upstairs. Soon the herbalist and Rafe left. I could tell that the herbalist was troubled. He continually watched Rafe from out of the corner of his eye.

Weeks passed uneventfully. The mother and child improved in leaps and bounds. The owner thanked me for making him call the herbalist. He spoke at length about the skills of the man. He also talked with his wife about the birth, and I believed he knew the true nature of the help his wife received.

Then one day, everything happened at once. From all doors, armed men appeared with drawn swords and large round shields. They were wearing helmets which covered the heads and necks, but left their faces visible. Their surcoats were torn and soiled, and their mail and weapons showed signs of rust. Even through the dirt and grime, the surcoats made the men easily identifiable; they were Eligere mercenaries.

Five Eligere entered the tap room and seated themselves at one of the corner tables. A chest was then carried in by one of the mercenaries. This he placed atop the table, before the Eligere. The mercenaries had spread themselves about the room, some at doors and windows, others at the stairs.

Food was placed on the tables and drinks were served to the mercenaries, but remained untouched. The messenger staying at the tavern rushed down to greet them. He was shown a seat and a quiet discussion began. At one point he looked up and allowed his look to pass around the room. There was a look of shocked and total disbelief on his face.

I repeatedly crossed the floor of the tap room carrying platters of spiced meats and roasted joints to replace those being ravenously devoured. Freshly boiled vegetables and fruit were also placed before them.

The conversation continued during this time. The lad I sent on an errand returned with Elred. I told the landlord I needed a few more helpers for the duration of the Eligeres' stay. He agreed. There was a look of terror on his face every time he was forced to look across the room to where the Eligere were sitting.

Elred stood beside the table in the corner. His role was to ensure nothing was lacking at the Eligeres' table. He continually signalled for fresh drinks or for an empty platter to be cleared away. All throughout, the Eligere ignored him totally.

Of the five Eligere, two wore rings. If one of these had been a Seeker, we would soon have been discovered, as he would have been able to tell that Elred and I were Usare. Fortunately, as they had entered the Tavern, I had sensed that neither of them wore the Seeker's ring. One was in fact a Caller, the other a Healer.

At last, the Eligere left the tap room for their rooms upstairs. The mercenaries formed a solid body about them as they climbed the stairs. They had taken the entire floor, one room for each of the Eligere. The mercenaries positioned themselves at windows and doors, and in every alcove. The floor above and below was also well-guarded, and a like number of mercenaries were outside the building, and at the stables.

At the first opportunity, Elred and I found a secluded spot where he could pass on what he had learnt. What he told me was incredible and shocking.

Elred said, 'Sixteen of the Eligere True Ones were killed in the gaining of the Talisman. Only eleven were Knights, the rest were Kyklos. From what I can gather, that is their equivalent of the Usare.'

'By all the Gods! What did they find in that city? What could possibly have killed the equivalent of eleven Vahian Lords and five trained Usare?' I asked him.

'What's worse,' he continued, 'is that their Kyklos are trained to operate in a Kyklos, or circle of seven. They are trained to work as a team with each individual Kyklos adding his power to that of his companions, similar to our Usare. Their armed Knights then form a defensive barrier around them. The mercenaries are used to clear areas and hold the flanks and rear. Only a handful of mercenaries were left after our rescue and escape, and the fifty-seven here are all who remain of that handful, and the two hundred replacements who arrived later.'

'Perhaps it was wise not to try for the city a second time,' I stated. 'I don't believe the eight of us would have fared all that well. Did you find out what it was that caused such casualties?'

'No,' he said. 'But I found they plan on leaving at first

light. They will be riding south to Bertal, then taking the river west to Kunack, on the coast. From there, believe it or not, they intend to take a ship south, home.'

'How are they going to pass the monsters?' I asked.

'One of the Kyklos, the Caller, will ward the monsters,' he explained. 'As well as enticing creatures, a Caller can repel them. With him on board, they will be safe to sail anywhere they wish.'

'What of the other Kyklos?'

'It was only through his skills that the Eligere succeeded at all. It seems many of those you saw out there were wounded beyond the skills of normal physicians. Without his Healing abilities, there would have been too few to have fought their way out of the depths of the city,' he answered.

'You spoke of a Talisman?'

'In the chest. It is the crystal bust of some creature long dead in these lands. They removed it from the crypt, which had been its home for thousands of years, on the same day, believe it or not, that we felt the change in our powers.'

'Perhaps this is the power they spoke of . . . the power to increase the strength of the rings. We all felt the increase. If the Talisman is responsible we must find out more about it.'

'There is more,' Elred continued. 'They plan to use the power of the Talisman to attack the lands of the north. Those lands are Thay, the Land of the Plains; and Nuevah. They have the aid of the Navealozans in the attack on southern Thay, with the Plastrals attacking the east. The Corsairs have been paid to stop all sea traffic, and then to ferry the Eligere forces north across the Uskery Sea.'

'But how will they be able to land? The Corsairs do not have enough vessels to allow them a major landing. The

Plains people will be able to hold them till help arrives from Nuevah.'

'Normally, yes, but the scavengers will rise in the west and create havoc, as will the Brigands of the Southern Plains. This will split the forces of the Plains, and allow the Eligere to land. Help will not come from Nuevah, as the Eligere have made an agreement with the Regent not to send aid south of the Erg, and to close the borders so none may escape north. The only Vahians they seem worried about are those of the Free States. They do not believe the Free Vahians can stop them, but they are afraid they may cause great damage before they are crushed.'

The last statement left me stunned. Without the aid of Vahian troops, the Plains would definitely fall. With the mastery of the ocean creatures, given to them by the Callers, the Eligere would be able to sail up the coast attacking the Vahian cities at will. The Vahians had never perceived the ocean as a threat, so there was little in the way of defences on the coast.

'I must get word to Ransyn,' I told him. 'We must send word to the Prince of the Regent's latest betrayal.'

The others were told what Elred had learnt. I told the Vahian Ambassador to Thayik what he had discovered.

'This news confirms what I have been hearing for some time,' the Ambassador replied. 'The Regent has ordered all Holluchon troops home, and the borders have been closed till the killers of the Prince are found. All other troops from the remaining provinces were withdrawn from their duties and returned to Nuevah weeks earlier. Things are beginning to look very bad indeed,' he said. 'I have a little over a hundred men here. Unfortunately, only twenty-seven are Liegemen with any fighting skills.'

'Is there anything that can be done?' I asked.

'I will pass on the information you have given to me. Perhaps something can be done about the Regent, if the

Prince can get through to Cruzeramba. With warning, they may be able to fortify many of the coastal towns. Is there anything you need on your mission? I don't pretend to understand anything of what you have told me concerning this Talisman, but if you believe the loss of it will weaken the enemy, then may the Goddess of Good Fortune smile on your venture.'

I bade him farewell, and made my way back past the Black Boar, where Ransyn was to have the horses and supplies ready. With my position on the inside of the Golden Fowl, it was hoped the others would be able to gain entry to the tavern without the alarm being raised.

In the early hours of the morning, I was woken by a soft tapping on my door. Wondering what could have gone wrong, I crossed the floor towards the door. Opening the door a crack, I found the landlord in the hall.

'One of my cousins has just brought me word,' he whispered. 'Your friend has been arrested. The herbalist reported him to the Administrator and soldiers were sent to take him.'

I drew him into my room and began to dress. 'Why do you do this?' I asked. 'Things could go bad for you if this becomes known.'

'Your friend did a great service for me. Should I, or my family ever be of service to you, feel free to call. I am now, and will forever be, in your debt.' He left the room, and was nowhere to be seen by the time I entered the corridor.

Now I had to decide whether Rafe or the Talisman was to be stolen. The choice was easy. Slipping out the rear of the tavern, I made my way quickly towards Rafe's lodgings. As I entered the street where Rafe was staying, I heard a squad of soldiers approaching. The clank of armour and the stamping of feet echoed loudly in the quiet and narrow city streets.

Drawing my cloak about me, I slipped into the shadows of an archway. I had only a dagger, as my weapons had to be left with the rest of my gear so as not to seem out of place with my role as an out-of-work cook.

As I watched from my hiding place, I saw a squad of soldiers appear out of the darkness. There were ten of them: two forward carrying lanterns; two officers; four clustered around a smaller figure, obviously Rafe; and another two at the rear, also with lanterns. The soldiers were wearing leather armour, and, were carrying short halberds and small rectangular shields.

As the last pair passed me, I stepped out from the shadows and brought the dagger's pommel down hard on the back of the neck of the right hand lantern bearer. As he began to fall, I snatched the lantern from his unfeeling fingers, and swung it at the head of the second soldier as he turned to see his friend fall. There was an explosion of light as the lantern took the second soldier on the side of the helmet, knocking him unconscious, and drenching him in burning oil.

The sound of the lantern crashing against the helmet warned the others of my presence. Two of the soldiers clustered about Rafe turned and drew their weapons. Rafe lifted his arms, and placed one hand on the temples of the two closest guards. Both of them crumpled soundlessly. Before the officers could rally the remainder of their forces, he pushed between the two facing me and ran towards me.

I threw the lantern at the remaining soldiers, and followed Rafe into the darkness. We turned down several streets before coming to the inn where the others were waiting. We ran inside and told the others what had happened.

'Do we still try for the Talisman?' Ransyn asked.

'Too late,' I answered. 'I feel the Talisman is no longer

where it rested. It is possible I was seen leaving the Black Boar.'

'What choices do we have left to us now?' Elred asked.

'First we have to get these chains off Rafe,' I explained, lifting the chain which joined the bracelets on each of his wrists. 'Then we have to follow the Talisman. It has not left the city yet. But I doubt they will tarry.'

Elred and Ransyn took Rafe to the rear of a local blacksmith shop in the hope of securing tools to free him. Meanwhile Lyn and I checked on the progress of the Talisman, while the three Janissaire remained with the horses. We were three streets from the tavern, when I felt the Talisman was moving again.

'It's on its way,' I informed Lyn. 'But I think we'll still pay a visit to the tavern to ensure all is well with the landlord and his family. Without their warning, we would have lost Rafe.'

We reached the tavern; it seemed deserted. We entered quietly and headed for the stairs. Lyn stopped. He looked at me, and cupped a hand to one ear, and then pointed towards the kitchen.

Before leaving our companions, we had armed ourselves. I drew my gladii, while Lyn produced his wicked looking kris from beneath his cloak. I followed him towards the door. As I did so, his shape seemed to flicker, and when it cleared, I was no longer following Lyn. Before me was an Eligere, slightly taller than myself, wearing surcoat over ring mail, and armed with a small sword. When I focused my ability on the Eligere, I saw Lyn beneath the illusion.

An Eligere small sword was not a little sword as it suggested. It was, in fact, a long sword with a narrow blade, and a basket hilt for the protection of the hand. The Eligere's legs were free of mail as seemed to be the way of the Eligere. And the boots, though high, were soft and offered no protection from a blade.

On reaching the door, we saw a scene which enraged us. The landlord's wife and children were gathered on the far side of the room, while the husband and his brother were lying on the floor. Above them stood six of the mercenaries, their swords drawn.

There was a startled shout as we were seen—an order was barked. Two of the mercenaries remained watching the two on the floor, while the others turned to face us. Lyn stepped into the room, and the confusion was clear on the faces of the armed mercenaries. He waved them back from the door as I entered. They stepped back several paces and then stopped. They were glancing from Lyn, who they saw as an Eligere, to the obvious leader of their group.

Lyn walked calmly across the kitchen to stand between them and the children. He then flicked his kris in a short arc and caught one of the watchers by surprise. The kris took him across the throat. Lyn allowed the momentum of the kris to swing him around, so as to aim a blow at the head of the second watcher. Their swords clashed, and some of the children called out in fear.

I still had not forgotten the massacre of the innocents at Dienall, and even though these mercenaries had nothing to do with it, I felt myself explode with anger against men who would carry out such an act. If we had arrived a few minutes later, I believed we would have found another massacre.

Even as Lyn was swinging towards his second assailant, I was dispatching my first with a straight thrust. Pulling my sword free, I turned to meet the charge of the nearest mercenary. A block with my right, a quick step closer, and my left sword was buried deep in his midsection.

I had no time to see how the others in the room were faring, as the last two mercenaries bore down on me. They fought well, but they were not Vahian trained. To them the sword was a weapon, not a way of life. Even though my sword skills were relatively new, weapon handling taught by Vahians was an art form rather than a fighting skill, and they were no match for it.

The last of my antagonists was down, and I turned to lend my aid to Lyn, but no aid was required. His attacker was dead, and he was helping the landlord and his brother from the floor.

'Again I am in debt to you, but you had best be gone. The City Guard will soon arrive to investigate the disturbance. Of course they will arrive after the deed is done. There is no chance they will interrupt anyone in the course of business. The Council of Thayik has recently changed, and the new Administrator tends to look the other way when things happen which could benefit him financially.'

'Do you have a wagon we can borrow?' I asked the landlord.

He nodded.

With the aid of the landlord and his brother, we loaded the bodies of the dead mercenaries on the wagon.

'I have need of their armour and weapons. When we have finished we will dispose of the bodies. Where shall I leave the wagon?'

'Leave it anywhere which suits you, and I will find it. Thank you for your aid.'

I took his hand in mine. 'I have simply repaid the debt to you.'

Lyn and I climbed aboard, and, with a flick of the reins, the wagon moved forward.

21

REYA

IT was two hours before we rode through the southern gate of Thayik. Sergeant Ransyn, Rafe and the three Janissaire were wearing the cloaks and helmets of the Eligere mercenaries and carrying their weapons, while Elred, Lyn and myself had acquired cloaks similar to those worn by the Eligere Knights.

We had to wake up several shop owners before we found exactly what we wanted. My stature would be sufficient to allow me to pass as an Eligere and Lyn would be able to use his Usare Weaving ability as he had done in the Golden Fowl. Elred looked the least like an Eligere, but he was the only one who could speak the language. It was hoped that would be enough to get him by if questioned.

Our disguises were not good enough to stand a close inspection. We were simply hoping we would be able to follow the fleeing party with the Talisman, and not look too out of place. We could possibly be a group who had been left behind and were trying to catch up.

We had decided there were too many of them for a direct approach out here in open country. We were going to wait till they reached a town or village, and hope that they stayed there long enough for us to try for the Talisman.

The Eligere were riding hard, but they were not pushing their mounts to the limit of their endurance, and we were making no attempt to close the gap between us and our quarry. At first they rode hard south, towards the Bertal Mountains, but once they reached the foothills they swung west, following the natural slope of the terrain. We were now riding south again. This time we were following the Bertal River, which we would follow all the way into Bertal, a large city on the Kunach-Bertal river junction. Once they reached Bertal they would be able to arrange river transport from there to the sea, where Elred said they were to book passage on a ship home.

I had just returned from checking the horses, and was squatting beside the small fire, when Ransyn walked over and sat beside me.

'If they do stop at Bertal for any length of time,' he said, 'they will be ready for an attempt on the Talisman. They will also begin to wonder why the mercenaries they left behind in Thayik have not caught up to them as yet. There is also the chance they have more help waiting there for them.'

'What is it you believe we should do?' I asked.

'If we ride hard before the sun rises, we should be able to catch them still encamped. They will outnumber us, but I believe it is the best chance we have.'

I thought about what he had said. He was right about one thing; they would be ready for an attempt on the Talisman. Our only hope was to try for the Talisman when the odds were in our favour, which at the moment, they were not.

'I don't think surprise will be enough to help us as it did

214

in the swamp,' I answered. 'We will need more in our favour than that.'

'Such as?'

'Have you ever been down the Kunach before, Sergeant?'

'Yes, once, but that was a long time ago.'

'Are there any rapids where they will have to portage their boats?'

'Yes, there are a few places where they will have to unload the barges or rafts, and cart them around rapids or falls. Most of the places have inns, of one sort or another where crews spend the night and rest before the trip continues.'

'Would it be possible for us to cut across country and arrive at one of these places before our quarry?' I asked.

'Yes, it would, and once there we could take over the place and wait for the boats' crew and the mercenaries to be split during the portage. We could then strike for the Talisman and be away before they could arrange mounts to give chase,' the Sergeant answered.

'Then you think it could work?' I asked.

'I can see no reason why not. As long as they intend to journey to Kunach and try for a ship,' he answered.

Sergeant Ransyn then went on to sketch a quick map. If correct, we would be able to beat the Eligere to the first inn by four days, plenty of time to look over the area, and work out how the theft would be carried out.

We made good time after exchanging the dense vegetation of the river valley for the more sparse flora of the surrounding plains. I guided the party southwest towards the Kunach River. All the while, I continued to search for the Talisman. It was now stationary, in the direction of Bertal.

'Another two days at this pace will bring us to the inn,' I explained, while we rested the horses. Even though they had not been forced to exert themselves fully, they were just about all in. Ransyn said a small number of horses were always at hand at the inns along the river. I hoped he was right—though I had no reason to believe otherwise. Everything he had told us as yet had proved true—his experience was proving priceless.

'The Talisman is again on the move,' I continued. 'We had best be on our way.' That night we were able to have a larger fire. We were in a large depression about a mile from the river. The Talisman was still several days away, and there had been no sign of life all day. I lay by the fire, wrapped in a blanket, more for security than the cold. I had been trying to find out more about the Talisman, but when I concentrated, all I could sense was power: intense, unimaginable power.

I fell asleep still locked to the Talisman. I dreamed we had surprised the Eligere, and were about to take possession of the Talisman. But each time I reached for it, it moved away from me. The more I stretched out, the further it got from my grasp until I could barely see it; it was only a shadow on the edge of my dream.

Suddenly I was awake. I was sitting bolt upright in my blankets by the fire. There was a chill about my body, even though the fire still burned. I searched the edges of the camp site, but could find no sign of danger. All my companions were still asleep, and I could see the shape of the sentry by the horses. I pulled my thoughts in and tried to arrange them, so as to isolate the danger I felt. I began to rerun the dream. It flowed through to the point where I awoke. This time there was no feeling of dread. There was just a great emptiness, and a sense of loss.

'The Talisman!' I cried, causing those around me to wake. 'It no longer travels the river. They have turned south with the Talisman, and have left us stranded this side of the river, with no hope of crossing.' The others had climbed to their feet, weapons drawn. Sleep and surprise showed on their faces.

'Somehow they predicted our actions,' I continued. 'It is impossible to cross here as the banks are too steep to manoeuvre the horses down, and too heavily wooded for the horses to be forced to jump. We are still thirty hours from the inn, and we have no definite knowledge we will be able to cross there either. It will take us days to ride for Bertal, and continue the pursuit from there.'

'How did they manage to predict our movements?' Rafe asked, as he hurriedly gathered his belongings.

'Perhaps they had a Seeker waiting for them in Bertal,' Elred added, as he secured his bedding to his saddle.

'Regardless of how they did it, we now have to devise a way across the river, and quickly, before they have a chance to try another trick,' I explained.

Our only hope was the inn. There might be a raft or barge there which could ferry us across the river. We pushed the horses to their limits. If there was no way over, then we would have no need of the horses, and if we did cross, it might be possible to buy mounts on the other side. Ransyn warned that to cross the border into Navealoza at any but the correct Border Keeps, was very dangerous. The Navealozans at the best of times believed all Northrons, or Whitlows, as they called us, were fit only for menial work. If we were discovered, they might take us as spies, and kill us on the spot without further thought.

The inn was a two-storey building, the lower section made of stone, the upper made of timber with a slate roof. At one time it must have been a small keep or watchtower, because all the windows were slits to be used by archers, and there was a metal portcullis lowered before the stout door to the lower level.

We reined in our horses and were about to dismount, when one of the Janissaire called to me.

'My Lord, over here.'

I crossed the dusty compound before the keep, and looked down the slope in the direction he was pointing. Tied up to the riverbank was a large flat platform. There was a thick cable running from this bank, across the river to where it was secured to a large tree. There was a great deal of activity about the barge.

'Blackbirders. You can find them operating the length of the river. It is a dangerous business to be in, but very rewarding,' the Janissaire commented.

'What exactly do they do?' I asked. By now the rest of the party had joined us.

'They operate as smugglers, since smuggling goods into Navealoza is an enriching business. Then, once they have gained the confidence of the Navealozans they are dealing with, they spring a carefully set trap.' As if to prove him right, several ebony figures appeared amongst the people below us.

'The Navealozans,' he continued, 'believe they are above menial tasks, so all low work in the land is done by slaves—Whitlows. You will not see one black lift his or her finger to do any type of manual labour at all. Slavery, trading, warring and hunting are the only labours of the Navealozans.'

'But what use are the black slaves to those of the north, if all the labours are performed by whites?' Rafe asked.

'The Navealozans are terrified of the ocean. They believe drowning does not allow them to enter Paradise. Because of this, they make great galley slaves. Many northern merchants use them. They will never attempt to jump ship and are continually in a state of fear. Many of the ship's Masters do not even have to chain them. At any sign of unrest amongst them, one of their number is simply dropped overboard as an example.'

'Barbaric!' Rafe cried.

'Barbaric, but effective,' Ransyn answered.

'How can people treat other people like that? It's inhuman,' Rafe claimed.

'It is quite obvious,' Ransyn added, 'that you have never seen anyone who has been enslaved by the Navealozans. They treat their livestock better than they treat their slaves. If a cow should die it would be hard to replace, but to lose a slave just means another raid across the river into Thay. Many do not treat the slave raids as work. To them it is a pleasure, merely a way of amusing themselves.'

While we were speaking, the crowd worked its way up the path from the river. There were about thirty of them, and as they neared, the stench was overpowering. How people so close to water could smell so bad escaped me. The pungent smell brought back unpleasant memories of the swamp.

As they drew closer, I saw they had captured five blacks; four males and a female.

'The men will be sold,' Ransyn said quietly. 'But I fear the girl will have a hard time of it. There is not much of a calling for female galley slaves.'

'We should help them,' Rafe said.

'Why?' said the youngest of the Janissaire. 'They would not lift a finger to help you if you were taken south of the river. In fact, they would probably bid along with the rest of them.'

He was right in one way. They would probably bid. The clothes they were wearing, though torn, were of the finest material.

'We are going to need aid once we are over the river. Our mounts are done in, and we will need fresh ones and

219

supplies. If we are to help these people, could we count on their help in return?' I asked Ransyn.

'If they are of a high caste, yes. They would honour any word given,' he answered.

'Good. Take the three Janissaire and circle around towards the inn, but don't dismount,' I told him.

He turned his horse's head, and, nodding to the three, kicked his horse into a slow walk towards the front of the inn. As he rode, he was talking quietly to his men. 'Rafe, once the trouble starts, I want you to get the captives away. Elred will aid you. Get them down to the ferry and be ready to cast off when we arrive. Lyn and I will stay to ensure there is no pursuit.' Lyn nodded, and loosened his kris in its scabbard.

I kicked my horse forward towards the now agitated crowd. They were calling for the girl, and jugs of drink were being passed around. The males tried to come to the girl's aid but were beaten back for their troubles. One of them was unconscious or dead.

We worked our way into the crowd, before the ring-leader of the mob noticed us.

'Come, dismount, there is no need to remain aloof. We are all friends here.' On hearing this, the crowd burst into laughter.

'How much do you want for the girl, friend?' Lyn asked. I moved slightly away to his left as he spoke. The action did not go unnoticed by the leader.

He threw back his head and laughed. The rest of the crowd followed his example. His laugh turned to a splutter as the knife I had flicked underhand buried itself deep in his open mouth.

Before the stunned crowd could react, Lyn and I had drawn our weapons and were laying about us with the flats of our blades. With a cry, Ransyn and the others charged

220

into the crowd from the other side, bowling over many of the now fleeing crowd.

Some of the crowd drew weapons, but they were soon dispatched. We moved our horses back and forth, forcing the crowd away from the captives and the river. A glance behind me showed Rafe had the captives away. I called for the others to begin a withdrawal towards the path leading down to the river. I was last to enter the path, and as I did so something whizzed past my head. One of the Blackbirders had emerged from the inn with a crossbow and was cocking it, ready to take another bolt.

I urged my tired mount down the path which wove downhill towards the river. Its twists and turns ensured the crossbowman did not get a chance at a clear shot.

Lyn was walking his mount onto the ferry when I arrived. I quickly dismounted and did the same. We cut the rope securing us to the bank, and began to haul on the cable. A bolt splintered itself against one of the hardwood rails. Ransyn had removed a crossbow from the rear of his saddle. Resting it across the back of his mount, he whispered soothing words to the creature while he focused on the figure moving down the path towards us. There was the twang of a cable being released and the crossbowman fell and tumbled down the slope.

We were in a stand of trees several miles from the river. Ransyn had cut the cable on the ferry to make sure we were not followed. Rafe and Ransyn were on sentry at the edge of the trees to ensure we were not surprised by any Navealozan border patrols.

'Elred, ask the older one if he and his people are from around here, and if they are, tell them we will help them reach their home,' I said.

He did as I had asked, and was soon in deep conversation with the older of the freed captives. The girl had recovered, it turned out, with nothing more than a few scratches and a bad fright. She was sitting on the far side of the camp with the three young men. They did not seem at ease, and I didn't think their near brush with slavery was the total cause of their disquiet.

Elred turned aside from his conversation. 'I think the good Sergeant should be here when I tell you the latest piece of news,' he said.

I sent one of the Janissaire after Ransyn, and soon we were joined by him and Lyn.

'Right. To start with, they are a family, or rather what's left of one. They were not at the river to trade, but to find a way across.' Sergeant Ransyn gave a low whistle. 'Exactly, Sergeant. They have been found guilty of crimes against the Crown and have been sentenced to death. They lived not far from here and were attacked yesterday morning by Ayahs of a local family.'

'Will they help us?' I asked.

'We saved them from the Blackbirders,' Lyn added.

'The old man is grateful, but to him there is no difference between those men and us. They captured them for a reason, and we freed them for a reason. He asked me if we would help them if we didn't have to cross the river. I told him we would have, but he doesn't believe me.'

'Now what do we do?' Ransyn asked, toying with the hilt of his dagger. 'If we leave them here, they are sure to be taken, and they may tell about us in an attempt to lighten their sentence.'

'Would you have us kill them in cold blood?' I asked, with a cold edge in my voice.

'No . . . I suppose not,' he answered.

'Ask him anyway. He may offer to help us,' I told Elred.

Elred turned back to the old man and was soon in deep conversation. This time the answer was not long coming.

'He says if he is caught, he and his family will be killed

and we will all probably be enslaved. If, on the other hand, he crosses the river, he and his family will be enslaved, and without his help, we will certainly be killed.

'He doesn't have much to offer, but because we saved his life and the lives of his remaining family, he will help us. He says we should not be under the impression the help will be great, as he has nothing apart from his word to offer us.'

I faced the old man. 'Tell him we thank him, and his word and his help will be all we need.'

Elred repeated this to the old man who smiled, and straightened his back so his eyes were almost level with mine. He took one of my hands in each of his and placed them on the pommels of my swords, then he spoke several words and smiled again.

'What was that about?' I asked.

'He has pledged his life, and that of his family to you. He also wishes you increased skill and long life,' Elred said.

The old man had walked over to where his family was sitting. A few cries and shouts were heard and then all was quiet. The young girl, who I suspected was about fifteen, got up from where she was sitting and walked over to stand before me.

'My father is impressed with the way you helped us, and by the fact your companion speaks our language so well. He says he knows a place, the home of an old friend who might aid you in the replacement of your horses. Do you wish to try him?' she said.

'Yes.'

She called to her brothers, who immediately climbed to their feet, and began to saddle the tired horses. With the old man and his daughter mounted, we headed off in the direction of his friend's home. The three brothers, along with Ransyn and one of the Janissaire, scouted the countryside ahead of us on foot.

The old man sat his mount well; he was obviously a soldier in his younger days. It did not take us long to reach the home of his friend. He insisted on approaching the gate alone. There was a brief argument between him and one of his sons, but it was soon over and the old man rode towards the gate.

The son he had argued with picked himself up and worked his jaw in his right hand. The blow which had felled him was enormous and he was lucky it did not break his jaw. Soon the old man returned with the news his friend would shelter him and his family, and supply us with fresh mounts.

We rode into the courtyard and dismounted, handing our reins to the slaves who approached us. We were then ushered away into one of the larger buildings. Ransyn insisted on seeing whether the horses we were to be sold were adequate, so he followed the grooms to the stables.

We were supplied with warm water so we could bathe. We were even offered a fresh change of clothes. Once clean and dressed, we were led downstairs to where an enormous meal had been prepared for us. While we bathed, Ransyn returned. He told us the horses were fine and he could see no problems with them.

After the meal we were entertained by bards and acrobats, and then shown to our rooms for the night. The old man and his friend, our host, bade us goodnight.

'Wake up, Teal!' a voice called out. I felt myself being shaken rather violently, while the quiet voice continued to call out to me.

'What is it?' I asked, at last managing to get my brain working enough to ask the question. I opened my eyes and saw Ransyn and the young girl standing beside my bed.

'We have been betrayed,' the girl said. 'My uncle, our host, has sent word we are here. We must leave quickly.'

'How?' was all I was able to ask.

'When I checked on the horses, there was a beautiful grey mare in the stables,' said Ransyn. 'I went down a short while ago to give her an apple I kept from the meal. When I got there, I found the horse gone, yet when I asked the Ayah on duty at the gate about the horse, he claimed no one had left, and he did not remember ever seeing the horse I was speaking about.'

'It was then he ran into me,' the girl explained. 'I was just coming from my father's room. When he told me of the missing horse, I immediately took him to my father.'

'I woke Rafe,' Ransyn added, 'and he is waking the others now. We had better hurry. Reya says the nearest military post is only a few hours' ride from here.'

Within minutes we were all assembled in the main dining room. Reya's father was the last to arrive. His face was long and drawn, and he gripped a bloodied knife in his left hand.

'Betrayed by my own brother,' he said. 'But he will never betray anyone again.' With these words he rammed the dagger into its sheath.

'Lord Teal!' cried one of the Janissaire from the door to the room. 'There are Ayah blocking the approaches to the stables. It is hard to tell the exact number from here, but there seems to be quite a few of them.'

'Is there another way to the stables from here?' I asked Reya.

'No. We will have to fight our way through to the horses,' she answered.

We gathered our gear and made ready to fight our way to the stables. Reya, her father and her brothers had armed themselves from a small room at the rear of the dining room. Her father had a large club, while two of her broth-

225

ers had armed themselves with falchions—heavy sabres. The other brother had found a cavalry sabre. Reya herself had a long light staff, which looked about as strong as she did.

Lyn had the Janissaire remove two of the large doors from the other side of the room. Handles were made out of tapestry cords, and soon we had a wedge-shaped shield built out of the two solid doors. With the doors thrust before us as a barrier, we hoped to force our way into the opposition ranks and scatter them.

22

THE PURSUIT

'**WHAT** are they doing?' I called.

'They have stopped at the far end of the corridor and seem to be waiting,' answered one of the Janissaire. 'They don't seem to be in too great a hurry.'

'Why should they?' I said to those around me. 'All they have to do is keep us bottled up in here till help arrives, then, with the extra swords, they will be able to force their way into the room. While we hold the door, they can only advance on a small front, and they do not have the men for the losses we would inflict. But, once in the room, their overwhelming numbers would come into play.'

'Then we have to get to the horses. We have no other choice,' Ransyn said.

'To get to the stables we have to travel the length of the main corridor, then pass through the large entrance doors. Once in the open, we have to cross the entire length of the courtyard, before we enter the stables,' I explained. I turned to Reya. 'That's correct, isn't it?'

'Yes,' she answered.

'How will the gate be secured?'

'There are two large bars which slide into place once the gates are closed. These fit into brackets on the gates, and slide back into the guard room on the eastern side of the gate. It is from this room alone the bars may be withdrawn and the gates opened.'

'So we need to get one or two men into the guard room, as well as the stable,' Ransyn added.

'Those in the guard room, if they get that far, will be able to hold out, but there will be no chance of escape for them. Those who make it to the stable, will have to saddle the horses as well as keep attackers from their backs,' Reya said.

I turned my back on them and walked slowly across the room towards the door. There might be one chance.

'Get that wedge into the corridor. We are going to try for the horses,' I told them. 'Lyn, I have something for you to do.'

Rafe, along with Reya and her family, carried the wedge. The rest of us packed in close behind them. At a word from me, the wedge carriers gave a cry, and rushed down the corridor towards the large doors.

The defenders had not expected the mobile fortification and were taken aback by the sight of it charging down the corridor towards them. We pushed them back as far as the door, where they held for a short time before being pushed out into the open courtyard.

As soon as we entered the open ground, the defenders swarmed around us. They probably expected us to fall easily before their superior numbers, but they had not allowed for the skill of Vahian fighting men.

Ransyn and his men fought in a diamond-shaped formation, which allowed them to travel in any direction— one man forward, one on either flank, and one at the rear.

They opened the way for the rest to follow. They were magnificent to watch as they cut their way through the defenders. No stroke was wasted nor any opportunity missed. Reya and her father were shepherded across the open ground by her brothers. Rafe and Elred followed to help any who might fall, and I brought up the rear.

The Navealozans fell back before the blistering attack of the Janissaire under Ransyn, and had no time to regroup for a concentrated attack on the family. By the time the defenders had reformed their ranks, the family was safe in the stables. I was only halfway across the courtyard at this time so they attempted to cut me off from the rest of the party.

Up to this point I had held back from the fighting, trying to coordinate the breakout, but now it seemed the others would have to watch for themselves. I could not afford to be cut off from them now.

With both weapons drawn, I leapt at the thickest point of the attack. There was not much time for the finer points of swordsmanship. Trusting in my scale mail to protect me from the lesser of the blows, I disregarded defence and simply cut my way through the press of bodies. Sometimes I was so pressed I was unable to swing my swords. When this happened, I used my size and weight to force my way through the straining bodies around me.

With the gate safe, and the others trapped in the barn, I was bearing the brunt of the attack. Already I had been slowed to a crawl—if many more assailants appeared, they would stop me cold. Just as I thought I had come as far as I could, there was a great deal of noise and confusion around me. The Ayahs before me seemed to melt away, and were replaced by my companions on horseback. As they passed me, I swung up into the saddle of one of the spare mounts. We paused, and I took in the situation.

Most of the Ayahs had taken up a position in front of

the gates, while the rest had formed up before the guard room. To attack the guard room would allow those at the gate to encircle us, and to attack the gate would be fruitless, as there was no escape while the gates were barred.

But so far everything had gone as I had hoped. I waved a sword in the air, and we kicked our mounts forward toward the gates. In the confusion, none of the defenders noticed that the bars across the gates were slowly being moved to one side. But we had been waiting for this to happen, and as soon as the last bar slid away, we wheeled about and charged the gate once more.

The Janissaire had readied their crossbows, and at a command from Ransyn, began to pick off the defenders at the guard room's door. Suddenly, there was a cry as someone noticed the gates were unbarred. A wounded Ayah rushed from the guard room shouting hysterically and incoherently, pointing behind him. The Ayahs began to race into the room. The wounded Ayah staggered free of the crowd, and began to run across the courtyard towards us. The further he travelled, the faster he ran, until no sign of his injuries were to be seen. Even as he approached us, the air around him seemed to shimmer, and suddenly, the wounded Ayah was gone, replaced by Lyn, unharmed and grinning madly.

He jumped into the saddle of the second spare horse, and cried, 'What are we waiting for? Let's go!'

We rode forward, and two of the Janissaire dismounted, and pushed the gates open. The remaining Ayahs at the gate made a half-hearted attempt to stop us, but we brushed them aside. The two mounted, and we rode out into the countryside. The horizon to the east was lost in trees, so I turned my horse's head, and spurred it in the direction of the forest.

We rode only a short distance into the cover of the trees before I called a halt to our mad dash. Finally calming my horse, I turned in the saddle, and began to call orders to the party.

'Ransyn, take one man and ride back to the forest's edge and watch out for any sign of pursuit.' Turning again, I said, 'Rafe, see if there are any injuries that need attention.'

'Right,' Rafe called. He dismounted, and began to move amongst the party.

'Reya, could I see you and your father for a moment?' I asked.

She nodded and said something to her father, who answered and dismounted. I caught Elred's eye, and signalled I wanted to see him as well.

'Reya, do you or your father know of any villages or towns nearby?' I asked.

She did not translate to her father, but answered my question immediately. 'You will find no towns, villages or cities, in the north of Navealoza. They are too easy a target for reprisals launched from over the border. All you will find are Family Holdings, like the one we just left.'

'Surely there must be a place for trade and such?' I asked. I was beginning to see why the northern peoples had never wiped Navealoza clean of the slave traders. To do that, each Family Holding would have had to be laid under siege, or taken before aid could arrive from families further afield.

'Trade is carried out along the river's length, and at places set aside for such things. But, before you ask, each meeting place is changed every few seasons, so as not to become a target.'

'Is there anywhere you know of where we can trade fresh horses and replace supplies?' I asked.

'Which direction are you intending to travel in?' she answered. I did not think she trusted, or needed us, as much as her father did. To her we were probably nothing more than future slaves.

'South,' I answered. The Talisman was getting further away with each hour; it would take considerable time for us to catch up to it.

Her father spoke for the first time during our conversation. 'What exactly is your business?' she translated.

'We are searching for a group of people like ourselves who are travelling south,' I explained.

'Are they rich?' she translated.

'Yes, and powerful.'

'Do they know you follow them?' she asked.

'Yes.'

With that answer, her father turned his attention to the surrounding area, to watch each of my travelling companions in turn as they relaxed, carrying out the work they seemed to have been chosen for.

Rafe was seeing to the few minor wounds which some of our party had received. Elred was sitting beside me, not speaking, but listening to all that was said, and translating where necessary. Lyn was a short distance from us using hand gestures to communicate with Reya's three brothers. Nyasa, Reya's father, had seen Lyn's Weaver abilities at the holding, and knew something of his strange abilities.

Ransyn and his companion had not returned, but the two remaining Janissaire were sitting to one side, cleaning and oiling their weapons. Every once in a while, one would say something to the other who would laugh out loud. I could see Nyasa noticed the calmness and difference of my people compared to his family. It was hard to tell we had just escaped from a trap which could have spelt death or slavery for all of us.

'My father says you are powerful and skilled at the art of killing. Your men share your skills as well, though not as great. He wants me to ask if the ones you seek are Eligere?'

'Yes,' I answered.

She did not have to translate for her father. When he heard my answer, he turned and spat.

'My father holds the Eligere responsible for the attack and sacking of our Family Holding. He has never shared the dream of conquest they have been spreading.' She paused, while her father continued. 'My father would like to thank you for your aid in protecting what is left of his family.' Again, she stopped, while her father spoke. This time she answered him and a heated argument erupted. Finally her father quietened her down, and gestured to me. Reya turned. There was a cold look in her eyes.

'My father believes you are to be trusted. He says our goals are the same: an end to the Eligere. He wishes me to tell you he places himself . . . ,' she turned, and said something to her father. He did not answer in words, but turned his head away from her questioning stare. Her head dropped and she turned back to me, ' . . . himself and his family at your disposal.'

'Tell your father I thank him, and I assure him the end of the Eligere is my aim.'

She repeated this to her father, then jumped to her feet and stormed away. Her father leaned forward and placed his hand on my arm. Elred translated what he said.

'He says, "My daughter is angry that I seek your aid in the destruction of our enemies. I see you and your men are skilled at what you do. Myself and my sons are Ayah, but we are not enough. Together, we shall succeed." ' When Nyasa finished speaking, he rose and followed after his daughter.

'Well, Elred?'

'The girl doesn't like us—to her we are Whitlow. She believes her father has lowered himself by claiming to be in our debt. She also feels we are not good enough to travel with,' he answered.

233

'Not bad for a first impression. Wait till she really gets to know us!'

'Yes. She's likely to cut our throats while we sleep.'

There was no sign of pursuit, so we mounted and rode. We had a great deal of time to make up. With Reya's help, Nyasa explained that there were many trade roads criss-crossing the northern lands, but if the Eligere were in a great hurry they would make for the Tlaxmilch River. They would be able to get a packet boat south from anywhere along the river. If we travelled fast, it was possible we would be able to get ahead of them.

Two of Reya's brothers, Lobito and Ndola, were going to travel ahead of us to reach the river as soon as possible. They would watch to see if our quarry passed. The rest of us would follow at the best pace possible. I couldn't under-stand how the brothers were going to get to the river that much earlier than us. I was even more confused when I saw they were leaving without their horses. But a short time later I found out why.

The so-called trade roads were merely paths through the forest. A man riding could barely pass beneath the branches of the trees which crowded both sides of the road. Occasionally a lower branch would rake an unsus-pecting rider from his saddle. This was made worse by the fact that the light was dim due to the foliage overhead.

We rode two abreast, continually on watch. Reya rode beside me and I took the opportunity to question her about her knowledge of our language and her obvious hatred for whites.

'Being a female I was not allowed to accompany my brothers or father on their northern raids. Because of this, I was responsible for the Whitlow at our Family Holding. It was my responsibility to teach the new arrivals our language, so it was inevitable I would learn your language in the process.'

'You didn't learn my language. You learned the language of the Traders, a common tongue used by many northern countries. This still does not explain why you hate whites so much.'

'The Thayians are weak. For decades we have raided their lands, and only on a few occasions have they had the strength to retaliate. The people of the Plains are weak as well, but their weakness lies in the fact they are a people divided. Each Land of the Plains takes care of its own problems, and does not trust its neighbour.'

'And the Vahians?' I asked.

'Your people are not much better than the Eligere. You are proud of your skill at arms, and you rule your lands fairly. But what of the people who were originally there? You have pushed them into the Erg, and those who remained you enslaved and trained as your Janissaire. You know the names of my brothers whom you have only just met, but do you know the names of your own men?' She did not give me a chance to answer, and soon I was riding alone.

Her words had struck deep. She was right. What was the difference between the Eligere mercenaries or the Purusmayon Janissaire, or for that matter the Holluchon Wolves or Ferropean Liegemen? Only the Free Vahians and their Skirmishers mixed freely. In Nuevah, all things were owned by the Lords—the True Bloods—and from what I had heard, the Eligere—the True Ones, as they called themselves—were the same.

I began to think about what I had learnt lately, and about what Reya had said. I turned the thoughts over and over in my mind as I rode through the Navealozan forest. Was it possible that she spoke the truth? Were the Eligere and the Vahians of the same race? Were we really no better than the ones we pursued? I would have plenty of time for my thoughts in the weeks to follow.

We spent considerable time on foot. Only a few places were open enough for us to ride for any distance. Reya was correct about one thing. It would be next to impossible for any nation to attack the lands of the Navealozans and succeed to any great length. No army would be safe moving along roads such as these, forced to move continually on foot at this snail's pace.

Even though the distance we needed to travel was only a little over three hundred miles, it took us seventeen days before we sighted the Waystation on the Ixtehcogan River.

'What now?' Ransyn asked.

'We sell the horses and hire a boatman to take us downriver to where the Ixtehcogan River merges with the Tlaxmilch River,' Reya answered. 'It is the quickest means of transportation in these parts.'

'I heard,' I told her, 'all Navealozans feared the water and drowning.'

'Most do,' she said, 'but my family has lived and worked by the Kunach River for generations. It is hard to fear something which gives you the food you eat.'

'What about the boatmen—are they the same?' I asked.

'It is said most boatmen are mad, and that they dare the river to try to take them from their boats, and draw them into the darkness of the water. I do not know if this is true, but we will soon find out.'

We needed to disguise the fact that some of us were white. We also needed a reason for travelling the land. Beira, Nyasa, Reya, and Lyn were to be couriers, riding south with a message from one of the northern families. The rest of us were to be common Ayahs. When in company, we were to keep well back and have our cloaks drawn close about us.

236

It was hoped no one would pay any undue attention to us. Elred would be able to converse with any who approached, and keep them busy till one of the Navealozans came to our aid.

Soon we were on the water. Instead of barges, the locals used a flat-bottomed boat. The river ride was different from our last journey, when we travelled from Beestrone to Lyram with Jon. This ride was wild and fast. We were surrounded by white water for the entire journey. Reya was right — the river boatmen were quite mad. At one point a crewman from one of the other boats was lost overboard. There was a brief search for the man but nothing was found. The remaining crew seemed to think little of the incident and carried on as if nothing had happened.

At last we reached the river junction. There was another Waystation here, much larger than the other we had encountered upriver. Lobito and Ndola were waiting for us with word that nothing had passed downriver since they arrived six days ago. They also told me they had questioned the locals, and no one matching the description of the ones we followed had passed by the Waystation.

Reya translated for me, but as soon as the conversation was over, she turned and stalked away. I had not been able to talk with her since the first day we entered the forest. I couldn't help but feel she was right about the Eligere and the Vahians, and she realised I was beginning to come around to her way of thinking.

The Waystation was a circular building. The bottom storey was made of stone while the upper section and roof was constructed totally of wood. Inside there was one enormous room with a large fire in the centre. The second floor was a simple balcony which was sectioned off into separate sleeping areas. Each area could only be reached by a ladder from the floor below. The ladder was drawn up before sleeping. This allowed no others to gain access to the sleepers. The side nearest the fire was open to allow the heat to enter the room.

Reya's brothers and the three Janissaire took one room, while the rest of us shared another. We explained our problem to Nyasa, through Reya. We had to stop the boats moving downriver, and retrieve an object from them. All I could tell him was that the object was close, perhaps only hours away.

Nyasa and Reya talked for some time before Reya turned to us. 'My father says he has a plan for stopping the boats, but he will need aid to do so. He wants you and your Ayah to remain here while he puts his idea into action.'

23

THE TRAP

THE Navealozan sitting on the edge of the balcony turned and smiled at me. Even this close, without the use of my Usare abilities, it would be impossible to tell it was Lyn who sat before me. With him was Elred wrapped deeply in his large travel cloak. I sat slightly back from the edge so as not to be observed from the large room below.

Rafe was in the adjoining room with Reya and the Janissaire. Nyasa and his sons were in the large room below us. They had descended to the lower level, and had taken seats while the place was still relatively empty, but now, at midday, the room was full and the air was thick with smoke and the smell of unwashed bodies. Several large packet boats had put ashore to use the facilities of the Waystation. This Waystation, it seemed, though popular, was not one of the better quality establishments.

Ndola and Lobito were sitting together near the door of the lower level. Nyasa and his youngest son, Beira, were seated at the base of the ladder which led to this sleeping chamber. Nyasa stood and raised his tankard above his head. 'I would like to stand all those in the room a drink, so we may drink to the continuing victories of our armies,' he shouted.

Elred translated for Lyn and myself, while the landlord busied himself with supplying liquor to his customers. As soon as this was done, the toast was drunk, but Nyasa did not sit down.

'I have been on the road for many days,' Nyasa said, and Elred translated. 'Are there any here who can tell me of the latest victories?'

Several men called out at once, but these were soon quietened by the landlord. 'I can tell you, brother. Our armies have reached the capital of Thay—Thayik—and if not for the high walls and Administrator's soldiers would have taken the city days ago. Rumour has it the Administrator is holding out for more money and will not open the city gates until his price is met.'

'And further afield? How goes our victories there?' Nyasa asked, ordering another round of drinks for all.

His answer was delayed while the landlord brought out more drink. 'Our forces are advancing everywhere.'

'Not quite,' a voice called from the rear of the room. 'I have just returned from Hocheken, where our Ayah have again been victorious. But they speak of pockets of enemy entrenched on the northern shore of the Uskery. One such place is Lyram. I was told the Brigands and Scavengers who were to aid us in our conquests, were virtually destroyed by a large force of Vahians who had been encamped not far from the city. These Whitlow had not been reported by our scouts and outriders, and had taken our forces completely by surprise.'

There were cries of anger around the room as many shouted what they thought of the northern scum. Lobito then stood up.

'I have heard there are large parties of Whitlow here, in

240

Navealoza,' Elred translated. 'They are here to disrupt our Whitlow, and cause a revolt which will force us to bring Ayahs back from the fighting.'

Again there were cries from around the room. This time they were more violent, and lasted much longer.

'I know what I would do if such a thing was to happen,' one man called. 'I'd cut the throat of every white I have.'

'And I,' cried another.

There were cries of agreement from around the room.

'I,' Ndola called, 'would rather cut the throats of the Whitlow who are here to cause the trouble.'

This was met with cries which threatened to shake the walls of the Waystation from their foundations.

'He's right,' Beira called. 'It's them we want, not our own Whitlow.'

'Yes, yes!' was chorused around the room. Men leapt to their feet and began to cry out for blood.

'But where would we find this scum?' one asked.

'I have been told,' Nyasa said, 'it is possible there is a group of whites upriver not far from here. Now!'

'How did you come to hear of this?' someone asked.

'On our way here, we were stopped by a company of Ayah. They told us they were chasing a band of renegades, who had joined with a party of whites who had crossed the border and destroyed a Family Holding. They told us this party was heading south and would probably try to use the river as transport.'

'How do they expect to pass the Waystations undetected?' Lobito asked.

'It is supposed they will use the renegades to gain passage for them, and then once on the river try to disguise themselves as travellers,' his father answered.

'What disguise could they possibly use which could fool the people of the river?'

'Eligere,' Nyasa answered.

The room was now quiet, as all there thought over what had been said. The Eligere were an ally, but they were still white and not to be trusted.

'It is possible for them to impersonate Eligere. We do not mix with their kind,' the landlord said. 'But what we speak of is only rumour, there is nothing solid about one part of it.'

It looked as if Nyasa's attempt was bound to fail.

'I arrived this day, not two hours ago,' a stranger called. 'Behind me on the river travelled three boatloads of whites.'

The Navealozans looked about the room in amazement.

The stranger continued. 'There were several river people with them, and they were in a hurry. Three of the whites claimed to be Eligere. But if they are Eligere they are the most miserable ones I have ever seen. They are stoop shouldered, and their appearance is not like any Eligere I have ever seen. They also travel with a large party of Whitlow troops, heavily armed and also in the same state.'

'Do you think they are the ones who attacked the Family Holding north of here?' someone asked.

The room was full of chaos as questions and answers were thrown about. Finally, it was decided a blockage should be constructed across the river and the boats stopped to assure the people of the identity of the travellers.

Nyasa agreed with the plans and bought several large kegs of drink from the landlord to ensure the workers did not go thirsty during their work. It would also ensure they did not sober up and realise exactly what they were doing.

Two hours and three kegs of spirits later, the blockade was finished. Only three legs and one arm were broken; two men nearly drowned, one diving in after a keg which fell from the bank. The dive had been spectacular, but the diver had tried a little too hard and landed headfirst on the keg, knocking himself out and breaking the keg. His injuries were not sustained in the dive, but in the treatment his companions handed out for breaking the keg.

The blockage consisted of four large cables stretched across the river from one bank to the other. They were to be kept below the level of the water and raised only at the last minute.

The first two cables were higher than the gunwales of the boats, to sweep the men off the boats as they passed beneath them. The other two were set to trap the boats themselves.

Nyasa explained that with most of the mercenaries surprised and in the water, it should be simple to take over the remaining boats. Because all the Navealozans wished to stay on the bank with the drinks, Nyasa volunteered us to cross to the western bank.

Everything was soon in readiness. The Navealozans were singing and crowding around the ropes which were to spring the trap—the Eligere would take the sight of the drunks as anything but an attempt on their boat.

We were indeed lucky because it was not long before the boats did appear. They were keeping to the centre of the river, and moving at a rather brisk pace. I couldn't help but wonder what had held them up for so long. They should have passed this point long before we arrived.

Even though the men were drunk, the trap was sprung at the exact moment the first boat reached the submerged cables. Years of slave raiding could not be suppressed by the drink, and with screams for blood, the men charged down to the river's edge.

The first boat was wiped clean of mercenaries, but we were not as lucky with the other two. Many mercenaries were scraped off the second boat, but the Eligere remained untouched. The third boat passed unscathed.

The first boat was drawn to a halt by the cables as was the second, but the Eligere began working on the cables with their swords. The third boat had been deflected by the cables and was beached on the eastern bank where the Navealozans rushed them.

Sergeant Ransyn had the Janissaire positioned in the trees above us. As soon as the second boat came to a halt, he and his men opened fire on it with their crossbows. I saw two Eligere take quarrels in the chests: one dropped from sight in the boat, while the other fell overboard. The last Eligere, seeing his companions die, sheathed his sword and threw himself over the side into the fast-running water.

'Quick!' I called, 'get the grapple and snare that boat.'

Beira stepped out onto the river's edge and whirled the grapple around his head. He let go of the rope and watched it fly out over the water and snare the gunwale of the boat. With Lobito's aid he began to draw the boat closer to the bank.

A cry drew my attention from their efforts. Ndola was confronting the Eligere who had thrown himself into the river. The current had carried him downstream, but on reaching the bank he must have made his way upstream, back towards us.

Ndola had drawn his falchion and was holding it in his right hand, with the blade resting across his left arm. The Eligere advanced, small sword drawn. The Knight's surcoat had been torn from his body in the process of escaping the river. His ring mail shirt was now quite visible. His head was bare and there was the faintest trickle of blood from the corner of his mouth.

Ndola attacked with a cry of rage, and swung his sword at the Knight's unprotected head. The Knight's reflexes were incredible; his hand holding the small sword moved in a blur, and steered Ndola's blow away to his right. The deflected blow left Ndola unbalanced, and he staggered forward. As he passed, the Knight raised his left hand and brought it down on the back of Ndola's exposed neck. Ndola's momentum carried him forward and he fell to the ground, unconscious.

With a cry of rage, Nyasa raced to his son's aid. But he was too far away to reach him in time. The Eligere turned without haste, and looked down at the unmoving form. He threw one quick glance towards the straining Nyasa, before he turned and thrust his sword through the body of the fallen figure.

Nyasa cried out and launched himself across the remaining distance at the Eligere Knight. Nyasa would have been a man to reckon with in his younger days, but too much time had passed.

The Knight plucked a dagger from his weapon belt, and crouched slightly to meet the attack of the enraged father. With the small sword, he deflected the blow from the club aimed at him by Nyasa, and, without any sign of emotion, stepped forward and drove the dagger deep into the old man's belly. Nyasa crumpled to the ground before the Knight.

Reya and her brothers tried to close with the Knight, but I reached him first. We began to circle each other, the forest to one side, the river on the other. My eyes were locked to his, as we searched out weaknesses in each other's defences. The Knight moved first in our dance of death. He aimed a blow at my chest with his sword, following it up with a slash at my face from his dagger. I warded off both blows, and sent a left backhand at his unprotected head.

The dagger in his left hand suddenly changed as a section on each side of the blade flicked out. The weapon now had a normal central blade, with a smaller one on each side protruding at a slight angle.

The weapon was obviously designed to parry a blow from a sword. I now realised this could be the greatest threat to my life since my travels began. I closed with my opponent; each of us repeatedly blocked and parried blows. Beneath my armour, I was drenched with perspiration. We circled one another for some time without any opening showing. Then suddenly one was found.

I stepped back, and the heel of my foot came in contact with the body of Nyasa. I felt myself falling, and for the first time the expression on my opponent's face changed. As I fell backwards, I saw him break into a smile.

I rolled as I fell, and landed on my shoulder. I continued my roll till I was up on one knee, looking up at the Knight as he stepped over the body of Nyasa. My right sword was lost; my left still in my hand, but on the ground as I attempted to steady myself. He did not pause but raised his sword to finish me. I began to bring my sword up to defend myself, but even as my weapon rose, the Knight's fell.

As the sword was about to strike, there was a flash of colour which collided with the Knight, sending him sprawling. I was on my feet in an instant, as was the Knight. He had lost his parrying dagger and was backing away. He stopped and stooped to draw a long-bladed stiletto from his left boot.

I retrieved my second sword and moved towards him. Only now I saw the true reason for his lost dagger. Before me lay one of the Janissaire, the hilt of a dagger protruding from his chest. I looked up at the Knight before me and saw only death. Three people who had entrusted me with their lives were now dead because of this man. Silently, I walked towards him. There would be no dance for openings this time. We whirled and twisted, forever getting closer to the river's edge, until we finally parted.

I stepped back and looked down. Piercing my mail was

the Knight's stiletto. The blade was surrounded by a growing stain of red. My right hand crossed my body to grip the hilt of the weapon and draw it out. Holding the bloodied stiletto in my hand, I looked once more towards the Knight.

He had dropped his small sword, and was holding the hilt of my short sword, the blade of which had burst the links of his ring mail, and entered his lower chest. He looked up in surprise. His head continued up, and he toppled backwards into the river. This time the river claimed him.

I slipped to one knee. I felt very weak. Rafe was beside me, talking, but I was unable to hear what he was saying. As I slipped further, I saw the body of the Janissaire who had given his own life to save mine—the Janissaire whose name I had not even known.

I opened my eyes, and slowly the light grew, till I could see shapes suspended over me. My vision cleared further, and I could make out the faces of Elred and Lyn.

'Rise slowly,' Elred said. 'Rafe has spent many hours on you, and will be quite upset, should it be in vain.'

I looked down at my side. My mail had been removed and the wound cleaned. I looked closer at the wound and saw that it was more than clean; it was almost healed. I looked to my friends, surprise showing on my face.

'Rafe's work,' Elred told me.

The wound had closed, and the area surrounding it was red and swollen and sore to the touch. But with the help of my friends, I was able to get to my feet. I had seen Rafe heal wounds before, and I knew of the difficult birth he handled in Thayik, but I did not truly take in the scope of his healing powers.

'The Talisman. Did we get the Talisman?' I asked.

'Yes. Ransyn has not let it from his sight. The Talisman,

or the other thing we found in the boat,' Elred answered.

'What else was there?' I inquired. I released my friends, and began to walk to where I could see Ransyn sitting.

'Once the boat was grappled to the bank, Ransyn boarded it and found the Talisman. He also found this,' Elred said, pointing to a girl seated on a log at the water's edge. Reya was watching over her.

The girl was dressed in loose, blue robes, which covered her from neck to ankle. The sleeves were wide, and long enough to hide her hands, which rested on her lap. She looked up at me, as we stopped before her.

'This is what was in the boat when Ransyn boarded it.' As Elred spoke, the girl lifted her hands. They were tied, but they were also enclosed in a black bag. The bag was so black it seemed to be a shadow on her lap. Though it was obvious that it contained her hands, the bag was shapeless, as if empty.

'I suppose we should release her,' I told them.

The girl stood, and began to talk. She spoke for some time, and then resumed her seat in silence.

I looked at Elred for a translation.

'It is the language of the Eligere. She says if we do not release her at once she will personally see we are all blinded, and every finger which touches her is removed slowly and painfully. She went on in detail about some of the other things she would ensure were inflicted upon us, but I think you get the idea,' Elred said, with a slight smile on his lips.

'All right, then. We don't release her,' I told him.

'We should kill her,' Reya said.

The death of her father had left her face stained with tears, and her voice was strained from crying.

'If she was a prisoner of the Eligere, then it is possible she may be able to help us. If she accompanied them to the

248

city, and helped in the gaining of the Talisman, then her knowledge is very valuable,' I answered.

Reya snorted and turned back to watch the captive.

'Have you managed to get anything else from our not-too-happy guest?' I asked.

'Not a great deal, but if you have nothing else for me to do, I would like to ask her a few questions,' Elred said.

'Go ahead, but from the sound of her, I wouldn't get too close,' I told him.

'Rafe is asleep,' Lyn told me. 'The instant he finished working over you, he walked off, and then fell into a deep sleep. The remaining Janissaire have buried their dead sword brother, while Beira and Lobito have seen to their father and brother. It seems Nyasa did not die immediately, but lasted long enough to learn the outcome of the fight. He told his son Lobito, the oldest surviving member of the family, that he was to pledge his aid to the defeat of the Eligere and to the return of the Talisman.'

Crossing over to Lobito I said, 'I am sorry about your father and brother. I wish I could have given aid sooner,' Elred translated.

Lobito looked up at me and spoke slowly. Elred translated. 'You avenged them, which is more than we would have been able to do. The Eligere are too skilful in battle for us to better.'

'I did not defeat him alone,' I told him. 'I had help.'

'Your Ayah merely gave you a second chance. He was a brave follower. My brother and I have said words over his grave to help him find his way to Paradise. It is the first time we have spoken those words over a white man. But,' he continued, 'my brother and I are concerned about our sister. Should anything happen to us, she will be left without family or protection. Yet we have promised our father to aid you in your quest.'

'Couldn't you leave her behind with a friend?' I asked.

'We have no friends in this land, not since we were driven from our Family Holding. Surely the attack on us by our father's brother showed you this. Even if we knew of someone, we also pledged to watch over our sister. We cannot do this if she is not with us.'

What he was saying made sense. He was trying to carry out all his father's wishes. Unfortunately it was impossible to do so—or was it?

'If I can find a way for your sister to travel with us and help in our cause, but at the same time be protected—not just protected, but in a position to protect you and Beira—will that help you?'

'It will, if such a way is possible,' he answered sceptically.

'I believe I have a way. Lyn, will you watch our guest and send Reya over to me? I'll be at the edge of the forest close to Rafe.'

Lyn nodded and walked off. I turned, and slowly walked towards the sleeping figure of Rafe. I was tired, and my side ached, but I had an idea which might help the entire group.

24

CHAGRIN

AFTER the fight and wounding, I had slept all night and most of the following day, and by the time I finished talking with Reya it was almost dark.

Beira and Lobito had just returned from the far side of the river. Not one of the mercenaries had escaped. All those who had made the other bank had been cut down by the Navealozans. The mercenaries, though outnumbered, caused several casualties. When the fighting was over, the bodies were stacked in a large heap and soaked in coal oil, then ignited.

It would have taken many weeks for the Eligere to reach their homeland. Knowing this, my companions decided to wait, rather than take off north as soon as the fight was over, thus allowing me time to recover.

Elred questioned the captive all morning and found out some interesting things.

Her name was Beth au Vieja, and she was the only daughter of a high-ranking Knight of the Great Forest. When her grandfather died, his ring was passed to her brother Piet. He was to join the hunt for the Talisman in the Perdu. However, he did not believe in what the Eligere were doing.

He claimed the Eligere were superior, because they remained segregated. Once they mixed with the northern animals, then they too would be tainted. Many agreed and the war nearly stopped before it began. But her brother was murdered—a thing unheard of in their land. The Kyklos claimed the antiwar factions were responsible because they heard Piet was going to support the war effort.

Many, including her father, denied the accusation and blamed the ruling Kyklos for the death. This was taken as treason and her father was executed. Her elder brother heard of this and rode to the Capital for justice. He disappeared somewhere between the Family Residence and the Capital.

Beth fled, and, with the aid of friends, found out that the Kyklos were, in fact, responsible for the deaths of both her brothers. She vowed to be avenged and rode north in search of her brothers' executioners who were assigned to the Talisman hunt.

She caught up with them at Bertal, which was why they suddenly changed their plans and fled south. She used her native language with the sentries to gain entrance to the camp. Once in the camp, she cut the throats of both Kyklos, as they were two of the seven responsible for her brothers' deaths—the other five had perished in the gaining of the Talisman.

She killed many of the mercenaries before being overcome and bound. The Kyklos had ruled the Eligere for many generations, in which time they had found it necessary, when the need arose, to secure any of their number who had shown wayward tendencies and deny them the use of their powers. For this they used a large black bag, similar to the small ones which contained the rings. The hands were placed in the bag and then tied. The bag was made of a special material which neutralised the power of the ring.

'How was she able to kill so many, before being over-powered?' I asked. 'Are the Eligere females trained for fighting as well as the males?'

'No,' Elred continued. 'The females are not trained. Before she left her murdered brother, she took his ring from him. She intended to pass it on to their older brother, but once her father was killed, and her brother disappeared, she placed the ring upon her own finger.'

'The ring is that of an Elemental, perhaps one of the most potent and destructive Usare powers. She is not trained in its uses, but all Eligere, whether male or female, know of the powers of the rings.'

I thought about what Elred had just said. 'Would she be willing to help us return the Talisman to Perdu? Without the power of the Talisman, the Eligere would not have the edge over the people of the north and would possibly stop their bid for conquest.'

'I have asked her this. She said she will think about it and give her answer in the morning,' Elred answered.

'Will it be safe to remain here till then?' I asked. 'A great deal of time has been wasted so far because of me. I do not want any more to pass us by.'

'Beth assures us more Eligere were to have met this party far to the south. It will take weeks for the others to realise something has happened. By then we will be long gone.'

'Very well, we will watch her closely till the morning and then have an answer from her. But I want a Janissaire, armed with a crossbow, watching her for treachery when she is released.'

Later, as we were sitting around the fire, Lobito asked if I had given any more thought to Reya, and what was to be done about her. Elred translated.

'Surely,' Rafe said, 'she is old enough to look after herself.'

Lobito looked about cautiously before he answered. 'She may look to be of an age where one can look after oneself, but I assure you she is far from it.' As he finished speaking, he raised the mug to his lips to drink, but before he could take a mouthful, the mug slipped and Lobito was soaked. He cried out and leapt to his feet.

'Perhaps it is you brother who should be watched and cared for—not our sister.' Elred translated for Beira who began to laugh loudly. But before too long, he too was drenched and standing with his brother.

Both were looking about the camp site. Nothing could be seen in the dim light, except the shadows thrown by the fire. Rafe was next to cry out as his mug tipped itself into his lap. Now all my companions were on their feet looking about them.

Reya danced from one to the other until all had been visited. Then she turned towards me, smiling as she approached. She cockily walked to my side and reached for my mug. As she did so, I pulled it back and dumped the contents on her head. She squealed and leapt back. In doing so, she allowed her concentration to slip, and became visible to the rest of the camp.

Lobito asked a question which Elred answered without translating. As Elred explained, Lobito looked towards his sister, first with anger, then with the knowing smile that I had seen him use many times.

In the morning we gathered our equipment and shouldered our packs. Ransyn and the two Janissaire were ten minutes ahead of us. The rest of us were to follow, with Beira and Lyn bringing up the rear.

The packs were light and the terrain was level. We made good time. We walked in silence; only the noise of the occasional disturbed forest creature was heard.

A month after gaining the Talisman we reached the Focharbers, a large cluster of mountains, which was the source of the Tlaxmilch River. We decided to rest for a few days in the quiet surroundings of the mountains. We had seen only two parties of local hunters since entering the high country, neither of whom gave us a second glance as we strode passed them.

We had plenty of water, and there was a great deal of game in the mountains. Ransyn was able to keep us well supplied with meats, while we rested and healed our bodies. The returning party of Eligere would have been missed by now, and a search party was sure to have been sent out. But we felt secure because of the lead we had.

Beth was proving to be a fountain of information about the Eligere. Since she decided to join us, she had picked up a great deal of our language, which made conversation with her much easier.

I had still not thought of a way to return the Talisman to the lower levels of Perdu, where it belonged. To meet the creatures of the city head-on, as the Eligere did, would be suicidal for our small force. But the only way the power of the Talisman could be diminished, was to return it to the place from which it was taken.

'Long ago,' Beth told us, 'a Kyklos of much strength, decided to make an object of power. He travelled the world until he came upon a creature of enormous strength and power. He watched the creature and learnt its secrets. Then he returned to our land and began his work. It took many years of work to construct the object and to infuse it with power. Eventually it was finished and he set out to make a land for himself. He formed a great nation using the power of the Talisman, as it became known. But all things fall with time, and his empire crumbled, and at last he died.

'The Talisman was lost for over a thousand years, until the city in the swamp was discovered by the Plastrals.'

'Has no one else looked for the Talisman?' I asked.

'One did, many years ago. He was Fria ir Tolten, a Knight of the Great Forest. He went north to find the Talisman. He did not intend to remove it from its resting place, simply to take a small section from it. He believed the power of the Talisman would not be lessened by his action, but only those who came in contact with the piece of the Talisman would feel the increase of power.'

'How would the object be used?' I asked.

'Fria had an amulet made to take a small piece of the Talisman. It was made of gold, to be worn around the neck.' she answered.

I touched the bulge in my tunic at the base of my neck. I crossed to where the Talisman had been placed. Opening the travel box, I examined the object closer than I had done before. The Talisman was in the shape of a horse's head, a horse with a horn centrally located on its forehead. As I suspected, the tip of the horn was missing—a small tapered piece of crystal, about an inch long.

'Did Fria know the true shape of the Talisman?' I asked.

'Yes, he had the opportunity of studying some of the ancient drawings the Powerful One had made while constructing the Talisman. Fria was so taken with the creature the Talisman was modelled on, that he had the head of the weapon makers add smaller versions of the Talisman to the pommels of all his weapons. They carried no power, but Fria was supposed to have treasured those weapons above all else,' she answered.

Later that night, I dreamt of mercenaries; there were many of them and they were hunting. Among the armed men were tall figures, not armed or armoured, but wearing loose flowing blue robes. They were also hunting. I watched them for some time. It was hard to see exactly what they hunted. I saw other men too—they were black and were not clothed at all. One of the robed figures drew a knife from his sleeve and threatened a naked man.

It was the sight of the knife which brought back memories; a dark hallway lit only by a solitary lamp, a figure at a door with a knife in his hand, the piercing gaze of the stranger as he had straightened and turned towards me. I could see those eyes in the figure of my dream.

I awoke. The perspiration was pouring freely from my body. I climbed to my feet and began to wake the others in the camp.

'What is it?'

'What's the matter?'

'Is there someone out there?'

I refused to answer as I rushed about the camp. I was trying to hold the image of the figure with the knife in my mind's eye. It was as if I was seeing the same man I had tried to catch in Harnet's tavern so long ago. But he was dead. I watched him die. At the time we had thought he was an assassin sent by Raimend. But now it appeared that he was really an Eligere, sent to do . . . what?

'What in the name of the Gods is wrong, Teal?' Lyn asked. He was sitting in a tangle of blankets, a drawn dagger in each hand.

'They are following us,' was all I said.

My friends climbed to their feet and began to pack up

the camp. No other words were spoken until we were ready to leave.

'How far away are they?' Ransyn asked.

'Close. Somehow they have masked their approach and hidden their presence from me. I don't know how.'

'They must have a Seeker with them; he would have been able to cover their approach until they were almost upon us. It is good you see them while they are so far away,' Beth said.

'Can they sense us?' Ransyn asked.

'I don't think so. They were asking questions of a local; they weren't all that gentle either. But now I know they are there, I will be able to cover our trail. Their Seeker will not be able to sense us. If they want us, they are going to have to do it the hard way. Ransyn, hang back and make sure we don't leave any sign for them to find. I'll lead off; the rest of you keep close—it will be easy to get separated in the darkness.'

I moved off at a fast pace. I could sense the others behind me as we moved through the almost total blackness. The sun rose and we continued—there would be no morning meal that day. I had expected the Eligere to follow, but not this quickly. Something must have happened to warn them earlier than I had expected.

We swung wide around the mountains. It would mean more distance to travel, but the going would be easier. Soon we were beyond the mountains, and again following a river. This time it was the Osseaux, which would lead us straight to the swamp of the same name. The river was too wild to think of a raft at this stage, but hopefully we would have enough time to construct a raft when the water quietened downriver. Even the river's slower pace would be enough to outdistance our pursuers.

We rested in a small clearing of the forest. All of us were

exhausted. I had pushed us continually since sensing our hunters. Reya and Ransyn had gone ahead to see if the way into the city was clear. The city was Murztal, the only place of habitation along the length of the Osseaux.

We had opened our lead over those behind us, but we could not afford to take any chances. There might be Eligere ahead of us and waiting in the city.

Our scouts returned with word that there were no Eligere in sight, nor had any people fitting their description been seen. It was the best we could hope for, so we again rose and continued our trek.

The city did indeed prove to be free of Eligere. We enquired about the purchase of a boat, but were told there were two large sets of rapids downriver which were impossible to navigate or portage around. We thanked them for the news and left the city immediately.

Rafe was continually treating us for sprains and other small injuries. But they increased daily and were starting to take a toll on Rafe's strength.

We were five days away from Murztal when we heard the sound of baying. I stopped, and tried to locate the source of the noise. It did not take long to find it, once I was aware of it. About three miles behind us, and closing fast, was a large pack of animals: wild dogs or something similar. I had not been watching for native animals, only for our hunters and for other humans.

'Can we outrun them? It's only a few hours since sun up. Hopefully they have been travelling all night and will be close to exhaustion,' Rafe said.

'The only trouble is the creatures who have found our trail are not likely to tire so soon. I have known the creatures who chase us to run for days once a scent is taken,' Ransyn said ominously.

'What are they?' I asked.

'That baying we can hear is the hunting call of the

Chagrin, large wolf-like creatures, who hunt the fringes of the Todismal Forest. As I said, once they are on a trail, they are hard to shake,' he answered.

We broke into a run. If what Ransyn said was true, and unfortunately he had been right on everything so far, then it was useless. But we had to try. Ransyn said the creatures may have been running for days already, just to get this close. I couldn't count on that, so as we ran, I looked for a place to make a stand. The trees would provide safety, but that would only let those following us catch up. If we were treed, the Chagrin had only to wait. The longer we were held, the more desperate our situation would become, and the more rested the Chagrin would be before our inevitable confrontation.

25

RHYHL

WE couldn't keep up the punishing pace for much longer. We were going to have to stop and make a stand soon, or drop from exhaustion.

'This will have to do,' I called, and stopped my headlong dash. 'If we keep going, we won't be in any condition to meet the threat.'

I spread the party out in a half-circle, giving everyone plenty of room to fight. Beth and Rafe had dropped to the ground and were building a small fire. Ransyn and his two men were readying their crossbows. The rest of us had turned, and were waiting for the Chagrin to arrive.

'Reya,' I called, 'you had better take cover in one of the trees nearby. That staff you carry will not be of much use against these creatures, and if you should use your Stealth abilities, they would soon sniff you out.'

She looked at me, and gave a small laugh. Holding the staff like a spear, she brandished it, and with a sound of metal against metal, and a definite click, a long blade slid out of the staff and locked into place. Two smaller blades slipped out either side of the larger one, locking into place at slight angles. The staff now looked like an Eligere parrying dagger, except the blade was longer and it was a four foot staff rather than a dagger.

'Impressive, but can you use it?'

'Watch,' was her only reply.

Suddenly something came crashing through the undergrowth, and stopped before us. It resembled a wolf, and was of enormous size. Its head would have come level with my waist. The Chagrin stopped and examined us for several seconds before raising its head and baying to the rest of the pack.

Its cry was cut short as a crossbow bolt thumped into its chest. A second bolt struck the creature, then a third. It was in pain, but far from dead, as it raised its head and howled again.

Three more bolts were fired; one struck between the eyes, only to glance off, while the other two took it in the throat. Finally the creature fell. It was still not dead and lay there trying to snap at the shafts protruding from its throat.

Five more Chagrin burst from the forest, followed by another six. The beasts spread themselves out and paused. Their number was swollen by four more creatures from the forest.

Ransyn and the two Janissaire were firing on the same creature in the hope of cutting down the number before they charged.

'They are taking their time,' Rafe said.

'It's as if they are making sure we're the ones they are after,' Reya added.

'They may be doing just that.' Beth said. 'If a Caller is travelling with our pursuers, then it is possible he may have set this pack upon us.'

'You mean they are being controlled?' Ransyn asked.

'No, not controlled. The Caller just places a thought in

the minds of the creatures—usually fear — to keep them at bay. But in this case, I'd say it was hunger, and we are the closest game.'

'Is there any way to break the thought?'

'Yes,' she answered.

'How's that?'

'Kill the Caller or all the creatures,' she stated calmly.

'Well, that makes it easy. Seeing as how these creatures are closer, we may as well make it these,' Ransyn said, firing another bolt into the same creature.

With a short cry from one of the animals, the pack leapt forward. I had my gladius in one hand and the stiletto which I had taken from the dead knight in the other. With the loss of so many friends at the river fight, I had hardly noticed the loss of my other sword. The Knight took it with him when he fell into the river.

One of the Chagrin leapt at me. I braced myself and threw my right arm in front of my face. The creature hit, driving me back several paces. It had locked onto my arm, and was beginning to shake its head in an attempt to tear my arm off, but my scale mail could not be penetrated. I disembowelled the creature with the stiletto.

Whirling around, I saw one Chagrin dead and Reya wrestling on the ground with another. The creature had taken hold of her pilgrim staff, and was trying to tear it from her hands. I stepped up beside the Chagrin, and cut its throat. Reya smiled weakly, and climbed to her feet.

The small area was littered with struggling bodies. Reya and I began to give aid to our companions. One of the Janissaire was down, a bad tear in his leg, and Beira had a bloodied arm where one of the creatures had caught him. But apart from these two injuries, we were unhurt. A large number of the creatures were dead, and the rest had fallen back and were watching us.

'Will they run now, Ransyn?' I asked.

'Usually, but if they're ravenous, or being made to think they are, then they will probably stay.'

Another few Chagrin emerged from the forest, and joined their brethren. They waited only a few seconds, and then began to move towards us.

'Wait!'

It was Beth. She stepped before us with a blazing torch. Holding it before her like a spear, she advanced on the Chagrin. When the creatures were almost upon her, she thrust the torch forward with both hands. The flames of the torch grew in size, and there was a roaring which filled my ears, as flames leapt from the torch to engulf the Chagrin. Beth moved the torch from side to side to catch all the creatures.

She lowered the torch, and as she did, the flames returned to normal. The smell of burning hair filled my nostrils, and the sickening odour of burnt flesh began to rise from the dead Chagrin.

'I had to wait till they were in one small group before I could act. These creatures are cunning, and would not have fallen for the same trick twice. They would have dogged our trail snapping at us from here on.'

'You did well,' I told her. 'Now we had better get moving, or we will be having other company soon.'

Rafe had stopped the bleeding of our only two injuries, and with Ransyn and Lobito supporting the injured Janissaire, we continued our northward trek.

The hunters were much closer now. The Chagrin attack had given them enough time to close the gap between us. If they tried the same trick again, I feared they would be on us before we were able to win our way free.

We reached the southern edge of the Osseaux Swamp, and stopped for a much-needed rest.

'What would you say is the best way to enter the swamp, Ransyn?' I asked.

'Turn east, and follow the swamp to Velliach; resupply, and then turn west into the swamp,' he answered.

'Then that's what we will do,' I stated.

The Eligere hunting us reached the edge of the swamp. The party was made up of at least fifty mercenaries, with seven Knights and seven robed Eligere: Kyklos. They stopped at the same place we did, and examined our trail. Orders were given, and a small group of mercenaries broke away from the rest, and began to trot eastward along the trail we had left. After another quick search of the area, the pursuers followed the smaller group eastward.

Once the last one was out of sight, I emerged from the bushes which had concealed me. Ransyn and Beira had taken off eastward, intending to lose their followers after a couple of miles, and rejoin us. In the meantime, we struck out north towards the heart of the swamp.

We had been travelling for four hours before Ransyn and Beira caught up to us.

'How did the ruse work?' Ransyn asked.

'Perfectly. They saw your trail and followed almost immediately. How far did you take them?' I asked.

'We travelled about six miles, then cut across a small section of swampy ground. It will look as if we did it to save time. When they fail to find our trail on the far side, they will keep searching, giving us a bit more time.'

'You sure they won't be able to sense us here, like you sensed them?' Elred asked.

'If they could sense us, they would have attacked us where we started the false trail, besides, I'm certain they can't sense us. I don't know why—it's just a feeling.'

We travelled only a few miles more, then stopped. We needed a good night's rest before we encountered any Plastrals. A small sheltered fire was lit, and we ate a hot meal, the first in many days. After the meal I felt much more relaxed. I settled down to a few hours' sleep before my turn on sentry.

We were up before first light, and, having eaten the remainder of the evening's meal, were on our way as soon as it was light enough to see. By keeping to the higher ground, we were able to keep a good pace, and in a couple of days we reached the area of the sloping tunnel which we had used to escape from the buried city of Perdu. Lyn wove the shape of a Plastral about himself, and ventured out to ensure the way was clear.

'We will have to find a different entrance to the city. The one we entered by last time is too close to the Plastrals' camp, and our exit was somewhat blocked in our escape,' I told the group.

Lyn returned with the news that the area was free of Plastrals.

'Perhaps the creatures left once the excavation was over,' he said.

'More likely they are fighting in this war on the side of the Eligere,' I answered.

With Lyn leading, still in the guise of a Plastral, we made our way towards the closest entrance to Perdu. At the downward sloping tunnel we paused, while Lyn and Ransyn searched the immediate area. Ransyn returned with an armful of torches.

'There is a large pile of them not far from here if you want more,' he said.

'These will be enough,' I answered.

We lit the torches, and started down the tunnel. It was similar to the one we had used to escape when we were last here. The tunnel brought us to the second level, and almost immediately, we came upon several bodies of mercenaries, some half-eaten, and the carcasses of many strange creatures. The creatures had been killed by sword strokes, but the mercenaries seemed to have been torn apart.

We had slept twice since entering the city. We had enough rations for three more days, and sufficient water for four. My senses had been guiding me to where the Talisman once rested. Only on a few occasions had we seen signs of life. Each time, whatever it was scurried away before we could see it clearly in the light thrown by the torches. We were now at the thirty-seventh level, and my senses told me we had a fair way yet to travel.

My thoughts were interrupted by a call from ahead of us. It sounded like a involuntary shout for help from a human throat. We moved cautiously ahead, and soon found the source of the call.

Before us, in a large chamber, was a collection of the strangest creatures I had ever seen. They were all trying to reach a man perched on a ledge above them. He was injured—bleeding from the forehead—and his left arm hung limply at his side.

As we watched, several of the creatures abandoned their attempts to reach the man, and turned and walked towards the far entrance. When they reached the opening, they stopped and returned to the press of creatures.

'Do we help him? Or do we let him entertain the creatures a while longer, while we slip past?' Reya asked.

'Leave him,' said Beth. 'He can be of no use to us, apart from as a distraction for the creatures which would otherwise seek us.'

I watched the scene before me. Some of the creatures were slowly climbing the sloped wall towards the ledge which sheltered the man. The creatures climbing towards the trapped man looked like pulsating rocks. It was hard to believe something like that could be alive.

The creatures waiting at the bottom of the wall were more acceptable. There were cave wolves, smaller cousins of the Chagrin. Standing next to them were small, squat men, armed with an assortment of weapons and armour stripped from the dead Knights and mercenaries. The last members of the bizarre scene were Plastrals. They were standing well back from the other creatures, and were not armed, but they were wearing tattered robes of Eligere Kyklos.

'We help him!' I declared, and drawing my sword stepped out into the chamber.

One of the wolves saw us, and sent up a howl which was echoed by its brethren. One of the Plastrals let out a cry, and suddenly the wolves turned from their trapped quarry, and rushed across the room towards us.

These cave wolves were not like their forest cousins in strength, and halfway across the floor, three fell to the quarrels of Ransyn and the Janissaire crossbows. Lobito and Beira, who was wielding his sword left-handed because of the injury caused by the Chagrin, chose to meet the attack of the wolves halfway. Their advance had split the wolves into two groups.

Ransyn and his men took one, while Elred, Lyn and myself took the other. Reya, Beth and Rafe moved forward to protect Reya's brothers from attack from behind.

The wolves were no match for us. We cut them down as soon as they came within reach, but despite the carnage, they did not give up. They kept attacking.

Then the small men joined the fight. They wielded their weapons without skill, but they more than made up for it by strength. One blow to Beira's falchion sent him reeling backwards. As the squat man followed up his advantage, Lobito, ever watchful of his younger brother, sent the man's head spinning from his shoulders with a well-timed blow.

Suddenly there were screams of fear, as those before us turned and ran. Weapons were discarded and the creatures clutched and dragged at one another to get from the room. Even the Plastrals were startled by the actions of their allies.

'They wear rings!' I called. 'One of them is a Caller. That explains why the creatures attacked us.' I turned to see how our party fared, and gave an involuntary cry, as I saw the creature in our midst. Before I could do anything, the creature shimmered and Lyn appeared in its place.

'I remember during one work party on the third level, we came upon a creature like the one you just saw. It grabbed the first slave and literally tore him apart, before we could even turn and run. I thought if these creatures lived down here, they may well fear it,' Lyn said.

'Well, it worked, but next time warn me first,' I answered.

With most of the creatures gone, it was easy for us to cross to the wall with the ledge.

'Beware! The wall climbers are deadly. Do not let them near you,' the man called down from the ledge.

'Stand aside,' called Beth. 'If we are to save this wretched fellow, let's have done with it and leave this place before those others return.' She raised her torch and a stream of fire leapt from it to each of the wall climbers. They sizzled and smoked and gave off an extremely unpleasant odour.

'There,' she called again. 'Can you climb down unaided or would you like me to climb up there and carry you down?'

The injured man lowered himself over the lip of the ledge, and dropped to the ground beside us. Rafe moved to his side, and began to treat him.

'Thank you,' he said. 'I fear they would have soon had me if you had not intervened. I am Rhyhl, Guardian

Ceallian of the Fortieth Level. I am in your debt.'

'What exactly do you guard?' I asked.

'That which is power. That which has rested in the lower levels of this city for a thousand years. That which was stolen by people such as you,' he said, giving us a searching look.

'It was not we who took the Talisman, but our enemies,' I told him.

'How do you know the name of the sacred object?' he asked.

Rafe interrupted. 'He's fit to travel. But, we will have to rest soon, or none of us will be any match for whatever lurks ahead.'

I nodded to Rafe, and waved for the party to move out.

'We have come to help your people,' I said to the Guardian.

'How will you help them, if the Guardians could not?' he asked, getting unsteadily to his feet.

'We will help you return the Talisman to its rightful place.'

He examined my face for a long time before he spoke. 'How are you going to do that?'

'Ransyn.'

Ransyn stepped forward and drew the travel box from the sack he carried it in. Then, kneeling down, he opened the box and lifted out the Talisman.

Rhyhl threw himself to the ground and began to speak in a fast gibbering tongue. Before I could ask Elred for a translation, Rhyhl rose and turned to me.

'The Guardians are all but destroyed; the creatures of the sub-levels have revolted and armed themselves. My people have gone into hiding. The only help I can offer you is myself. Will you accept this?'

I took the Talisman from Ransyn, and handed it to Rhyhl. 'If you are indeed one of the last Guardians, then it is your place to return the Talisman, and we will aid you.'

Tears filled his eyes, as he looked from one to another of the party. Each one smiled, and nodded in agreement. Rhyhl placed the Talisman back in its box and then in the sack. 'Then let us go.'

26

THE CIRCLET AND THE DAGGER

'ELRED!' I called quietly.

'Yes?'

'He wears a ring.'

'I thought he would have to, when he said he was a Guardian of some sort. Would the ring be that of a Caller?' he asked.

'Yes. How did you know?'

'It is the only Usare power which has not made itself available to you, and the only way he could have kept so many creatures at bay.'

'How do you mean?' I asked.

'As I told you some time ago, a Seeker is always the leader of a Usare Circle, as he is the only one who can see the rings uninvited. But that is not all. When a new Seeker comes to power, the ring draws one of each of the abilities to him, for him to accept or deny. Most deny, as they do not want the responsibilities of the role. But a few accept the challenge. It looks like you are one of the few, Teal— you now lead a Circle of Usare.'

Rhyhl was true to his word, and led us quickly from level to level. We had a few encounters, but nothing on a large scale. We saw no more of the Plastral ring-wielders—I believed they had withdrawn to a lower level. Soon we were passing through rooms, and travelling down hallways with walls covered in mosaics. Rhyhl had provided us with more torches. Even though he and his people lived far below ground, they were often forced to the surface for one thing or another. Because of this their eyes had not grown accustomed to the lack of light over the years.

We were travelling down a hallway when I sensed something ahead of us.

'What is around the next corner, Rhyhl?'

'Nothing but a series of connecting rooms—why?'

'I can sense something there, something large and dangerous. What could it be?' I asked.

'You . . . sense,' he repeated.

Lyn and Elred moved closer, and I called for Rafe and Reya. Beth came over of her own accord. I made a fist of my right hand and extended my arm. The others did the same and soon Rhyhl was looking upon a row of rings, gleaming in the torch light and identical in every way. He too raised his hand and made a fist, and another ring joined ours.

'This is how you sense the danger ahead? You are a Secan,' he said.

Suddenly, ahead of us, a roar tore the stillness.

'A Chimera!' Rhyhl cried. 'Those ignorant fools have released a Chimera.'

'What exactly is a Chimera?' Ransyn asked, as the roar sounded again.

'Death,' was Rhyhl's simple answer.

'How can it be fought?' I asked.

'It cannot. I know of no one who has fought a Chimera and lived,' he said. 'Though I once heard a tale about an

273

ancient ancestor of mine, who claimed he had killed a Chimera by attacking it from behind, but I believe it was nothing more than a story.'

'Then we avoid it,' I told them. 'Quickly, through this door.'

The door opened at a touch, and we found ourselves in a long room. The ceiling was lost above us, and the only other exit was a door at the far end of the room.

'Will that door take us to the rooms you spoke of?' I asked.

'Yes, but we must hurry. If they have released the Chimera, they may have released other creatures, more dangerous,' Rhyhl said, as he rushed across the room.

'More dangerous!' I heard Ransyn mumble, as he helped the injured Janissaire across the room in the wake of Rhyhl. 'If you can't fight that thing, what could possibly be more dangerous?'

'Wait—we cannot expect to avoid dangers if we continually race from place to place. Reya, get rid of the torch and scout ahead. Try to keep us in sight as much as possible.'

She handed the torch to Beira, and stepped into the shadows. Instantly she was gone from their sight, but I watched her as she strode to the door and slipped through the small opening. 'Beth, you stay with Rafe and the injured. Ransyn, take one man and cover our rear. Don't get too far behind, or we won't be able to help you. Elred, you and Lyn follow Rafe's group and tell Lobito he is to stay with me. He'll be travelling behind Reya.'

With everyone in position, we moved off. Reya scouted the halls and rooms. Sometimes she had only to wave to have us scurrying for cover. Other times, because of obstacles between us, she had to return to tell of a danger ahead.

'There's a large number of those squat men—

Troglodytes Rhyhl called them, I think. Well, anyway, there's a large number of them coming down the hall in front of us. All of them are armed,' Reya said.

I glanced behind me to Rhyhl. 'What's through those doors?' I asked. I had sensed the way was safe, but I had to know what else we might encounter.

'It leads to one of the older sections of the city, unused for many years,' he answered.

'Well, we are about to use it.'

The great age of this section of the city was obvious. Inches of undisturbed dust lay on the floor, and there was not one piece of timber which had not rotted away completely. All the rooms and chambers stood open; at each opening a deep pile of dust marked where once a door had stood.

We travelled the corridors slowly and in silence. To move at too great a speed caused the centuries of dust to rise in a choking cloud. I was thinking we should soon stop for a rest and something to eat from our diminishing rations, when I sensed a feeling of wellbeing coming from ahead of us.

'What lies in that direction, Rhyhl? I sense something, but not danger. It's hard to tell exactly what it is.'

'I do not know,' he answered. 'This section of the city was used only after the builders moved below ground. The population then slowly decreased over the generations and this section was abandoned.'

'We will wait here. Reya, you search out a place for us where we may rest for a while. You know what to look for.'

She nodded and slipped into the shadows again. A short time later she returned. 'There is a large chamber a short distance from here. Around the chamber are seven doors leading to seven small rooms. The only way into the rooms is through the chamber, and the chamber itself has only one entrance.'

'Sounds fine—we'll rest there for a while then.'

The chamber was perfect. We found that one of the rooms had a small spring in it, but when we tasted the water we found it was undrinkable. We settled down in the larger chamber. Lobito was on sentry at the entrance.

'Is there anywhere we can obtain water and food?' I asked Rhyhl.

'There are plenty of creatures which are edible roaming these chambers. I will hunt for some shortly. I am afraid water will be much harder to find.'

I turned to Beth. 'There is a spring in the second room. The water is quite undrinkable. Is there anything you can do about it?'

She rose and entered the small room. The Elemental powers were new to all of us. All the powers we possessed could be used and hidden at the same time. The power of an Elemental was quite different. Being able to control the four elements, earth, wind, fire and water, made the Elemental the most powerful of the Usare. But none of the skills could be used in a land which did not allow magic. For this reason Elementals were virtually unknown in the northern lands. Even the actual extent of the powers were not known.

Beth returned carrying a full waterskin, which she passed to me. I raised it to my lips and sipped at the water. It was cold and fresh, with no trace of the taste it had carried before. I took a mouthful this time, and passed the skin to Rafe. The skin was passed round to all.

'I can make foul water pure, and pure water foul,' Beth said simply, and walked across to the far side of the chamber where she sat down by herself. Even though she had joined us, she was not really one of us . . . not yet.

For two or more days we travelled the dark corridors of the old city. When finally we entered more used areas, we were only a few rooms from where the Talisman was taken. Rhyhl had informed us that the replacing of the Talisman would bind many of the more dangerous creatures to the levels below that of the Talisman.

We had had no contact with any of the strange creatures since Reya had taken the point. Using her Stealth abilities, she had been able to steer us clear of the trouble, slipping back to warn us when necessary.

'There are eight Troglodytes in the next chamber; we must pass through it to reach our goal.' Reya explained, when she returned from one of her invisible scouting trips.

We were too close to be stopped at that stage. Three of the Troglodytes dropped with crossbow bolts in their chests, while the other five were rushed by the remainder of our group. Rafe, Beth and Beira kept out of the fighting and made for the door on the other side of the room. They reached it and disappeared into the next room.

We dispatched the remaining five and followed. The next room was smaller; there was only one more before the room of the Talisman.

'Behind us!' Ransyn called.

I turned and saw dozens of Troglodytes pouring into the room we had just left.

'We'll have to hold them here,' he called, and added, 'The doors can only be barred from the other side.'

'We can at least close the doors and make them pay for opening them again,' Beira said, testing the edge of his falchion.

'All right, close them and see if there's any way of securing them from this side,' I told them. The Troglodytes had stopped their headlong rush. Knowing we could not lock the doors from our side, they were now in no hurry.

The second door was almost closed when the wounded Janissaire slipped through. 'I'll bar the door from this side, and hold them as long as I can, Lord,' he called.

Beira leapt for the door as it closed, and he too slipped into the other room. The doors closed with a thump and we heard the bolts being shot home. Then came the ring of steel on steel as the two prepared to sell their lives to give us more time.

'We can only help them by returning the Talisman to its rightful resting place. Hurry—they cannot hold long,' I urged.

We entered the last chamber. Reya and Beth were already there. 'There is a niche in the side wall; it is the only place we can see where the Talisman could rest,' Reya explained.

Rhyhl crossed the chamber and removed the box from the sack. He placed the box in the niche and then opened the lid. He removed the Talisman and stepped back. A section of the wall opened and a smaller room could be seen. Rhyhl entered the room and placed the Talisman upon a dais. Alongside the dais was the body of a man. There was a Silver Dagger in his heart and upon his head was a Circlet of gold.

'This was the Altar Guardian; he slew himself when the Talisman was taken,' Rhyhl said. 'For too long he had told people that we were safe, and no harm would befall us. Because of this we were not expecting the attack when it came.'

He took the Circlet from the man's head and placed it on his own. Then he pulled the Dagger from the man's chest and stepped onto the dais. He touched the Talisman with the Silver Dagger, then placed the Dagger in his belt.

The instant he touched the Talisman, a strange feeling came over me. The room had been quiet before, but now the silence seemed absolute. Rhyhl walked out of the small room, and the wall closed behind him. He took the Dagger from his belt and raised the hilt to the Circlet on his head. His lips moved in silence, then he replaced the Dagger in his belt and walked toward the outer room.

When we got to the barred doors we found they were closed, but no longer barred. I pushed the doors open. The room was full of bodies but it was the two closer to the doors who got my attention. Beira and the Janissaire were dead. They had held the door and allowed the Talisman to be replaced. The addition of the Circlet and the Dagger, had increased Rhyhl's Caller abilities to enable him to send all the creatures away. But the deed was done—two more of our companions were dead.

The bodies of our two fallen friends were taken to a room put aside for burial by the Guardians. While this was being done, many of Rhyhl's people began to creep back into the city. After the funeral of our friends, we rested for a day. During that day, Rhyhl used his increased Caller abilities to call all the creatures of the lower levels to him. The wolves were penned and the Troglodytes unarmed and sent to the sublevels to wall off the chambers holding the bound creatures. The Plastrals were called last. These were slain, and the rings removed and given to those who would become the new Guardians.

Some of the Plastrals had not answered the call. Rhyhl explained that these beasts probably wore the rings of Callers, and had managed to block out the call with the power of their rings.

An expedition was mounted to hunt down the last of these creatures. Reya and Lobito wished to avenge their brother's death, while Ransyn and Bryan, the last Janissaire, wished to avenge the death of their sword brother. The rest of us accompanied our companions and many of Rhyhl's people.

The trail led to the upper levels. Finally we had the rogue ring-wielding Plastrals cornered in a large cavern. As well as the Plastrals, there were a score of Troglodytes. These were able to overcome the call because they were under control of the Plastrals at the time.

Our forces met in the centre of the cavern. Swords flashed in the flickering light of the torches. Realising their Caller abilities would avail them little, the Plastrals took up weapons from the fallen and aided their beleaguered slaves.

One pocket of Plastrals was forced back into a corner where Beth incinerated them. She did this only once more before becoming too weak to help further. The loss of the Talisman had returned all our powers to normal.

The last few Plastrals were forced back against a wall. One of the larger ones forced his way from the others and attempted to escape. I intercepted him before he could leave the room and killed him. In the process, my one remaining short sword was broken.

We were to return to the lower levels where we would rest and be resupplied. Beth commented that the weapons of her people did not break so easily. When she said this, I remembered her story about Fria's obsession with his weapons.

I detoured to the chamber where I had found the ring. I dug carefully amongst the fallen rubble until I uncovered more of the skeleton. Reaching into the rocks, I felt about. At last, my hand rested on something familiar. I drew the weapon belt slowly from the rubble. The belt was wide and stiff from its great age. The two sheaths were the same, but the swords they held were the finest I had ever seen. The blades were as long as my arm, and three fingers wide. They were untarnished and gleamed brightly in the torch light. But the most breathtaking of all were the pommels: each was an exact copy in miniature of the Talisman.

Having gathered fresh supplies, we were guided out of the city. All the entrances but one were to be closed, and the power of the Circlet and Dagger would be used to ensure the Plastrals living near the one remaining entrance protected it from any who might search for it.

Rhyhl said his people had agreed to send warriors and some of the Guardians north to help with the war. We told him we were grateful and word would be sent as to where the troops should go.

We said farewell to our new allies, and made ready to leave. We had learnt from the Plastrals that the coastal towns of Hocheken and Chorenz were still held by the Thayian armies. It was our hope we would be able to leave the swamp and join up with these forces before these cities fell. We didn't know what the chances were of returning to the Plains before the war spread further north, but we intended to try.

Reya, still grieving over the loss of her second brother, led with Sergeant Ransyn, Lobito, Elred, and the last Janissaire brought up the rear. The rest of us, Rafe, Beth, Lyn and myself—were in the centre. Also with us was Rhyhl. He had handed the Circlet and Dagger over to his son, and named him the Guardian of the Altar.

He intended to travel north with us. The Talisman was safe, deep within the city. No power was greater than that of the Circlet and the Dagger when wielded by a trained Guardian. Now that the Guardians were alert to the dangers, no force would ever penetrate the city again.

27

RETRIBUTION

THE journey to Hocheken was long and troublesome. Many times we were forced to detour around a superior force of the enemy. Their camps seemed to be everywhere. The replacement of the Talisman, and Rhyhl's handing over of the Circlet and Dagger had returned all our powers to normal. The Eligere with their greater number of ring-wielders — Kyklos — would be the ones to suffer most. It was our hope that the loss in ability would force the Eligere to give up the northern war and return home.

The others had all commented on the diminishing of their abilities. I, however, had found that my abilities had suffered no loss of intensity. I had still been able to seek out and locate the enemy, and find the safest paths and trails to follow.

I mentioned this fact to Lyn and Beth—the two of them were always together since leaving the city. Beth asked about the two swords I now wore; I had not placed them in my sword belt till we were clear of the City. Fria had also been a thief in his way, and although he did not try to take the Talisman, he had removed a part of it.

I told them about finding the skeleton, a tale Lyn had heard before. This time I also told them about the third bag containing the strange piece of jewellery. I pulled the amulet from beneath my tunic. Beth reached out a hand and gently touched the small tapered crystal. Her face brightened, and she threw back her head and laughed.

She got to her feet and, taking a burning branch from the fire, held it up high. Then she raised her other hand and sent a tongue of flame into the heavens. She did this over and over again, laughing constantly.

She turned and saw our surprised looks. 'Don't you fools understand? Once the Talisman was replaced I was exhausted after two such uses of power, but now I feel as if I could continue all night.' To prove the point, she sent more flames skywards. 'That is the Amulet Fria made from a fragment of the Talisman. It magnifies the rings' powers like the Talisman, only it isn't as powerful—it only works on those who have laid hands on it.'

Now I knew why my powers had not diminished. I had placed the Amulet around my neck. As soon as I had taken the ring, the Amulet had magnified its abilities. My companions gathered round, and gently touched the crystal.

'You realise if the enemy find out about this they will stop at nothing to get the Amulet from you?' Lyn said.

'True, so none must know of it. Only we ten know and we must pledge here to take the knowledge to the grave with us,' Elred said.

We all made the pledge. On the hills around us, the flickering fires of the enemy camps could be seen: a reminder we should always be on our guard. Because of Beth's indulgence in her abilities, we were forced to move camp.

'Try to restrain yourself if you feel the urge to burn something coming upon you again,' Ransyn said.

We reached Hocheken and sneaked into the city under the cover of darkness. The enemy had the city well ringed but were watching for those trying to escape from the city, not enter it. A few questions told us all we needed to know. The Vahian Ambassador from Thayik and his retinue had made it as far as Hocheken before the enemy's advance cut off their route home.

'On the day you say you returned this Talisman, all assaults on the city stopped, and the enemy fell back and began to strengthen its own defences,' the Ambassador said.

'Is there a chance we can break out of the city and return home, or at least aid Lyram in its defence? On the way here, all I heard in the streets was talk of surrender and overwhelming forces. This city is lost—the enemy just hasn't realised it yet,' I told him.

'That's true, but at the moment there is no way a size-able force of men could leave the city undetected. We could force our way out onto the Plain, but the enemy would soon trap us, and with its superior numbers, it would destroy us, and that would help no one,' he answered.

'Could we go by sea?' I asked.

'There are sufficient vessels in the harbour. The problem is getting them and then breaking the blockade. Easier said than done.'

'What we need is for the owners of the vessels to give us permission to use them, and at the same time a storm arise to scatter the blockading ships, and then provide a good wind to speed us on our way,' I stated.

'Yes,' he answered smiling. 'That's all we need.'

'Then, this is what I propose we do,' I answered, returning the smile, but for a different reason.

The preparations were complete, and all we waited for was

the setting of the sun as a signal to all those concerned. As the sun set that evening, hundreds of men in dozens of locations would begin to move towards the waterfront. All day, parties of merchants and slaves had been leaving the building that the Ambassador had made his headquarters. As soon as these people were out of sight in warehouses and storerooms, the parcels they carried were opened to reveal weapons. Cloaks and robes were removed to show armour-clad bodies.

Since early afternoon, Lyn and Elred had been travelling the waterfront, relaying messages to Captains. In many instances, they rowed out to the vessel in question so that the owner could give his orders to the Captain personally.

Beth and Rafe were situated in the tower of an old abandoned temple. It was the highest point in the city, and allowed Beth to work more freely.

The rest of us were spread amongst the waiting battle companies.

In the instant of time that the sun touched the horizon, the city seemed to freeze. Then the sounds of armoured men moving through the streets could be heard. The docks were alive, as boat after boat moved out across the harbour to the waiting vessels.

The weather had worsened. There was a wind blowing from the east which had even the sheltered vessels dancing at their moorings. As the last of the men climbed on board, the wind dropped. All vessels got under way, save ours. We were waiting for a solitary longboat from the city which we could see making its approach. The crew were striving at the oars to pull the boat through the swell in the harbour. The boat came alongside and the crew and passengers climbed on board. Beth looked exhausted, but she was still capable of a smile as she was taken below deck.

The storm had blown the blockade ships well to the

west before it died down. With the storm gone, a light wind had picked up from the west which moved the small fleet along at a goodly pace. As the days passed, the wind freshened and the speed of the small fleet increased.

At the mouth of the Osseaux River, where it appeared from the swamp, a tall spiral of smoke was seen by the mast lookout. The fleet hove to and longboats were sent ashore. They soon returned loaded to the gunwales with armed men.

While still in Hocheken, Rhyhl had dreamt to his son of a meeting. The son had replied. So the longboats brought twenty Guardians and one hundred and forty warriors, each wearing a cuirass of old coins and a helmet which was fully enclosed with only a slit to see through. On the hip of each man was an aor, the ancient sword of their people. The Guardians and the warriors were soon placed below decks and the fleet continued.

Our force now totalled eight hundred fighting men: the one hundred and forty Perduans who had just boarded the vessel; the four hundred and fifty Janissaire under Sergeant Roelf, an old friend of Ransyn; and the two hundred and ten Thayian marines who the Ambassador had managed to borrow, and who were under the command of Sergeant Lorima, as no volunteer officer could be found.

Apart from myself there were four other Vahians: the Ambassador, Aron Haryss, and two others, Sub-Arons Symes and Whyte. The fighting men were spread over eleven vessels of all types and sizes; the only thing they had in common was the Eligere battle standard at the fore of each vessel.

With all the galleasses and privateers blockading the ports which had not yet fallen to their allies, the voyage across the Uskery was uneventful. Lyram was sighted on a clear morning, with no other vessels in sight. The latest information we could obtain before we left was that the city as a whole had fallen, but the centre of the city was still held by a large band of fighters from many different cities and lands. None could explain what was holding the mismatched force together and why they were enduring the hardships which were being heaped upon them by the besiegers.

The sun was high overhead by the time our small fleet put into Lyram harbour. There were many soldiers on the waterfront, watching as our vessels tied off at the docks, supposedly there to unload supplies for the entrenched troops. Their waves and cheers soon turned to cries of disbelief as squad after squad of Janissaire swarmed from the vessels.

Those vessels carrying the Thayian marines had placed themselves alongside vessels belonging to the enemy. The marines were experts at ship to ship fighting, and it was their role to board and capture as many vessels as possible.

The Perduans had been split into squads of twenty. Used to the caverns and corridors of their buried city, they were perfect for the job of clearing the buildings of enemy soldiers. All their lives they had lived and fought in such surroundings. There were few who could match their fighting skill, and backed by their Guardians, they were truly a force to be reckoned with.

The Janissaire had been formed into nine squads of fifty. Two would remain and secure the docks while five squads, taking one street per squad, would clear a path to the beleaguered defenders. The remaining two squads would be a reserve force, called forward should any one street prove to be too heavily defended.

My companions and I had been placed with one of the reserve squads. The enemy had expected help to come to the defenders from the plains around Lyram, not from the sea, as the Corsairs had swept all the shipping into harbours and then blockaded them until the town or city fell. It was obvious that the Eligere wanted as many vessels taken intact as possible.

Only an advanced force of Navealozans, backed by Brigands and Scavengers, made up the forces already on the Plains. The Scavengers and Brigands had risen on word from the Navealozans. They had cut communications between cities and towns and spread rumours that many of the towns had fallen or surrendered. The Corsairs had then blockaded the harbours and cut off food and help to those cities and towns holding out against the attackers.

Once all this was accomplished, the Navealozans, using captured vessels, began to cross the Uskery to reinforce their allies. Many of the Ayahs had to be forcibly secured below deck as their fear of large bodies of water was almost driving them mad.

They had but to keep the remaining forces bottled up in the towns and cities, until the bulk of the Navealozans finished in Thay and marched north to aid them. The Eligere had been keeping their forces in reserve, should Nuevah send troops to aid their southern neighbours.

Our troops found only little resistance as they cut a path across the city towards our comrades. In the process, our forces had come upon several large groups of soldiers, captured and interned, who were to be sold later as slaves or used as manual labourers. These men were freed and armed with the weapons from the dead enemy. By the time we reached the defenders in the free section of the city, our numbers had trebled.

Our troops were billeted and given food from the meagre supplies which remained. I was taken to the Ambassador's residence.

All my old friends were there. I greeted them with tears.

The Ambassadors greeted each other formally and then embraced, as old friends should.

'You are welcome, my friend,' the Ambassador of Lyram stated. 'The troops you brought are sorely needed, as most of the city has surrendered itself to those scum on the plains.'

'Then why do you stay?' I asked.

'Where else is there to go?' he answered.

'Home,' I told him.

Our discussion was interrupted by the arrival of the Prince. 'It is good to see you again, Teal. Tell me of your mission.'

I told him and my old friends all that had happened since we parted. I introduced Reya, Beth and Rhyhl to them and told them of the aid they had given us, and of our losses. When I was finished the Prince rose and stood before us.

'From what you have told us here today, and what we have learnt from prisoners taken, I believe the replacing of the Talisman was the turning point in the war for the remaining free people of all the lands. The Eligere are still a force to be reckoned with, but with the loss of the extra powers they had gained by the theft of the Talisman, their strength has been severely set back.'

He placed a hand on my shoulder. 'I heard the word home as I entered. What were you discussing?' he asked.

'Why stay here and fight for a people who have already given up?' I asked. 'With us are nearly two and a half thousand fighters, either brought here or released from the enemy's slaves compounds. With the troops already here, we are more than a match for the forces holding this city.'

'You would have us escape the city and return home for help?' he asked.

'Yes,' I answered.

'We have the men to leave the city, and we can get the

food to feed them from small towns and villages; but what do we do when we come to the pass into the Erg?' the Prince asked.

'We will defeat the Wolves holding the pass and then cross the Erg,' I replied.

'Then,' the Prince said, 'there will be no more supplies once we leave the pass; most of the troops will have to be left there. The Tribesmen of the Erg will know about the trouble down here and will be ready to take advantage of it. With the number of troops away, and those used to block the pass, it is my opinion our families will be at this moment fighting for their very lives. If we travel to Nuevah, it will be to aid our families, not to ask for help from them. From this time on, it will be up to us to do the aiding. We are the only large force unopposed in all the lands.'

All in the room were silent. Those Vahians present believed, like myself, that Nuevah would be safe, and it would be the force to end this war. None of us had thought about what the Prince had just told us, yet each man hearing it realised the truth of it.

'What can we do?' the Ambassador of Lyram asked.

'What can we do?' the Prince repeated, conviction ringing in his rising voice, 'We are going to clear this city and the lands surrounding it of the refuse that infests it!' He paused to allow the cheering to die down. 'Then we are going to take this army of ours and free every city, town and village of the Plains!' More cheering erupted. 'There is no force which can stand before us! If we strike fast and hard, we will have an army at our back to match any the Navealozans can throw at us.'

Word spread throughout the city, as did the provisions we brought with us. With new hope, the defenders pushed outwards. The enemy fell back continually. When they held their ground, they found themselves under attack by men wearing strange armour, who used wedge-like swords with great skill. The Perduans were wreaking havoc in the buildings, and our renewed troops pushed the enemy from the streets. Within days the city was ours.

The Prince had us gathered in the large conference room at the Ambassador's residence. 'The east is too strongly defended. To the north are the Cordilleras—impassable. Behind the enemy and to the east is the Todismal Forest—impossible to move large bodies of troops through. To the south is the Uskery—still controlled by the Corsairs. The only approach is from the west, either across the Wastelands or at Esherweld. The strongest concentration of troops is to be found along the Esherweld River. We must be in a better position before we attempt the east.

'With this in mind, I intend turning our forces north, using the Wyernt River for fresh water, supply transport, and messages.'

We took Merbah and Boarric.

Boarric was an old garrison town, but it fell easily to our advancing forces with the aid of the town's people. Once the enemy had been cleared, the Prince set up his headquarters there. The Navealozans were landing in force in the east. Lyram was a thorn in their side. No matter what the enemy threw at it, the city would not surrender. The Prince had withdrawn all the troops that we had brought to Lyram, to Merbah and Boarric, as well as all the Vahians and their Janissaire.

All those freed by our troops in the clearing of Lyram had stayed to bolster the troops who were already there. They also had the crews of the eleven ships which carried us there, and the Thayian marines. The Corsairs had again blockaded the harbour, so there was no way for them to leave.

We received a courier from the town of Liechen. The

town's people aided by the people of the surrounding lands who for generations had fought the Natives of the Wastelands, had turned their attention to the invaders, and had swept the enemy from the town.

The people of Liechen had heard of the Prince's advance from the coast and had offered their town as another stepping stone for the Prince's army, which had doubled in size since striking out from Lyram.

Troops were sent to Liechen, under Kyle, while Kryss was in Merbah helping with the defences. The Ambassador to Thayik was to hold Boarric. It was hoped the Ambassador in Lyram could continue to hold the city until help could be spared to send to him.

'I intend,' the Prince told us, 'to take the Janissaire and cross the western plain and reinforce the coastal town of Holsmer. Once we have this town, we will control the southern half of the Western Plains. Teal, I want you and your companions to go with me.'

Holsmer was a town of average size. Its isolated location had kept it from the attention of the advancing enemy, but if the Eligere did intend to sail the Great Western Ocean, then Holsmer would be their target. From there, they could strike anywhere they wished.

The town greeted us, and especially the Prince, with great enthusiasm. They too had watched the enemy army creep closer to them each day.

'Teal, I have another role for you,' the Prince said. 'The five towns and cities which we hold are easily defendable and contain large stocks of food. What I need you to do is ride north, past Carnnoc, to the lands of the Free Vahians. If they can strike the enemy from the north while we have them cut off from their forces and supplies, then I believe they will surrender. If, however, it is as I fear, and you find them under siege and unable to help us, then ride further north. Try to make it to the Capital.' He pulled a ring from his finger and passed it to me. 'My father gave me this ring when I graduated from the Collegium. My sister will recognise it and hopefully aid you. You are to tell her all you know of Raimend's treachery, and that I am alive.'

'Then, you think they will be able to send help?' I asked.

'No, I doubt they will be able to help us, but the news of the Regent's crimes may help Nuevah to survive. They have to rid themselves of that killer and be ready to defend themselves. The Eligere will not stop here. I believe they intend to rule all the lands.'

28

THE VRIJBANE

'IT'S going to be very difficult to make our way through the enemy forces in the north,' Ransyn said. 'This is just the type of manoeuvre they will be expecting us to make.' He walked to the window of the room and looked out across the open plain to the east. 'We hold much of the south, but the enemy gain in strength as we weaken. They know we will seek aid, and, it can only come from the north.'

'Their patrols are going to be numerous and alert,' Lyn added. 'They can't afford to let us find help. If we do, they know they will have no chance, trapped between us and the forces which will arrive from the north.'

I took a piece of cheese from the platter in the centre of the table, and taking a bite from it, walked across the room to the second window.

'That is why we are not going to travel overland,' I told them.

'What other way is there?' Lyn asked.

I took another bite of cheese. 'I intend to take a ship north to Whalestrone.'

Ransyn and Lyn slowly turned to look at one another and then finally at me. There were looks of disbelief on their faces, and I couldn't say I blamed them. Since the increase of the monsters in the Great Western Ocean, no vessel which had left any of the western ports had ever been seen again. But it would be different for us: we had a Caller.

'With the use of Rhyhl's Caller ability, we will be able to travel north in relative safety, keeping well out from the coast to avoid Plastrons. At Whalestrone we can buy horses, and send messages to the Princess and to Danel's father, explaining what we have learnt. The letter to the Princess will contain the ring the Prince has given to me. Then, with the messengers safely on their way, we can ride southward to the Free State and present our plea for aid to the Free Vahians,' I explained.

'Are you sure Rhyhl has the strength to ward off the dangers for so long a journey?' Ransyn asked. Lyn also seemed concerned that our newest travelling companion would not be strong enough to ward off the larger creatures all the way to Whalestrone.

'I have mentioned my idea to Rhyhl. He says it would be impossible for him to protect the vessel continuously, but if he is warned of an approaching creature he will be able to erect a barrier which will repel any creature of any size, and he will be able to hold it for a considerable time if need be.'

'Who would be needed for this mission?' Ransyn asked. He crossed to the table containing the platter of food. He, like the rest of us, had been given new clothing, having lost his Janissaire tabard weeks ago. His new tabard was black, and showed no rank or embellishments. The Prince had thought it best not to announce what province we were from.

Ransyn's problem was that he feared he would be left

behind because he lacked a ring. He did not realise he was needed for his other skills, skills which had saved us on many occasions.

'You will be one, Ransyn. Your knowledge of the lands we are to travel will be needed. Rhyhl will keep the creatures at bay, while Beth is to ensure we have a continual favourable wind. Rafe's Healing and Reya's Stealth abilities may also prove useful.' I turned towards Lyn. 'You will also be needed—a Weaver is always a good edge to have.' I again turned my attention to the ocean, this time taking in the size of the waves as they crashed against the north shore of the harbour. 'Lobito will not be coming with us. I believe he would come for his sister's protection, if asked, but I will not ask him to come. He will be too hard to disguise, and he does not speak the language well enough yet.'

'What about Elred?' Lyn asked.

'I have not yet decided. I would like him to accompany us, but we will have no need for a Speaker where we are going. On the other hand, the Prince will need to know how we are progressing and with Elred here we will be able to inform him through dreams.'

'I do not think Elred will agree with you about that,' Ransyn said, and gave a small laugh. 'He has travelled far, and I think he would like to travel further.'

'I will see him alone. I am sure I can persuade him to remain behind.'

Elred was not persuaded that remaining behind was his best role. He felt that if his Speaker ability was not needed, then at least his swordsmanship would gain him a place on the mission. Beth, Reya and Rafe had been practising at every spare moment. Reya was quite able to defend herself without the use of her powers. Beth, though totally untrained in weapon handling, was picking up the use of

296

weapons at an incredible rate, another reason to believe that the Eligere and the Vahians were cousins. Rafe was, however, not destined to be a swordsman, nor, it would seem, a fighter of any description.

Lobito agreed to remain behind. He was to form a company of Ayah made up of freed slaves, captured from the enemy. At first it was thought they would fight with their people, but it seemed many of them were sold by neighbours or sent north to slavery by so-called friends, when they disagreed with the alliance between the Navealozans and the Eligere.

Elred was to accompany us. I had wished for him to journey with us, but did not have sufficient reason to ask him. I had grown close to the bondsman in the time we had travelled together. While in Lyram, I had approached Ardemus about releasing Elred. Ardemus had agreed, but the law insisted a bondsman could only be sold, not freed, until his indenture was done, or his debt was repaid.

I had agreed to buy out Elred's bond—the cost was set by the local authorities, who even in times of war, still functioned. Instead of money, I gave Ardemus the aor and cuirass I had taken in Perdu. As a collector of weapons Ardemus was delighted with the payment. His excitement over the weapon and armour was incredible.

'I am probably the only person in the Lands of the Plains to have antiques such as these in his possession,' he had claimed excitedly.

All the while he had been talking I was watching from the corner of my eye the gathering of a group of Perduans. Their cuirass showed signs of battle, but the men seemed unhurt. They still wore the large helmets, and from every hip hung an aor. I hoped Ardemus was not too upset when he found he was the only non-Perduan with such antiques, and that there was an entire race of people who still used these weapons.

The Silver Sail was the largest tavern on the Holsmerian waterfront. It was built in the shape of a capital letter H. The centre area was the kitchen. The city side housed the stables and store rooms. The harbour side contained a small tap room and several rooms which were used by lesser Captains when in harbour.

Lyn, Rhyhl and myself were there to hire a vessel and crew capable of taking us north to Nuevah. All we had met with so far was disbelief. No one could believe we actually wished to travel the Great Western Ocean. There were many vessels in the harbour, but most were without Captains or crew, and those which had a crew did not wish to venture away from the shelter of the harbour. It looked like we might have to find a skilled Captain and crew from amongst the army.

After having no luck in the tap room, we decided on a drink before moving on to the next establishment. We ordered drinks from the landlord, which he brought us, along with some advice. 'There may be one who'd take your money, though I'd put no trust in the man myself. I didn't mention him earlier, as I thought you'd be able to do better.'

'There seems to be no one who wants our money,' Ransyn said, possibly a little louder than he should have. 'I had heard those who sailed from Holsmer were men to be reckoned with. Obviously I have heard wrong.'

Several of the drinkers began to stand, while more stopped drinking and silently scrutinised the black-shrouded talker. Ransyn's black hair was now quite long, and held back by a band of gold, the one I had taken from the dead Guardian in Perdu. As well as the black tabard, he wore high black boots and a wide weapon belt. Hanging from the belt was a new cavalry sabre, and on the opposite side was the Eligere stiletto I acquired at the river in Navealoza. I had no need for it, so I had given it to

Ransyn. The beautifully worked and bejewelled grip of the stiletto stood out in stark contrast to Ransyn's garb.

Lyn was dressed in the same way, except his dagger was not as fancy, and his kris had the basket hilt favoured by the Eligere. I was wearing a light, loose-flowing robe, which completely covered my armour and tabard. My swords hung from either hip; a knife bought to replace the one Tomas gave me after we had fled Dienall was in a special sheath attached to my left boot.

One of the customers was about to speak when three men walked through the front door into the tap room. 'That's the one you seek,' the landlord said. 'When you stopped for a drink instead of leaving, I sent my son for him. I hope you don't mind.'

Ransyn waved a hand above his shoulder, dismissing the landlord. The three who had just entered turned their attention towards us. One was tall and thin, with a womanish air about him, the other two looked like common down-on-their-luck seamen.

'Are you the gentlemen seeking to hire a ship?' the tall thin fellow asked. His voice was soft, and sounded more like that of a woman than a sea Captain.

'Yes,' I answered. The customers had seated themselves and were returning to their drinks. Many still stared at Ransyn with open anger.

'This way, gentlemen,' the thin man said. 'I have a private table.'

The table was in a secluded corner. Even during the day the table was cast in shadows.

'Be seated, gentlemen. I am Captain Carney and these are two of my crew,' he said, waving at the two who stood at either side of him. 'How may I be of service to you?'

'We need a ship to take us north, past the enemy forces at Carnnoc. We will travel well out to sea to lessen the chance of Plastron attacks,' I told him. Ransyn and Lyn had positioned themselves beside me, each facing one of the crewmen.

'What about the large creatures which frequent the deeper waters?' he asked.

'They will be no problem—I have a member of my party who can guarantee they will not bother us in any way.'

'That is indeed a useful person; is it possible you know of others who are able to . . . guarantee this?' He gave a half-smile which drew up the right side of his mouth, but even as he smiled, his eyes remained the same: cold and calculating.

'No, I know of no other,' I answered. The more I saw of this fellow the more I began to dislike him. Any other time I would have left the tavern and sought another Captain elsewhere, but time was short.

'How many will there be in your party, and who?' he asked, again showing the half-smile. Before he could continue, Ransyn interrupted.

'There will be eight, and who they are is of no concern of yours, . . . friend.'

'Captain!' one of the seamen growled, taking a half-pace forward. 'It's Captain Carney to the likes of you.'

Ransyn continued without even glancing at the one who had spoken. 'All you have to do is take us where you're told; and that's all.' Now he looked up at the seaman, who had stepped forward. 'Friend.'

The seaman's hand dropped to the hilt of his knife. His companion followed suit. Ransyn and Lyn both reached for their weapons. Carney seemed quite content to let the four come to grips, but I had other plans.

While Ransyn and Lyn both wore the light, Janissaire mail coats beneath their tabards, beneath mine I was wearing the heavy Vahian scale mail. Raising my right arm, I brought my first down hard on the table between us. My fist was empty and clenched. Carney looked down at it and noted the heavy mail glove.

He raised one hand and the two seamen stepped back and removed their hands from their weapons. 'Do not worry,' he said, 'I would have stopped it before either of your men were hurt too badly.'

'My only worry,' I answered, 'is that I would not have been able to stop it before both of your men were dead.'

He regarded me for several minutes before speaking. 'I think this will be an interesting voyage. My ship is the *Vrijbane*. You will find boats waiting to take you out to her tomorrow morning, three hours before the high tide—if that is suitable.'

'It is,' I nodded. 'And the cost?'

Carney seemed to study his hands for several minutes. 'Four silver pieces per head,' he answered. 'Payable once you are aboard.' Rising from the table, I turned and walked towards the door of the Tavern. Ransyn and Lyn kept a careful watch on our Captain and his men. We stepped out into the street. The air was fresh and cool compared to the stuffiness of the Silver Sail's tap room.

'Do you trust him?' Lyn asked.

'He will probably take our money and then once out of sight of land, try to feed us to the fish—or something worse.'

'What did he say his ship was called, . . . the *Very Jane*?' Lyn asked.

'The *Vrijbane*,' I told him.

'It's from a little used coastal language,' Ransyn added. 'Men of smaller fishing villages use it when discussing prices in company when they do not want strangers to know the outcome. Loosely translated, Vrijbane means unhindered or unowned destroyer.'

'I think Captain Carney is right,' Lyn said. 'This *is* going to be an interesting voyage.'

When we returned to our lodgings, we found unexpected but welcome guests.

'Well, you certainly have changed since we parted company,' Jon said. 'For the good, it seems.'

'I didn't know you were in the city,' I said.

'I knew you were here. There are not too many Vahians who carry twin swords. Though when they described the swords I thought I had been mistaken. Where did you get such fine-looking swords?'

'I lost one of my original pair and broke the other. I found these in Perdu when we visited it the second time.'

'From what the Prince has told me, you did a fine piece of work there. Now where are we off to this time?'

I explained the mission and my idea to him. He was silent until I told him the name of the Captain we had hired.

'Carney! I have never met him but I have heard things about him. You are sure there are no other vessels you can hire? A raft crewed by three monkeys would be better than Carney and the *Vrijbane*. You know what that means, don't you?'

'Yes, Ransyn told me. But we have no choice; time is short, and he is willing. We will just have to keep both eyes on him at all times,' I answered.

'I may be able to help you there,' he said.

The longboats were waiting as arranged, with a motley assortment of seamen to help with the luggage.

We decided that the best way to hide was to be obvious. We were all dressed in frills and finery and looked the part of rich travellers out for an adventurous voyage. I was the first to climb from the longboat. As my companions reached the deck of the ship, I introduced them to the Captain.

'Captain Carney, I would like to present my sister, Beth and her husband, Rhyhl.'

Carney bowed and took Beth's hand in his and raised it to his lips. He did not seem to kiss the hand; rather his lips seemed only to brush the skin. 'A pleasure to be of service, my Lady. I hope you did not find the trip out to the ship too tiring.'

Beth was dressed in a long gown of flame red silk. Her neck was circled in white lace, and a belt of pearls hung from around her trim waist. 'Unfortunately, the trip was tiring and quite horrid. I would like to be shown to my cabin now if you please.' She turned from the Captain, and waving for her 'husband' Rhyhl to follow her, began to make her way below decks.

'First Officer!' Carney called. 'Show the Lady Beth to her cabin, and if there is anything she requires, provide it for her.'

Carney now looked at the rest of the party.

'This is my sister's maid, Reya.' Reya bowed slightly and ran off after Beth. 'This is our linguist, Elred and our physician, Rafe. You have already met our men at arms,' I said, pointing to each of them in turn.

'And these?' Carney asked, pointing to the last two members. 'I remember you saying there were eight in your party, surely these two make ten?'

'These are simply servants my sister picked up in Holsmer. They can stay with your crew and work their passage if you like,' I answered.

'Excellent—good crewmen are hard to find. Most have left for the Uskery Sea, and those who remain are not worth the money they want.'

Jon and Tryell were led away by the ship's bosun. We would not see them till we reached our destination, but Jon believed it would be safer that way. With some of our people in amongst the crew, we might pick up any sign of trouble long before it would normally become evident.

The wind that time of year blew steadily from the south-west, so once clear of the harbour, we began to increase speed. I sat in the stern cabin which had been put aside for Beth. Rhyhl was beside me. I began to search the surrounding ocean for signs of any creatures, but there was nothing close by.

The first evening out of harbour, there was an accident in the rigging. One of the crewmen fell to the deck. He was not seriously injured, but his arm was broken in at least three places. Rafe was soon beside the injured man. He took him below, and began the process of resetting the arm. It took most of the night before Rafe was again seen on deck.

'How is he?' Lyn asked.

'I saved the arm, and he'll be fine in a few days with rest, though he won't have use of the arm for a few weeks,' Rafe answered. 'There was a bit of trouble with some of the crew.'

'How so?' I asked.

'It seems many of the crew are Thayians, and they know enough to realise that if I were a physician, as I am meant to be, then the only way I could have healed him was to remove his arm—it was too badly broken for a normal physician to save.'

'It's a pity there are Thayians on board, but you did what you felt was right. Ransyn will stay outside your cabin tonight. We don't want you to have any . . . accidents.'

There were no accidents, but a few of the crew were found wandering where they weren't supposed to be, although Ransyn soon convinced them it was not healthy to be in that particular part of the ship.

On only a few occasions over the next three days did Rhyhl

have to use his abilities to deter creatures large enough to damage the ship. Each time I was able to give him adequate warning so he could set his wards in place. None of the monsters were seen, though once a huge fin was spotted and I sensed a fanatical driving hunger.

On the third day, while closer inshore than we had been so far on the voyage, smoke was sighted rising from the east, presumably from the coast, somewhere inside the Free States.

'Could they see us from the coast? Is it a signal of some kind?' Beth asked.

'No. I doubt they can see us. It is probably the results of a skirmish with either Plastrons or Tribesmen of the Erg and nothing to do with us at all,' Ransyn answered.

'We could go closer if you wish,' he added.

'Yes, I think we will. Have the Captain change course and take us in closer to the shore,' I told him, then, turning to Rhyhl, 'I know your abilities work on Plastrals and larger creatures, but what about Plastrons?'

'As long as the creature is not too intelligent, I will be able to manipulate it,' Rhyhl said.

'If that's the case, then you should be able to manipulate most of the crew,' Lyn laughed.

By the time we gained sight of the coast, the smoke could no longer be seen.

'Whatever caused it has gone,' Ransyn said. He had a large telescope, and was studying the coastline with interest.

'Can you recognise anything?' I asked.

'Maybe—I can't be certain. I've never viewed this area from out to sea before,' he answered.

'Anything of interest?'

We turned, and found Carney standing behind us. He had his two men with him as he always did.

'No, there seems to be nothing there,' I answered.

'Shall I go in closer?' he asked. If he gave me his half-smile again, I was sure I'd wipe it from his face.

'No, that won't be necessary.'

Later that day Reya approached me. 'I took a look around below deck as you suggested. It is quite dark down there so I wasn't seen.' I glanced down at her hand and saw the ring. 'It seems there is something going on. What exactly I don't know, but it has to do with Rhyhl and Rafe. I think they have seen Rhyhl at work warding off some creature. I get the idea he is to be taken and Rafe killed. But that is only an impression I got—I heard nothing definite, just hints.'

'That's good enough for me. Tell everyone I want them in Beth's cabin in twenty minutes. Tell them to make sure they come armed,' I told her. She nodded, and rushed off to tell the others.

'What's the problem?' Ransyn asked, as I entered Beth's cabin. I was the last to arrive; the rest were seated, waiting for an explanation.

'Reya has been doing a little listening. It seems the crew are not happy with Rafe, and are planning something special for him. The Captain, I have found, is very happy with what Rhyhl is able to do. He plans on making him an offer the first chance he gets—an offer Rhyhl won't be able to refuse.'

'What are we to do?' Beth asked.

'We wait till the Whitlow scum try something, and then we kill them all and burn this ship around their ears. That's what we do,' Reya answered angrily. She looked around for agreement and then, realising what she had said, she actually blushed. 'I didn't mean . . . ' she began, but was interrupted by the laughter which exploded from the rest of us.

'Don't you think it may be an idea to leave the ship

before we think of burning it?' Elred asked, as he placed a hand on her shoulder.

There was a tapping at the door. Everyone reached for a weapon, but I waved them to stop. We were far too packed into the room to try to fight. I signalled for Reya to see who was there.

'It's your friend, Jon, and he's with two others,' she said.

'Open the door,' I told her.

'You have to hurry,' Jon said. 'The crew have persuaded the Captain that Rhyhl should stay with the vessel and Rafe should die. They are planning to kill the rest of you. They will be here soon. If not for this fellow,' Jon continued, pointing to the man whose arm Rafe had saved, 'the first Tryell and I would have known about it would have been when we were helping them throw your bodies over the side.'

29

PLASTRONS

THE crew were noticeably absent when we reached the deck. Jon, Tryell and Lee, the injured crewman, began to swing the longboat out, and prepared to lower it to just above the water. The ship was hardly moving, and we were dangerously close to the shore. Details of the coast could be made out without the use of a telescope, especially the waves breaking on the numerous shoals, any one of which was capable of tearing the bottom out of the *Vrijbane*.

All the equipment was thrown into the boat as it disappeared over the side. Before anyone could climb aboard, there was a shout and the crew began to swarm from the forward hatches. They were carrying cutlasses and boarding axes, and a few were armed with pikes. Carney was now on the bridge, surrounded by men. He was calling orders to his crew.

'Let none escape save the husband. I want him alive and unhurt. Should any ill befall him, the guilty one will live to regret his mistake.'

Rafe, Lee, and Tryell helped Beth into the boat while

the rest of us threw off our cloaks and prepared to meet the attack of the crew. At first, the sight of so many armed and armoured men seemed to take the fight out of the crew, but the Captain began to yell fresh orders and the crew responded.

'I have put up with that one long enough,' Ransyn snarled, pointing with his sabre to the Captain yelling from the bridge, 'and I'm going to do something about it. Right now.'

He drew his stiletto and charged the surprised crew. Lyn and Elred followed him. The crew was disturbed by the sudden attack and fell back. Just as they were regaining some semblance of order, Jon, Rhyhl, and myself attacked. The fight continued for some time, the crewmen not having the skill needed to best us.

They outnumbered us, and we were forced from the side of the vessel to the stern. It was obvious it was going to be very costly for the crew to kill us, and many were beginning to hang back.

Suddenly a scream was heard above the din of combat. The scream was long, and was cut off before it reached its climax. The crew turned at the sound and found themselves confronted by five creatures straight from their darkest nightmares. Plastrons. Four of the huge grey-scaled creatures were climbing over the side rail to the deck of the *Vrijbane*. The fifth Plastron held the remains of a crewman—the broken and bloodied body, almost unrecognisable as that of the remains of a human being, was casually thrown from the vessel.

Water dripped from the scaled creatures as they slowly began to advance across the deck towards the terrified crew.

One of the Plastrons seized a frozen crewman by the throat and crotch, and with a gigantic throw, sent him spinning from the vessel well out towards the shore. None of the creatures were armed, but that did not stop them from attacking the armed crew. They waded into the crew, throwing bodies, and portions of bodies to left and right. The creatures towered over the stricken crew by at least three feet, and their strength was beyond measure. The crew fought back desperately, but in vain. Nothing could stand against the Plastrons, as they passed from a battle rage into a feeding frenzy.

'Quickly—this way!' I called.

I sensed a feeling of safety from the stern of the vessel. Running to the rail, I looked over and saw the longboat with the rest of the party still aboard. They were busily fighting off smaller creatures, similar to the Plastrons; their young.

Beth had managed to light a small torch and was keeping the creatures at bay with it. Tryell and Lee had erected the sail of the boat. Rafe was waving for us to climb down to them.

'Over the rail,' I called. 'Don't jump—use the rope. There are creatures in the water which may not be strong, but they are quite capable of drowning a tired, armoured man.'

While Ransyn and I watched to ensure we were not surprised by either Plastrons or crew, the remainder of the party slid down the rope into the waiting longboat. As we were about to join them, a Plastron charged through the remaining crew and rushed straight towards us. Its huge mouth was gaping, revealing triangular bloodied teeth, and its arms were covered in blood to the elbows.

Ransyn and I separated to confuse the creature, but this worked only momentarily, as the Plastron turned and charged me. I ducked beneath its outstretched hands and stepped out of its path. The creature hit the railing with a crash, and it looked to me as if the Plastron was going to topple over the rail, and fall into the waiting longboat. But the rail held, and the creature turned. Again it rushed me. Again I stepped to one side. This time I flicked out my right sword as the creature passed.

There was a cry of pain which turned to rage as the Plastron grasped the stump of its left arm. The hand of the creature was on the deck at its feet. Slowly the Plastron turned, and began to move towards me. It moved slowly, to make sure I did not evade it this time.

Something whistled through the air, and struck the creature just below what would be its ear. The creature cried out again and turned to face the new source of pain, Ransyn. The stiletto could be clearly seen protruding from its head. The creature attacked, and Ransyn tried to do as I had done, but he was not quite quick enough, and the creature caught him on the shoulder and knocked him across the deck.

As the Plastron turned back towards me, I rushed towards it and threw myself at its good arm. Both swords were dropped, as I scrambled to get a hold on the creature's wet hide. I had wrapped my legs around the creature's right arm, with both hands locked under its throat. Its left hand was gone, but it was still striking me with the stump, trying to knock me from my precarious perch.

From the corner of my eye, I saw Ransyn slowly rising to his feet shaking his head groggily. I released one hand from the creature's throat, and I was instantly drawn towards the gaping mouth. I reached down, and wrapped my hand around the hilt of my knife. Then, drawing it from its sheath, I drove it into the right eye of the Plastron.

I was thrown across the deck, and ended in a heap next to Ransyn. The Plastron was charging about the stern, its remaining hand grasping at the knife, trying to pull it from its eye.

'Erebus! What creature can take a wound like that and still live?' Ransyn cried in awe.

'I don't think this is the place to call upon Erebus the Devourer of Souls, nor is it the time to question the strength of the Plastrons. I suggest you get yourself over the railing and into the waiting longboat.'

As he lowered himself towards the boat, the Plastron finally succumbed to the wound I had given it. With a crash it fell to the deck and stopped moving. Ransyn was climbing into the boat, and the other Plastrons were still interested in the remainder of the crew defending the bridge. I slipped across to the creature, and removed Ransyn's stiletto from the still body. My knife was stuck firm, and no amount of effort would free it. So I left it there, and stepping to the rail, climbed over and slid down the rope into the waiting arms of my friends.

Beth increased the slight breeze into a wind which filled the sail. Soon we were racing towards shore, Jon steering us between the shoals. The Plastrons and the *Vrijbane* were left well astern.

'I did not know whether there were any Plastrons between us and the shore, so I took no chances and placed a warding about the vessel,' Rhyhl explained, as we reached the safety of the shore. 'The older creatures are beyond my power to ward off, but the females and young are easy enough to repel.'

'Good, I want you to keep watch with Elred while we salvage what we can from the boat and set up camp,' I told him. He nodded, and walked off to find Elred.

There were several water casks and a large waxed box of biscuits in the longboat. As well as these, we took the sail to use as an awning, and a length of rope. Each of us carried a light blanket, and a small packet containing dried rations—not very edible, but sustaining. Apart from these few things, we had only our weapons and armour.

'How far are we from the closest outpost, do you think?'

Lyn asked, as he stared into the east. 'I wish we had brought that telescope along.'

'Here, try this,' Lee said. His left arm was still strapped across his chest, and his right carried the small canvas sack he brought with him when he warned Jon of the impending danger. He placed the canvas sack on the ground and opened it. He then offered a small telescope to Lyn.

Lyn thanked him, and took the telescope and began to quarter the southern horizon. After this, he searched to the north, east and finally to the west. 'The *Vrijbane* is underway. It looks like they managed to beat off the attack, though I wouldn't have thought it possible.'

All eyes turned westward after hearing this. The *Vrijbane* was hardly visible on the horizon, and was soon gone from sight.

'If the Plastrons are no longer busy with Carney and his crew, I think it would be advisable to move further inland,' I told them. They agreed, and soon we were moving inland carrying all we had in the way of equipment. Unfortunately, it wouldn't be enough if we did not find help.

Even though the Plastrons were afraid of fire, we agreed that the first night should be a cold camp. The canvas awning was set up as a windbreak for Beth and Reya, while the rest of us bedded down where we could. The wind was blowing in from the ocean bringing cooler weather with it.

'It doesn't snow this far north, does it?' Rafe asked.

'I've not heard of snow falling in these parts, but the further east we travel the closer we get to the Cordilleras, and those ranges are always covered in a blanket of snow,' Ransyn answered. 'If this wind keeps up, the weather is going to get much colder. First thing in the morning, we should travel further inland, and try to find a place to hole up in, out of this cutting wind.'

Our sentries were set and the rest of us were soon rolled in our rather inadequate blankets trying to get some sleep. The night was the coldest I could remember—the wind seemed to find even the smallest opening in clothing or bedding. I woke several times during the night—each time I was awoken by the chattering of my teeth.

At last the night ended, and we dragged ourselves from our beds in the hope of catching the warming rays of the morning sun. Our equipment was quickly packed, and we again set off east. As the sun rose higher, we began to shake the chill from our bodies.

'I don't care if there are hundreds of those devils about tonight. I'm not going another night without a fire,' Ransyn declared, as he rubbed feeling back into his fingers.

It was almost midday when Rafe, who had been scouting ahead with Ransyn, rushed back to us. 'There is a group of people a short distance ahead of us in some kind of trouble. Ransyn has gone ahead to help them.'

'What type of trouble?' I asked, dropping my bedroll.

'Some kind of fight, I didn't see it. He just called back. I was to fetch you, and he was going down to help them,' Rafe answered.

'All right. Rafe, you and Lee bring up the equipment. Beth, you and Jon and Tryell watch over them. The rest of you come with me.' I began to run in the direction from which Rafe had come. I could sense that Elred, Lyn, Rhyhl and Reya were right behind me.

We came to a small crest. The sounds of fighting could be heard coming from beyond it. When we reached the top we saw a group of wagons bunched in front of a large cluster of rocks, with people fighting all around them. Gear was strewn everywhere, and a large fire was burning in the middle of what looked to be a camp site.

Ransyn in his distinct black tabard was fighting his way

in towards the rocks. We hurried down the slope to lend a hand in the fighting.

As soon as we were off the slope, a number of the attackers turned their attention to us. They were obviously deserters. You could smell them long before they got within sword reach, and they were wearing scraps of armour, probably taken from those they had ambushed. At first, they swarmed around us yelling and laughing. After three of their number died, they stopped laughing. The next five deaths brought an end to the yelling. Three more, and they turned and ran.

We kept after them, cutting down another seven before they reached their friends. We began to fight our way towards the rocks where Ransyn had last been seen. By the time we reached Ransyn, the enemy were giving us a wide berth.

The rocks were full of women and children. A few men protected the only entrance.

'They were ambushed,' Ransyn shouted above the noise. 'They only had a few defenders, and most fell to the first wave. If not for the protection of these rocks, they would all be dead by now.'

There was another outbreak of yells, and we looked up and saw Beth and the others had come over the ridge, into sight.

'Quickly,' called one woman. 'Your friends will need your help.'

'I doubt it,' I answered. Beth was leading the others down the slope. She was carrying a lit torch. Even as we watched, the wind began to pick up, blowing dust across the open area into the eyes of the attackers. Beth continued to walk calmly towards the deserters. One of them, a great fat man covered in sections of chain mail tied together with scraps of leather, grabbed a burning brand from the fire and called out to those around him.

'If the bitch wants to play with fire, then let's oblige her.' He waved the brand over his head, and his men cried out in agreement.

Beth was quite close by now. Without stopping, she raised her left hand and pointed at the fat man. Suddenly the brand in the man's hand erupted. A great ball of flame consumed it and the fat man, who began to run about screaming. The deserters were horrified as they watched their leader fall to the ground, engulfed by flames and writhing in pain. Finally his screams stopped, and he became still.

The wind had resumed once more, and her long hair was being blown about her face. The flames from the torch she carried had lengthened, and resembled a burning sword. She raised it, and whirled it around her head, then, as the wind dropped, she pointed it at the deserters and screamed.

Weapons dropped from trembling fingers as the deserters fought each other in their efforts to flee. Beth continued into the camp, the burning torch extended, the wind once more howling about her. Many of the women were mumbling prayers of protection, and children began to cry.

When the last of the deserters disappeared from sight, Beth extinguished the torch and allowed the wind to drop. Jon and the others walked over to the scattered fire and dropped the bedrolls they had been carrying. Ransyn looked down at the now smouldering fire, and then looked back to Beth. She glanced at the coals and instantly there was a blazing fire, which Ransyn began to feed with pieces of timber from a nearby pile.

'I knew she would have her uses eventually,' he said, and laughed.

The laugh turned into a howl as the fire reached out and caressed his armoured seat. Ransyn began to tear off his tabard in an effort to remove the heated armour, much to the amusement of all. Finally, the offending armour was removed, and Ransyn also began to laugh.

'With the bodies cleared away, this depression is the perfect camp site,' Gayle, one of the women, told us. 'The hollow escapes the wind, and there is a small spring located in the rock cluster. This was why the wagoners decided to rest the teams here. We had no idea that rabble was following us. Once the wagons had been unhitched and everyone relaxed, the deserters attacked. We thought we were lost. Then we saw the dark-haired one approaching.'

'What are you doing in this desolate area?' I asked.

'Our men folk are serving at a post nearby. When word reached them that deserters and Scavengers were seen in the area, they sent men to fetch us,' she explained.

'They did not send many to escort all these people,' Ransyn said. There was a slight hint of anger in his voice.

'This is the third time we have been attacked. The other times we defended ourselves quite easily, but each time we lost several men. Now I fear we have only a few of the older men and children left.'

'How far do you have yet to travel?' Ransyn asked somewhat quieter.

'About twenty miles,' she answered.

Ransyn turned to me, but did not speak. 'We will escort you,' I told them. 'We will leave first thing in the morning.'

I left Gayle and Ransyn to work out the details of the move.

'Well,' Lyn asked.

'It seems that the Prince is correct: the Free Vahians have enough troubles of their own, without our problems as well. All we can do is get these families to safety, then head north to Nuevah. The Vahians are our only hope.'

30

WELCOME TO THE FREE STATES

THE oxen for the wagons were hidden in the rocky cluster, under a small overhang at the rear. The next morning the wagons were loaded and the oxen hitched. The Free States lacked the horses that the rest of Nuevah had in abundance. Any horses they did have were highly treasured, and used only as mounts for the Skirmishers and Lords. Oxen were used for all other aspects of transportation.

We had been pushing the oxen to their limits, in the hope of reaching the outpost before the deserters built up enough courage for another attack. The question was not so much whether they would attack, but rather when.

'The outpost is just over the next rise,' Gayle called. 'It is in the centre of a large depression, which keeps the wind out. There are sentry towers located around the rim of the depression, to give warning of any impending attack.'

'Then they will have noted our progress?' I asked.

'Most assuredly,' she answered.

'We have visitors,' Ransyn called. 'Those rabble have

worked up enough courage to give us another go.'

Reaching out behind us with my abilities, I sensed the rabble closing on us. 'It seems strange they would make an attempt when we are so close to the outpost. Surely the outpost will send out Skirmishers to aid us?' I asked.

'As soon as they sighted us from the sentry towers, I thought Skirmishers would have been dispatched,' she answered.

'What if they haven't seen us?' Ransyn asked. 'Suppose their sentry towers are not manned.'

'But the positions are always manned,' Gayle stated.

'Manned, yes. But by whom?' Ransyn asked.

I ordered the wagons to halt and sent Ransyn forward to investigate. He soon returned.

'The closest sentry tower is empty and half-burnt. There are at least a thousand men, surrounding what has to be the outpost, and from the looks of them they are either deserters, like our persistent friends, or a rather ragged advance force of the enemy,' he reported.

'So that's why the deserters picked this time to attack. It's them, not us, who will get aid from the outpost,' I answered. 'The families of these people are trapped behind their own walls, and we are trapped out here between two forces.'

'If we wait till dark, I can enter the outpost and they may be able to open a gap in the encircling forces long enough for us to pass through,' Reya said.

'I don't think our friends will give us till dark,' I told her, throwing a look over my shoulder at the growing dust cloud behind us. 'We have to move now, or we will be caught in the open by both forces.'

'But how do we get through all those troops?' Elred asked.

'First, empty the lead wagon, and spread its load

319

amongst the others. Then gather combustibles and bring them to me,' I told them.

With the oxen moving at their best possible speed, we crested the rim of the depression and started down the other side. The wind was almost immediately cut by the protecting rim, and there was a distinct difference in the vegetation. Where the grasses of the open areas had been brown and dry, the grass in the depression was lush and green.

The lead wagon was a considerable distance ahead of the rest, which were travelling bunched together. It was being driven by the fat deserter, who had led the group we chased off some time ago. Beside him was a ragged clothed deserter, with black hair held back by a golden band. A long cavalry sabre rested across his knees.

I was riding in the second wagon. We were midway down into the depression before the wagons were noticed by the besiegers of the outpost. Within a few minutes, a welcoming committee detached itself from the mass and rode towards the lead wagon.

The fat man was standing, pointing to the horizon behind him. His wagon drew to a halt but the rest of us continued. The welcoming committee had reached him by now, and having brought their mounts to a stop, had started a heated argument

As we passed them, I heard the man with the golden headband say, 'They are only about three miles behind us.'

'How many did you say there were?' one of the horsemen asked.

'Are you deaf as well as ugly?' the one wearing the gold headband shouted. 'There are five Vahians and at least three hundred of their boot-licking Skirmishers. Have you got it now?' Both raised their weapons but were stopped by another of the mounted men. 'Get the wagons past the outpost and over to the far side of the depression.'

'Shall we take the wagons in close to the walls, so the defenders can see who we have as entertainment for tonight?' the fat man asked.

'Yes, that's a good idea. It may make the boot-lickers sit up and take notice.'

'This wagon is full of treasures,' the gold-banded man said. He threw a wineskin to the leader of the mounted men, who raised the skin to his lips and took a long drink.

'That's good stuff!' he said.

'You're right there—what say I leave this wagon a bit apart from the others?' the gold-banded man said with a wink and a smile.

By now the wagons had passed the small group and their conversation was lost. Our wagons kept rolling towards the outpost. Now came the tricky part. If we were to gain entry to the outpost, they were going to have to believe we were truly who we said we were, and that we were here to help. If they waited for any length of time, we would be caught out here in the open and decimated.

A glance over my shoulder showed that the lead wagon had stopped and the driver and the passenger were walking after us. A large force of deserters had broken from the main force and was riding towards the rim. The dust from over the crest was much nearer now.

We were passing the gates of the outpost. The Skirmishers who manned its forward wall were silent as they watched their captured families drive past.

I stood and raised my arm, then I brought it down in a chopping motion. Our wagons turned towards the gates as Beth stood up in the rear wagon. She extended both arms towards the unattended stationary wagon, and it exploded in a shower of wooden splinters. We had placed several barrels of coal oil under the wineskins, and a lit lantern had been hanging from the tailgate of the wagon.

The fat man and his passenger broke into a run. The fat man shimmered and became the familiar form of Lyn. As they ran, Ransyn cast off the rags he had been wearing. Jon, Tryell, Elred and myself jumped from the wagons. Gayle stood in her wagon and began to call for the gates to be opened.

The deserters were still in confusion. Those who had ridden away did not know whether to meet the threat of the coming forces or return to see what was happening with the rest of their band. To make matters worse, all the mounts of the remaining deserters had begun to rear and throw their riders, thanks to Rhyhl.

The wagons were almost to the closed gates. If they were not opened soon, all this would have been for nothing. Finally the gates began to swing inwards just in time for the first wagon to enter. Lyn and Ransyn had reached us now, and we formed a line across the rear of the last wagon.

The second and third wagons had entered by the time some of the deserters realised what was happening. A sizable force began to move towards us. They were in groups of eight or so and held no formation, which was lucky for us. We clashed with one such group and dispatched them before a second approached.

All but one of the wagons were safely within the walls, and a unit of Skirmishers had positioned themselves at the gate to cover our flanks as we withdrew.

We were almost safe when Elred was hit in the chest by a bolt from a crossbow. Jon sheathed his weapon and scooped the wounded man into his arms. Tryell had stayed by his friend's side and was being attacked by four of the deserters. Stepping in to help, I slew one of them from the side, and killed the second with a thrust to the heart as he turned to face me.

Tryell had killed one of his attackers, but the second

had caught him in the chest with a blow from a short spear. He drew back the weapon and was about to finish Tryell, when a blade flashed passed me and buried itself in the man's throat. The man grasped the hilt of Ransyn's stiletto as he fell to the ground.

Ransyn passed me, and putting a foot on the head of the dead man, withdrew his stiletto. Keeping the weapon in one hand, he turned and faced the deserters approaching him.

'Neither of us is going to make it if we both try for the gate,' he said. 'You go, and I'll hold them.'

'No,' I told him. 'We have lost too many already. If you stay here, then I stay here with you.'

He did not take his eyes from the approaching deserters, but nodded, and slowly began to move backwards towards the waiting gates.

Just as the deserters were about to rush us, a wall of arrows struck them, dropping many. Ransyn and I took the chance given us. We turned and sprinted for the gates, which were almost closed. Falling through the gates, we tumbled to the ground, drawing air into our starving lungs.

Many hands helped us to our feet, and a Vahian stepped forward and said, 'Well done! Welcome to the Free States.'

We had been sharing the hospitality of the outpost for three days. In that time, most of the besieging forces had melted away. They had lost faith in their ability to take the outpost now that we had arrived with fresh supplies and equipment. Many of them were only there in the hope of a bit of easy killing and looting. When they found the defenders so well entrenched they just gave up and left.

I was on the northern wall of the outpost when I saw Rafe approaching me. His face was drawn, and it looked as if every movement was an effort. For the three days we had been here, he had stayed by the side of Elred, only leaving his friend to see to Tryell's wound.

Both were in a bad way, but Elred had been close to death many times in the past three days. If not for Rafe, Elred would be dead, and probably Tryell with him.

'What news, Rafe?'

'No change. Tryell is still too weak to move, and Elred has not regained consciousness.'

'I am sorry, my friend, but I cannot hold any longer. The more I delay, the more lives are lost in the war,' I told him.

'I know, but I cannot leave them,' he answered.

'That is as it should be. The rest of us will leave tomorrow. The sooner we are away the better for all.'

The next morning, the remainder of our party gathered in the open area before the gates. Since arriving, I had told the Lord in command of the outpost what was happening. He agreed to send word to all other outposts and garrisons of the Prince's return. He also furnished us with mounts and supplies.

The outpost now had a large number of mounts, thanks to Rhyhl. Once inside the outpost, he called all the unrestrained mounts to the gates. The Skirmishers had been more than willing to open the gates again to allow the horses in.

Lee was to stay here. His arm was still not healed and he would be of little use if we had to fight our way through the pass into Nuevah. I hoped to reach Nuevah by travelling north from here but the Lord commanding the outpost explained the Tribesmen of the Western Erg had gathered in great numbers, and were attacking all along the border. It was because of this that the deserters of the southern lands had become such a problem.

'If I had a hundred more Skirmishers, and no responsibilities, I would sweep this rabble from our lands. But we are short of men and equipment. We had to wait till the last minute with our volley of arrows to help you reach the gates because they were the last we had,' the Lord explained. 'At least I now have enough horses to mount all my Skirmishers, thanks to you.'

We decided that speed was the best way to escape the few deserters who still circled the outpost. Once the gates were open we would ride east for the edge of the depression. Ransyn and myself were to lead, with Reya and Beth following. Lyn, Jon and Rhyhl were to bring up the rear.

We bade our new friends and travelling companions farewell. The gates were opened and we spurred our horses forward. At first, some deserters pursued us, but Rhyhl sent a warding to their horses and they soon forgot about us as they tried to stay in the saddles of their uncontrollable mounts.

At last we reached the shelter of the Cordilleras. We crossed the border into the Plains after two more days of hard riding, a total of twelve since leaving the outpost and our friends. I was hoping we would be able to follow the foothills of the Cordilleras around to the south and then pass through the forest at the source of the West Wyernt and Wyernt Rivers.

The war had not reached this far north, and the few miners and trappers we met did not seem to care one way or another about its outcome.

The third night in the forest we came across a group of four trappers. They were small men, and were dressed in a mismatched collection of furs. They had already set up camp in what seemed to be the only suitable place we had come across all day.

'Do you mind if we join you?' I asked.

They looked at us rather suspiciously, and then talked

quietly among themselves. 'As long as you be toting your own vittles, you be welcome to stay,' the shortest of the four answered.

'Thank you,' I answered, and we dismounted. The trappers backed away when we removed the travelling cloaks we were wearing and revealed our armour beneath.

'We be poor trappers,' the shortest one said, 'You be wasting your time if you be thinking of robbing us.'

'We only wish to share the clearing with you. If you like, we will make our own fire away from yours,' I told him.

'No, it be fine for you to share our fire,' he answered.

At first, both groups kept to themselves, but as the shadows closed in across the camp, we began to merge for mutual protection. The trappers had the knowledge of the creatures that prowled the forest at night, and we had the skill to see them off should they stray near the camp.

We learned a great deal from the trappers during the night. A large force of Wolves had blocked the pass and were allowing none to enter. The trappers seemed to find this incredibly funny, though they refused to explain why. They also told us a large force of Brigands was located this side of the pass, trapping all who tried to flee. Once trapped, they were put to work or killed out of hand. This topic upset the trappers considerably, and when pressed, one simply answered, 'What they do to those poor fools, be not for the delicate ears of the young ladies.'

The next morning we left the trappers, and rode eastward again. At one point we were forced to ride north into one of the many canyons of the area to avoid being found by a large band of Brigands that I had sensed nearing us. Once it was safe to do so, we left the canyon and continued on our way. Several hours had been lost in the detour, and it was nearly dark before we found a suitable place to stop for the night. I almost expected the trappers to be there, but our delay would have placed them miles ahead of us.

We had seen to the horses and were about to eat when a cry of object terror and pain filled the forest. The scream was repeated a short time later, even more terrifying than before. Rhyhl, Ransyn and I went to investigate the screams. I led the way through the darkness, trusting my Usare abilities to find the source of the screams.

Ahead I could see a large fire flickering between the trees. As we neared it, another scream broke the silence of the forest. When we reached the edge of the trees, we saw a small clearing ahead, smaller than the one in which we had set up camp. Around the fire were thirteen Brigands, and over the fire were the four trappers we had met the night before.

As we watched, a Brigand reached up and released a rope, lowering one of the trappers headfirst into the flames. His scream echoed around the clearing. The trapper thrashed about while his hair and then clothes caught alight. I saw that two of the trappers were already dead, and the third still burned. When the same Brigand reached for the rope of the last trapper, I could no longer hold myself in check.

With a scream to compete with those vented by the trappers, I leapt from the cover of the trees and raced across the clearing. All thoughts had gone from my mind except to save the one remaining trapper. As I raced towards the startled Brigands, several scenes flashed before my eyes.

I saw the fake Prince fall from the saddle, and Danel drop with an arrow in his shoulder. I saw the crewman on the *Vrijbane* torn apart by the Plastron, and a Janissaire lying at my feet with the Eligere dagger in his chest. And last of all, I saw Elred lying on a bed with an arrow protruding from his chest and the front of his tunic covered in blood. None of the Brigands were responsible for any of these things, but for too long I had kept them held within me.

With a cry of vengeance, I released my pent-up hatred upon the Brigands.

31

DEATH LORD

THE hatred finally drained away, leaving me kneeling in the centre of the clearing, drawing in great shuddering sobs of air. Before me on the grass were my two weapons, the Talisman likenesses on the pommels staring up at me. The fight was a blur of sounds and motions—I could not remember one part of it clearly.

Turning my head, I took in the sights surrounding me. Ransyn and Rhyhl were lowering the remaining trapper gently to the ground. The remains of the other three were still hanging above the embers of the now dead fire.

'How long?' I asked.

'Not long at all. They never really understood what was happening. One minute they were sitting around their fire having fun, the next minute you were in amongst them. It was beautiful,' Ransyn answered happily.

'It was truly magnificent,' Rhyhl said. 'Your swords were almost invisible as you cut your opponents down, yet through the entire fight I could clearly see the twin Talismans mounted on their hilts.'

There was a crashing of underbrush as the rest of our company came running into the clearing. All had weapons drawn. In the half-light Beth resembled an Eligere knight; she had chosen the small sword and parrying dagger as her weapons.

Lyn's kris was at the ready, as was Reya's pilgrim staff. Rhyhl had his ancient aor at his side and Ransyn brandished his newly-acquired sabre. Jon's cutlass was still sheathed, but his hand rested on the hilt.

'It seems it was hardly worth the effort of the run,' Beth said, with a glance at the corpse-filled clearing. She flipped one of the dead Brigands onto his back. A look of terror was frozen on his face. 'It seems not all of you enjoyed yourselves,' she added, sheathing her weapons.

The trapper was now standing on shaky legs. 'I be thanking you for my miserable life, Lord Thanatos. I be Hersal, and I be your servant,' he said, and bowed deeply and solemnly.

I was about to question him about the name he used for me when Ransyn interrupted. 'I'll scout the area—the rest of you best get back to the camp.'

Hersal rushed forward and picked up my swords, and with a flick of each wrist, reversed the weapons and presented them to me hilts first. I could not help but notice the touch of ceremony in his movements.

We were in the saddle early the next day. The incident last night still disturbed me, as did the actions of my newly-acquired shadow. When I woke that morning, I found Hersal curled beside me, a look of peace and contentment on his small face.

Once awake, he did not leave my side—even when mounted, he rode his pony silently beside me. Perhaps that was what seemed so strange. Since the greeting he gave me last night, he had not spoken. We paused to water our horses and I took the opportunity of moving away from Hersal. As I did so, I motioned for Ransyn to join me.

'Why is Hersal so quiet?' I asked.

'Hersal,' Ransyn answered, 'is of a different race from the people of the Plains. To most they appear simple trappers, but we of the north have many stories of the strange small people of the Cordilleras. Hersal's people believe in ceremony. There is not much else for them in these rugged lands. You saved him; now he will serve you.'

'But why the silence?'

'You have not given him permission to speak,' Ransyn answered. 'He takes the role of your servant, which he has chosen for himself, quite seriously.'

'What was it he called me last night?'

My question seemed to make Ransyn uncomfortable. 'The locals believe in several beings of power: the Gods of Life and Death, the Goddesses of Fertility and Love, and many other Gods.'

'And Thanatos?' I asked.

'The Lord Thanatos is Death,' Ransyn answered.

Somehow I had known he was going to say that.

'Not to worry—it is a compliment. The way you stormed into the clearing and dispatched the Brigands, little Hersal could hardly think anything else,' Ransyn said with a smile.

Once the horses were watered, we continued our trek towards the pass.

'Have you given any thought to how we are to pass the Brigands and then the Wolves?' Ransyn asked as we rode together at the head of our small force.

'No,' I answered.

My attention was caught by a movement I saw out of the corner of my eye. 'Do you know a way through the pass?' I asked.

'I be knowing a way, but not through the pass,' Hersal answered.

'Impossible,' Ransyn laughed. 'The pass is the only way to cross the Cordilleras east of the Wastelands.'

'If you be knowing so much, why do you ask?' Hersal replied.

'Where is this previously unheard-of pass?' Ransyn asked.

Hersal studied him for a moment and then answered. 'My people makes their living by selling the pelts of animals we trap. There is not much market to the south for our goods, so others were found.' Hersal tapped his nose with a small finger. 'The pass be too well watched for our liking, so we found our own way through to the north.'

'Can you show us?' I asked.

He nodded.

'Is it near?' I asked.

He nodded again.

'When will we be there?' I asked.

'Now,' he said, and reined in his pony.

If we had searched for months, we would not have found the opening. Hersal led us to a small canyon, from which many smaller ones branched. Without hesitation, he stopped and dismounted. Leading his horse, and with us following rather sceptically, he led us behind a bush into what I thought to be solid stone. But hidden behind the bush was an opening just large enough for the horses to pass through.

On the rock above the opening many strange symbols were drawn. I wished Elred were with us. He would have been able to make some sense of the markings. I then realised just how much I had come to depend on his Speaker abilities.

The tunnel was in darkness, utter and complete darkness. I tried to follow Hersal using my Seeking abilities, but found I was unable to locate the small trapper—yet I could hear him moving ahead of me, and if I called out, he answered. A panic began to well up deep inside me.

A speck of white appeared ahead. The speck grew to an opening filled with light. Hersal blocked some of the light as he left the tunnel, but soon I was bathed in the most welcome light I had ever known.

I almost panicked when my Usare abilities failed me in the tunnel. It seemed I had become too dependent upon the abilities granted by the ring.

We followed a narrow winding path from the tunnel opening down into a small valley. In the distance, a small tendril of smoke could be seen snaking its way into the sky. I tried to focus on the village and found again that I was unable to. The discovery was not such a shock this time, but I still felt almost naked.

The smoke was coming from the chimney of one of several small dwellings. As we approached the dwellings, many curious people gathered around us. It was only as we stopped and began to dismount, that I realised the people were all smaller than Hersal.

Hersal began to talk to the onlookers in a fast, almost musical tongue. First there were cries of sorrow, which were soon replaced by cheers and smiles. Lastly Hersal pointed towards me and there was wonder in the eyes of the small people.

Hersal turned to me. 'I have told my people of the circumstances of our first meeting, and of the tragic death of my travelling companions. I also told them of your timely intervention which saved me from suffering the same fate as my friends.'

Ransyn leaned closer and whispered in my ear. 'Is it just me, or does he make more sense than he did before?'

Ransyn was right. Gone was the rough trapper we had met and helped in the forest. He looked like the same small trapper, but his speech was now as good, if not better than any of our party.

'You are much easier to understand, Hersal. Perhaps the sight of home has eased your worries?' I asked.

'A necessary deception, I assure you. No disrespect was intended, Lord Thanatos,' he answered.

I had hoped the title would have vanished with the bad grammar.

We stayed in the peaceful valley for three days, during which we rested and the horses regained their strength. We learned that the village had been hidden there for hundreds of years, the little folk having moved there originally to escape persecution. My friends were the first outsiders to have ever seen this valley. I, Lord Thanatos, had apparently been here before. Hersal explained that even though I saved his life he would not have led us to the secret valley were I not one of the Chosen, the Death Lord, Thanatos.

'For the benefit of the young and those who have not heard the full tale, I will tell of your first visit to us,' Hersal said.

'From this hidden valley there is another tunnel which will take you north into the pass, beyond the blockage built by the Wolves. We, the Gamin, as we have been known since our arrival here, use the secret tunnels for the purpose of trading. Even before the blockage was erected the pass had been guarded. We had found it wiser to keep out of sight as much as possible. The taller of our people can pass for trappers of the Plains, but the average person would soon be picked out as something different.

'We have been plagued recently by one disaster after another. First the Brigands swarmed up and overran our trapping grounds. Then the blockage forced us to use a little-travelled section of the northern tunnel. Then came the deaths . . .

'There is something alive in one of the side sections off the northern tunnel. At first traffic passed without incident; then there was the first death; then others followed. The village Chronicler tells a tale of a dark force which had been confined to a cavern during the time shortly following the arrival of our first ancestors. It seems that when the valley was first settled, a strange creature attacked the village using great powers. None of the men had been strong enough to defeat it.

'Then one of the wiser of the men left the village for a time, and when he returned you were with him,' Hersal said bowing to me. 'The Death Lord then demanded the lives of three of the villagers as payment for his service. The villagers agreed. The Lord then went and battled the creature of Darkness, and banished it to its lair.

'When we again began to travel the old tunnels we somehow woke or released the creature to prey on the village once again.'

Hersal went on to remind us of the deaths of his partners and of my appearance and skill. It seemed I was their Death Lord returned to help rid them of the creature once more, and worse, I had already been paid.

Ransyn, Hersal and myself scouted the area where the first attack had taken place. We then moved on to the areas of more recent attacks. All of the deaths had one thing in common: all had occurred close to the entrance of the northern tunnel.

'Have any of your people used this tunnel since the deaths started?' I asked.

'At first a few did, but they told of strange things in the

depths of the mountain so no one has used it since then,' Hersal answered.

'What sort of strange things?' Ransyn asked. Ransyn believed the people had disturbed a cave bear, probably one too old to hunt its normal quarry, or perhaps injured and in pain.

Hersal said it was not a bear, but a creature of Darkness.

Ransyn had brought his crossbow and a quiver of quarrels. I had a long spear made from a small sapling with a large metal head provided by the village blacksmith. With Hersal carrying several torches, we made our way into the tunnel.

The others had wanted to accompany us at first but I explained that the tunnel would be small and cramped and there would be hardly enough room for the three of us. They agreed to wait in the village for us. Ransyn assured them he would soon return with a warm bear skin.

'What were the marks over the opening to the tunnels? I noticed the same ones over the southern tunnel as we entered,' I asked Hersal.

'They are wards. They allow none to know of the valley, and let no powers operate within their boundaries,' he answered.

That was why my Seeker abilities did not work when we arrived. It also meant they would not be used in the hunt.

32

CHIMERA

WE paused at the entrance to the northern tunnel while Hersal lit a torch. The little trapper was armed only with a small knife.

'Is that all you intend to bring?' I asked.

'I am only here as a guide,' he answered. 'You, the Lord Thanatos will best the creature and confine it to its lair once more.'

Hersal began to whistle a soft tune as he led the way into the tunnel. Ransyn brought up the rear, crossbow cocked. I followed Hersal with the large spear held at the ready. The tunnels were cold and dark, and with my abilities gone, all I could perceive was a smell, which must have been coming from the burning torch.

We searched the tunnels for several hours before finally stopping for a bit of food and a mouthful of water. Hersal had a small sack slung over one shoulder containing two small loaves and some goat's cheese. There were biscuits made of a grain I couldn't identify, as well as a flask of water.

'Hersal?' Ransyn asked. 'What happened to the three the Lord received in payment the last time he was here?' Ransyn glanced over his shoulder at me as he asked the question. He wore the same annoying smirk he had when he spoke of the Death Lord in my presence.

Hersal looked at me questioningly. I nodded.

'The three accompanied the Lord Thanatos into these tunnels, but they did not return with him after he vanquished the creature. We searched the tunnels for sign of them but all we could find were three small piles of ashes,' he answered.

'Hersal, apart from the fact that I saved you, and that your three partners were burnt to death, as were the three who went with the Lord, why do you think I am the Death Lord?' I asked.

'Your skill at arms, my Lord Thanatos,' he answered.

'Is that all?'

'And those,' he said, pointing to the sword hilts protruding above my shoulders. I had chosen to wear my weapons on my back in the crossed sheaths to give my legs more freedom.

Before I could question the trapper further, a terrifying roar echoed from the stone walls about us. The noise was deafening, so loud in fact it seemed to surround us, stifling, almost paralysing us with its sound. I had heard of creatures which immobilised their prey with a roar, paralysing them with fear. Could this be such a creature?

Finally the echoes of the roar faded, leaving us in a deep silence. Ransyn scooped up the crossbow, while I lifted the spear. Hersal was at last showing some signs of fear as he ran behind Ransyn and grasped the Janissaire's legs so tightly he almost fell.

Moving cautiously down the tunnel, we came upon the scuffed prints of several cave wolves, and those of a goat. Obviously the wolves had been stalking the latter. The cave wolf was a smaller cousin of the Plains' Chagrin, but just as dangerous when confronted.

We continued to move silently down the tunnel. Hersal held the torch low, throwing a flickering dim light about our feet, but not revealing what might be waiting silently ahead of us in the thick blackness of the tunnel.

Even though the tunnel was silent, the sound of the terrifying roar still echoed in my head. I was finding it extremely difficult to continue towards the unknown deadly killer which could send such fear through my body from so faraway.

An animal's tortured scream tore through the silence, ending abruptly. Without warning, the tunnel opened up into a small cavern. An opening in the roof allowed a faint light to filter into the centre cavern, revealing the rock-strewn floor. In this light, I could see another opening on the far side of the cavern. As I was about to enter the cavern, another roar reverberated about us, so close that I felt the full power of the roar as my body seemed to lock with fear. With great effort, I managed to keep the spear raised, as I waited for the beast to appear.

Suddenly a cave wolf darted across the floor of the cavern. As it neared the second opening, another creature flashed through the centre of the cavern, cutting off the escape of the panicking wolf. With a swift bound, the strange creature leapt on the wolf and raised it in its massive jaws, before a casual toss of its head sent the torn and bloodied carcass flying through the air to strike the wall of the cavern.

Left alone in the centre of the cavern was a nightmarish creature straight from the deepest pits of Tartarus, underground world of Erebus, Devourer of Souls. As the creature moved slightly, its hooves made a clipping sound on the stone floor. Its coarse-haired body rippled with power as it turned to face the last of the cave wolves.

A low snarl escaped from between the rows of dagger-like teeth as the creature tilted back its head. Its small triangular ears were pressed flat against the top of its head as it watched its paralysed prey. All this time, the creature's tail had moved rhythmically back and forth. The tail stretched itself up above the back of the creature, and a faint hissing filled the cavern.

Straining into the dimness of the cavern to see what was making the strange noise, I realised to my horror that the sound came from the creature's tail, a green, scale-covered snake, as thick as my wrist, which danced through the air above the creature. What we faced was not one creature, but an abominable mixture of three.

The serpentine tail now began an exotic dance as it mesmerised the wolf cowering before it. Then without a sound, the mouth of the creature opened and a green flame leapt out, flashing across the cavern to wrap itself around the frozen wolf. The burning wolf threw itself into the air, biting frenziedly at its own body, as it tried in vain to extinguish the flames. By the time the wolf struck the ground, it was dead.

Slowly the creature turned to face us.

'You have to kill that!' Ransyn snapped. It had gone from 'we' to 'you' in a very short time.

'Try your crossbow,' I told him.

Ransyn leaned slightly into the cavern and fired. The bolt took the creature between the eyes, causing it to leap backwards. It must have leapt in surprise, as the quarrel bounced harmlessly from the creature's skin. It then shook its head, and began to cross the cavern towards us. Ransyn had another shot, but this had as little effect as had the last.

The creature's tail was thrashing about in a frenzy of motion. The scales of the snake were green, darker at the base than around the neck.

'Well, so much for the crossbow,' Ransyn said, as a fourth blow struck the creature in the head with no effect.

My brain was racing. Why had Thanatos brought the three villagers with him? As I watched the creature's movement, I realised why.

As we had noted with the attack on the cave wolf, the creature preferred to play with its victim before the kill. I explained my idea to Ransyn who agreed to act as decoy for me.

As Ransyn backed along the wall, away from the tunnel, the creature followed. The whole plan rested on the creature not attacking Ransyn till it had played for some time. Ransyn was keeping as far away as possible, wary of the fire the creature could expel. He was also constantly on his guard, due to the creature's speed when attacking.

At last Ransyn reached the far side of the cavern, followed by the stalking creature. I stepped into the cavern and proceeded slowly across to the rear of the creature. For no apparent reason, the creature whipped around and faced me. I crouched ready to meet its charge.

Ransyn leapt forward, and with an enormous two-handed blow struck the creature across the back. The sound of his sabre striking flesh was loud in the confines of the cavern. With an enraged snarl, the beast whipped round and struck Ransyn a blow across the body which sent him reeling across the cavern, crashing into the rough wall.

Before I could strike, the beast had turned once more to face me. Dark blood oozed from the cut on its back, but already I could see that the previously gaping wound had begun to heal, closing itself even as I watched.

The beast began to move in a circle, never removing its eyes away from me. I thrust the spear at its head, but the beast stepped quickly to one side, avoiding the attack. A savage, but somewhat strange expression came over the beast's face, almost as though it was enjoying itself.

Suddenly, Hersal landed on the creature's back and buried his knife deep into the creature's right shoulder. The creature leapt into the air and spun sharply about, throwing Hersal from its back. I threw the spear, and even as it struck the beast, I was drawing one of my swords. With a shout of anger, I attacked the creature, trying to draw its attention from the slowly recovering Hersal. Ransyn pushed himself off the wall at the same time, staggering across towards the back of the beast. The creature ignored Hersal and attacked me, knocking me from my feet. Then, with great speed, it spun round to face Ransyn, bringing the Janissaire Sergeant to a sliding halt.

As I was about to regain my feet, I realised I could hear the ominous hissing sound once more. Looking up, I saw the serpent tail of the creature weaving before me. The eyes of the serpent locked on mine and held me. Even as I watched the creature prepare to attack Ransyn, there was little I could do to free myself from the serpent's stare. The body of the creature expanded slightly, and I somehow knew that it was about to send its green flame at Ransyn.

As fast as the cold stare had grasped me, I found myself free. My left hand was bunched at the front of my tunic, holding the Talisman which was hidden beneath it. I leapt to my feet, and as the serpent's head struck forward, I brought my sword down across the tail of the beast, removing the serpentine head.

The head of the snake fell writhing to ground, and the creature froze. As the tail continued to twist on the floor, the creature began to crumble; turning to dust as I watched.

There was great excitement in the village as Hersal told of what had happened.

'But how did you know the tail was the weak point?' Beth asked.

'The scales around the neck were different from those on the rest of the tail. They looked newer. Thanatos used the three villagers as bait, while he attacked the creature from the rear. With the head cut from the tail the creature is finished,' I answered.

'Far from it,' Rhyhl said. 'If you have described the creature correctly, it is far from dead.'

'But it turned to dust,' Ransyn said.

'True, however the Chimera—the creature you just fought—had many unusual properties, several of which you have already seen for yourself. But the most interesting and important, is the fact that while the brain lives, the creature can regrow,' Rhyhl said.

'But the brain turned to dust along with its head,' Ransyn added.

'No, it did not,' Rhyhl answered.

Before Rhyhl said another word, I realised he was right. The Chimera was far from dead.

'The Chimera's brain is located in the snake's head. The new growth Teal saw was not the replacement of a new tail, but the regeneration of an entire body,' Rhyhl said, and turned to Hersal. 'The head must be found and burnt. It is the only way to stop the Chimera from regenerating.'

Hersal and several of the men rushed to the northern tunnel, but the snake head was nowhere to be found.

We said our farewells and led our horses into the northern tunnel. Hersal's people had loaded us with food and other gifts. They were not too concerned that the Chimera was not killed, for it would take centuries for the creature to grow a new body.

The journey through the tunnel was uneventful, and we

were soon in the pass at the rear of the blockade. Mounting up, we spurred our horses forward. We had not ridden more than a mile when we ran into a patrol coming in from the Erg.

There was no time to think. I kicked my mount into a run, and rushed the surprised patrol. Many of the Wolves were caught off-guard, but a few managed to keep some semblance of discipline. By the time the Wolves were dispatched, most of the mounts had fled, including three of ours. Rhyhl was down and so was Reya. She had injured her arm in a fall from her horse. After all this time, she was still not comfortable in the saddle. Rhyhl was the more seriously injured. He was unconscious and no amount of water or face-slapping could revive him.

Lyn crossed to where I was standing. He was wiping the blade of his kris. 'Several of the Wolves escaped on foot. It won't take them long to reach help and return. With three horses gone, there is no way we can outrun them. So we are going to have to outthink them.'

'How?' I asked.

'The most obvious thing to do is to ride straight out into the Erg. But if you ride along the foot of the Cordilleras for several days, and use your Seeker abilities to cover your trail, they are sure to miss you,' he answered.

'Possibly,' I answered.

Lyn continued. 'They may even go the wrong way.'

'And why would they do that?'

'We don't have enough food or water for all of us to cross. If I remain here, and weave the illusion of a Wolf about me, I could send them off in the wrong direction,' Lyn explained.

'And I will stay in the shadow in case any of them see through this illusion,' Reya said.

I was about to protest.

'There's no use arguing. They will be here any time, and

you must get out of sight. We will be fine. Once they are gone we will make our way back to where we left Rafe and the others. Good luck.'

Lyn and Reya ran back to the opening of the pass. Beth mounted Rhyhl's horse and Jon passed the unconscious Rhyhl up. Ransyn kicked his horse forward. 'We must go now. They will be quite safe.'

We watched the two in the distance. Suddenly they passed through a section of shadow and there was only one. Next the air shimmered around the remaining figure and a Wolf turned and waved.

Our food and water ran out after five days. If not for Rhyhl's Caller abilities we would all have died. Any living thing which came within range of his influence succumbed to his call. Beth was unable to make rain as there had to be moisture in the air to start with, and without a breeze for her to change into a wind, there was little chance of her finding any.

The last of the horses died. If it were not for the detour at the beginning we might have made it. The wind was beginning to pick up but it was as dry as the rest of the inferno. At about midday we realised that the wind was turning into a storm, and we would have to find cover soon or die.

'There to the east: mounted men,' Beth croaked through parched lips.

We looked to the east, and saw the figures getting larger by the minute.

'Tribesmen,' Ransyn said. 'At least twenty of them. Well, at least we won't die of thirst,' he said. With a flick of his right hand, he loosened the sabre in its sheath.

'When they are close enough, I will panic their mounts,' Rhyhl said softly. He was lying on the ground at Ransyn's feet. He had suffered from the heat more than anyone.

'Perhaps Rhyhl could steal several horses with a little help,' Jon said, 'while Beth and I keep them occupied.'

As the Tribesmen rode down on us, Rhyhl lowered his head and clenched his fist. Suddenly the mounts were reeling and jumping. Many riders were thrown while the rest tried to control their mounts. Rhyhl, Ransyn and I took the opportunity to rush the terrified horses and their riders. Some turned and fled; the rest were too busy to worry about us.

The three of us mounted and turned to the others.

'No time,' Jon called, and pointed towards the south. Riding hard towards us was a large company of Wolves.

Beth raised both hands and the wind began to increase. Dust was whipped around her and flung at the approaching horsemen. She turned her head slightly and said something to Jon who shook his head, and turned towards us.

'She is too tired. If she takes even the smallest portion of her concentration away the wind will drop, and the Wolves will be on us. She says you are to ride. She will keep the wind blowing as long as she can.' Jon turned and watched the tall Eligere girl as she strained to maintain the storm. 'I'll wait with her,' he said, 'she'll need help when she is too exhausted to continue. Now go!' he shouted into the wind.

The pair were almost hidden by the storm. Ransyn grabbed my arm.

'We must go!' he shouted above the mounting wind.

'If we do they will die,' I cried.

'If we stay they will die anyway,' Rhyhl said. 'We cannot stand against so many when we are so weak.'

'We must get the Prince's message through to Nuevah. If we stop now all the injuries and hardships will have been for nothing,' Ransyn added.

I nodded and turned, not speaking for fear of betraying my emotions. Rhyhl looked at me. His face was streaked with tears. I turned to Ransyn and found even the veteran Sergeant wiping tears from his eyes.

'Damn sand,' he cursed.

33

THE MESSAGE

THE water was cool and refreshing, and brought me choking to my senses.

'Easy — just lie there for a moment,' a voice said.

I tried to speak but my tongue seemed to take up the entire inside of my mouth. I opened my eyes and immediately closed them again as the blinding sun cut straight into them.

Some time must have passed, as I felt cooler when I next awoke and the sun was not burning at my eyelids. Again I tried to open my eyes and this time there was no blinding light to force them closed. I slowly raised my head and looked about. I was under a lean-to made of several saddle blankets. Beside me were Ransyn and Rhyhl, both silent and unmoving. I sat up and examined my friends closer. Once assured they were fine, I got to my knees and crawled from the lean-to.

It was much brighter outside, and I was forced to shade

my eyes. Sitting a short distance away were twenty men dressed in the white tabards of Purusmayons. As I started towards them, one of the Janissaire noticed me, and nodded to the man next to him, who rose.

'Take it steady first off. You were all in a pretty bad way when we found you,' he said. 'I'm Sergeant Drynan, and you have just crossed the border into the Purusmayon Province of Nuevah.'

'I realise that, Sergeant. My name is Teal. My companions are Rhyhl, a Perduan, and Sergeant Ransyn, also of this province,' I told him.

'Ransyn!' Sergeant Drynan crossed to the lean-to and examined Ransyn and returned. 'You're right. That's Ransyn. I never would have recognised him. Not with the long hair and all.'

I reached into my pocket and pulled out the ring. 'I was given this ring, several weeks ago by Prince Nels.' All of them stopped, and turned towards me. 'He is alive and leading an army in the southern war. His troops are of all races and lands and he needs aid,' They were all watching me in disbelief. 'I realise it is hard to believe, but what I am telling you is true. I have a message for the Princess from her brother, and another for the Lord Daived from his sons Danel and Tomas.

'You know where the two young Lords are?' he asked. There was almost a pleading tone in his voice.

'Yes, they are with the Prince, as are many other Vahians,' I answered.

The Sergeant turned and began to talk to his men in the Vahian tongue.

'You're wasting your time,' Ransyn said, as he stopped shakily beside me.

'How are you feeling?' I asked.

'Fine ... Lord,' he answered. I couldn't help but note the

way he stressed the title; nor, for that matter, could the others.

Sergeant Drynan and his men looked at me in a different way now. No longer was there a look of disbelief. It had been replaced by a look of understanding.

'I should have known you would have been mixed up in this war somewhere, Ransyn,' Drynan said. 'I've never known you to miss a good fight.'

Ransyn laughed.

'Is it true then? The Prince is alive and well?'

'More than that. He has raised an army and has driven the invaders from most of the Western Plains. For all I know, he may have ended the war already. But I knew how much you liked a good squabble, so I thought I'd see if you and a few of the lads wanted to come and give us a hand.'

The men laughed. 'I'm afraid there's not much chance of that. The Regent has closed the borders.'

Ransyn spat and looked into the face of Drynan. 'It was the Regent who had King Elfred and Prince Jaymes killed. That is why we must reach Lord Daived.'

Drynan and his men looked shocked at the news. The shock turned to disbelief and then quickly to realisation. Tears filled the eyes of many of the Janissaire. 'You have proof?' Drynan asked.

'The ring is proof,' Ransyn said. He turned his back on the Sergeant and spoke softly, almost to himself. 'When we last saw the Prince, there were ten of us, good friends all. We three are all who remain. That's how much we believe in our mission,' Ransyn's face dropped as he mentioned our missing companions. Rafe should be safe at the outpost, but what of Tryell and Elred? Reya should be safe with Lyn as long as her wound was not too severe. Beth and Jon were my true concern. Even with the storm, I doubted they could have escaped the Tribesmen and the Wolves.

Drynan saw our grief, and, being Vahian, sympathised with the pain of our losses. He left us alone while he organised his men to leave. When all was ready, he again stood before me. 'I'm sorry to disturb you, Lord, but we had best leave now.'

I nodded and walked to the horse he indicated. I mounted and the rest followed suit. Three of the Janissaire rode double, one supporting the conscious, but groggy Rhyhl.

We changed horses many times over the next few days and at last found ourselves approaching the lands of the Lord Daived. After the desolation of the Erg, the lands of Nuevah were magnificent. They were exactly like Mikal had described them to me: wide open expanses of fertile land, bordered by low, tree-covered hills; shallow streams criss-crossed the fields, sustaining a wide variety of flora along its banks.

Soon we were riding beneath the raised portcullis of Lord Daived's Stronghold. Grooms took the mounts for us as we were ushered into the presence of the Lord. Sergeant Drynan had sent a messenger ahead of us to warn the Lord of our message. As well as Lord Daived, his eldest son Grieg was present, as were six of their neighbours.

I gave the Lord the ring and told him of the Prince's plight in the south. I told him that the Prince could have presented the ring personally but had chosen to remain with the army he had raised. When I told the tale of the Regent, there were cries for vengeance that made even my blood run cold.

'We must take this news to the Princess and the late King's brother, Grehem, immediately. The longer we delay, the greater the risk to the Prince's life and the more evil can be done by that Jackal Raimend,' Lord Daived said.

I couldn't help but note that no mention was made of the fact that hundreds of men were dying south of their borders and they were in a position to stop this. Reya's words again came to me, and once more I realised how close to the truth she really was. There was no great difference between the Eligere and the Vahians—all they were concerned about was themselves.

Preparations were made and we were soon on our way towards the Capital. Every man who could be spared rode with us, and as we passed the Strongholds of Lord Daived's neighbours, our ranks swelled even further. The sight and sound of so many Vahian Lords and their battle companions was an event I would never forget: high-stepping, spirited horses; flashing armour; and snapping pennants.

By the time we crossed the Purusmayon Province and entered the Province of the Ferropeons, we had thirty-seven Lords and their combined battle companies. Each stronghold was left under the protection of a Lord and enough Janissaire to hold it against attack.

In most cases, the eldest brother remained in charge while the fathers and uncles rode northwest to the Capital. Word reached the Capital well ahead of us, and by the time we arrived there was a large force of Wolves waiting to meet us.

'Stand aside and let us pass or we will ride you down,' Lord Daived ordered from astride his charger. All of the Lords were riding huge chargers, called coursers. They were bred for battle and stood many hands taller than the largest of the Plains' horses.

The order and tone of voice momentarily confused the

Wolf Aron. Suddenly from behind the force of Wolves, a tall figure approached. It was a Wolf Lord, only the second I had ever seen. His helmet was shaped like a timber wolf's head and made him look quite formidable.

'Stand aside, Wyest. We have proof that the Regent ordered the murder of the King and Heir and we are here to see justice done,' Lord Daived called.

Now the Wolves looked apprehensive. They realised that if a wrong word was spoken from either side, a large number of men would die.

I kicked my horse forward and placed myself between the two opposing Lords. My black tabard had been laundered and repaired, and my swords were on either hip. 'There is no need to fight! The Princess can identify this ring,' I called, holding up the ring, 'as her brother's, Prince Nels. The Prince is alive and he bade me ride here and inform the Princess. The Prince is the Heir to the Throne of Nuevah—any effort to stop me will be considered treason, and the man responsible, whether Lord or common soldier will hang for his troubles.'

Once finished, I spurred my mount forward. Ransyn and Rhyhl followed me on either side. As I approached the ranks of Wolves, I held the ring before me. The front rank parted, as did those behind. As I passed the Wolf Lord, he turned his mount and rode beside me.

'Should you prove to be lying, it will be you and your friends who will hang, and I will be there to ensure it is done properly,' he said.

Our strange gathering reached the Palace. The Wolves fell in behind as we rode past them. The Purusmayons in turn followed them. On the way through the city another force of Wolves, with several Lords, joined the rear. On entering the main courtyard before the Palace, the entire force was surrounded by Ferropeon Lords and their Liegemen.

'What is the meaning of this show of arms before the Palace?' a tall armoured Lord called from the top of the stairs which led to the main entrance of the Palace.

Several of the Lords began to speak at once, but the Lord on the stairs raised a hand and silenced them.

'That's Grehem, the late King's brother. All the Lords respect him or fear him. He is a very powerful Lord and has a large following of Lords who believe he should have taken the Throne for himself once his brother was dead,' Ransyn explained.

'Now, one at a time! I want some explanations.'

Daived spoke his piece first, followed by the other Lords who were present when I told my tale. Next Wyest recounted what happened at the entrance to the Capital. Grehem turned from the speakers at one stage, and gave orders to a follower.

By the time it was my turn to speak, the Liegemen had returned. He whispered something to Grehem which caused the tall Lord to snap several more orders to those around him. Another force of Liegemen arrived. In their midst was a tall woman. In stature she was like Beth, only her features were softer, more at peace.

'Where is my brother's ring?' she asked.

I dismounted and approached her. Several crossbows were trained on me as I walked towards her. I stopped and gave her the ring. 'It was given to me several weeks ago with a message for you, your Highness.'

'The message?' she asked, turning the ring over in her fingers.

'It was for you alone,' I answered. I could almost feel the fingers tightening on the triggers of the crossbows as I spoke.

She leaned forward and I whispered something in her ear. She straightened and there were tears in her eyes. 'The ring is indeed from my brother,' she said.

'Yes, your Highness, but how do we know the Prince is still alive?' Wyest asked.

I was about to speak when I sensed something strange. It took me a short while to place what it was, before I noticed a small thin ring on the Lord Grehem's middle finger of his right hand. I raised my hand to my face and as I did so, I caught Grehem's eye. I allowed my ring to become visible for only a second, but it was enough. Grehem's eyes widened in surprise and his right hand was whipped behind his back.

He steadied himself and turned to the Princess. 'Your Highness, I believe several points of interest should be brought forth at this time. One is the strange order from Raimend to close the border. The second is the large number of Wolves in the Capital. And thirdly is the fact that shortly after the arrival of our messenger from the Prince, Raimend and his battle company left the Capital riding east in somewhat of a great hurry.'

The last statement drew oaths from all Lords assembled.

The Princess stepped forward as weapons were drawn on those Wolves present. The Wolves drew their weapons in answer, and prepared to sell their lives for the creed they believed in.

'There is to be no fighting,' she called out. Then she motioned for Wyest to approach her. 'I do not believe that anyone, other than Raimend and his personal Wolves, was involved in this foul plot. I charge you Lord Wyest, Wolf Lord of the Holluchon Province to find Raimend and return him here for trial. I give you this task and expect all in Nuevah to give you aid.'

'I accept, your Highness,' Wyest answered. He turned and mounted, and ordered his men to do the same. All others in the courtyard parted to allow him to leave. Soon

Wyest and his battle company were gone from the court-yard.

The Princess turned and walked back into the Palace. Grehem waved for me to follow.

'All Lords present,' he called, 'are to keep themselves in readiness for the Princess' orders; and all troops are to be readied for war!'

34

THE REGENT

'DAMN this waiting!'

'There's nothing much more we can do, Ransyn. The new Regent, Grehem, has been told everything we know abut the Eligere and their allies,' I told him. Ransyn was taking the waiting worse than Rhyhl or myself. It was now two months since Raimend had fled, and, looking from the window of our room in the palace, you would not think the nation was preparing for war.

There was a soft tap at the door. Rhyhl walked in; seeing the look on Ransyn's face, he said nothing.

'For Krodil's sake, Ransyn, sit down!' I shouted. Ransyn had spent almost the entire two months pacing back and forth in that very room.

'All right,' he said, and threw himself into the closest chair which gave a groan of protest.

'The Regent Grehem has given the orders to all Commanders concerned.' This got Ransyn's attention. 'The main force of troops is to cross the border into the Erg tomorrow morning.'

'About time. For a while I thought the Lords were waiting for the Eligere to die of old age,' Ransyn snapped.

'Ransyn, I think I liked it better when you were a simple Sergeant who did only as he was told. Do you have any idea how many supply wagons are needed to carry food and water for six thousand troops and their mounts?' I asked. He didn't answer.

'How long are they expecting to take to cross the Erg?' Rhyhl asked.

'Four weeks.'

'That's pushing it a little,' Rhyhl said.

'They could only manage to find four weeks' supplies. Transport is another factor. They cannot have their supply line too long or too many troops will be needed to protect it from the Tribesmen. As it is, one thousand troops will return to Nuevah with the wagons.'

'That's not going to leave many for the actual fighting,' Ransyn stated.

'Worse yet. Another thousand are to stay at the pass to improve the fortifications,' I answered.

'But that will only leave an army of four thousand. There are ten times that number in Navealozans alone,' Ransyn complained.

I shook my head.

'What more?' he asked.

'Once through the pass, five hundred will turn west into the Wastelands. It is hoped they will be able to surprise and take Beestrone from an unexpected quarter.'

'Only five hundred for an entire town the size of Beestrone?' Ransyn asked, incredulously.

'It is hoped the populace will rise and aid our people,' I answered.

'I've heard enough about the army,' Ransyn said. 'When do *we* leave?'

'Tomorrow morning. Grehem has picked a mixed force

of three hundred Liegemen, three hundred Wolves and four hundred Janissaire. There will also be fifty-seven Lords.'

Our vessels were several hours south of Whalestrone before Grehem was free. I had asked Ransyn if he had any idea of the amount of planning which went into an operation of this size and, of course, he hadn't. The problem was, I was only just beginning to realise myself how much planning was involved. I had fully expected to ride into the Capital and give my message, then ride south almost immediately with an army.

'Sorry to keep you waiting, Teal, but an unexpected problem arose.' Grehem walked to the rail and leaned over. I crossed the deck and stood beside him. He was watching Swimmers as they kept pace with the vessel.

'Do you think Wyest will find Raimend?' I asked,

'I hope so,' he answered. Then he smiled and said, 'In another way I hope he doesn't.'

'Why's that? Don't you think Wyest is good enough to catch him?' I asked.

'Oh, I think Wyest is a match for Raimend. It's Raimend's Aron who worries me.'

'His Aron?'

'Yes. I know it sounds strange, but by the Gods, the man was strange. He was always with Raimend, no matter where he went, yet, when I think back I can't for the life of me remember what he looks like.'

'He was probably the type of person who is always around but never noticed because there is nothing outstanding about them,' I answered.

'No, there was more than that. He was the exact opposite of the person you just described. He stood out in a crowd more than his Lord Raimend did. I think the most remarkable thing about him was his eyes,' Grehem answered.

The Swimmers were forgotten. Grehem had my total attention. 'How do you mean, the eyes?' I asked.

'It's rather hard to explain, but if our eyes met it seemed as if he was looking deep inside me. On several times I found I was unable to move until the eye contact was broken,' he said. 'Strange?'

'No, not strange at all. I have had the same experience on two occasions. Once in a hallway with a killer. His eyes locked onto mine and filled me with cold fear. Then he beckoned for me to come towards him, and even though he held a knife, and I knew he was going to kill me, I could not help myself. I had to do as he wanted.'

'And the second?' he asked.

'In a dream far into the land of the Navealozans. We were being hunted, and I was watching the hunters in a dream, when suddenly one of the Eligere began to question a local. He had a dagger similar to the one the killer in the hallway had had. But when he looked up and I saw his eyes, it was as if I was looking at the same person.'

'Could it have been?'

'No, the other was killed—I watched him die. But now that I think back, I find it impossible to remember one feature of either of the men.' As I recounted the tale to Grehem, I remembered that I had had another similar experience. That one was in Dienall when my companions had first arrived. One of them had locked eyes on me in much the same way, though without the fear.

My thoughts were broken as Grehem continued. 'I still can't see how you got through the pass,'

'It was dark, and with Reya as scout we simply slipped by the defenders,' I answered. I must admit each time I was asked how we used the pass unchallenged, I was forced to admit I was slightly fuzzy on exactly how it was done.

I remembered leaving the trappers. Then we struck out north till we reached the pass. The next thing I remembered clearly was the Erg as we rode away from Reya and Lyn.

'Sergeant Ransyn tells me you were helped briefly by some trappers.'

'Yes, he . . . no, *they* showed us the pass,' I answered. Why had I thought there was only one? 'I think I'll go below deck for a while,' I told him.

In the cabin put aside for my two friends and myself, I found Ransyn. He was sitting at the table running a whetstone along the edge of his sabre. 'Ransyn, do you remember exactly how we got through the pass undetected?' I asked.

He gave me a strange look and then a half-laugh. Then he saw that I was waiting for his answer. 'You're serious?'

'Yes.'

He shrugged. 'It was dark and with Reya as scout, we simply slipped by the defenders,' he answered.

Virtually what I had told Grehem. No! It was exactly what I had told the Regent. Word for word, it was exactly the same answer I had given.

'Is something wrong?' he asked.

I walked across the cabin, and as I passed the bunk, I glanced down at my swords lying there. The Talisman replicas on the pommels seemed to be watching me. Head . . . something about a head. I remembered leaving the trappers. There was a fire, a huge fire, and I was tired. There was a different type of fire as well, and a head — a snake's head.

'What's the matter?' Rhyhl asked, as he entered the cabin.

'Rhyhl, do you remember how we got through the

pass?' I asked. There was a look of confusion on Ransyn's face.

'Yes,' answered Rhyhl. 'It was a dark night and with Reya as scout we simply slipped by the defenders,' he answered.

'That's what I said,' Ransyn added. 'What is the matter with you, Teal? Your face is almost white. You look like death warmed up. Why is it so important?'

Death! That was it! Death ... I remembered it now: The Gamin, Hersal, the tunnels and the Chimera. I remembered all that had happened in the small valley. Most of all, I remembered Hersal's answer to one of my questions. When I had asked him what other reasons he had for believing I was the Death Lord, he had pointed to my swords.

Over the next three days, no matter what I tried, I couldn't convince my friends that we had travelled the pass in any way other than the way they remembered. They were totally blank about Hersal and the valley, and all that happened there. Perhaps that's what Hersal meant when he said the wards above the tunnel entrances stopped people from discovering the valley. Maybe they wiped the memory from the mind of any traveller.

Without incident, we were soon off the coast of the Free States, and the unloading began. Half the men went ashore while the rest laboured on board the vessels to get all the stores and equipment ashore as soon as possible.

Several hours after landing, a large force of Free Vahians appeared. With them were the mounts required for our troops. Coursers had been brought for the Lords on one of the vessels, and I had dreamt to Rafe to have the Free Vahians gather as many of the deserters' horses as possible.

With our squadron mounted, the combined force moved south towards the border. Outriders were placed well ahead of the main body of troops in the hope of keeping the enemy from learning the exact size of our force. We hoped to get close to Beestrone before the enemy knew of our relatively small size. The Free Vahians made up the majority of our force. All the available Skirmishers had been gathered, and placed under the command of Grehem. With the six hundred Wolves and Liegemen, our total forces numbered three thousand. Not a huge army by any means, but a host of trained men, the likes of which the Navealozans were not likely to forget.

We also had the advantage of having seventy-eight Vahian Lords, each mounted on a courser. The sight of the armoured Lords mounted on their huge coursers was indeed inspiring. Pennants flapped from lances, and swords and axes slapped thighs. Never, not even in Ardemus' training room, had I seen such an assortment of weapons.

Just north of the border, we met up with the supply wagons of the Free Vahians. Elred was with them.

'It is good to see you again, my friend,' I took Elred's hand in mine. I had refrained from hugging him when I saw he was still weak. He was walking towards me unaided, but his stride lacked his usual determination, and his face was pallid and drawn.

'You look better,' I said.

'Better than when we parted company,' he replied.

'How are you?'

'Fine, though still weak. Even after all these months, I find I have to rest every once in a while to keep up my strength,' he said smiling.

'And Rafe?'

'As soon as he passed on your message regarding the horses to the Free Vahian Commander, he and Tryell left.

They planned on travelling through the forest to just south of Beestrone then making a raft to take them south into safer lands. If nothing has gone wrong, they should be with the Prince now. I have been too weak to dream to Rafe to see if all went well,' he said.

'Don't worry—I will try to contact him tonight,' I answered.

Rafe was indeed well, and he and Tryell had reached the Prince as planned. In my dream, I showed Rafe an image of Carnnoc under attack by Janissaire. Then I showed him the setting of five suns. He answered that he understood and projected the likenesses of the others. I showed him Ransyn, Rhyhl and myself and then I conveyed to him the last few seconds of our parting with the others.

The effort of dreaming over such a long distance left me weak. But what was worse was the sense of loss I felt when I woke, after thinking of my missing friends.

Five days later, as scheduled, our forces attacked Carnnoc. The Skirmishers assaulted the eastern wall while the Wolves sent showers of arrows over their heads into the defenders. Using battering rams hung from their mounts, the Liegeman tried for several of the gates on the eastern and northern sides of the city. We did not press the assault to the very walls of the city as we were not yet ready for the main attack.

As we began the third assault, smoke was seen to be coming from the city in the area of the harbour. As soon as they saw this, the Liegeman concentrated their efforts on one gate, while the Skirmishers attacked the walls on either side of it.

The gate soon fell and the mounted Wolves rode into the city.

'I doubt we would have taken the city so cheaply, if not

for your idea, Teal,' Grehem said. We were riding through the streets of Carnnoc, which were lined with people waving and cheering.

'If the Eligere had visited the city, then one more ship entering harbour under their flag would not seem unusual, and if they had not arrived yet, the defenders would not be expecting a force to appear from the ocean,' I answered.

Rhyhl and all the Janissaire had taken the largest of the vessels and had entered the harbour while most of the defenders were busy at the eastern wall. Once free of the ship, they lit several fires and began to make their way into the city.

The fires were built well clear of vessels and buildings; there was not much sense in capturing a town if you had to burn it down to succeed. But the defenders only saw the smoke, and heard that troops were marching towards them from the docks. Most surrendered; some fled; a few decided to fight—but these were soon overwhelmed by the Janissaire and the mounted Wolves.

Rhyhl carried word of our victory south by fast courier ship, as we began the task of repairing the damage we had done to the city's defences, and seeing to the arming and training of the population.

In the months to follow, the western Plains were cleared of all who opposed us. The only enemy left was entrenched in Beestrone, with no way to escape nor to receive aid. With the west secured, the Prince left a garrison in all cities and towns, and then took the remainder of the forces south to Lyram. Grehem's forces were left at Carnnoc, in case the assault on Beestrone should fail and more troops were needed.

35

THE STRANGER IN GREY ROBES

THERE was a pounding on the door. Rhyhl leaned across and opened it. Standing in the hall was one of the Skirmishers.

'Lord, the Regent wishes to see you immediately,' he said. He seemed very excited and eager to be gone.

'Yes, I'll come at once. Is there news?' I asked.

'Yes, Lord, there are messengers from Beestrone.'

'Beestrone!' Ransyn exploded. 'What by the names of Gods do those scums want?'

'It wasn't one of the enemy . . . Lord,' the Skirmisher answered. Ransyn still wore the black tabard given to him by the Prince at Holsmer. His hair was even longer now, and he had an air about him which marked him as anything but a Sergeant Janissaire.

'You mean it was a message from the Commander of the attacking troops?' I asked.

'No Lord—it is from Beestrone. I heard the Aron say so,' he answered.

'Well, there's one way to find out for sure.' Grabbing

my weapon belt I followed the Skirmisher.

'Gentlemen, I have just received word from Beestrone.' The audience chamber fell silent. 'It is from the new Commander of Beestrone. It simply states the city is now in our hands,' The Regent lowered the message and smiled. The room was in an uproar. Weapons flashed through the air and men were laughing and crying at the same time. Pennants of all forces located in Carnnoc were lifted from where they rested and waved above the head of the Regent.

The Regent raised his hands and the noise died down. 'Four days ago a large party of Natives attacked Beestrone.' Sounds of surprise echoed about the room. 'The attack was repulsed. The enemy then decided to finish the natives off before they could regroup for another attack.'

'Most of the defenders rode from the city, and began to ride down the Natives. As the last scavenger and Navealozan rode from the city, the gates were closed. Before the defenders knew what was happening the Natives turned and attacked. The rout had turned into a second attack. At that precise moment, five hundred Wolves broke from the cover of nearby trees and split the Navealozan's ranks.'

More cheering and laughing erupted as the Regent paused. 'The Navealozans were cut to pieces. The Natives would gather until numbers were sufficient, then they would swoop down on a pocket of them, and ride right over them. Every time a larger force of Navealozans tried to gather, the Wolves would launch themselves at the force and break it up.

'Those who fled towards the city were met with barred gates. The people of Beestrone had risen and taken the gates, thus dividing the forces of the enemy.

'Once those on the plain had been dealt with, the gates were opened and the Wolves rode into the city. What they found was a massacre. The people had had no weapons, but with their bare hands they had stormed the enemy positions at the gates, and those who had survived, had held them with captured weapons against repeated attacks of overwhelming numbers.

'Eight out of ten of the populace died holding the gates, so that the enemy on the Plains could not reach shelter.' The Regent lowered the message again.

'And what of the enemy who were still within the city?' someone called.

'The Wolves were under orders that there was to be no blood bath. Prisoners were to be taken if possible; all attempts at surrender were to be recognised,' the Regent answered.

'Were there many attempts?'

'The Wolves killed hardly any of the Navealozans. Instead they forced them from the city,' he answered. Heads bowed and fists clenched at the news. All knew the Wolf Lord or Aron present would not go against orders, but the number of the populace killed raised anger from all in the room.

'They forced them from the city into the arms of the waiting Natives. There has been no loss of love between the two since the war began. The report continues to say, "No prisoners were taken due to the overzealous reaction of the Natives assisting in the attack".'

The news was good. With Beestrone in our hands, and with the Natives to watch the Wastelands, the entire force under the Regent could move south and join with that of the Prince. With the four thousand Vahians who by now had left the pass and were moving south, many of the enemy would be forced to flee or be trapped between the two forces.

Messengers were sent to the New Lord of Beestrone telling of the Regent's plan to join his forces with that of the Prince. Preparation began immediately, and before long we were on the move once again. We travelled west to the Wyernt River, a few miles south of Beestrone, where barges were being prepared for our use.

We reached Lyram. The Prince had been forced to march without us as the Navealozans were beginning to mass north of Esherweld. If allowed enough time, they would be able to build fortifications along the length of the river which would take months, and more men than we had, to capture.

Grehem pushed the men hard; they had had sufficient rest on the barges, and he wanted to overhaul the Prince as soon as possible. Three days from the river, we were attacked by a force of four hundred Brigands who had been hiding in the foothills of the northern mountain range.

They were easily dealt with, and this convinced Grehem that the enemy were trying to slow him down. He pushed the men even harder, and at last reached the Prince's force. With this increased army, the Prince crossed the Esherweld River, and linked up with the Vahian army moving towards the sea. With his now sizeable army, he began to push back all who opposed him. His forces were stopped at the Faiharn River. The enemy controlled the western bank in incredible numbers. Neither side wished to cross in the face of the opposing forces, so a parley was called for.

The Prince and I with Elred as translator, were to take part in the parley. Ransyn, Rhyhl and Rafe were also to attend. The Prince wore ceremonial armour and the green tabard of the Ferropean Province, while I wore a new tabard of black. Ransyn also wore a black tabard, while Rhyhl was dressed in a cuirass identifying him as a

Perduan. Rafe wore the plain yellow robe of a healer of the Plains.

The previous night, the Prince was crowned King by the assembled Lords of all provinces. The Council members of all freed towns and cities had also chosen him as leader of the free forces of the Plains.

The parley was to be on a barge anchored centrally in the river. Each side was to make their way to the barge by small boat which was to return to the bank immediately.

'What's the matter?' the Prince asked me.

'There is an Eligere Seeker on the far bank, trying to find you. I sensed his searching, and have placed a barrier about us—as long as you stay close, they will not be able to find you.'

'But soon we will be in the centre of a river for all to see,' he said.

'I know—that is what worries me. Why seek you out now? All they have to do is wait,' I answered.

A raft had been fashioned for the Prince, as no boats were available. Ten Janissaire took their place on the raft alongside us, and began to pole the raft across to the waiting barge. The six of us climbed from the raft which was poled back to the riverbank.

The Prince sat in one of the chairs provided, and watched a small boat pull towards us from the other bank. Rhyhl and myself stood on one side of the Prince with Rafe and Ransyn on the other. Elred stood behind the Prince ready to translate all he heard.

We were all armed, as the arrangements had said nothing about weapons.

'You are to keep your weapons concealed beneath your cloaks, and try not to reach for them at the first insult, real or imaginary.' He looked at Ransyn as he said the last.

The boat contained six Eligere as well as the slaves who propelled it. As soon as the boat touched the barge, the

Eligere stepped from it and snapped a series of orders to the slave master, who ordered the boat turned.

One of the Eligere sat in the chair opposite the Prince, while the other four adopted positions beside him. Two were armoured Knights while two others were robed Kyklos. The last member of the party was robed like the Kyklos, but the colour of his robe was ash grey, rather than blue. He was a head taller than the tallest of the Eligere and he positioned himself behind the seated one.

'It seems we are at odds with one another,' the seated Eligere said in slightly accented Vahian. 'I would suggest we come to a compromise.'

'Such as?' the Prince asked.

'Withdrawal.'

'Whose?' the Prince asked sceptically.

'Why, ours,' the Eligere answered. 'I am Syat ir Habel, and I am empowered to come to any agreement to end this stalemate.'

The Prince nodded.

'And you, Sir?' Habel asked.

'I am Lord Nels, King of Nuevah and defender of the People of the Plains,' Nels answered. 'Now, about your withdrawal?'

'Perhaps withdrawal was the wrong word. I propose the lines stand as they are now. We control the Eastern Plains, while you have the Western and Southern Plains.'

'And what of the Plains people behind your lines . . . slavery?' Nels asked.

'Possibly—who is to say what our Navealozan allies will do with their booty?' Habel answered.

All the time the two had been talking, I had been watching the Knight opposite me. His eyes had not left mine since his arrival, and there was something strange about him. Then I understood what it was. He wore a golden band identical to the ones worn by Ransyn and Rhyhl. The only place a band of that design could be found was in Perdu. All but five of the Eligere who had stolen the Talisman had perished in the buried city. Two of the remaining had been killed by Beth, while I had slain another at the river ambush. This Knight must be one of the other two who had both been struck by bolts and fallen into the river, believed dead. He must have survived, which was why the pursuers had caught up to us so fast.

'I see you recognise each other,' Habel said, looking at me.

'Yes,' I answered. 'I believe we just missed each other in Navealoza.'

'That's true,' Habel answered. 'You did well, "Two Swords", I doubt you would be as lucky again.'

I shrugged.

Nels spoke. 'I have an alternate suggestion.'

'Speak,' Habel said.

'I propose that I hold my forces here, and that you withdraw your forces east beyond the Kelturk River.' Nels paused for any objections.

'Continue,' Habel said.

'The towns of Wirrilac and Kelturk are in your hands and will remain so. Firnall and Faiharn are to be evacuated and the people moved to Tharrac, which will be returned to us,' the King paused again.

'So far we give and you take, but continue,' Habel said with a slight smile.

'The lands between the rivers mentioned will act as a buffer between our forces, giving each warning of an attack,' Nels stopped and leaned back in his chair.

'You will give us two towns we already have, and in return we will leave two others and give you a third. Pardon me if I do not jump at the offer, but your generosity overwhelms me,' Habel sneered.

'The towns are not yours to take. We are here to stop

372

the senseless slaughter of your army,' Nels answered.

'Pardon me,' Habel said. 'I had thought it was your troops we were saving.'

As the discussion went back and forth between them, the weather began to change. The clouds which filled the sky earlier were gone and the sun beat down upon us. I reached up to loosen the cloak when I noticed a movement from beneath the grey one's robes. My own cloak dropped from my shoulders.

Hands on both sides reached for weapons, and Habel and Nels were on their feet.

'What is it, Teal?' the King asked.

'That one,' I said, pointing to the tall grey-robed figure. 'He has something beneath his robe.'

Eyes turned to the grey one. He opened his robe to show a small reptile sitting on his left forearm. As we watched, the reptile spread small wings and arched its back.

'Simply a pet,' Habel answered.

'Slightly more than that,' Rhyhl answered. 'A Wyvern is a somewhat dangerous pet.'

Habel looked at Rhyhl in surprise. 'You know the creatures of the eastern lands?' he asked.

'I know nothing of the eastern lands,' Rhyhl answered. 'But the history of my people goes back far enough to mention that those creatures once lived in these lands, and that they were used as hunters. They also kill on command.'

'Your people?' Habel asked.

'I am of Perdu,' he answered. 'The city you attacked without warning.'

Habel was indeed surprised by this statement and he turned and talked to those about him using the Eligere language. Once finished he turned back towards the Prince, but before he could speak Elred gave the Prince a

373

translation of what had just been said. Habel was even more surprised to find someone other than one of his people who could understand his language.

'You seem to have surrounded yourself with people of great interest,' Habel said. He looked at me then continued. 'Two Swords has new weapons, so I've been told, that have quite an interesting pommel design, and the quiet one,' he said, pointing to Ransyn, 'wears an Eligere stiletto which he has yet to pay for. You have one who understands the Eligere language, and another from a city believed long dead. Do you have more surprises for me?'

The King did not answer.

'Well, allow me to tell you what I have decided. Your proposals have been accepted. Evacuation of our troops will begin immediately. How do you propose we ensure none enter the buffer lands between the rivers?' Habel asked.

'There are few places where the Faiharn River can be forded, I intend that garrison houses should be built there to deny all the use of the ford, and that the western side of the river be patrolled to ensure none cross anywhere else,' he answered.

The Wyvern again extended its wings. This time the robe of the grey clad one opened further. He reached to close it and as he did so his cowl moved back slightly. For the first time I saw his face. It was rather plain, until he looked up, and I saw his eyes. A look of fear started in my stomach and began to expand throughout my body. I couldn't draw my eyes from his stare.

Suddenly I realised his stare no longer held me, yet his eyes were still locked on mine. I found that my right hand had bunched the front of my tabard as it grasped firmly on the amulet beneath it. The grey ones eyes opened in wonder, and perspiration appeared on his brow. But no matter how hard he tried he could no longer hold me.

Our battle of wills had not gone unnoticed by those on the barge. The Eligere showed surprise and the Knights just the hint of fear.

'It seems those about you are truly powerful. No wonder you were able supposedly to return from the grave to inherit your late father's throne. We must meet again sometime, when things are not so pressing,' Habel said, and rose to leave.

That night, I dreamt of the Gamin. Hersal was before me, smiling as he was when we last parted. I saw a small grey spot appear beside him. The spot enlarged until it was the size and shape of a man. It was a tall man wearing loose grey robes.

The grey one raised his right arm and pointed at me. 'You have eluded me several times now, but I will have you in the end. Neither dreams, amulets, nor the Gamin will save you when next we meet.' After saying this, the grey figure faded and Hersal remained. I was shaken by the fact that for the first time I had been spoken to in a dream; usually there was no sound at all.

'Several times,' Hersal said, 'the Gamin have come to your aid; the quarrel which struck the counterfeit Prince was directed by one of us. The dream from Rafe, which called you into the safety of a certain bay, was also engineered by one of my people. We allowed him to see the storm building, and planted the thought he should call you. The storm which wrecked you off the Osseaux Swamp and led you to find the ring you now wear, was of our design. How else do you think the other six Usare found you . . . ? *With our help.* The Chimera was a test, a beast of Darkness which even we could not destroy.

'Just as dark forces have been manipulating all that the Eligere do, we have been trying to influence you in the right direction. The Talisman and the war were merely the first step in a long journey you are to take. Your friends Beth and Jon have already started on this journey, and your other friends Lyn and Reya await you here. The journey will be hard and many times you will meet Dark forces at work upon this world ...

'We have awaited your return for centuries, Death Lord. . . .*For now, the search truly begins.*'

ARMOURY

AOR —Straight, double-edged, wide-bladed sword.

ASSAGAI —Short spear for hand to hand combat— not meant to be thrown.

BEVOR —Pivoted neck and lower chin protector.

BUCKLER —Small round shield generally used by swordsmen.

BOLT & QUARREL —Missiles fired by a crossbow.

BREAST PLATE —Plate armour to protect the front of the body.

CLAWS —Four curved blades which are fitted to the hand to protrude between the fingers and thumb.

COIF —Hood and strip that wraps across the lower face to protect the head, made of mail—can be part of or separate from the cuirass.

CUIRASS —Mail shirt for the protection of the upper body.

CUISSE	—Plate metal thigh protection.
CUTLASS	—A short, heavy, single-edged slightly curved sword.
FAKIR	—Small buckler with two opposing blades.
FLAIL	—Spiked metal ball attached to a wooden handle by a length of chain.
FORK	—Long-shafted weapon consisting of two prongs, an axe blade and a reaping hook.
GLAIVE	—Double-edged, long, heavy sword.
GLADIUS	—Double-edged, short sword.
GAUNTLETS	—Heavy leather gloves, reinforced with steel rivets, or metal scales.
GREAVES	—Plate armour to protect shin and calf.
HALBERDS	—Long-shafted weapon, combining the axe and spear.
HARPE	—Short sword with a considerably curved blade, similar to modern day reaping hook.
KRIS	—Short sword with an undulating, double-edged blade.
MACE	—Spiked metal ball mounted on a wooden shaft.
PILGRIM STAFF	—Wooden staff with three extendable blades which appear when brandished.
PAULDRON	—Plate mail worn to protect shoulder and upper arm.
PARRYING DAGGER	—A dagger with a smaller blade recessed on either side of the main blade.

RING MAIL	—Armour made from rings of metal attached to a leather shirt.
RAPIER	—Long thin-bladed sword, very light.
TRIDENT	—A military fork with three tynes.
SABRE	—Slightly curved single-edged cavalry sword.
STILETTO	—Dagger with a long, narrow blade.
SURCOAT	—Short sleeveless outer garment worn over armour, showing heraldic designs.
SCALE MAIL	—Armour made of scales of metal or bone, attached to a leather shirt.
SMALL SWORD	—Long sword with a narrow blade, double-edged, generally fitted with a basket hilt.
SWORD BREAKER	—A device used to trap a sword blade and then break it with a twist.
TABARD	—Sleeveless coat worn over armour.

Brian Stableford
The Empire of Fear £4.99

'Imaginative . . . fearless . . . a book to be proud of'
STEPHEN DONALDSON

NOMINATED FOR THE ARTHUR C. CLARKE AWARD

THEY COULD LIVE FOR CENTURIES AND THEIR EMPIRES SPANNED
THE WORLD. MEN CALLED THEM VAMPIRES . . .

In seventeenth-century London, Edmund Cordery, Mechanician to the
Court of Prince Richard, seeks out the sinister formulae that sustain an
aristocracy of vampires as immortal overlords holding whole continents
in sanguinary thrall.

His son Noell carries his father's dangerous knowledge into the dark
heart of Africa and on to the fortress island of Malta at the head of a
company of soldiers of fortune. There he awaits the coming of the
awesome armada of Vlad the Impaler and Richard Coeur-de-Lion across
the Middle Sea when the battle lines are drawn up for the last great
conflict between subversive science and sinister superstition . . .

Brian Stableford's *The Empire of Fear* is a fabulous adventure
spanning three centuries and three continents, an epic feat of
imaginative storytelling . . .

'A tremendous story . . . beautifully written, carefully researched . . . a
remarkable book. Highly recommended'
CRITICAL WAVE

'Original, thoughtful and hugely entertaining'
INTERZONE

Brian Stableford
The Werewolves of London £4.99

'Truly magical'
FEAR

THE MOURNFUL HOWLING OF WOLVES
ECHOES THROUGH ETERNITY.
FOR WHEN THEY ARE NOT WOLVES
THEY MUST BEAR THE IMAGE OF MAN . . .

In 1872, David Lydyard accompanies his guardian to Egypt. Lured into a search for the 'real' Egypt by a priest they encounter a land of tombs and snakes and fiery desert demons . . .

David now finds himself possessed by uncanny visionary powers. At the same time Gabriel, a foundling boy brought up by nuns, experiences a mysterious force developing within him.

Others covet these powers for their own purposes . . . the heretic priests of the secret Order of St Amycus, the occultist and reputed Satanist Jacob Harkender . . . and the legendary werewolves of London.

'By far the best book he has ever written, a scientific romance of very great scope . . . the most intelligent novel yet published in 1990'
INTERZONE

'So absorbing . . . you're in for some surprises, right up to the last page'
LOCUS

Brian Stableford
author of **The Empire of Fear** and
The Werewolves of London

The Angel of Pain £4.99

The final book in a brilliant fantasy trilogy.

England, 1893. David Lydyard has been beset by strange visions since he returned from Egypt over twenty years previously. Now the visions are becoming ever more extravagant and ever more urgent, undulled even by the potent drug laudanum . . .

Soon he is caught up in the net cast by the fallen angels, those newly awakened beings who need humankind to serve as their eyes and hands on earth.

David's task, to discover the truth about the fallen angels, starts him off on the strangest journey in human history: a journey he cannot undertake alone. But will his own companions prove to be his deadliest enemies?

And David's mission cannot ever succeed, unless he can come to terms with the Angel of Pain . . .

'An absolutely extraordinary book'
JOHN CLUTE, INTERZONE

'A bright light in a shining abyss'
FEAR

'The breadth of an epic, the dense intellectual texture of pure science fiction . . a fascinating and successful experiment'
LOCUS

'One of the most inventive and original writers working today'
THE TIMES

Charles de Lint
Yarrow £4.99

A NEW TALE OF ENCHANTMENT AND WONDER FROM THE AUTHOR OF *MOONHEART* AND *GREENMANTLE*

Cat Midhir lives in a land of dreams, crossing nightly over the borders of sleep into a magic realm.

YARROW

A land where gnomes hide among standing stones and selchies dwell beneath the waves, where the harper Kothlen tells tales of the ancient days and the antlered Mynfel walks by moonlight . . .

When Cat wakes she weaves stories around the Otherworld. Her books are labelled as fantasy, but Mynfel's domain seems more real to her than the humdrum streets of the city.

Until a thief comes stalking – and steals Cat's dreams away . . .

'You open a de Lint story, and like the interior of a very genial Pandora's box, the atmosphere is suddenly full of deep woods and quaint city streets and a magic that's nowhere near so far removed as Middle Earth'
JAMES P. BLAYLOCK

'The storytelling lyrics of folk music lie at the tender heart of Charles de Lint's fictions. His work reaches to the very heart of humanity'
FEAR MAGAZINE

'Classical folklore with modern settings full of power and beauty . . . one of the most gifted storytellers writing fantasy today'
LOCUS